THE SOPHISTICATES

• Book One •

DEVIATION

CHRISTINE MANZARI

This book is a work of fiction. Any references to historical
events, real people, or real places are used ficticiously.
Other names, characters, places, and events are products of
the author's imagination, and any resemblance to actual events
or places or persons, living or dead, is entirely coincidental.

Copyright © August 2013 by Christine Manzari

Second Edition Copyright © 2014

www.christinemanzari.com

Cover Design: VLC Photo

Cover Photo: Vania Stoyanova

Cover Model: Krista Gibson

To Johnny Manzari —

No matter how many Prince Charmings I read

or write about, you will always be the only

one who truly matters.

I love you.

Always.

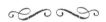

1

SPONTANEOUS COMBUSTION

Access Denied.

What did I do wrong? This worked earlier. I was in earlier.

I tried again, starting over and going through the same process, wishing I had downloaded the files when I first found them.

Why didn't I do that?

My fingers angrily attacked the keyboard, searching for a way back to those secure files.

Sitting cross-legged on my bed with the laptop nestled on the pillow, I could feel the panic rising in my chest. All the work I'd done the last few weeks. All the time spent hunched over these keys. All the meals missed. All the lies told. I finally found a way in and now I was locked out again. Why?

Tap. Tap. Tap. My fingers briefly hovered over the keys, then I clicked enter and held my breath.

Access Denied.

The letters were small and innocent as they spanned across

the screen, but I felt the accusation in their simplicity and I felt warm. Too warm.

I punched the bed on either side of my legs with my fists, fighting the urge to scream in frustration. The laptop slid off the back of the pillow, falling on the mattress with the keyboard straight up in the air. It looked like a beetle trapped on its back. If I weren't so angry, I would've laughed. Instead, I glared at the offending words on the screen as if they were to blame.

Access Denied.

Two little words with so much power. I would just have to try again. There was a way in. There was always a way in. I slid my hands through my hair, and then rubbed my palms along the side of my face as I stared at the bed. Thinking. There was a way. There had to be a way.

The unmistakable "ping" of the computer let me know that a new email had arrived.

"What is it this time?" I mumbled, pulling the laptop back up to its pillow perch. More limits to solve? Professor Garner was notorious for sending extra homework right before Lights Out and I'd noticed earlier that the workload was lighter than usual. I seriously hoped it wasn't an email from Garner; I was in no mood for Calculus.

When my eyes found the new email sitting in the email box, I could feel my confusion crease into a tight "V" in the skin between my eyes. It wasn't from Garner, it was from a Program Security Advisor. I'd never gotten anything like that before, but given the fact that I'd been trying to hack into password protected Program files only moments before, I knew it wasn't good.

An unruly chunk of hair dangled in front of my eyes and I

tucked it behind my ear, wishing I could ignore the email. Sweat trickled down my temple and slid down the side of my face to my neck.

I was so unbelievably hot right now.

I licked my lips, knowing I couldn't put it off any longer. I clicked the link, cringing, expecting the worst.

————————————————————

Subject: Genetic Donors
Date: Sun, 17 Sept 10:29
From: J.M., Program Security Advisor
To: Dracone, Clementine

Dear Ms. Dracone,

It has come to our attention that you have been accessing Program files that you are not authorized to view. We have since fixed this issue and you will no longer be able to gain access to top secret information. Your genetic donors are not your concern and it is imperative that you cease and desist all efforts to discover their identities. It is not in your best interest, or theirs, to be privy to this information. You are property of the Program and need to accept the fact that your future is that of a Sophisticate.

As punishment for your indiscretions, your Internet privileges have been revoked until further notice. Internet access will only be given under the supervision of a Professor until we determine that you can be trusted.

Thank you for your cooperation in this matter.

Sincerely,
Program Security Advisor, J.M.

———————————————————

Property? Property?

My hands were shaking. My blood was on fire and my skin was crawling as if my insides were actually boiling. Air. I needed air. I tried to crawl off the bed and get to the window, but the words from the email were blazing through me — a bellowing inferno of indignation.

Donors.

Cease and Desist.

Property.

Punishment.

Indiscretions.

Revoked.

Trusted.

My hands covered my ears as the words screamed through my head. Or was I screaming?

Pressure was building inside me and I just wanted to let it go, to feel relief. It was too much. I was too hot.

Exhale.

The computer exploded, throwing flaming plastic and metal across the bed. The television answered with its own death, spewing its fiery innards onto the desk and floor, igniting the carpet instantly. The rage in my chest echoed like a heartbeat and with each pulse, something in the room burst into flames. In less than a minute, I was surrounded by broken and burning bits of my room, all of them melting or on fire. A small untouched circle of floor under my feet was my haven, my island in the disaster. Flames raced up the drapes, licking at the ceiling as shards of glass from the window fell inward with an eerie tinkling.

I stared in disbelief, unable to move, as the room burned around me and smoke curled to the ceiling like agitated ghosts. The goldfish flopped helplessly among the wet rubble of his shattered home. Pictures hanging on the wall curled up in the heat, catching flame and falling to the floor in large, ashy flakes.

What had I done?

TARDY

Late again.

The bell above the library at the end of the grassy mall tolled its deep song, mocking me as I ran.

Late again. Late again. Late again.

I sprinted, slipping on the wet grass, nearly dropping the book bag that was slung clumsily over my shoulder. What was it, the second or third time this week? It didn't matter. Professor Waverly made it clear yesterday that one more tardy was going to land me in Dean Younglove's office. I shuddered at the thought. That was one place I'd rather avoid. It was dark and creepy and smelled oddly like old, wet cats — and Dean Younglove didn't have cats, wet or otherwise.

My sneakers slapped the concrete as I escaped the slick grass and ran along the sidewalk that led to my destination. The brick, white-columned building looming in front of me had the look of a bleached skull — mysterious, empty and devoid of life. Yet, it was anything but empty — it was full of my fellow students. It's where I should have been five minutes ago, if only I hadn't gambled with the snooze button this morning.

But I had gambled. I'd been afraid to wake up this morning and find out that last night had really happened. And I was right, it had. I swiped my fingers across my forehead, catching the clump of hair that escaped my hastily-made ponytail, and tucked it behind my ear. I attempted to tuck the memories from last night away, too — shards of glass littering the floor, blue flame devouring the sheets on my bed, Cassie pounding on the door demanding to know what was going on, my desperate pleas for Cassie to go back to bed before the Hounds showed up.

I forced the thoughts out of my mind.

When I reached the massive, building known as Jiminez Hall, I took the stairs two at a time and wrenched open the heavy door leading inside. The bright light of the morning blinked out as the door slammed shut behind me and I found myself in the cool, hushed foyer of the first floor. I ran up the deserted staircase and hurried past the closed doors of classes that were already in session. When I reached the last door at the end of the hallway, I stopped momentarily to catch my breath and tuck the loose hair behind my ear one more time.

The door groaned noisily as I eased it open. Nearly every head in the room swiveled around to see the latecomer, even though they all knew exactly who it was. I was the only student who seemed to have a problem with being on time. Professor Waverly was at the head of the room, reviewing the material we were supposed to have read the night before. He spared me a brief look as I slid into a seat at the back of the room and pulled my heavy textbook onto the desk in front of me.

Relief washed over me as I realized Professor Waverly wasn't going to send me directly to Younglove's office. Perhaps he'd had a change of heart. I silently basked in my good luck as my finger lazily traced the complex pattern on the cover of the Thermodynamics book while Waverly's voice droned on.

"Psst. He's calling on you," Cassie hissed from two seats over.

My head snapped up to meet the stony gaze of the professor. Under the severe lights hanging over his desk, Waverly's bald spot gleamed — a beacon declaring he wasn't a Sophisticate. Educated, yes, but he'd never be a Sophisticate. No matter how much he studied, no matter how much he learned, he'd never measure up to the genetically-altered superiority that was sitting in each and every one of the seats in front of him. I was sure that was the main reason for his bitterness, why he was always determined to catch one of his students screwing up — as if to say, "See, you're no better than me after all."

"I'm sorry, I didn't hear the question," I said.

"Didn't hear, or don't know the answer?" Professor Waverly asked smugly, folding his arms over his grey sweater vest.

I bit the inside of my lip to keep my anger in check. There was no need for a repeat of last night. When I didn't acknowledge his insult, Waverly asked, "What is the second law of thermodynamics, Clementine?"

He fixed me with an arrogant smile, confident I hadn't done my homework. Oh, I'd done it — too well in fact.

"The second law?" I repeated.

Waverly nodded.

"The second law states that the entropy of an isolated system

8

not in equilibrium will tend to increase over time, approaching a maximum value at equilibrium."

Waverly continued to stare at me.

"Basically, heat can't spontaneously flow from a colder location to a hotter location," I added. Yeah, right. So much for laws.

Waverly pursed his lips in defeat. "Thank you Clementine. Even though you seem incapable of making it to class on time, you are at least proficient enough at memorizing." He turned and continued his lecture, assaulting the blackboard with his chalk stub, reproducing the diagrams I'd studied the night before. He didn't bother to call on me again for the rest of the class, which left me free to let my mind wander. Unfortunately, it wandered exactly where I didn't want it to. As if echoing my thoughts, a ball of paper bounced onto my desk. I unraveled it.

"What happened last night? Why wouldn't you open the door? I thought you were hurt. I almost called the Hounds!" was scrawled on the note.

I looked over at Cassie, shook my head no, and then went back to tracing the patterns on the cover of my textbook. Another ball of paper came flying through the air and bounced off my head, landing on the table in front of me. I ignored it until two more balls of paper joined it. I unraveled them.

"Oh no! You're not getting away with that. I'm your best friend," the first one said.

"You won't answer my texts and emails so I'm going to keep throwing these until you answer me," the second taunted.

And the third . . . "I have three notebooks of paper with me. Trust me, you'll get tired of this game long before I do."

Classic Cassie. I hastily scribbled, "Later, I promise," at the bottom of the third note and discretely tossed it back to Cassie while Waverly wasn't looking. I couldn't have answered Cassie's texts or emails because my phone and computer had both been destroyed last night, but I could explain that later. No need to put anything incriminating in writing, especially since Waverly took great pleasure in intercepting passed notes. Cassie seemed to be pacified for the time being — at least no more paper balls came my way.

I spent the remainder of class wondering how I was going to explain last night to Cassie. Not that I didn't trust her, I did. Implicitly. I knew Cassie would never tell Younglove or any of the other administrators. The problem was that I was more worried that she would think I was crazy. If I was having a hard time rationalizing to myself what happened, how was I going to explain it to Cassie and expect her to believe it? And I had to tell her, because . . . well . . . I told Cassie everything. My biggest problem right now was going to be how to repair and clean up the destruction in my room without the administrators finding out.

When the bell rang I quickly stuffed my textbook in my bag, which still smelled like smoke. I was intent on escaping before either Waverly or Cassie could interrogate me.

"Clementine, I need to speak with you please," Waverly called over his sweater-vested shoulder as he wiped his blackboard clean.

I groaned inwardly, rolled my eyes, and then shrugged apologetically at Cassie.

"I'll talk to you later," Cassie said pointedly as she met my gaze before stalking toward the door and disappearing into the hallway.

When I reached the front of the room, I set my backpack on the floor and started to take a seat.

"Don't bother," Waverly said. "You need to go to Younglove's office."

"But sir, I was almost on time today. I promise tomorrow I'll be early. Please," I begged.

Waverly tugged at his untamed beard. It ran along his jaw, ragged and bushy like a garden that needed weeding, and joined the unruly mustache that hovered unattractively under his large nose. I always thought it was unfair that his face was so overgrown and shaggy while the hair on his head seemed in an ever-increasing state of retreat. How could the top of his head be so shiny and barren and his face be such a scraggly tangle of unkempt whiskers? It was an enigma.

Waverly twirled a section of beard between his fingers. "It's not because you were late Clementine, although you have been warned repeatedly to be on time for my class. This was on my desk when I arrived this morning." He lifted a folded piece of paper off the table and handed it to me. The unwelcome scent of damp feline wafted up as I opened it.

Professor Waverly,
Please send Clementine Dracone to my office after class.
— Delia Younglove

I hated when the professors used my last name, as if there were any other students with the name Clementine. Just another cruel jab reminding me that I was nothing but an object to them. All of the Sophisticates born the same year as me had the same last name — Dracone. My parents had given me life and their DNA, most of it anyway. They had even been allowed to give me the name Clementine. However, they couldn't give me their last name, their legacy. I wasn't even sure I really wanted it. I'd never met them and had no idea what their last name was and so I was left with Clementine Dracone — one half a gift from my parents, the other a curse from the Program. Sometimes, I felt the only identity I had was the one the Sophisticate Program gave to me.

I looked helplessly up at Waverly, silently begging him to give me permission to ignore the letter and head to Calculus class. He looked away and cleared his throat.

"You had best be on your way Clementine; Dean Younglove doesn't like to be kept waiting." He turned back to his desk and began shuffling and re-stacking his books and papers in a desperate attempt to not have to look at me.

I exited the classroom into the hallway, crushing the note into a tight wad in my fist.

"It's later."

I jumped back a step, startled that Cassie had stuck around, risking being late to class. "You scared me."

Cassie tapped her foot, considering what to say. She flicked her dark curtain of hair over her shoulder and her delicate almond-shaped eyes narrowed. "Not nearly as bad as you scared me last night. What were you doing in your room? Glass breaking, things crashing. I even smelled smoke and it definitely wasn't burnt popcorn. What happened?"

I ignored the questions, lifted up the letter from Younglove, and shook it open so that my best friend could read it.

Cassie's expression immediately softened. "Oh no. Younglove? That's not good. What does she want?"

I shrugged. "Whatever it is, it's not good. You only see Younglove for two reasons; when you arrive and when you leave."

"But you still have the rest of the year to finish before we specialize."

"Maybe she's kicking me out?" I suggested hopefully.

Cassie gave me a withering look. "You wouldn't be so lucky. This isn't good."

I sighed. "Nothing ever is when Younglove is involved. I better get going before she sends out the Hounds. You should too or you're never going to make it to class on time."

"Never mind that," Cassie said with a wave of her hand as she used the other one to push me down the hallway toward the stairs. "I'm escorting you there so you can tell me what happened."

My stomach did a nervous flip at the thought of trying to explain the unexplainable. "You can't, you'll be late," I argued. My steps were quiet as I descended the stairs but Cassie's heels chattered noisily, just like her personality.

Cassie tilted her head so that she could stare at me from underneath her perfectly arched eyebrows. "Unlike you, I'm not regularly late to class. I think I'm due for a fashionably late entrance to Calculus. I'll just tell Garner I was sick. Cramps," she said patting her stomach. "He's twitchy nervous like a squirrel; he'll be too embarrassed to give me a hard time." Cassie pushed open the door that led outside and sunshine rushed through the opening, spilling across the dark floor.

"Cassie, I know your cycle. The entire faculty knows your cycle. They know everything about us. It won't be too hard for him to figure out that you're lying. Knowing the Program, I bet there's a Sophisticate PMS spreadsheet for just this very reason."

"Whatever," Cassie snapped as we descended the steps. "I'll

think of something. But don't think I'm going to let you slide on this. I'm your best friend and you can't keep secrets from me."

That was true. There had never been any secrets between us and there was nothing we wouldn't do for one another. When Cassie first started using pointe shoes in ballet and developed a painful case of dancer's heel, I was the one who massaged and stretched her feet every night, the one who wiped away her tears when the pain was unbearable. When my martial arts classes went full contact, Cassie was the one to bandage me up at night, the one to help me dress when my arms were too bruised and sore to lift. And when we were little, it was always Cassie's bed that I crawled into when I had a nightmare. I often thought that the only reason I was able to cope with life as a Sophisticate was because Cassie was always there, unconditionally. She was my best friend and deserved to know what had happened last night, but what would she think of me once she learned the truth? Did the truth fit into the unconditional love category? After all, this was more than just a harmless nightmare or sprained wrist — nobody ever wants to be friends with the nut job.

But I knew I couldn't lie to her, this was too big. If there was anyone I could trust with the truth, it was Cassie.

"All right," I sighed. "So, it's like this. I was eating dinner in my room last night while I was doing homework."

"What else is new?" Cassie asked, sharply. "You haven't had dinner with me in the cafeteria in at least three weeks. You're a sucky friend."

"Exams are coming up," I argued.

"And your social standing is going down. You're the invisible girl."

I shook my head as we walked past the old bronze terrapin statue that stood guard in front of the McKeldin library. Absent-mindedly, I ran my hand along the shiny nose for good luck as we passed, just as so many students had done over the years. Good luck for exams, good luck in the big game, good luck in relationships. This time I was hoping for good luck in Younglove's office. I knew I'd need it.

"Do you want to know what happened or not?"

"Just telling it like it is," Cassie said. "So what was the invisible girl up to last night while her better half — that's me by the way — was left to entertain the Homework Harpies all alone?"

The Homework Harpies were what Cassie lovingly called our friends Justin, Brad, and Sam. The guys managed to spend most of any meal or study session asking, "Are you going to finish that?" while snatching-half eaten food off our plates. The Homework Harpies needed the study group more than we did. I was convinced that most of their need, however, was centered around the extra calorie intake of pilfered meals.

"How much of your dinner did you actually get to eat?" I laughed.

"Let's just say I won't have any problem fitting into that sinful red dress I just bought."

"Cassie. You have a genetically-altered metabolism. You could eat your dinner and the dinners of all the Harpies and you'd still fit into that sinful red dress."

"I'm just saying, it'd be nice to have you there so I could at least get half my meal to myself. I'm in a constant state of starvation," she said dramatically, showing off her slim figure.

I did feel guilty. I'd been skipping out on Cassie way too much lately.

"Sorry. I promise I'll be there tonight." I knew the promise was a hollow one. After all, I'd turned my room into a biohazard last night and was now on my way to an appointment with Younglove. I knew the two events were not just coincidence.

Cassie grabbed my arm and pulled me to a stop as we walked alongside the reflecting pool that waterfalled its way down the McKeldin Mall. The long rectangular fountain whispered as the water flowed over the edges of the short walls, splashing into each subsequent pool. Younglove's office was located in the administration building at the end of the mall. We were nearly there.

"What happened?" Cassie demanded.

I looked around warily, but none of the groups of Sophisticates walking by seemed interested in our conversation. They had classes to get to, rules to follow, expectations to fulfill. Their futures were all planned out for them and they asked no questions. I was an anomaly.

"I got an email. About my parents."

Cassie's face softened and she grabbed my hand, pulling me closer. "Cleo, honey. We're Sophisticates. We don't have parents; we have donors. Pretty awesome ones, apparently," Cassie said as she indicated herself. "But don't go hoping for something that's not there. You have to stop obsessing over this."

"That's what the email said. That I needed to stop trying to find out who my parents are." My voice shook as I tried to calm myself. Not here. I couldn't let it happen here.

"What do you mean stop trying to find out who they are?" Her gaze narrowed accusingly at me.

I sighed. I hated that I'd been keeping things from her. "I've been trying to hack into the Sophisticate Program computer system, to find out who my parents are. That's what I've been doing instead of coming to dinner."

"You tried to hack into the computer system of the Sophisticate Program? Are you crazy?" Cassie hissed, looking around as if she expected Younglove to leap out of one of the trees and pounce on us at any moment. "Did you think they wouldn't find out?"

I shrugged. "I hoped they wouldn't, I'm pretty good with computers."

"Well," Cassie pressed. "Did you find anything out?"

"Aside from the fact that the Program knew I was trying to hack them?"

"Yes, aside from the obvious," Cassie huffed.

"Their names, Michael and Sarah."

"That's it? No last name?" When I shook my head, Cassie asked, "Did the email say anything else?"

"It said that my Internet privileges had been revoked. And that I needed to accept the fact that I was the *property* of the Program and that my genetic donors were not my concern." I recited the awful words with biting hatred and my body trembled just as it had last night when I read the email. I glanced over at the reflecting pool that spanned the length of the mall. The water was gently roiling, overheated just like my temper. I took a few deep calming breaths and watched uneasily as the water calmed itself into a perfect reflection of the blue September sky above.

"Ouch," Cassie empathized. "Property? I mean, I know it's true, but to come out and say it like that is just crude. At least they could let us live in our fantasy world that we have some choice and control over our lives. Take the sinful red dress for example. See the amazingly good decisions I can make when given the chance? I think they..."

"My room exploded. It was my fault," I interrupted.

"What?"

"After I read the email I got so angry. It was like I was burning up. My computer exploded and caught the bed on fire."

"Your computer exploded?"

"A lot of stuff exploded. That was just the thing I was most worried about," I said, biting my lip and nervously tucking the stray chunk of hair behind my ear again, remembering the panic of being suddenly surrounded by flames.

"Well," Cassie said cautiously. "That sucks, but I'm sure they'll give you a new computer, even without Internet privileges. How else are you going to do your classwork?"

"You don't understand; I made it explode."

"It got too hot?" Cassie suggested.

"There's something wrong with me," I explained as I fidgeted with the strap of my backpack, tentatively looking around to make sure none of the other Sophisticates passing by were eavesdropping. "My temper somehow made the things in my room explode and catch on fire."

Cassie shook her head. "That doesn't make sense."

"My computer, the television, the dresser, my camera. Everything. Even the fish bowl."

"Marcus?" Cassie asked, unbelievingly.

I ignored the question. I already felt bad enough without the guilt of a goldfish death weighing me down as well. "My entire room was on fire. I barely managed to put the flames out, which is what I was doing when you knocked on the door. I had no idea what was going on, I was too freaked out to open the door. Almost everything was destroyed and I'm actually kind of surprised the smoke alarms didn't go off."

Cassie was still shaking her head. "Impossible."

"My room was on fire. I made things explode."

"Maybe it was a power surge or something."

This was exactly what I'd been afraid of — that Cassie would try to explain away the truth and replace it with a logical answer. I knew what had happened and I knew it wasn't logical. I was afraid of not being believed.

"Impossible," Cassie repeated quietly.

My shoulders slumped in disappointment. "Tell that to my back. I spent the night sleeping in my bathtub."

"Why did you sleep in your bathtub?"

I turned and looked at her sadly, "Because it was one of the few things that didn't catch on fire."

WET CATS

Even before I knocked on the door, the overwhelming smell of wet cats slapped me in the face like a soggy towel. What was it with the smell? Couldn't the Dean get someone to steam clean the carpets or something? A little air freshener might not hurt either.

"You may come in, Clementine Dracone," Delia Younglove announced from behind the closed door.

Dracone, I repeated hatefully, yet silently. I fisted my hands at my sides, keeping tenuous control of my temper. Using the name Dracone was Younglove's way of reminding me, and every other Sophisticate, that any feelings of control or hope or choice we had were merely an illusion allowed by the Program. It was an illusion that could be yanked back into nothingness at the smallest indiscretion, such as unintentionally setting one's room on fire.

I uneasily entered the shadowy room. The bright blue of the morning sky was held back by thick, heavy, mustard-colored drapes that were pulled across the windows. They gave the room a sickly, yellow glow. There was so little light in the room that there could easily have been hidden mounds of waterlogged felines in the darkened corners and I'd never know. Hidden piles of wet cats was the only explanation I could come up with for the odor that clung to the room.

There was an army of lit, scented candles scattered around the office furniture and I assumed their purpose was to mask the overwhelming animal stench. It wasn't working.

Younglove was seated at the desk, her dark bobbed hair perfectly molded around her gaunt face. I wasn't positive, but I guessed it was probably a wig. Younglove had somehow managed to fold her gangly form into the leather chair in a way that exuded power and danger, despite her lack of body weight. The only other time I'd been in Younglove's office was four years ago when I graduated from the primary education school of the Program and was admitted to the secondary level here at the University.

Years ago, the University had been a college campus complete with Terrapin fans and Engineering majors. After *Wormwood*, however, what had once been known as the University of Maryland became the property of the government and was turned into the East Coast Campus for the Sophisticate Program. I always found it rather sad that droves of hopeful college students were displaced for the pampered, over-educated, orphans of the Program. The Program had taken a beautiful University with rich history and turned it into a boarding school for their genetic experiments who had no appreciation for all that they had inherited. There were still colleges for those displaced students to go to, places of higher education, but nothing like it used to be. That sort of education was reserved for the Sophisticates. We were the ones that had the best education and the jobs of power — politics, business leaders, government positions. Non-Sophisticates got everything else that was left over. Fast food management, postal delivery, and trash collection? No wonder they hated us.

But then again, they had something we didn't have. Freedom. I'd gladly give up my life of ease for freedom and a family. But those were only day dreams. Sophisticates didn't have family.

I apprehensively made my way across the room and sat only when Younglove motioned with long, bony hands at the chair across the desk from her. I sat on the edge of the hard chair, my arms resting on the sides, my hands clenched — nails digging into my palms.

"Professor Waverly gave me a note that you wanted to see me," I said.

"Yes, Clementine," Younglove answered as she opened a folder, took out a sheet of paper, and held it toward me. "You are to be transferred to St. Ignatius this afternoon. Here is your transfer slip. You can go straight to the Transfer Office now and they will have a driver take you there."

"What? Now?" I asked, caught off guard. I'd joked with Cassie that the only time anyone saw Younglove was on arrival and departure, but I never really thought I'd be leaving the University. I expected punishment yes, but not transfer.

"Yes, now."

"But don't I need to pack?"

"Do you?" Younglove's yellow-eyed gaze seemed to nail me to the chair, daring me to answer.

She knows. She knows what I did last night to my room. She knows I don't need to pack because I destroyed nearly everything

I own.

"But I can't go to St. Ignatius," I argued. "I'm not supposed to specialize until next fall."

"Recent events have proven otherwise," Younglove countered smugly. "Apparently, you are advanced." She said the last word like it tasted badly.

"But, St. Ignatius is for Mandates. I'm a Vanguard."

I'd always known as a Vanguard I'd eventually be working for the Program in one of their offices, perhaps doing communications or computer programming, since those were my strengths. Maybe I'd even get to be a code breaker, hacking into enemy computer systems. I was a Vanguard and Vanguards were the intellectuals of the Sophisticate Program. It wasn't the best scenario in life, but as a Sophisticate, it was better than the alternative — being a Mandate.

The Mandates. They were an entirely different breed of Sophisticate. The Homework Harpies — Justin, Brad, and Sam — would most likely specialize as Mandates. They were physically superior — bigger, faster, stronger. They were designed to be fighters. I knew that the Program didn't waste Mandates on superficial jobs like physical labor. Mandates were the first line in the War on Terror. The War that had been going on for decades. The War that had birthed the Sophisticate Program after *Wormwood* wreaked havoc across major U.S. cities more than thirty years ago. 9-11? That had been a drop in the bucket compared to *Wormwood*.

"You were a Vanguard." Younglove responded, jerking me out of my thoughts and back to the reality of the musty office. Her haggard face twisted into what I thought was an attempt at a smile, but it was hard to tell. There were rumors among the Sophisticates as to why Delia Younglove looked the way she did, rumors of failed genetic mutation. She looked like a sphinx, one of those hairless cats. Her skin was tanned and leathery and hugged each crevice and curve of her body. Her eyes were large and wide, dominating her cadaverous face. And she didn't have any eyebrows, which is why I assumed the perfectly styled, bobbed hair was fake. The rumor circulating was that Younglove was one of the first experiments of the Sophisticate Program — an experiment in genetically modifying a child. Apparently, the experiment hadn't worked as well as the Program had hoped, which is why now all Sophisticates were genetically altered at conception. Younglove had been permanently disfigured physically, emotionally, and — in my opinion — morally. The woman had the personality of a rabid bobcat. I was pretty sure those failed experiments were also responsible for the woman's unique brand of cat stink and I wondered just what the Program had done to Younglove to create such a horrible side effect.

"I don't understand," I responded. "I don't belong at St. Ignatius. I belong at the University. The fall semester just started and it's my last year here. How can I be a Mandate? I'm good with languages and computers, not guns and dumbbells."

"As you were so recently reminded, you are the property of the Program. You go where we tell you. You do what we tell you."

My temper had always been quick to surface, but I'd never really worried about it until after last night. It'd never actually caused any problems. I silently bristled at Younglove's crassness but kept my composure, refusing to rise to the bait. Being called property of the Program wasn't something new. Every Sophisticate was well informed on the importance of following the rules and doing as they were told. Like everyone else, I'd seen the propaganda videos of the Sophisticates who'd been punished for not following rules or not meeting the expected standards. It was easier to do as you were told. After all, the life of a Sophisticate wasn't all bad. Sure, there was the problem of lack of freedom, but we had free education, good health, plenty of food and shelter, and a guaranteed successful future. After *Wormwood*, most people would have gladly given up their freedom for the benefits that Sophisticates enjoyed. Many had given up their children. I was one of those children.

But I'd always assumed that I'd be a Vanguard and that I'd always be with Cassie. That had made everything seem bearable.

"But what about my friends? What about Cassie?"

"You have no friends, Clementine. You have no family. You have no choices. The sooner you accept that, the easier things will be for you. You exist because the Program says it is so."

"But . . ." I started.

"I suggest you make your way to the Transfer Office sooner rather than later. I told the Hounds you would be there by 11:00, which gives you . . . " Younglove raised her emaciated wrist to check the watch dangling from it. " . . . fifteen minutes. You should hurry. The Transfer Office is on North Campus and the Hounds won't be happy if they have to come hunt you down and escort you there."

She lowered her arm back to the desktop with a clatter that sounded like bones knocking together. "Good luck." Younglove's thin lip lifted into a sneer as she flicked the form out of her hand, causing it to skid across the desk and then come to a stop in front of me. Standing, I snatched the paper up without looking at it, stuffed it into my backpack, and hurried out of the room without glancing back. I was afraid that if I locked eyes with Younglove, I might do something I'd regret, like setting the Dean's office on fire. Charred cat smell was probably no better than wet cat smell. In fact, it was probably far worse.

Once outside, I hesitated, considering my options. The sidewalks in front of me led away from the administration building like rays from the sun. If I went straight, I could go to Calculus and find Cassie — and a whole mess of trouble for not following orders. If I turned left, I could leave the campus. I could run. Run from the Program, and Younglove, and a future as a Program soldier. If I turned right, I'd be heading for a fate I knew I was neither prepared for nor wanted — a future as a Mandate.

My heart pulled me toward Cassie and the Homework Harpies, the only family I knew, the only source of comfort I'd ever known. I needed that human connection — the love of a sister and brothers, even if they were only related through given names and shared memories. I needed someone to tell me everything was going to be okay. Even though Cassie hadn't believed me about the room exploding, I knew that she'd always be there to support me. I yearned to find my best friend and tell her all the other things I learned while hacking into the Program's system, all the things I'd been keeping secret. At the very least, I wanted to say goodbye. But I knew running off to find my friend would only delay the inevitable and get us both in trouble.

As much as my heart pulled me straight ahead, my fear urged me to the left, to an unknown future. The unknown, I rationalized, at least held potential. It held the possibility for knowledge, happiness, maybe even love. But there was also the possibility for danger and punishment. Sure, Sophisticates were the best of the best: the smartest, brightest, and most talented. They were the military that protected the country and the businessmen and women who ran it. But the average American had no love for the Sophisticates. A Sophisticate was an ideal that the typical person could never attain, no matter how hard they tried. Science had finally surpassed hard work. The best jobs? The best bodies? The best minds? They all belonged to the genetically-altered Sophisticates. I could run from the Program and I might have a chance at true freedom, but there was also the likelihood I'd be discovered. I wasn't sure the hopeful possibilities outweighed the negative ones since I was fairly certain I'd get caught eventually. Those who tried to run always got caught. And punished. I shivered, remembering the gruesome videos. If I ran, I'd get caught. If I was lucky, I'd be discovered and caught by the Program, not the average man who was overcome with bitter jealousy.

As my heart and fear waged a tug of war on my emotions, I was faced with yet another choice, the only choice Younglove had given me. My mind urged me to go to the right, to do what I was told to do. To go to the Transfer Office and sacrifice myself to the Hounds and become a Mandate.

I licked my lips, hitched my backpack over my shoulder, and started to jog across campus. My mind had won out. I knew that to consider running anywhere but to the Transfer Office was a lost cause.

I'd been a fool to think I actually had a choice in my future.

4

THE LION'S DEN

I made it to the Transfer Office with only minutes to spare. The security guards, known to most of the faculty and students as the Hounds, hastily shuffled me into the back of a waiting vehicle where I was surprised to find a box of my meager belongings. I immediately rummaged through the box to find my bathroom toiletries, the clock radio that survived the raging inferno of my temper tantrum, and a few other random items that managed to remain unscathed, even if slightly charred in places. There was nothing of value in the box. Nothing that a normal person would have with them when making a life changing move. There were no pictures, no mementos, no books, no valuables. Hell, there weren't even any clothes in there.

I dropped the alarm clock back into the box where it rattled against the shampoo and conditioner. I was leaving everything behind. The life I knew, my friends, even my few personal belongings which were now nothing more than smoldering ash. I was going to be alone and stranded in a military academy — a place I didn't belong. I considered the age old question people sometimes asked themselves: If you were stranded on a desert island, what would you take with you? I realized that not only did I not know the answer to that question, but I was positive that whatever it was I would want to take, wasn't in the box sitting with me in the back seat.

Overcome with a feeling of loneliness, I stared down at my hands, my eyes falling on the tattoo that was on the inside of my right forearm. It was the size of a quarter, a circle with two inter-twining lines slashing across the center. The left side of the circle was black, the other side was red. It was the symbol every Sophis-ticate wore, declaring them as one of the elite. The best of the best.

And now you're a Mandate, I thought to myself.

I wasn't sure what part of the current situation was worse: leaving everything behind, or becoming a Mandate. Being without Cassie was going to be hard, but I had a feeling becoming a Mandate was going to be far worse.

I'd spent my entire life on school campuses of the Program — with the exception of the occasional field trip — so riding along I-95 in the massive SUV was an interesting distraction from having the proverbial rug pulled out from under me. I tried not to focus too much on the panic and fear that were taking up residence inside my mind. Being one of the Program's soldiers had never been a thought I'd considered, and now it was my destination.

Looking out the window to the left, I could see the city skyline of Baltimore basking in the hard light of the midday sun. The University campus was situated perfectly between Baltimore and Washington D.C., which was why the Program took it over in the first place. They wanted access to the political goings on in the Capitol as well as easy access to the shipping industry in Baltimore. Although I enjoyed the architecture and monuments of Washington, I much preferred Baltimore since Washington was one of the cities that had been hit hardest by *Wormwood*. It had been all but destroyed. The museums, politics, and monuments were still there, but it was a scarred and shattered city. Almost everyone living in Washington had died from the "bitter waters" of *Wormwood* and those lucky few that survived fled and never came back. Homes that had once been beautiful were rundown and abandoned, now nothing more than mangled skeletons that sheltered a handful of lost and broken people. Washington, and all of the other cities hit by *Wormwood*, were now cursed reflections of their former glory — ghost towns and havens for crime and death. Baltimore remained untouched and I always felt it was a cleaner city for that.

As the SUV devoured the miles along the interstate in quiet efficiency, the University and Cassie drifted farther and farther away. I felt my composure cracking — tiny, spiderweb-like fractures that threatened to break my sanity into a million, screaming pieces. A lifetime in the Program had forced me to bear the situation, any situation, with calm detachment. If the Hounds had bothered to look back at me, they'd see nothing but a bored teenage girl with not a care in the world, except for the care the Program gave her. But I felt my composure clawing for purchase on the slippery slope of my fear. The fear of the unknown, the fear of being alone, the fear of being a soldier — possibilities I'd never bothered to consider before were now slowly smothering me.

I closed my eyes and leaned my head back into the seat, trying to control my breathing, remembering a time not too long ago when I'd felt a similar sense of smothering panic.

****

I hugged my knees and rocked back and forth on the bed, muttering to myself. "I can't believe they signed me up for Martial Arts. I can't do it, I just can't."

Cassie sat beside me and pulled me into a one-armed hug, rubbing my back. "What do you mean? Of course you can. You always worry needlessly about this stuff and then breeze by easily. You're a Sophisticate — best of the best, right?"

"Yeah, breeze by easily when it's something I can learn from a book!"

"They have books on martial arts," Cassie argued unhelpfully. "Maybe you could use your super nerd powers and read your way to being a ninja."

I glared at her, momentarily forgetting my panic. "You know what I meant. I suck at this physical stuff. Why do I have to learn it anyway? I'm a Vanguard. Not likely I'll be battling it out with an enemy-roundhouse-kicking-laptop."

Cassie stared at me and was quiet for a moment. "That actually would be kind of nerdtastic, wouldn't it? How exactly would the laptop roundhouse kick, do you think? With the power cord or the mouse?"

"Shut up," I laughed, my fear ebbing away at the absurd turn of the conversation. "I just don't want anyone punching and kicking me, you know? I like my teeth and nose perfectly straight and my bones completely unbroken."

"Well then, I guess you better throw the first punch and learn to block pretty quickly." Cassie playfully punched me in the arm.

"Yeah, you're right. You totally suck."

"You hit like a girl," I bantered back.

"Thank you."

"I'm still scared," I admitted.

Cassie turned, her face sincere and serious. "You may not be able to control your future, but you can control how you handle it. Don't let the fear rule you, rule the fear."

****

Breathe, I reminded myself. Don't let the fear rule you, rule the fear. I smiled at the memory, the words that had helped me then were still helping me now. Only Cassie's advice could be that far-reaching. Of course, Cassie had been put into ballet and never had to worry about a roundhouse kick to the face, but I knew that didn't make the words any less true. The future wasn't something I could control; I knew that. I just had to control how I handled it. I tucked away the fear of the unknown and the despair of being alone and, as Cassie would've said, put on my big girl panties.

Twenty minutes after emerging from the Harbor Tunnel, the vehicle exited the interstate. Soon we were on Route 1, passing a series of rundown auto shops and crab shacks. The Hound on the passenger side cranked the lever on his seat to make it recline into my personal space. I shuffled to the other side of the vehicle, purposely kicking the back of his headrest in the process. Neither of the Hounds had spoken to me since I arrived — sweating and panting — at the Transfer Office. They had taken my form, given it a cursory glance, and led me to the SUV as if I were a prisoner. In reality, I knew that was just about the truth of it.

Heading along Rocks Road, it wasn't long before the derelict businesses on either side of the roadway faded into woods. I looked uneasily to the right where a wide stream hugged the edge of the road. The stream ducked underneath a bridge as we crossed over it, only to embrace the road on the left side. I'd only ever lived in cities so I was used to pavement, shiny buildings, and traffic. Thick woods, winding rivers, and desolate places in the middle of nowhere? They kind of gave me the creeps.

The SUV made a sudden turn onto an unmarked road forcing me, and my box of meaningless things, to slide across the leather seat as the vehicle tunneled its way through overgrown trees. After a mile or so, the road dead-ended at a large, black iron gate which swung open at our arrival, allowing me my first look at St. Ignatius. Ahead, an imposing stone building glared down at us. Stretching out to either side were massive stone walls of sharp edges and Romanesque architecture. In the center of the building, a tall tower loomed overhead, featuring a large clock, smaller rose windows, and blind arcades. The architecture was intricate, like an overly-decorated wedding cake, only it was grey and drab — like an old, moldy, black and white postcard.

It was as if someone had taken an old European building and tossed it carelessly into the middle of the woods in rural Maryland. I'd seen a lot of farms on our way here. Old red barns, rows of corn, and grazing cows were to be expected out here in the boondocks. This building had no business sitting where it was, pretentious and unwelcoming.

A long driveway approached the building and then looped around a garden of flowers and bushes, which was manicured to feature the silhouette of a lion with the words "St. Ignatius" underneath. A lion — the perfect symbol for all the ruthless soldiers inside.

I really am about to enter the Lion's Den. I wondered if, like the biblical Daniel, I had an angel that would shut the mouths of the St. Ignatius lions and keep them from devouring me.

Doubtful.

The driver followed the driveway around, coming to a stop in front of the main door, which was flanked by two marble lions.

As I got out of the car, I glanced back down the driveway and noticed that on either side of the entry gate, there was a thirty-foot high wall that ran along the property and disappeared into the surrounding woods. I was fairly certain the wall went entirely around the St. Ignatius campus. However, whether its main purpose was to keep people out or the cadets in, I couldn't be sure.

The two security guards led me up the steps to a set of large double doors where a golden-haired boy, in a slightly rumpled school uniform, stood waiting.

"This the one?" the boy asked.

"She's all yours. Her name's Clementine, like the orange," one of the Hounds offered, chuckling at what he obviously thought was an amusing joke.

"Cleo," I corrected, glaring at the Hound. My box of random crap was propped under my arm and rested on my hip.

The disheveled boy appraised me and then said "Let's go Clementine, I'll show you around."

He entered the building with me and my box clattering in his wake. I was annoyed at his refusal to call me by my nickname.

"Don't I need to see the admissions office and get some sort of orientation?" I asked.

"The Hounds are checking you in. I'm your orientation so don't fall behind. I'm only doing this spiel once, Clementine."

"It's Cleo," I reminded him in a clipped tone. I knew it was stupid to be rude to the first person I met, but no one my age ever called me by my given name. That was an insult allowed only to professors and the other henchmen of the Program.

"Your genetic donors named you Clementine and that's what the Program calls you, so get used to it. Answering to your given name will be one of the easiest things for you to get used to here at St. Ignatius. Trust me."

"Exactly what else will I have to get used to?"

"Let's just start with the name for now."

"Okay then, what's your name?"

"Sterling."

Remembering the Hound's reference to my name, I asked, "As in silver?"

"As in shut the hell up," rumpled Sterling shot back. He seemed annoyed, but not cruel.

"You're a really pleasant tour guide. I can see how you got the job," I replied in a fake, bright voice.

"You don't want to know how I got this job, so why don't you give me a break? You think you're the first genius to come up with a joke about my name? I've had seventeen years of asshats making sterling silver jokes."

"Point taken," I conceded.

We walked in silence for a minute before I couldn't take the awkwardness any more. "So, what's it like here?"

"Do you want the welcome pamphlet description or the truth?"

"Is the truth really that bad?"

"That depends on your definition of bad," Sterling replied, turning the corner and leading me down a hallway — stony, grey, and dismal, just like the previous hallway. "If you enjoy getting up before the sun to run five miles every morning, you'll love it here. If you enjoy wearing dipshit uniforms that incorporate plaid whenever possible, then you'll be ecstatic. If you enjoy having absolutely no free time whatsoever, this is your place. If you . . . "

"I get it," I interrupted. "The uniforms alone will be my own personal hell," I said, indicating the various shades of gold, brown, and green that Sterling was decked out in.

Sterling laughed. "You think this is bad? Just wait till you see the girl's uniform. You get knee socks."

"Knee socks aren't so bad." In fact, they were kind of stylish if done correctly. Or so Cassie said.

"They're yellow," Sterling countered. "And they have tassels."

"Tassels?"

"Like on moccasins. You know that little leather fringe stuff?"

"You can't be serious."

"Remember the girl scouts in the 1970s? Those lovely little sock garters? You get to wear them — tasseled and brown."

"Please be joking."

Sterling laughed. "It's like your knees have beards. They look like little twin Abraham Lincolns."

"Why would they force us to wear something like that?"

"Because they can. Don't worry though, you only have to wear them to class."

I groaned. Uniforms. Well, considering all of my clothes were destroyed anyway, maybe it wasn't such a bad thing. It was much better than wearing the same jeans and t-shirt every day for the rest of the foreseeable future.

We continued down the cavernous hallway as Sterling pointed out various classrooms. He then led me up a set of stairs to a window that overlooked the grounds on the back side of the building. From that vantage point, I could see a large, open, grassy space that appeared to be an arena for athletic training. There was a track that circled the edge of the entire space while weight benches and pull-up bars mingled in organized rows in the middle. A shooting range was tucked away at one side. At the moment, large, grossly muscled cadets were using the equipment and working out. A few circled the track, but most were lifting weights, doing pushups, and knocking out pull-ups in rapid fire succession.

"Lunch break," Sterling muttered, noticing that I was studying the intense workouts taking place below.

"Do we have to do that at lunch?" I asked. The most activity I did during lunch at the University was attempt to inhale my food before the Homework Harpies got their talons on it.

"No. Those are the overachievers, St. Ignatius's finest stock," he said as he frowned.

I looked at Sterling. He was a tad disheveled, but aside from that he didn't look too bad. "You're not one of St. Ignatius's finest?" I asked innocently.

"Do I look like a typical Mandate?"

I noticed that although his uniform fit rather well, he wasn't bulging out of it like the cadets below — like the Homework Harpies bulged out of their clothes. For the first time, I realized he was probably as out of place as I was.

When I neglected to answer his question, he said, "Just wait. You'll see. You're not the only outcast here. We're a small, but obvious, group."

I felt uncomfortable discussing my lack of popularity with people I hadn't even met yet, so I changed the subject. "Is that where we do our morning run?" I asked, pointing to the track that circled the area below.

Sterling grunted. "You wish. The morning run is slightly more challenging." I noticed he said slightly in a way that really meant severely. "I don't envy you the first day," he continued. "It's a bit of a rude awakening no matter who your genetic donors were." He turned from the window. "Let me show you where your room is so you can change. I'm supposed to take you to your mentor before your first afternoon class."

"Class?" I asked in surprise. "Today?"

"This isn't a spa vacation, Tiger Lily. Just be glad it's History of Wormwood and not Conditioning."

"Conditioning?"

"Hope you've got a bottle of *Icy Hot* in there," he said, peeking into my box.

Reflexively, I tilted the box out of his view. I didn't have anything personal or embarrassing in it, but I didn't like the idea of him gawking at the only possessions I had left. They were meaningless, but they were still mine. "That's none of your business," I said stupidly.

He just shrugged and said, "Hey, I don't care if you have it or not. Just saying, you're going to need it."

Sterling guided me back through the maze of arches, columns, and hallways and I was positive I'd never find my way around. St. Ignatius was massive and confusing. Once back in the main foyer, we went down a central hallway toward the back of the building.

We entered a small hall that was dominated by a large desk that stretched across most of the room. A couple of guards sat behind the desk, staring intently at monitors in front of them. One looked up briefly as we approached the desk.

"I'm showing Clementine Dracone to her room," Sterling said.

"Ten minutes," the guard stated as he handed Sterling a key card.

Sterling led me past the desk toward a stairway to the right. He used the card to open the door and as we climbed the stairs, my curiosity got the best of me.

"Ten minutes?"

Sterling held up the card, waving it in front of my face. "This gets me into the girl's dormitory, but I have to be back out in ten minutes."

"Or?"

"Or they come looking for me." At my puzzled look he continued, "They figure ten minutes isn't long enough to get into any trouble. They obviously forget what it's like to be a teenage boy." He smiled mischievously, waggling his eyebrows.

"Well, don't get your hopes up," I warned. "I'm a lot more trouble than I'm worth."

"I don't doubt that," Sterling agreed. "I've never seen someone show up here with so little," he said, indicating my box of junk. "What did you do to get sent here?"

"I can't tell you."

"Because then you'd have to kill me," he said in mock fear.

"Something like that," I responded, shifting the box to my other hip as if I could hide my secrets as easily as I could hide the box and the dregs of my old life.

After several flights of stairs, we reached a door. Sterling slid the card through the reader and the door clicked open onto a hallway.

"Here's your room," he said, stopping in front of a door with the number 323 on it and handing me a key that he fished out of his pocket. "Go ahead and leave your stuff inside and then get changed. There's a closet full of plaid and knee socks in there."

"Where are you going?" I asked, suddenly afraid to be alone.

Sterling flashed the card in front of me. "Downstairs. Only ten minutes, remember? I'll be at the front desk waiting for you."

With that, he hurried down the hall and I could hear him jogging down the steps before the stairwell door clicked shut. I fit the key into the knob and pushed the door open. The room inside was small but neat. There was a desk with a laptop — completely uncharred, I noticed happily. Against the wall were a bed and dresser. There was a door across from the bed that led to a walk-in closet that was filled with brown, green, and yellow clothes and a few pairs of equally unattractive shoes.

Mounted on the inside of the closet door was a guide for wearing the uniforms and which styles were appropriate for different occasions. I located the diagram of the class uniform and quickly dressed. I looked myself over in the full length mirror on the back of the door. Sterling was right. The fringe on my socks made my knees look like they had Abraham Lincoln beards. I shrugged at my reflection, tucking the ever disobedient lock of hair behind my ear. It would have to do; Sterling was waiting and so was this mysterious mentor of mine.

I was standing outside my room locking my door when a painful sensation shot through my hand. I jerked my hand off the doorknob, which had just sent a stinging shock through my fingers. I shook my hand to ease the pain, afraid to grab the handle again to try to lock the door. When I heard someone clear their throat, I looked up to see a girl leaning against the doorway of a room two doors down.

"So you're the new girl, huh?" the girl asked, snapping a piece of gum between her front teeth. She had long, platinum blond hair that curled luxuriously like one of those shampoo commercials.

"Guilty as charged," I admitted.

A sly grin lifted the corner of the girl's mouth. "Are you really?"

I shrugged, allowing the girl to think what she would of that remark. "My name's Cleo," I said, holding out my hand.

"Quinnie," the girl replied, grasping my hand lightly.

Another shock bit into my hand, dancing uncomfortably between my palm and Quinnie's. I pulled my hand back, bending and flexing my fingers, working the sting out.

"Sorry about that," I said. "Static electricity."

Quinnie acted like she hadn't felt the shock at all. "So what are you in for?"

"Sorry?"

"No need to apologize." Quinnie smiled conspiratorially. "I was just asking what you did to get sent here."

"I'm not sure. They never told me."

Quinnie appraised me, from the top of my lumpy ponytail to the tips of my bearded knees. "It must have been pretty bad if they sent you here. You're obviously not Mandate material," the girl sneered.

I looked at Quinnie more closely, incredulous that the girl was being so rude for no reason at all. Quinnie was taller than average, but not excessively muscular or athletic looking. She definitely wasn't the typical Mandate either.

"I've got skills. I could definitely take you," I boasted, not fully believing the threat myself. The only battling and taking of anyone I'd ever done was when I was playing chess with one of the Homework Harpies and that didn't really count since they were such easy prey.

"Doubtful," Quinnie laughed as she sashayed down the hallway. She turned and added, "I'm shocked you'd even think that you were a match for me." And then she disappeared into the staircase.

Quickly regaining my composure and locking my bedroom door without touching the knob, I walked to the door of the stairwell — where Quinnie had just disappeared — and reached for the handle. I pulled the door open a little more forcefully than I'd intended and was rewarded with another painful shock. This one was strong and zapped up through my hands and into my arms.

"Ow! Shit!" I hissed loudly, my cursing echoing inside the stairwell.

Below, I could hear Quinnie laughing in response.

MENTAL MENTOR

Sterling was waiting by the counter, nervously tapping the girls' dorm entry card on the countertop. The guard glared at him for several seconds before snatching the card out of Sterling's hand and filing it away in his desk drawer.

I stumbled out of the stairwell, unused to the slight heel on the shoes I'd gotten out of the closet. Sterling looked up at the sound. "Nice Lincoln legs."

"I bet you say that to all the girls." Sterling was kind of growing on me. I liked his sense of humor.

"Actually, I do," he admitted. "Can't help it. All I can say is that someone needs to assassinate those socks. They do all sorts of horrible things to the female figure which, come to think of it, might be the purpose of them after all."

"How so?"

"Isn't it obvious? It's hard for me to find any female attractive when there are two miniature dead presidents peeking out from under her skirt at me."

"So what did Quinnie say when you used the Lincoln leg line on her?"

"Ah, I see you met our illustrious Quinnie."

"Yes, it was a bit of a shock."

Sterling looked at me sympathetically. "I know what you mean."

Did he? Was he agreeing that there was something odd about Quinnie or was he just agreeing that Quinnie was a mega-bitch? I mentally kicked myself. The latter, obviously. I decided not to mention that I thought that the pretty girl across the hall was somehow shocking me with some amped up static electricity. That sounded crazy, even for me.

"Anything I should know about Quinnie?" I asked instead.

"Basically, you just don't want to piss her off. She doesn't look like much, but she packs a punch. In fact, a good general rule around here is to keep your head down and your mouth shut."

"Are you speaking from experience?" I smiled halfheartedly.

Sterling didn't smile back. "Come on, let's go meet your mentor, Professor Younglove."

I coughed. "What? She's here?"

"You know her?"

"Delia Younglove is the Dean at the University where I just came from. I didn't know she was coming here too." I cringed at the thought of seeing Younglove again. Perhaps the only bright spot of being sent to St. Ignatius had been knowing that I wasn't going to have to deal with that woman anymore.

"Oh. Not Delia Younglove. Twyla Younglove. Maybe they're related?" Sterling suggested.

"Oh God, I hope not. One crazy cat lady is enough. Does Twyla

Younglove smell like wet cats?" I asked as we turned down a new hallway.

Sterling turned to look at me quizzically. "Wet cats? Not that I've noticed. Although I'm not sure I'd recognize the smell of wet cats anyway."

"Trust me, you would."

We reached a door with the nameplate "Professor Younglove" mounted on it.

"Here you go," Sterling said, indicating the door.

"Where do I go after this?" I asked. "I'm not sure I can find my way back . . . well, anywhere."

"No worries, I'll be waiting for you out here. I'm supposed to take you to your History of Wormwood class after your meeting. Go on. Get it over with," he said with a grimace, nodding his head in the direction of the door.

I knocked and a husky voice invited me inside.

Twyla Younglove's office was nothing like the Younglove office that I'd been in earlier this morning. It was bright and smelled mostly pleasant. The heavily perfumed smoke of incense hovered in the air around a woman seated at the desk. Her face was leathery and tan, but not completely unattractive. Her black hair hung down to the middle of her back, with small braids sprinkled throughout, looping and curling through the rest of her wavy hair. She held a long cigarette in her hand, the jade handle perched expertly between her first and middle fingers.

"Come in," Younglove beckoned, blowing perfect smoke rings into the air. When I was seated across from her, Younglove took another drag on her cigarette and then leaned her elbow on the table with her hand poised in the air like she was some black and white movie star. "I'm Professor Twyla Younglove, your mentor."

I mustered all the courtesy I could and leaned forward and held out my hand. "Nice to meet you," I said. Younglove turned her head and blew a stream of smoke, neglecting to partake in a handshake.

I was somewhat offended, but not nearly as much as I was relieved. Younglove's skin, upon closer inspection, looked like an old, cracked leather couch. I couldn't be certain that bits of that dried up old skin wouldn't flake off at the slightest touch. Younglove looked to be in urgent need of some moisturizer and I thought it was a bad choice for the desiccated woman to be smoking. It looked entirely possible that her parched body could go up in a tower of flames at the slightest spark. The overflowing ashtray on the edge of the desk proved that Younglove tempted fate quite often.

"We'll be seeing quite a lot of one another during your time here," Younglove promised, flicking the end of her cigarette over the ashtray, sending ash scattering across the desktop. "I'll be overlooking your education and training, making sure that you're where you should be in the learning process. I'll also be helping you with your specialization."

"My specialization?"

"Discovering your skills and helping you develop them."

"You mean like computer programming and my knack for foreign languages?"

Younglove took another long drag on her cigarette before answering. She looked me directly in the eye as she blew out another stream of smoke. "That's not what I'm referring to, Clementine, and you know it. You're well aware of what you can do and you know that's why you've been sent here. Don't play stupid, you're better than that," she said forcefully. It wasn't said in a supportive way, but more as a warning.

"You mean what happened to my room?" I questioned.

"Yes."

"Because I accidentally set it on fire," I ventured.

"It was more than that, as you are well aware."

"I'm not really sure what happened, honest," I said, holding up my hand as if I were swearing on the bible.

"Well, we'll have plenty of time to explore that — safely of course. Your specialization will be a very valuable asset to the Sophisticate Program, and to the Mandates in particular."

"Are you saying that I was sent here only because of what happened last night? Because if that's the case, you need to send me back to the University. Last night was an accident, it won't happen again," I promised.

"Oh, it will," Younglove assured me. "It will. But no worries, we're not going to explore that your first day here. I merely wanted to see you today so that we could go over your class list and discuss what team sport you will be involved in."

"Team sport?"

"Yes, as well as your job."

"My job?" I wasn't making a very good impression, I sounded like a damn echo.

"You have to have some way of earning money, don't you? From what I've heard, you didn't bring many belongings with you. St. Ignatius provides your uniforms and training clothes, but I seriously doubt you'll want to wear your uniforms outside of class."

I glanced down at my bearded Lincoln legs. Uniforms all day long? "No," I agreed.

"Very well then, you'll need to be able to afford to purchase clothes and other necessities, which is why you need a job. Don't worry, I think you'll enjoy the one that's been assigned to you. First things first, however, let's discuss your class schedule." She sucked in another breath of tangy smoke as she pushed an off-white card across the desktop.

I grabbed the card, which detailed my daily schedule, and scanned it. "We run for an hour and a half?"

"Five miles."

"Every morning?"

"Every morning."

"Even Saturdays and Sundays?"

"Yes, but you don't have to do the obstacle course on the weekend."

Obstacle course? Sterling didn't say anything about an obstacle course did he? I'd never run five miles in my entire life and now I was going to have to do it every day? And with obstacles on most of those days? I am going to die, I thought. I am literally going to have a heart attack and die the very first day.

Well, that's one way to get out of being a Mandate.

"So, there's your schedule," Professor Younglove said easily. "Cadet Sterling will show you to your first class today after you leave here. Any questions?"

Only about a million.

"What about Calculus and Physics and all of the other classes I was taking at the University? I see Weapons and Conditioning, but this schedule seems to be lacking some actual educational classes."

Younglove studied me thoughtfully. "You will be studying the things that a Mandate needs to know. Physics, Calculus, World History — they mean nothing to a Mandate."

I was disappointed. I may not have always liked my professors at the University, but I liked my classes. Another glance at some of the classes on my schedule — Weapons, Conditioning, Strategy & Statistics, and Foreign Politics — was a harsh realization that I was walking the path of a soldier now, not that of a student.

"Now, let's talk about your job, or as we call it here, your Work Detail."

I winced at the thought of having no control over my choice of jobs. I didn't mind working, I only hoped it had nothing to do with cleaning toilets.

"You will be the librarian aide for St. Ignatius. Not only will you help with retrieving and re-shelving books, but you will also be expected to help out with research, and to tutor other cadets when necessary."

Finally! Something about this day was turning out well. Library aide was a very acceptable job since I would have access to books and computers. Since I fully intended to keep trying to hack into the system to get the answers I wanted about my parents, being a library aide was a very fortuitous position to have. And even the tutoring part wasn't that bad. I was used to tutoring the Homework Harpies, so I didn't foresee having any problems tutoring Mandates.

I allowed myself a small smile of relief. The one thing I couldn't understand was if they knew what I had done to my room last night, why on earth were they allowing me to work in a library which was full of flammable objects? Well, I wasn't going to bring that oversight to their attention. I'd just have to make sure I was on my best behavior. And thankfully, a library was usually one of those places which was calm and serene. Perhaps that's why they'd put me there in the first place.

"And last but not least, we have to discuss your team sport. Everyone at St. Ignatius is required to participate in a team sport."

"Okay," I agreed apprehensively. "What sports are there to choose from?"

"No need to worry about that," Younglove promised. "I've already signed you up for the sport I coach."

I reassessed Younglove just to make sure I hadn't missed anything on my initial first impression. Nope. She was definitely a chain-smoking, bag of bones. What sport could this woman possibly coach?

"Croquet?" I asked hopefully.

Younglove laughed. A big belly laugh, which seemed odd coming out of someone as dry and fragile as a dead leaf. "Croquet? Have you forgotten where you are? No, not croquet. You're going to be on my roller derby team."

Now it was my turn to laugh. "Roller derby? I think you're mistaken."

"How so?"

"It's apparent you've mistaken me for someone who can actually roller skate. I can't skate and I'm pretty sure that's one of the prerequisites for roller derby, as is athletic ability and a certain disdain for one's own safety."

"That's not a problem; you'll simply learn to skate. You're a Sophisticate, you'll pick it up easily. And as for safety, you'll have helmets and pads. You'll be fine as long as you train hard. It's either roller derby or full contact football, since they are the only sports with openings at this point. I think once you get a look at the football teams, you'll agree that roller derby is just your thing." Younglove smirked.

There was nothing that I could say. I'd learned from experience that once a Program decision was made, it was final.

"Now run along," Younglove motioned with her hand. "Class starts in 15 minutes and we wouldn't want you late on your first day. Well, at least not twice in one day." Younglove's stern gaze said what her mouth didn't: "I know all about you. You have no secrets."

I grabbed my schedule and quickly made my way out of Younglove's office, wishing I had the power to be invisible, to hide from the Program. I couldn't shake the feeling that there were eyes all around. Always watching.

"Let's see your schedule," Sterling prompted when I met up with him outside in the hallway. I passed the sheet over to him. "Ouch. Work Detail every day for two hours a day?" he exclaimed. "That's rough."

"That's not normal?"

"Not if you have a sponsor."

"What do you mean?"

"Well, if you manage to get a sponsor, you don't have to work. They pay for all of your creature comforts — clothes, electronics, and other luxuries."

"Do you have a sponsor?"

"No, but my work detail is only an hour a day. You must have really pissed someone off before coming here." The statement hung in the air, begging me to fill in the blanks. I didn't. Sterling was starting to grow on me, but he was still a stranger and my secrets were still mine. Mostly.

"Pissing people off seems to be a talent of mine," I admitted. "My work detail isn't too bad though — I'll be a library aide."

"Double ouch! Can't get more boring than that."

DEVIATION

I was surprised. I thought I'd gotten off pretty easily in the grand scheme of things. I had, after all, destroyed my room back at the University. They could have decided to make me shovel out horse stalls or something.

"What's your work detail?" I asked Sterling.

"Data entry. I transfer a lot of old handwritten files into the computer."

"Talk about boring."

"Yeah," Sterling agreed. "But they only give me an hour's worth of work. Or, at least what would take a normal person an hour. I usually get it done in half the time," he bragged, wiggling his fingers like he was typing at supersonic speed. "So see, while you're stuck in the library polishing the card catalog for two hours, I'm spending most of that time kicking back and playing video games."

"That's how you spend your money? Video games?"

"How else would I spend it?"

I appraised my guide and his absurdly wrinkled clothes. "For starters, an iron and an ironing board."

Sterling took the barb in stride. "That, my darling Clementine, would be a terrible waste of money. Wrinkles are my trademark."

I laughed as we turned into another hallway and into the crowds of cadets heading in different directions for class.

"Everyone is staring at me," I whispered.

"That's because you're like a new car, you've still got that new car smell. Plus, they can sense your fear."

"I'm not afraid," I insisted.

"You should be. But don't worry, our classroom is right up here."

Despite my declaration that I wasn't afraid, apparently, my

stomach didn't agree. "Hold up, is there a bathroom around here anywhere?"

"Sure. It's right there," Sterling said, pointing down the hall, "but I don't think you have time, the bell's about to ring." He looked at his watch to confirm his suspicion. "You only have three minutes, and I don't want to be late. Can you hold it until after?"

"Definitely not. Don't wait for me, I know where to go now. I'll see you there."

Sterling nodded and jogged off to the classroom. I spun on my heel and threaded my way through the crush of burly cadets bulldozing through the hallway to be on time to class. A big guy ran by, thoughtlessly pushing me out of his way. He didn't bother to look back or apologize and I was caught in an avalanche of muscles and massive bodies, smashed against the wall, hardly noticed. I reminded myself that these were the people the Program sent off to fight terrorists. These were killers in training. What was I doing here?

As the crowd moved past, I scanned the hallway for the path of least resistance. I briefly caught the eye of a dark haired boy leaning against the wall, hands in his pockets. I couldn't be sure, but it seemed something was defective in the assembly of his uniform — it didn't look like Sterling's uniform. He also was either unaware or unconcerned by the surging mass of people around him, or by the fact that the bell was minutes away from beginning classes.

I didn't have time to worry about the mysterious looking boy. Using my forearm, I pushed open the bathroom door and darted inside, afraid I'd throw up before I could get to the nearest toilet. A few dry heaves later, it was obvious that my lack of meals had kept the incident from becoming a full-fledged disaster. My uniform was still intact and clean, even if I was utterly damaged on the inside. Was it just a few hours ago that Cassie was tossing notes on my desk?

I stumbled over to the nearest sink, splashed water onto my face and then leaned over the running water, bracing my hands on either side of the porcelain bowl. An overwhelming sense of loneliness threatened to crush me, stealing my breath and causing my vision to blur at the edges. I stared into the sink, willing myself to dissolve and seep into the drain, to disappear into oblivion. Yesterday I had wished I could just be a normal girl with normal problems. Today, I just wanted to go back to my old life and Cassie. I wanted my biggest worries to be whether I was late to class or if I'd get a decent meal with the Homework Harpies around, not whether I could physically survive the day.

I took a few, deep calming breaths and then dried my face off with one of the generic, brown paper towels in the dispenser.

You can do this, I promised myself. Rule the fear.

The bell rang and for the second time that day, I found myself late for class. I wondered if they would punish me on my first day. With a class schedule already boasting an hour and a half of running, an hour of conditioning, five hours of classes, an hour of team sport practice, and two hours of work detail, I wasn't sure where they would find the time to punish me or how my body could survive it. I was already exhausted and I hadn't even made it to my first class yet.

If Cassie were here, she'd have something totally inappropriate, superficial, and self-centered to say. She'd cheer me up for sure.

But Cassie wasn't here. I forced myself to keep my eyes dry.

Like Sterling said, "They could sense fear" here and I didn't want to give my fellow classmates any ammunition.

Balling up the paper towel, I tossed it into the trash can and then yanked on the handle of the bathroom door, stepping out into the now empty hallway. I'd only taken a few steps when he spoke.

"Late on your first day?"

I turned to find the dark haired boy still leaning against the wall. The top button of his shirt was undone and his tie was slung over his shoulder. He wasn't wearing his jacket and his shirt sleeves were rolled up, revealing his tan, muscular forearms. His tousled hair hung across his forehead, nearly falling into his eyes, and it appeared he hadn't bothered to shave this morning.

"You're late, too," I pointed out. I also wanted to point out that his uniform was far from uniform or acceptable according to St. Ignatius policy.

The boy shook his head and then ran his hand back through his messy curls, trying to tame them into submission. "Not late. Sick."

"Sorry to hear that," I said, because I couldn't think of any better response. It was obvious the boy wasn't sick, he was skipping class. "Look, I really have to go. It was nice meeting you."

"But we haven't met," he responded.

"What?" I asked, confused.

"We haven't actually met yet," he explained, pushing away from the wall. "Name's Ozzy," he said, holding out his hand.

I looked at his hand. "Is it contagious?"

He tilted his head causing the unruly curls to tumble back across his forehead. "I don't follow."

"Your sickness, I don't want to catch anything."

"Right," he said, a wide grin dimpling across his face as he pulled his hand back and returned it to his pocket. "Well then, I should let you get to class I suppose." He turned and walked down the hallway, the opposite direction from my classroom. "It was nice meeting you, Clementine," he called back over his shoulder.

"I never told you my name," I said calmly, even though I was a little unnerved that he knew my name.

"You didn't have to."

"Apparently, I do," I retorted. "I don't answer to Clementine."

Ozzy chuckled without turning around. "See you around, Cleo."

6

WORMWOOD

My suffering upon being late to class was minimal. Professor Lawless allowed me to take a seat at the front of the room, eliminating the awkward gawking and walk of shame that taking a seat in the back of the classroom would have induced. My only friend (if he could even be called that after only a few hours) was in the back corner of the room trying to look inconspicuous.

Unfortunately, the result of my seat location was that Quinnie was seated at the desk behind me. Since our earlier meeting in the hallway hadn't exactly been friendly, I had a bad feeling about the situation. As soon as I sat down, she kicked the back of my chair.

"What do you want?" I asked grabbing the back of my seat as I turned around to face her.

She ignored me, but the metal bar along the back of my seat sent a stinging shock into my fingertips. I pulled my hand away as my breath hissed through my teeth. I thought I saw a ghost of a smile on Quinnie's face. Annoyed and confused, I turned back around and watched as Professor Lawless outlined the topics for discussion on the blackboard.

Grabbing my backpack, I shuffled through it to find a notebook and pencil. I didn't have a book for the class yet, but I could at least take notes. I found a notebook and flipped through the pages, passing endless numbers and complex equations from Garner's Calculus class until I found a blank page. I grabbed the spiral of the notebook to pull it closer to me and pain zapped through my fingers. I gasped loudly and pulled my hand away, noticing a series of small black lines along my fingertips. It felt as if the metal spiral had burnt me with an electrical shock. Not possible. I sucked on my fingers, trying to get the pain to go away. I thought I heard laughter behind me.

"Clementine," Professor Lawless called, returning my concentration to class and away from my personal pain. "I know this is your first day here, but I'm assuming that they covered a little History of Wormwood at the University. Unfortunately, you'll have to make up the first three weeks of classes you've missed here. So far, we've covered the events leading up to *Wormwood*."

I was relieved since I knew just about everything about *Wormwood*. At least everything that wasn't classified or restricted. Forgetting about the pain, I rubbed my thumb along my fingers and answered him. "That won't be a problem Professor, I'm well informed on the subject matter."

"Really?" Lawless rubbed his hands together hungrily, eager to test my knowledge. "Excellent. Can you tell me where the name *Wormwood* originates from?"

"It's from the book of Revelations in the Bible."

"Ehhh. Wrong," Quinnie said under her breath, imitating the

buzzer of a quiz show.

"Correct," Lawless praised. He turned around to write on the blackboard.

I looked over my shoulder to throw a triumphant glare at Quinnie only to find that she was diligently studying her nails, feigning innocence. When I turned forward again and leaned back against the chair it felt as if I had been stuck in the back with a needle. I jerked instinctively and had to stifle the urge to curse. Quinnie was laughing quietly. When I reached back to feel my shoulder for a wound, my hand brushed up against a metal bolt and I felt another stinging shock. Not a needle then. More random static electricity. Or more accurately, electrical shocks.

What the hell was going on?

If I hadn't caused everything in my room to explode the night before, I might have considered Quinnie and the random shocks a strange coincidence. Now, however, I was certain that Quinnie and I were more than average Sophisticates. I also suspected that these strange afflictions we had were also the reason we were both at St. Ignatius, even though it was obvious that neither of us truly belonged here.

Professor Lawless was facing the class again. "Clementine, can you tell us what *Wormwood* means in the context of the bible?"

I swallowed nervously, eager to make a good impression. I leaned forward, avoiding my notebook and every bit of metal in my immediate vicinity. "Basically, in Revelations it says that a star falls to the earth and poisons a third of the waters, causing them to be "bitter waters," and that it kills many men. The name of the star is *Wormwood*."

"Exactly."

I noticed that only a few of the other students in the class were listening to the answer. Either they already knew it, or didn't care. I assumed it was the latter. *Wormwood* was the whole reason there were even Sophisticates at all and I was always surprised to find that no one else in the Program ever seemed to care how or why we existed. *Wormwood* happened over 30 years ago. As far as my fellow Sophisticates were concerned, that was eons ago, when our genetic donors were just children.

I, however, was infatuated with *Wormwood*. I needed to know everything about what had happened and why the Program had been developed. Not many Sophisticates bothered to know their history. They didn't care about who their parents were or why they belonged to the Program; they just accepted it. Many of them thought being a Sophisticate was better than the alternative — being normal. A Sophisticate never really had to worry about anything. All of our needs were provided for by the Program and success came with very little effort. It was the normal people outside of the Program who struggled. To many Sophisticates, giving up freedom seemed a fair trade. I couldn't understand that blind acceptance, so I studied and searched and learned as much as I could. Knowledge is power. And in a world where I didn't have many choices or freedoms, that was the only kind of power I had.

A boy a few seats over seemed to rouse himself out of lethargic drooling. "I thought it was just a name they made up. I didn't know it had anything to do with the Bible."

"It doesn't, really," Lawless explained. "When the terrorists poisoned the drinking water of major U.S. cities, no one understood what was happening. Thousands of people began to die unexpectedly. At first it was thought to be a new virus or plague of some sort.

It took a very long time for the government and the CDC to discover that the source of the problems was the water."

Lawless' gestures were animated and his voice dramatic as he recounted the details of the attack. To listen to him, one might think he was talking about a blockbuster movie and not real events that had nearly destroyed the American way of life.

"When they finally declared the source of the deaths," he continued, "it was still unknown that terrorism was responsible. No one knew why the water was deadly. Religious fanatics claimed the end of the world was upon us and that *Wormwood* had caused the bitter waters. In time, terrorists claimed responsibility, but by then, *Wormwood* had become the adopted term for the attack."

Lawless continued his speech, explaining the type of poison used, how it had been administered, and how many deaths had resulted. It was horrific when one actually considered the facts. Ten of the largest U.S. cities were wiped out. Men, women, even children — completely gone. The people affected by the poisoned water suffered long, agonizing deaths. The cities became a modern version of leper colonies. In all, almost 29 million people died. Nearly 10 percent of the American population killed in one act of terrorism. It was sickening.

What was left of the government reacted aggressively to the attack. They needed a new weapon in the Global War on Terror and so, the Sophisticate Program was born. They created the Sophisticates — designer babies who were stronger, faster, smarter, and completely loyal to the government. Well, maybe not loyal, but property of the government. The Vanguard Sophisticates were created to help U.S. businesses excel and flourish, to help the country to be competitive in foreign markets, and to replace the political leaders and business owners that were lost when *Wormwood* took its toll. The Mandate Sophisticates were created for one purpose and one purpose only: killing terrorists and other enemies of the U.S. Mandates were the ultimate predators, which is why I was completely baffled to find myself one of them now. I was no predator. The only thing I ever preyed on was books and that was the nerdy, honest truth of it.

Reviewing *Wormwood*'s history dredged up unpleasant thoughts as I became lost in memories of my past. I didn't have a normal childhood, at least not what could be considered a normal childhood for a non-Sophisticate. I grew up in the Program schools and dormitories, surrounded by other designer babies. We had nannies to raise and take care of us and some of those women had actually been capable of genuine hugs and emotions at times. But the Program kept the nannies on a frequent rotation to keep the attachment to us nonexistent. As far as the government was concerned, we were an investment. We were tools and weapons for war. The Program couldn't risk allowing the nannies to create attachments to us because, one day, they might have to send one, or all, of us off to die. Of course the Program never came out and said it exactly that way.

As for the nannies, I didn't really remember any of those women, just minor bits and pieces of memories here and there. The person I remembered most clearly was Cassie — happy moments, sad moments — it didn't matter. There was always Cassie and the Homework Harpies. The five of us had been together as long as I could remember. Well, we'd been together up until this morning when the Program decided to send me to St. Ignatius, essentially ripping Cassie out of my life like it was nothing — just like they ripped out all those nannies over the years.

My anger smoldered and I had to tamp it down to keep from losing control. I knew that nothing good would come of letting destruction run loose and I didn't want to punish Lawless by turning his classroom into a battle zone. As far as Program professors went, he wasn't bad at all. Besides, I didn't know who was watching or what they knew. If something was destroyed, I'd probably be the first suspect and who knew what kind of punishment they dealt out here?

"Clementine," Lawless said, interrupting my thoughts of mayhem. "Since you seem to be my star pupil today, I was wondering if you could tell the class what *Wormwood* actually is?"

"It's another name for a plant," I explained uneasily. I hated being the center of attention. "Artemisia absinthium. Sometimes also called Mugwort," I continued, almost as if I couldn't help myself.

"Excellent," Lawless said happily. I guessed it wasn't often that students knew the answers to his questions.

"Know-it-all," Quinnie whispered in a voice that was barely audible.

"Yes?" Lawless asked, peering past me to Quinnie. "Quinby, do you have something to add?"

I nearly choked. Quinby? Oh, that was far worse than Clementine. I unsuccessfully tried to stifle a laugh as I turned and was caught in the blaze of Quinnie's glare. Quinnie chewed on the end of her pen as she slid her right hand up to her face and discreetly gave me the middle finger.

"A bonus question. Does anyone know of any other historical reference to the *Wormwood* prophecy from Revelations?" Lawless asked, glancing around the room. Nobody answered. "Clementine?"

I was a little unenthusiastic about being called on again, but I also had a hard time acting like I didn't know the answer. "Huns. One historical interpretation of what the *Wormwood* prophecy was meant to predict is that it was actually about the army of the Huns. There are other interpretations, but that is one of the most popular."

Lawless was giddy at having someone in his class that was not only paying attention, but also knew the answers to his questions. My fingers drummed the desktop with nervous, fidgety energy. As soon as I grabbed my pencil and my skin came in contact with the metal band just below the eraser, a sharp pain shot through my fingers and arm as I was shocked by an incredibly strong electrical current far worse than static electricity.

I snatched my hand back with a gasp and Quinnie giggled quietly. There were actually a huge red welt on my fingers. My anger responded instinctively, overpowering the sting of the shock, filling me with rolling waves of heat. My anger was hot and vicious and looking for a target. I could feel it starting in the pit of my stomach, racing through my veins with burning speed until the heat and fury and burn felt like it was exploding out of every pore in my skin. Belatedly, I tried to grasp the energy and pull it back inside, but it was too late. A small popping sound, followed by a screech caused me to turn around in curiosity.

Quinnie was staring at her pen, which had exploded, covering her in blue ink. It was all over her hands and her face. Her uniform was speckled with dots and blotches of blue stain. The remains of the pen were a smoldering mass of melted plastic, tendrils of smoke drifting toward me, the smell of burnt plastic and hot ink filling my nostrils and making me want to gag.

What had I done?

I was terrified that I had so easily lost my grip on my temper. I felt feverish and overwhelmingly relieved that the pen was the only damage I had done. At the same time, however, seeing Quinnie's beautiful face covered in a smattering of blobs of ink was oddly satisfying.

She deserved it.

And in that one thought, I was even more afraid of myself than of my new life as a Mandate.

Just then, the bell rang. I quickly gathered my stuff, turned to catch Sterling's eye, and motioned that I'd meet him outside of the classroom.

"Wow, you really know your *Wormwood*," Sterling muttered when he caught up with me in the hallway.

I shrugged. "It's a minor obsession. I read a lot."

Sterling studied me. "Are you all right? You look a little flushed."

I will not cry. I will not cry. I will not cry, I repeated to myself. "Yeah, I'm just trying to get adjusted."

"Did you see what happened with Quinnie? She seemed really upset at the end of class."

Lie. Lie. Lie. He won't believe the truth anyway, my brain argued. "I didn't see anything."

Sterling was in a different class than me for the next hour, so he escorted me to the door of the Technology classroom so I'd know where to go before he took off in a sprint to make it to his own class on time. He promised to come back afterwards to show me where I needed to go for roller derby practice.

Unsure whether Quinnie would be in this class too, I did my best to protect myself from being a shock experiment all class long. I sat down in front of a girl who looked like she was just barely five foot tall. The girl had long black hair that was streaked with blood red chunks that had been sloppily pulled into jagged ponytails high up on her head. Another large chunk of red and black hair hung across the left side of the girl's face, obscuring my view of her. I assumed that behind the curtain of outrageously long bangs there was most likely plenty of black and purple makeup. The girl was wearing all of the required elements of the St. Ignatius uniform, complete with bearded socks, but her arms were inked with colorful tattoos and she wore a ridiculous amount of leather bands with spikes and skulls on them.

The girl may have been tiny, but everything about her said, "I'm not scared of you, so piss off." She reminded me of a yapper dog — small in stature, but huge in attitude. I decided I'd take attitude over downright cruelty any day.

Right before the bell rang, Quinnie entered the room, panting and damp. It looked as though she had unsuccessfully tried to clean off the evidence from the exploded pen. Splotches of blue ink were still spattered on her skin and clothes. Even her thick blond hair had blue stains in it. Quinnie's eyes scanned the room and when she caught sight of me, she pointed a long lacquered nail at me and mouthed, "You're dead, whore," before taking her seat in the front row.

"I've never understood why girls do that to each other," a voice from behind said.

I turned around to find I was staring into the bright blue eyes of the girl behind me. And just as I thought, those eyes were lined with so much black and purple it looked like she had been the unfortunate victim of a fistfight.

"What's that?" I asked the girl.

"Call each other demeaning names. Slut, whore, skank. It just perpetuates negativity of women and their worth. However, that being said, anyone who is an enemy of that juiced-up witch over there is a friend of mine," punk rock girl said, pointing to Quinnie with a very chewed up pencil. "Name's Arabella."

"I'm Cleo, nice to meet you."

"When did you get here?"

"Right after lunch," I said, realizing that despite my nervous stomach before my History of Wormwood class, I was now starving.

"And you've already made an enemy? You work fast."

"I didn't really make her my enemy; I guess I just didn't make a very good first impression."

"You're not missing much," Arabella promised. "So, what do you think of St. Ignatius so far?"

"I haven't really had much time to think about anything yet."

Arabella nodded. "Classic method of operation for the Program. Keep us busy and distracted so we don't have the time or energy to question the insanity that is our lives."

I had to agree with Arabella on that one.

"So, what do you have next? What sport did you sign up for?"

"Younglove signed me up for roller derby," I confessed.

"Wicked. I'm in roller derby too, you'll love it."

"Somehow I don't think so. I can't skate."

Arabella laughed. "Good thing roller derby doesn't have much to do with skating."

I tilted my head and looked at Arabella in confusion. "Isn't skating kind of the whole point? *Roller* derby, right?"

"Nope. Derby is the important part of that term. Roller derby is basically road rage, only on a track. And, unlike on the road, in roller derby you're dealing with the same assholes over and over and over again in every single lap. It's great for releasing frustration, and I have a feeling you need plenty of release." Arabella grinned wickedly.

She'd hit the nail on the head there. I only hoped that in releasing frustration, I didn't do any permanent damage. Before I could ask any more questions about roller derby, Professor Dashwood entered the room and began class.

My computer skills were so advanced and beyond the subject matter in class, I didn't bother to pay attention. And since Dashwood seemed content to lecture nonstop without asking questions or requiring student involvement, it made daydreaming far too easy. Before I knew it, class was over and the students excitedly headed for their sports team responsibilities. When I exited the classroom, Sterling was already waiting outside. Upon seeing Arabella chatting with me, he grinned. "You've met Arabella, I see."

Arabella looped her arm through mine. "I've asked Cleo to join my witch hunt and she's agreed," Arabella said, glancing toward a still ink-spattered, pissed off Quinnie. "You in? I've got an extra pitchfork."

"You know I'm in," Sterling responded, glancing warily at Quinnie as she trounced off down the hallway followed by two girls who looked just as haughty. "Hey, would you mind showing Cleo to roller derby since you're going there?" Sterling was already slinging his bag over his shoulder, preparing to sprint away. He seemed to run everywhere. I noticed he finally used my nickname. Maybe he really was a possible friend.

"No problem. I'll make sure she gets to dinner too."

"Thanks," Sterling said, darting in and out of the other students as he made his way down the hallway.

"Where's he going?"

"Track and field," Arabella answered.

"Lucky. I wish I got track and field assigned to me."

"No you don't," Arabella said firmly. "It's not what you think, trust me. Roller derby is perfect for you. For your sake, hope you're on my team."

"Is your team the best?"

Arabella shrugged. "There are only two teams and Quinnie is on the other one," Arabella explained. "I'm pretty sure you'll be on our team though, we still need another jammer."

"A what?"

"You'll see," Arabella smiled. "Now let's go so we can get you a pair of skates."

"Wheels of death. Can't wait."

7

WHEELS AND SQUEALS

"Oh my God. I'm going to die." I wiggled dangerously on the skates before Arabella reached out to steady me. "I thought roller derby was played with roller skates. These are definitely NOT roller skates."

"They're inline skates," Arabella explained, tightening the buckle on my boot. "They're faster, more agile, and dangerously hot. You didn't expect St. Ignatius to play roller derby like everyone else did you?"

"Why not? Sterling gets to do track and field."

Arabella laughed out loud. "Yeah, but it's not track and field like in the Olympics. Trust me. He has a meet in a few weeks, you'll see."

"Can we go watch?" I asked out of curiosity. I wondered what they could possibly do to track and field to make roller derby a better choice of sport.

"Of course. We have to go, it's mandatory."

"Really?"

"Pretty much all of the sporting events are. Just another way for them to distract us from the reality of the Program," Arabella said quietly.

"You mean because eventually, we're all going to be out there. As soldiers."

"Exactly. What do you think this place would be like if everyone was focusing on the future? And I mean the Big Picture future, not What Homework Do I Have Due Tomorrow future? They don't want us thinking about things like terrorists and suicide bombers and the danger we'll be putting ourselves in, so they create these modified sports so they can still teach us the skills they want us to learn without us knowing we're actually learning something. The Program is constantly giving us freebies, distractions, and other things to look forward to so that we will be more likely to ignore reality."

"What kinds of distractions?"

"Work detail, sports . . . and the Autumn Formal," Arabella added, as if the Formal was on par with eating a bowl of roaches.

"You really have an Autumn Formal here?" I was astonished. The last thing I expected at a military academy was a dance. We didn't even have those back at the University.

"They have two Formals a year. I went to the one last spring when I got here, it was really boring."

"So when's this big dance thing taking place?"

"Six weeks. There's a football game and everything. Just like the Homecoming nonsense the normals have."

I may not have ever been to a dance, but I knew what Arabella was talking about. I'd seen enough movies and television shows involving Homecomings to know what the normals (non-Sophisticate kids) did. I just had a hard time believing the Program tried to replicate that at St. Ignatius. "You have two football teams here?"

"Yup. Male and Female."

"They make the girls play the guys?"

Arabella looked at me. "St. Ignatius is all about gender equality."

"Then why do they have the teams separated by gender?"

"Oh, that's easy. Locker rooms. As equal as we are, they still know we're teenagers and therefore slaves to our hormones. With the whole locker room situation, it's just easier that way."

Arabella and I had been the first ones in the locker room, but now other girls were arriving and getting dressed. As soon as Quinnie entered the room, Arabella ushered me out and onto the practice track.

"Take a lap around before everyone gets out here. You know, to get your derby legs," Arabella suggested with a smile.

The track was a large oval that was banked so it was higher on the outer edges than in the middle. It looked like a NASCAR track, but on a much smaller scale. The degree of the incline on the track wasn't much, but I still clumsily slid down toward the middle as soon as I coasted onto it. A stream of obscenities came out of my mouth as I fought to keep my balance.

"Don't just coast, push with your legs," Arabella suggested. She hopped out onto the track and her skates began to hum as she circled in a blur of black, red, and hideous plaid. I followed Arabella's example, pushing my feet out in an alternating rhythm, swinging my arms, and rocking my body weight from side to side for leverage. Arabella circled the track quickly and caught up with me. Once I got over my initial fear of falling, I found it wasn't as difficult as I thought it would be. It wasn't long before Younglove entered the training arena and sat down behind a panel of switches, clicking a few and causing more lights to flicker on.

"You're doing great," Arabella praised. "You're getting the hang of it a lot faster than I thought. I mean, you don't look like a Mandate, but you must have gotten a pretty nice physical genetic upgrade package to pick it up this quickly."

"Either that, or I ice skated once," I offered with a smile.

The arena was suddenly filled with the echoes of machinery grinding to life.

"Look out!" Arabella called.

Ten feet in front of us, a bar slid out of the wall and across the floor of the track. Arabella neatly vaulted over the obstacle, but I wasn't as fortunate. Lacking the confidence to try to jump, I attempted to step over the bar but was going too fast. My back skate caught on the metal obstruction and I fell forward — sprawled onto the track — legs and arms splayed wide as I slid several feet. The helmet protected my head from the inevitable smack and the pads protected my knees and elbows, but I fell painfully onto my right hip, initiating a vicious scrape up my side. That wasn't as painful as the blow my pride took, however. Quinnie was leaning against the wall in front of me, laughing and pointing.

Arabella skidded to a stop next to me, bent over, and reached under my elbow to help me up. "I'm so sorry. I had no idea that Younglove was turning on the obstacles. She usually doesn't do that until everyone is out here."

"Obstacles?" I asked as I turned around to look at the track. Various bars, blocks, and other dangerous objects undulated into the track area.

"It's how we train. Younglove thinks it helps make us better," Arabella explained. "Are you okay?"

"No big deal," I said, shakily standing up, only to start slipping down the track further. My arms pinwheeled in an effort to regain my balance, much to the delight of Quinnie who dissolved into a fit of loud giggles.

"Quinby, you need to meet your team on your practice track." Younglove reprimanded her.

"I was just leaving," she called over her shoulder as she was followed by her two giggling cronies. "Thanks for the show, Clementine." She laughed as she disappeared through the doorway.

"I know what I said about girls not calling each other names, but she's a total hag witch," Arabella whispered, eyes narrowed as they followed Quinnie and her friends.

I couldn't agree more.

"All right ladies," Younglove announced as the rest of the team came out of the locker room and gathered around the track. "Meet your new teammate, Clementine," she said, indicating me as if I were nothing more than a new piece of equipment. "Today we're going to warm up with the obstacles and then we'll do a little pack practice."

I understood the obstacle part, having just been victimized by one of them, but I didn't understand at all what pack practice was. I hoped someone would explain.

"Begin," Younglove called, as she brought her whistle to her lips with a sharp shrill. She then settled her brittle looking body into the seat behind the panel.

Arabella and the rest of the team clacked onto the track with an unexpected surge of speed, and what appeared to be a total lack of control. It was a flurry of skates, moving obstacles, and bodies hurtling around in dizzying circles. I didn't want to jump into the fray, but one look from Younglove and her pursed lips and I knew avoiding the obstacles and other skaters would be a much easier task than dealing with the repercussions of not doing what I was expected to do.

In the next breath of empty space, I jumped into the current of madness and fell into the rhythm. I got passed frequently by the other girls, but now that I knew there were obstacles, I avoided most of them by jumping or swerving. Every once in a while, something would come thrusting out of the wall at waist height and I'd have to squat low and duck under it. It was completely random and none of the passes around the track were similar at all. Either I was narrowly missing another skater or just barely avoiding an obstacle. Despite my best efforts, I still got knocked down several times.

Finally, the whistle blew and the skaters came to a stop. I was so bruised and battered I felt like I'd fallen down a flight of stairs.

"Great warm up ladies," Younglove said, standing up from behind the panel of buttons. The obstacles slowed and disappeared into their hiding places. "You did very well, Clementine." She smiled, pleased with herself. "I knew you'd catch on quickly." Younglove said it in a way that sounded like she knew more about me than I did myself. "Okay, now let's do some pack practice to acquaint Clementine to the living and breathing barricades of roller derby." There were nine girls besides me. Younglove gave five of them purple helmet covers and the rest green covers.

"These are called helmet panties," Arabella whispered to me as she twirled a green cover around her finger and winked impishly.

She then stretched the cover over her helmet and let it fall into place with an impertinent snap of elastic. The panty transformed her plain helmet into a striped one. Almost everyone else had a solid colored panty.

Younglove handed me a green panty with a white star on it, but then grabbed my arm and held me back as I tried to follow the other girls onto the track. "Just watch a few go rounds until you understand a little."

Eight of the girls grouped in a pack in the middle of one of the straightaways of the track. The girl with the purple helmet panty with a star on it was farther behind the pack, almost to the turn of the track. Younglove blew her whistle once and the pack of girls in the front began to skate around the track, bumping into one another, jockeying for position. They weren't going at top speed, but were skating at a pace set by the two girls in the front that had stripes on their helmet panties. One of the girls was Arabella.

As soon as the pack reached the curve, Younglove blew her whistle twice and the girl with the star on her helmet began skating quickly toward the pack. As soon as she reached them, the green helmeted girls attempted to block her using their hips and shoulders. She was roughly jostled around by the girls with the green helmets and aided by her fellow purple helmeted teammates. When she finally squeezed through the pack, she circled the track again in a frenzy of speed to catch up to the pack again.

"The girls in the pack are called the blockers," Younglove explained. "Each team of blockers has a pivot person — the girl with the striped helmet panty — that leads the defense and strategy for her team. She is also responsible for setting pack speed. In total, counting the pivot, there are four blockers for each team.

Katherine, the girl with the star on her helmet, is the jammer. Each team has one jammer."

I looked down at the helmet panty in my hand and noticed the star on it. Arabella said her team needed another jammer. It appeared I was filling that spot.

"The jammer is the player that scores points," Younglove continued. "Once she makes it through the pack the first time, she can skate back around and try to get through the pack again to start scoring. For each pack member from the opposing team that she passes, she scores a point. The first jammer to make it through the pack is the lead jammer and is in control of the jam."

"How long does it last?" I asked.

"The match consists of two half-hour periods. Within that, you have jams. Each jam lasts two minutes, unless the lead jammer calls off the jam earlier."

"Why would she call it off?"

"If she has scored more points and wants to keep the other jammer from scoring, she might call it off. There are other reasons and strategies. If the lead jammer wants to call off the jam, she merely puts her hands on her hips and there is a 30 second break before the next jam starts."

I watched as Katherine, the jammer, struggled to get through the pack.

"Right now, the pack only has one jammer to worry about. The green team is playing only defense, the purple team is only worried about offense. Once there are two jammers in there, however, it gets a lot more confusing and rough," Younglove explained with a wide grin that looked like it would tear the dry, brittle skin of her cheeks.

After a few minutes, Younglove blew the whistle in three short bursts and the skaters slowed to a stop. "All right, let's get Clementine in there for a few laps."

"Are you sure about this, Professor Younglove?" I asked.

"You're not going to learn anything sitting around watching them practice. You've got to get in there and take the hard knocks. You're going to fall. A lot. It's inevitable. Accept that now and you'll be fine. That's why you've got a helmet and pads." Younglove handed me a mouthguard and nodded toward the track.

Standing next to Katherine and holding on to the wall, I noticed how tall and muscular the girl was. Definitely a Mandate by birth. Her skin was a warm coffee color and her eyes were a dark brown. Katherine's hair hung out of her helmet, straight and golden. It was her muscles and size that I couldn't get over, though. I was pretty sure Katherine could lift a small vehicle without breaking a sweat.

"Name's Katie," Katherine said, smiling and holding her hand out to me.

"I'm Cleo."

"Nice to meet you, Cleo. I apologize ahead of time."

"For what?" The whistle blew once and the pack took off.

"It's not personal, it's the game. Better you learn it from us than the others."

"Learn what?" The whistle blew twice. Katie bumped into me, knocking me to the boards, and then sprinted ahead.

"How to take a block," Katie called over her shoulder as she raced toward the pack.

I pushed myself back into a standing position and struggled to start skating before I got lapped by the pack.

The next twenty minutes consisted of me attempting to

wheedle my way through the pack only to be shoved into the wall or knocked flat on my back over and over again. I noticed that Arabella and I were the smallest ones on the team — by a long shot — but Arabella was having no trouble at all staying on her feet. In fact, she was quite the tiny terror, causing frequent pile-ups from her strategically placed blocks.

I tried to skate around one of the purple blockers and was pushed into the wall where I rolled along the edge before tumbling to the track.

"Stay on your feet, Clementine!" Younglove hollered.

"Don't bother getting up, it's a waste of time since you'll be flat on your ass again in just a minute."

I lifted my head and found Quinnie leaning over the wall looking at me, a sneer plastered on her otherwise beautiful face.

"Shouldn't you be at practice?" I spat, annoyed that Quinnie should find me, once again, sprawled out on the track.

"Scrimmage time, Loser. Your team is taking it too easy on you. I'm here to give you a real education." She took off her helmet and shook out her long blond hair as if she were modeling for a hair commercial.

"Easy on me?" I'd just spent the last twenty minutes amassing a collection of bruises, most of them in unmentionable spots.

"Obviously," Quinnie laughed as she swiped her nail down my arm to the accompaniment of stinging shocks. "Easy on you. See? No blood yet. But don't worry, I'll fix that." She turned away, shaking her platinum blond hair again before jamming the red helmet on her head. There was a star on the side of it.

Of course, I thought to myself. She's a jammer.

Arabella's wheels screeched as she stopped next to me. "Rest time. We're scrimmaging against Quinnie's team. Katie's jamming first."

I breathed a sigh of relief. I needed a break.

"Don't worry, I'll be your pivot when you jam. I'll take care of you."

"Weren't you my pivot for the last twenty minutes?" I asked, trying to laugh. I displayed myself to Arabella in a mock beauty queen spin, showing off all the red blotches and scrapes I'd gotten from my numerous falls.

"Trust me, I was taking care of you. It could have been much worse. You really need to start making some hits instead of just taking them all."

"But everyone is like three times as big as me. How do I block that? I mean, look at Jane. I think she's half Yeti. Only pretty," I added, just in case Jane could hear me.

"Don't pull that crap. I'm barely five feet tall and I can put every one of those girls on their backs. You're low like me, use that to your advantage. You don't cut a tree down at the top, you take it out at the base, right?"

"Right," I agreed, reluctantly.

"Watch the next few jams, and choose at least one move you can use when it's your turn. That's it. If you learn nothing else today, learn one move. No one expects you to be an expert. Hell, no one expects you to even attempt to block today. My advice is pick a move, use it on Quinnie. She won't see it coming." Arabella grinned conspiratorially.

The minutes ticked by as I got to watch the carnage, for once, instead of being part of it. Younglove and the other coach weren't even keeping score, but from what I could tell, it was pretty much dead even.

"That one there," Arabella leaned over and whispered during the third jam. "Did you see that?"

I nodded.

"That's the Can Opener. Save that for Quinnie. I don't care if you score a single point during your jam," Arabella hissed, "just put her in her place — that place being the floor of course."

After five jams, it was time for me to take my turn on the track. Arabella had been out every other jam, but Katie remained jammer for the first five jams as Younglove allowed to me to watch and learn. Now it was my turn though. My body protested as I stood up. Every single part of me was battered and bruised. I took the purple panty from Katie and snapped it over my helmet.

"Go get 'em," Katie said, slapping my helmet so hard that I nearly fell down and had to reach for the railing to stay upright. From across the center of the track, I heard Quinnie's giggle.

I skated out to my place on the track, hoping I could manage to stay on my feet. I knew I had little hope of winning the jam, I just hoped I didn't make a total fool of myself. Standing close to Quinnie, I could almost feel the animosity crackling off the other girl's skin.

The whistle blew and the pack took off. The double whistle shrilled signaling the jammers' turn and Quinnie and I surged forward. Quinnie looked over at me with an insolent smirk and instantly leaned in for the block, but I was ready this time. I knew Quinnie would go for immediate satisfaction and maximum embarrassment. Dragging my skate behind me to brake, I leaned back to swerve out of Quinnie's reach. She lost her balance and stumbled toward the outside wall trying to stay on her feet. I took the opportunity to jump ahead of her and dash for the pack.

Apparently, the red pack members had been expecting Quinnie to come through first so by the time they realized that it was me, I was already ahead of every single red member and behind Arabella. Arabella grinned and then viciously blocked one of the red girls to the inside and out of the track border. Jane pushed me forward by my hips, hurling me out of the pack and into the first lap.

"Thank God for Yeti strength," I mumbled to myself as I looped around to catch up with the pack again. Despite being a klutz, I was pretty fast. Speed or not, though, I could almost feel Quinnie breathing down my neck. I chanced a look back and saw that the other girl hadn't been slowed down much and was only about ten feet behind me, and gaining. We were right behind the pack and I knew as soon as we were back in the fray, we'd be scoring points.

When I felt Quinnie come up behind me on the right side, I knew it would be my only chance to get in an unexpected hit — the block from jam three. Quinnie knocked her shoulder impatiently into me, doing minimal damage. I squatted low and then pushed outward with my left skate, maneuvering myself in front of Quinnie. I unfolded my body up and back with as much speed and force as I could. My shoulders slammed into Quinnie, right below her chest. I was rewarded with a surprised grunt and thud as Quinnie went down. Hard. A string of curses followed the thud.

The girls in the red pack turned to see what happened. They were momentarily distracted and I easily dodged past them. As soon as I skated out of the pack, Arabella yelled "You're the lead jammer, Cleo. Hips! Stop the jam!"

I did as Arabella instructed and tapped my hips with my fists. The whistle blew three short bursts and both packs slowed and then hopped into the center of the track, skating to their benches for the rest period. My teammates all took turns slapping my helmet in congratulations until I thought I'd go deaf from the racket.

"I'm going to dream about that Can Opener tonight," Arabella sighed. "That was textbook-perfect form," she complimented me.

"I wouldn't go that far," Quinnie's syrupy voice dripped as she rolled toward us. "She got lucky, that's all."

"Lucky or not, she put points up on the board. And as you well know, you can't score if you're on the floor." Arabella was downright giddy. I couldn't deny that it felt good to finally give Quinnie a dose of embarrassment.

"Let's make it best two out of three," Quinnie challenged me. She put her hand on my shoulder and shoved, adding a harsh shock to the push. I gasped in surprise and lost my balance, falling to the floor. As Quinnie skated past me, she purposely ran over my left hand with her skate. There was a sickening crunch followed by crushing pain and I cried out.

"Oops. An accident," Quinnie feigned innocence.

Arabella crouched down and grabbed my hand. "Are you all right?"

I cried out again, almost sobbing as Arabella checked my fingers for damage. I thought I was going to throw up. "No. I think it might be broken," I managed to say.

"Oh no. Wouldn't that be a shame," Quinnie said with a pretend pout. Her eyes sparked with malice. "Does this mean you forfeit the rest of our scrimmage tonight? You do know what a forfeit means, don't you?"

My anger boiled inside of me. It was all too much. Too much for one day. It didn't matter how frightening last night had been, and I wasn't scared about what would happen. What could they possibly do to me now? The fury was so intense I thought that maybe my skin was actually bubbling with my rage. I didn't even try to hold it back this time. It felt as if I was filled with the power of the sun — the fiery rays racing to get out of my body, screaming through my fingertips, and bursting through my skin.

Glorious release — a storm of rage liberated in a powerful exhale.

And then all of the lights overhead exploded in a shower of glass that rained all over the track.

The arena went as dark as my mood.

❧ 8 ❧

UNBROKEN HAND, BROKEN SPIRIT

My hand wasn't broken. I went to the infirmary and the nurse, Ms. Petticoat, gave me some pain relievers and a bag of ice. Ms. Petticoat didn't seem alarmed or surprised that a cadet would skate over another cadet's hand on purpose and I found that incredibly unnerving.

Luckily, I made it to dinner before it was over and sat with Arabella and Sterling.

"All better?" Sterling asked.

I shrugged. "The ice helps a bit."

"Well, this should make you feel better," Arabella promised. "Quinnie went to the infirmary, too." At my questioning silence, Arabella added in a whisper, "Multiple cuts and lacerations. Apparently, some of the glass from the lights cut her up pretty badly. Didn't happen to anyone else though, isn't that strange?" she asked, although it seemed like she didn't think it was strange at all.

I stared at my food as I picked through it with a fork. "Yes, very."

"Do you know what happened?" Sterling asked.

"The lights exploded."

It was Arabella's turn to lead the inquisition. "Yes, but how?"

I looked between my two new friends. "I'm not an electrician."

"You didn't have anything to do with it?" Arabella asked.

I rolled my eyes to hide my nervousness and tried to laugh. It came out shaky and tinny. "Exploding lights?"

They both stared at me expectantly, but I merely shoved food in my mouth, aware that dinner was almost over and I'd have to go to work detail soon. I wanted to deny that I had anything to do with the accident, but couldn't find it in myself to lie convincingly so I didn't say anything.

"Okay, fine," Arabella conceded. "I just have to say, though, exploding lights totally trumped the Can Opener. I'm guessing Quinnie isn't going to be too happy tomorrow. Word is she's pissed at you."

"She wasn't going to be happy anyway," Sterling answered. "Quinnie can't wait to sink her talons into Cleo and rip her to social shreds. Your only hope," he said turning to me, "is that someone new will come in that she likes even less than you."

"I don't get it," I said. "Why does she hate me so much?"

Sterling shrugged. "She sees you as competition. She never likes the new girl. It just happens to be you right now."

"Well, what's so great about Quinnie? Who made her queen of the castle?"

"Did you forget what I told you earlier about Mandates and sponsors?" Sterling reminded me. "Quinnie has a sponsor. A very powerful sponsor. Essentially, she could make your life a living hell."

I shrugged and then stood up. "It already is. Could one of you show me where the library is? I don't want to be late for work detail."

"Have a seat, Little Miss Catastrophe. You don't have work detail tonight. Younglove let you off the hook since it was your first night, and probably because you had to take a trip to the infirmary. Sterling and I can show you around and introduce you to people."

No work detail. I was relieved. I just wanted to hole up in my room alone and wallow in self pity for a while. "I appreciate that," I said, "but I think I just want to go back to my room."

"And do what?"

"Plot my escape," I answered truthfully.

"Don't bother," Sterling responded seriously. "Been there, done that. The attempt wasn't worth it. I still have the marks and I'm still serving the punishment." I eyed him apprehensively and he shrugged. "Why do you think I get to be a tour guide for all the newbies?"

I sighed. "Well, I guess since escape isn't an option, I'll just go to bed."

"What are you, 93 years old? It's not even seven yet," Arabella exclaimed.

"It's just been a long day."

"Give her a break," said Sterling. "You remember what it's like the first day."

"Yeah, all right," Arabella slumped. Even her wild hair seemed to wilt a bit with her disappointment.

I turned and walked away slowly, heading for the cafeteria door. My body hurt so badly I felt like I really was 93 years old.

"You need me to show you how to get back to the dorms?"

Sterling called after me.

"I'll be fine," I told him. "But thanks." I was pretty sure I wasn't going to be fine and I fully expected to get lost, but that wasn't necessarily a bad thing. I just needed to get away from everything and everyone and think.

After four or five turns in the massive, stony maze, I realized I was hopelessly lost. I didn't recognize the hallways at all. I found a dark corner next to a statue of a lion and wedged myself into the cool shadows. It was quiet and that's all I cared about.

Everything was happening so quickly. Last night my room exploded. I knew it was my fault, but I didn't know how or why. Nothing like that had ever happened to me before and yet all day, I had to fight off the ever-present urge to destroy things — twice unsuccessfully. I had to get a grip on this affliction. I couldn't go around making things explode every time I got mad about something. Although, to be honest, I wasn't feeling too guilty about the pen incident or the lights at derby practice. Quinnie deserved that, and more, for bullying. Especially since her obvious dislike of me was unfounded. I'd done nothing to warrant the maltreatment.

Lost in thought, I didn't hear him until he crouched down next to me and leaned against the wall too.

When I didn't acknowledge his presence, he said, "I see it's broken."

Surprised that the roller derby story had gotten around so quickly, I shook my head and lifted my hand, wiggling my fingers. "Not broken, just a serious bruise. Ms. Petticoat said it'll probably be really swollen tomorrow, but unfortunately, it won't stop me from doing the morning run."

"I'm not talking about your hand," he said, confused. Apparently he hadn't realized my hand was even hurt. "I mean your spirit. It looks kind of broken right now," Ozzy said.

I bristled at his brutal honesty and took a chance at looking up from my bandaged hand and into his face. Brown, wavy hair tumbled over his forehead, hanging over his lashes, and it bothered me that I couldn't see his eyes because of the shadows. Were they filled with kindness or cold curiosity? His voice didn't give away anything and I got the impression that he stumbled upon me accidentally and asked about my well being out of courtesy. Courtesy or curiosity — whatever had forced him to stop, it was like he could see right through me.

He was right, I did feel broken.

"I'm all right," I lied, bending and clenching the fingers on my injured hand to stretch them out. "What are you doing here?"

"On my way somewhere."

"Work detail?"

"I have a sponsor," Ozzy admitted.

"That must be nice."

Ozzy shrugged in answer.

"Having two extra hours a day to yourself sounds rather nice."

"It does. Which reminds me, I have some place to be. So, if your spirit is fine, I guess I'll be on my way. Nice to see you again, Cleo." He stood, slung his bag over his shoulder, and then disappeared down the hall.

I was alone. Finally able to let my fear rule, my despair reveled in its freedom and I promptly dissolved into quiet tears.

The blare of the alarm roughly tore me out of my dream — something about Cassie and a cat on a wall. Or was Cassie the cat?

And what was Cassie doing on a wall? I grasped for the meaning of it, but the dream skittered away like a crab scuttling across the beach. Before I could hold onto it, it buried itself in the sands of my troubled thoughts. I rolled over and attacked the alarm clock with my fist. Why was the snooze button so elusive? And honestly, it was a bit offensive that the stupid alarm clock would still work after nearly burning to a crisp in my old dorm room.

Last night, after finally finding my way to my room, I discovered that there was a brand new alarm clock on the nightstand next to the bed. But I unplugged it and put it in the closet, then took the burnt clock out of my tattered cardboard box and plugged it in. It was the only way to really hold on to something of my old life, and by association, a way to hold on to Cassie. The only other things in the box were toiletries and I didn't really think snuggling up with a bar of soap was going to make me feel any closer to my best friend. The alarm clock didn't either, but it did feel oddly sentimental.

But right now, all I wanted to do was get the wailing of the stupid clock to stop. My fingers danced across the top of the offending machine looking for the right button. Where was that button? It felt like I was trying to diffuse a bomb. And then the reality of that thought helped me shake off the remaining stupor of my troubled sleep.

I sat up and turned off the clock with a definitive click as the remnants of the strange Cassie dream faded away. Of course it didn't mean anything, it was just a result of my frustration. Last night I'd attempted to email Cassie. No matter what I tried, the email bounced back undelivered, as if Cassie didn't exist anymore. I also tried using the telephone to call Cassie's number. All I got was a busy signal. I wasn't sure if I was blocked on my end, or if Cassie was being blocked. Either way, it was clear that the Program didn't want us to keep in touch. I felt the stirring of my anger rising up and had to take a few deep breaths to calm myself down.

I got up and wandered over to the closet to look for something suitable to do the morning run in. Luckily, I found the appropriate uniform: brown running shorts and a gold t-shirt with a lion and the words "St. Ignatius" silkscreened onto it. I also found a pair of sneakers. As I shimmied out of my pajamas, I caught a glimpse of myself in the mirror and gasped in horror. Black and blue bruises were scattered all over my pale body. I must have fallen more than I remembered during derby practice. I quickly pulled on the uniform and added a sweatshirt just as there was a knock on my door. I opened it to find Arabella standing there. She was wearing the same uniform as me, but she looked different.

"Your hair . . . " I started.

"I know, you love it. Thanks," Arabella smiled.

"But yesterday it was black and red."

"Yes, and yesterday I was in the mood for multiple pony tails. Today, I'm in an orange mood." It was all orange. Not just orange streaks, but flaming orange. It looked like her head was on fire.

"Let me guess. Someone stuck you on top of a pencil and gave you a little spin this morning, right?" I asked with an attempt at a laugh.

Arabella didn't answer.

"You've got that whole agitated troll doll thing going on," I explained, motioning to the explosion of tousled hair hovering above her head.

Arabella's eyes narrowed. "You can do better than that, can't you?"

"It's still early," I complained.

"Don't worry, Sterling will make up for it."

Five minutes later, we met Sterling at the bottom of the girls' dormitory staircase.

"Hey, I think it's time to release that thing on your head back into the wilderness," Sterling teased. "What the hell, Arabella? It looks like two alley cats had a fight in your hair and one didn't make it out alive."

"See?" Arabella asked, pointing to Sterling who was wearing running shorts and a t-shirt so rumpled it was hard to read the print on the front of it. "He's witty. I don't mind you making fun of the 'do, just put some quality effort into it," she scolded me. "Don't worry, I'll give you another chance tomorrow. I rarely leave it the same longer than a day."

"Really?" I was surprised. "That sounds tedious."

"Not as tedious as running a five mile obstacle course every damn day. Ugh. Let's just get this over with," she groaned as she looped her hands through Sterling's and my arms and dragged us down the hall.

Stepping out the back of the St. Ignatius building, we followed the crowd walking down a large hill toward the start of the course. I looked around at the cadets, noticing that most of them were built like Jane — large, muscular, and likely able to rip appendages off an enemy without too much effort. I also noticed that Quinnie was nowhere to be found, although her cronies (whom I had discovered were named Sadie and Evie) were nearby, casting dark looks at me. They clearly wanted retaliation for what happened to their friend, but it was obvious they didn't want to risk getting too close to the unstable, possibly dangerous, new girl.

A large man with a viciously receding hairline and wobbly jowls stepped out onto the raised platform at the edge of the tree line where the course began.

"Dean Overton," Arabella whispered, pointing to the man.

"You're kidding, right?" I asked. What an unfortunately true name.

Sterling laughed. "Nope, that's his name. But uh . . . I advise not making fun of it in front of him."

"You know from experience?" I guessed.

"Something like that," he mumbled, rolling his shoulders around under his shirt.

Dean Overton lifted the whistle to his mouth and blew it. The sun had barely risen and hadn't even begun to stab through the thick canopy of leaves that shaded the woods, but cadets raced headlong into it anyway.

Sterling apologized before we even started, declaring he had to get the run over with quickly so he could finish his work detail before breakfast. "See you at breakfast," he called, sprinting into the crowd, quickly weaving his way toward the front.

"How long does it take him to get through?"

"I think he told me 20 minutes, give or take," Arabella responded.

"I thought it was five miles!"

"Yep. And don't forget the obstacles."

"That's super fast. How is that even possible?"

"He's kind of a freak," Arabella said affectionately. "Let's go. You're going to need every second of the 90 minutes we have."

Arabella, the punk rock saint that she was, stayed with me the entire time. I'd never sweat so much in my life. Running the trail wasn't bad at all, I actually enjoyed it. Every quarter mile, however, there was an obstacle — cargo nets, walls to climb over, bars to swing across, steep hills to climb. By the time we finally got to the end, I was doubled over, retching in the bushes.

"Isn't this fun?" Arabella teased as she held my hair for me. "And guess what? We get to do this all over again tomorrow!"

"I want to die," I moaned.

"Not an option. Let's go get showers and head to breakfast, I'm starving."

Neither Sterling nor Arabella were in my first class, Foreign Language. In fact, no one was in my class. It seemed I was an enigma at St. Ignatius. I was fluent in four languages, the four that were offered to all of the other students. While everyone was required to learn a language, it wasn't really a serious requirement at St. Ignatius. Younglove must have realized that putting me in any of those classes would be a waste of time, so I had a personal tutor to help me learn a new language — Arabic. At first it was awkward being in a class of one, but I soon found that it was nice to not have to worry about anyone else. I could learn at my own pace, which was a very fast pace, even for a difficult language such as Arabic.

After Foreign Language, I had Weapons. Sterling and Arabella weren't in that class either, but I did recognize one familiar face. He was standing at the edge of the shooting range, firing at a target that was easily 100 yards away. Ozzy.

I didn't like guns.

I sat at one of the outdoor benches farthest from the shooting range and waited for the rest of the class to arrive, wondering how

I was going to get out of shooting a gun. I almost wished they'd make me run another five miles instead. Almost.

When the bell rang, Ozzy took off his earmuffs and yellow tinted glasses and set them aside. I was surprised when he didn't take a seat with the rest of the class.

"Professor Farnsworth is out sick, so I'll be leading class today. We'll be working with handguns," Ozzy explained.

There was a lot of excited whispering.

"Ozzy, how about you give us the day off?" asked a guy on the other side of the room.

"Shut up, dude," hissed another guy that was sitting right next to him, who was obviously his twin brother. "We get to shoot at stuff."

"Oh, right."

Ozzy ignored the boys and proceeded to explain how to properly load the gun. I effectively tuned out. I had no desire, or intention, of firing a gun today — especially if the professor wasn't around. I had to figure out a way to get out of the class. Should I fake illness? I was feeling rather faint at the thought of even touching the gun.

Ozzy finished his lecture, unloaded the gun, and set it and the magazine on the shelf in his booth. "Everyone grab a gun, a magazine, and a booth. There's room for everyone to go at once. Cleo, you can take my spot," he offered with a smile as he walked up next to me. His smile nearly melted my bones right on the spot and I almost agreed and marched up into the booth. One look at the gun, however, made me come to my senses. I wasn't a coward by any stretch of the imagination, but guns, for some reason, freaked me out.

"Actually, I'm not feeling all that well. Maybe I should go back to Ms. Petticoat and get checked out?"

"What's wrong? Maybe I can help," Ozzy suggested.

"I don't think so."

"Here at St. Ignatius, unless you're bleeding or broken in some way, you go to class. You don't look like you're bleeding so is something broken?"

Broken? I didn't think I could get away with saying my spirit was broken after all. I panicked. I had to get away from the guns. What would Cassie do? I thought back to my conversation with her yesterday morning.

"Cramps." I grabbed my abdomen and made a face like my uterus was being torn to bits.

There were giggles from the girls and snorts from the guys. Ozzy just looked at me with a satisfied smile. "Right then. There's a bottle of painkillers in the first aid kit on the wall over there. Grab two and then come on back. I'm sure you'll be fine in no time."

I took my time meandering over to the first aid kit, wondering how long I could drag out the medicating farce. I took two pills and then leaned on the table, feigning an attempt to recover.

Soon, shots were being fired at the targets at the end of the football sized field. I winced with every crack of gunfire.

"Theo!" Ozzy shouted in annoyance. "Put on your earmuffs and glasses unless you prefer being blind and deaf." As Theo put on his safety gear, Ozzy walked toward me and leaned against the table next me. "Ready to come over and take some target practice?"

"Still not feeling too great, maybe I should lay down?"

"Let's pretend for a moment that I don't know you're lying." Ozzy held up his hand in defense to stop me from interrupting. "You don't think they'd actually let me teach a class without giving me the background information of all the students in that class do you? I know you don't have to worry about this whole cramp issue for at least another week, so do me a favor and get over there so I don't have to look like a complete jackass by sending you to the Dean's office for not following directions."

I was both embarrassed and angry that he knew I was lying. Mostly, though, I was angry. Even as a Sophisticate, some things should be private, especially from people my own age. Menstrual cycles definitely fell in that category. "You wouldn't," I accused.

"You don't know me," Ozzy shot back.

"I don't like guns," I snapped.

"I don't like people that lie."

"I don't —" I was interrupted by the whooping and hollering of the twins. Theo, the one that Ozzy had just reminded to wear safety gear, was now pretending to shoot his brother.

"Excuse me," Ozzy said, picking up the pill bottle off the table where I had left it. He brought back his arm and threw the bottle at Theo with the speed of a major league pitcher. The bottle hit the obnoxious twin square in the chest with such force that he dropped the gun and crumpled in a heap next to it. Everyone stopped shooting and stared.

Ozzy walked over, picked up the gun, clicked on the safety, and crouched down next to Theo. "You've got to go to Dean Overton's." His voice was quiet, yet dangerous.

"What?" Theo cried. "Dude, I was just playing around. It wasn't even loaded."

Ozzy stood up, clicked off the safety, pointed the gun toward the targets at the end of the field, and fired. Everyone gasped as the shot rang through the otherwise silent area.

"Take Wesley with you," Ozzy spat.

"What did I do?" the other twin yelled.

"You shot at the flagpole," Ozzy explained, pointing to the St. Ignatius lion flag on a pole to the extreme left of the shooting field. "If you hadn't noticed, the dorms are within shooting range. You could have damaged the building or hurt someone. You guys just aren't ready for this today. Go," he said firmly. I didn't think that Ozzy really looked all that frightening, not compared to all the muscle-bound Mandates in the class, but the brothers must have seen something I didn't because they couldn't leave fast enough.

After the twins disappeared, everyone began to whisper. " . . . I know, with a pill bottle . . . He's totally badass . . . Don't piss off the Oz . . . " I heard.

Ozzy grabbed my elbow and led me over to the booth. I reluctantly let him. He picked the unloaded gun off the countertop and put it in my hand. "Load it," he ordered. Gunfire began ringing out again, rattling my nerves. I struggled with one hand to slip the earmuffs over my head and then shakily tried to jam the magazine into the bottom of the gun.

Ozzy watched tensely, frustration evident on his face as he struggled against the urge to help me by doing it himself. After several unsuccessful attempts of trying to jam the magazine in, Ozzy snatched the gun out of my hand. "Open the action and put it on safety," he snarled, pulling the top of the gun back. He handed the gun back to me and I was able to finally get the magazine to click in. I gingerly touched the barrel of the gun, unsure of how to get the top to slide shut again.

"Pull back the slide and let it go," Ozzy hissed.

"The what?"

Ozzy reached up and pinched the top part of his nose. "Did you pay attention at all when I was demonstrating? No one else seems to be having any problems," he said, gesturing to the rest of my classmates. When I continued to stare at him, he grabbed the gun, yanked back on the top part again and it snapped close. He roughly turned me so I was facing the targets at the end of the field and he forced the gun into my hand.

"Shoot," he demanded.

The bell rang.

"Oh," I said happily. "Class is over."

"Not for you. Shoot," he repeated.

I glared at Ozzy, but he looked unconcerned.

"You may not have to listen to me any other day, but today, I'm the professor. Shoot."

I raised the gun, my hand trembling. Why was I so scared of guns? I didn't know why. Or maybe it was that I couldn't remember why. But I did know that there was a reason. My body was rebelling against me and my legs felt like they wouldn't support me anymore. My vision started to go black around the edges as I struggled to focus on the target. I squeezed the trigger and the gun kicked.

And then everything went black.

9

Perfect Aim

Someone was slapping me in the face. Gently, but still a slap. I pushed the hand away.

"Wake up," a familiar voice ordered, as the slapping ensued.

I opened my eyes. Ozzy was leaning over me, his wavy hair tumbling forward. I couldn't be certain, since I was so sore from roller derby yesterday and the obstacle course this morning, but I was pretty sure I was sporting a few new bumps and bruises. The back of my head was throbbing painfully.

"What happened?" I croaked.

"You fainted," Ozzy said drily.

"I did? Well that's embarrassing." I sat up and experimentally rubbed my head, which was extremely tender.

"Not as embarrassing as the fact that you completely missed the target."

I scowled. "It's on the other side of a football field!"

"And every other Mandate can at least hit the target even if they don't land a killing shot."

"Well, maybe my lack of perfect aim will prove to the Program once and for all that I'm not a Mandate. I don't belong here. I need to go back to the University," I added harshly.

Ozzy huffed, but said nothing. He got up and began putting the handguns and ammunition into a large metal locker against the wall.

I winced as I touched another spot on my head that seemed to be swelling into quite an impressively sized knot. "Did I hit my head?"

"I would've caught you," Ozzy said defensively, "but I had no idea that shooting a gun was going to totally make you lose your shit."

"I told you I don't like guns."

"You didn't tell me you were terrified of them."

"Same thing." I shrugged.

"No. Not the same thing. I don't like hot dogs. In fact I hate hot dogs. But I don't have nightmares about them. And I've yet to have the sight of one knock me unconscious."

"Are we done?" I sassed impatiently. The rest of the class was gone and I wasn't sure how much time I had until the bell rang for the next class.

"Yes," Ozzy answered through tight lips as he finished putting the guns away and locked the door to the cabinet. "You have Conditioning next, right?" he asked, his tone of voice more gentle. When I nodded he said, "So do I, I'll show you where it is."

I decided pretty quickly that Conditioning should really be called Medieval Torture. It was essentially a weight training class run by a woman, Professor Peck, who looked like she was a female gladiator. Hell, she was as muscular as a male gladiator. When I first caught sight of Professor Peck, it was from behind and I was completely disoriented when she turned around and I realized those ridiculously lumpy biceps and shoulders did not belong to a man.

"Push, Clementine! Harder!" Peck barked as she tried to force down the bar that I was bench pressing. After ten gut-wrenching reps, Peck allowed me to take a break. "That's what I'm talking about, Clementine! Way to finish up strong," she yelled as she slapped my shoulder in what she probably thought was a sign of encouragement. I nearly fell off the bench with the force of her excitement. Peck didn't even notice because she was already strutting across the room in search of another victim. I sat up weakly, my arms trembling. I wondered if Arabella would be willing to feed me at lunch because I wasn't sure I'd be able to lift my arms to get food to my mouth.

"It gets easier." Ozzy had sauntered up and was leaning against the barbell.

"It couldn't get much harder."

"It can if you start to stand out," he confided. "Do just enough and you'll be fine. St. Ignatius is one place where you don't want to be the super star."

"Why not?"

"Look around, Cleo. You don't fit in," he pointed out. "Vanguards have no business being at St. Ignatius, but they sent you here anyway. There was a reason. All I'm saying is they're expecting that reason to surface, so don't give them an opportunity to see it. Just do enough and maybe you'll get out of this with something easy."

"I don't follow —"

"Osbourne!" Peck growled. "Why are you just standing around?"

"Waiting in line for the bench press, ma'am."

"Clementine, you need to be working nonstop. No breaks. Or has it escaped your notice that you're far behind the rest of the class?"

"No, Professor Peck. I'm well aware that I'm the runt of the litter."

Peck glared, unsure whether I was being sassy or serious. "Squats, Clementine! And don't stop until class is over. Your legs look like they'd snap under the weight of a sack of flour. How do you walk around on those things?"

I looked down at my legs, which I'd always thought were a little too meaty. I supposed next to Peck's tree trunk legs, everyone else's looked like brittle saplings.

"I don't know, Professor. One foot in front of the other, I guess," I mumbled as I stalked off to do squats.

Ozzy laughed under his breath as he began adding weights to the barbell. "Just enough," he called after me. "Just enough."

Compared to the trauma and drama of the morning, my afternoon classes were a breeze. I liked my History of Wormwood class the best. Professor Lawless called on me a lot, but it was because I always knew the answers. Today, he discussed how the donor parents of the Sophisticates had been chosen. Lawless seemed pleasantly surprised that I knew as much as I did.

Even roller derby practice wasn't too horrible since there was no scrimmage against Quinnie's team. I secretly thought it might have something to do with the fact that the entire track had to be swept clean and new lights installed after the unexplained explosion the night before.

"You're really catching on," Arabella congratulated me in the locker room after practice. "Hey, did you notice that Quinnie wasn't at practice? She wasn't in any of our classes today either."

"I thought you said she just had a few cuts?"

"That's what I heard. Maybe it's more serious than we thought," Arabella said, a little too gleefully.

Despite how Quinnie had treated me so far, I felt guilty. I didn't really want to be responsible for permanently disfiguring her. A few cuts and bruises were one thing, needing plastic surgery or a bag for her head was another. I really needed to get my temper under control. When I let it run free, there was no telling who or what would be in it's path. What if it was one of my friends or some innocent person? I couldn't risk hurting anyone.

"So, what did you think about your first full day here?" Arabella asked as we hurried down the hallways to the dining hall.

"Tiring," I said. "The morning run was puke-inducing and Conditioning was brutal. I used up the rest of my energy on practice and I still have my work detail."

"Me too."

"What do you do?"

"I'm an assistant for Professor Lawless. I do whatever he needs — help with grading papers, getting him coffee and dinner while he does lesson plans, cleaning his office and the classroom. Just whatever he needs help with."

"Sounds boring."

"Nah. He's cool. He always gives me easy stuff to do and usually lets me out early. Plus, sometimes he sends me to the library to get research materials, so I'll get to come hang out with you every once in a while."

We were nearly to the dining hall when someone grabbed my elbow and spun me around.

It was Ozzy.

"I need to talk to you," he hissed.

"I'm on my way to dinner."

"You need to listen to me," he snapped angrily. "I just heard what happened between you and Quinnie. You can't let that happen again."

"I don't know what you're talking about." Technically, that was true. He could have been talking about the pen or the lights. But either way, I wasn't admitting to explosions of any kind. It had done nothing but cause problems so far.

Arabella forced her minuscule body in between me and Ozzy. "What's your problem, Osbourne?" she sneered. "Are you upset your girlfriend is mutilated for life?"

"I'm trying to help her," he growled.

"Then go look in the infirmary, that's probably where she still is."

"I'm talking about Cleo," Ozzy said. "This is none of your business, so run off to dinner. Cleo will meet up with you later." He attempted to brush Arabella to the side, but despite the fact that he was much taller and more muscular, she was immovable.

"My friends *are* my business. Are you trying to help her like you helped Sterling? Fat lot of good that did, he's lucky to still be alive."

"That wouldn't have happened if he'd just listened to me."

"Go tell it to your girlfriend," Arabella snapped. "We don't want your help." She grabbed my arm and pulled me toward the dining hall. Ozzy let go, but when I turned around, he was still staring at me angrily.

"What was that all about?" I muttered once we rounded the corner.

"He's probably mad about his beautiful Quinnie taking a face full of broken glass during the scrimmage last night."

"Why would he want to talk to me about that?" I swallowed nervously.

"It was a strange coincidence, don't you think?" Arabella looked sideways at me. "You give her the can opener, she skates over your hand, and then the lights explode and Quinnie's the only one that gets hurt."

I avoided the assumption. "So, Ozzy's dating Quinnie?"

Arabella shrugged, seemingly unaffected by the change in topic. "Not officially, I guess, but they're always together. From what I've heard, she knows where all his birthmarks are."

"Sophisticates don't have birthmarks."

"It's an expression, Cleo. Do I have to spell it out for you? You're not that naïve, are you?"

"Oh," I said uncomfortably. "I thought Sterling said that kind of stuff didn't happen around here."

"He did?" Arabella laughed.

"Yesterday he said that guys aren't allowed in the girl's dorms for more than ten minutes at a time. You know, so stuff like that won't happen."

Arabella laughed so hard her eyes watered. "You can't be serious. You really think teenagers with genetically altered, superior intelligence can't figure a way around alarms and curfews for a little hot and heavy time?"

I blushed. "No, of course not. I just . . . Ozzy and Quinnie just seem so different. He doesn't seem like her type at all."

"Ozzy? Mr. Perfect? He's everybody's type. He can have pretty much anything and anyone he wants in this school. He walks on water here at St. Ignatius, but you can't trust him. I suggest you stay out of his way and off his radar, okay?"

"Because of what happened between him and Sterling?"

Arabella's eyes narrowed. "Did Sterling tell you about that?"

"No," I admitted. "You told Ozzy that Sterling was lucky to be alive."

Her expression softened. "Look, Ozzy is nothing but bad news. You can do what you want, but if you want my advice, stay away from him. As far away from him as you can."

Quinnie showed up to dinner, hidden beneath an absurd amount of bandages and flanked by her sidekicks, Sadie and Eva. There were two other guys sitting at the table with them and Ozzy made the group an even six. Quinnie sat right next to Ozzy, looking pathetic, lobbying for his attention and sympathy. Ozzy leaned over and whispered in Quinnie's ear, which seemed to calm her down, and then he looked up, catching my gaze. The look he gave me clearly meant he wasn't finished with me. Not by a long shot. He didn't care what my guard dog Arabella said, he was going to have his say.

After dinner, Sterling walked me to the library for my work detail since I'd never been there before.

"I heard you fainted in Weapons class." He smiled.

"You did? News travels fast, I guess."

"Was it Ozzy's overwhelming good looks?"

"No!"

"Don't be embarrassed, you're not the first girl to fall prey to his supposed hotness and perfect aim."

"It wasn't because of him. I'm scared of guns, that's all." The strap of my backpack was digging into an exceptionally sore part of my shoulder and I adjusted it. It didn't help. It seemed every part of my body was sore. "What do you mean perfect aim?"

"You were in Weapons class with him, didn't you notice? He can hit anything. Bulls-eye, first time, any weapon."

"Well, he was teaching the class, so I didn't really get to see him shoot much. He did, however, knock some kid named Theo on his ass with a pill bottle."

"He threw a pill bottle at him?" Sterling laughed. "That's a first. I've seen him take people out a dozen different ways, but never with a pill bottle."

I nodded. "Theo and his brother both got kicked out of class and sent to Dean Overton's office. Theo was pretending to shoot Wesley with a loaded gun."

"Sounds about right. Those two are definitely not the sharpest tools in the shed. Well," he corrected himself, "they're tools, but not the useful kind. So, how was Mr. Perfect Aim as a teacher?"

"Okay, I guess."

"I'm sure he was more than okay; Ozzy is good at everything," Sterling said bitterly.

I bit the inside of my lip, afraid to ask Sterling what had been running through my mind since before dinner. But I had to know why Arabella didn't trust Ozzy. "What happened between you and Ozzy?"

Sterling's smile faded. "I don't really want to talk about it."

"Oh come on. You know all about me fainting. How bad could it be?"

He glared at me. "Bad," Sterling said irritably. We reached the library and he spun on his heel quickly to go back down the hallway, his head hung low. "Have a good night, Cleo," he mumbled.

"I'm sorry, Sterling, I shouldn't have asked."

"No, you shouldn't have. See you later," he said, stuffing his hands in his pockets and hurrying down the darkened hall.

Great, I only have two friends and I'm already turning one against me, I thought as I opened the large, heavy door in front of me.

The library was large, nearly as big as the one at the University. It had the unmistakable smell of old paper, ink, and leather. The kind of smell that made me want to curl up under a blanket on a rainy day and bury my nose in a book. Inside the door, there was a checkout counter to the left, and seated behind it was a tall woman with long hair tied back into a loose and messy ponytail. She was wearing the designated librarian eyeglass chain around her neck, attached to red horn-rimmed glasses that were perched on her nose. She looked up when I entered and smiled widely. She got up quickly and shuffled around the counter to introduce herself.

"Hi, Clementine. I'm Zelda Cain, the Academy Librarian. So glad to finally meet you," she gushed. "I haven't had an assistant in so long."

"Glad to be here," I answered truthfully. If there was one place I felt at home, it was among books.

"Let me show you around and give you an introduction to some of your duties. We don't generally get very busy in here, but it's more than I can handle by myself. Especially the re-stacking of books." She sighed. "It's never-ending."

Zelda showed me where all of the various sections were, the room where I would tutor students who might need it, and how to check out books and enter them into the computer. I took special note of the locked door of the Restricted Section, but didn't raise Zelda's awareness of my interest by asking any questions. Once I got used to the routine of both the job and Zelda's comings and goings, I intended on getting a good look at the things inside that room. Maybe I could find out something in there that I hadn't been able to uncover in my unsuccessful hacking of the Program's computer system.

Twenty minutes later, we circled back to the front desk. "For tonight, I'd like you to re-stack this bin of books," Zelda said, indicating a large box of books on the other side of the wall behind the return slot. She provided me with a cart to put the books on and a map of the library to help me remember where the various sections were.

I quickly loaded up the cart and eagerly headed off into the quiet solitude of the library. Walking down the aisles between the book-laden shelves and empty tables, it occurred to me what a shame it was that the library was so deserted. All this knowledge just sitting here, waiting to be discovered, I thought sadly. If this had been a library at a Vanguard Academy, I knew every single seat, at every single table would be taken. However, since this was a Mandate Academy, I assumed that every single weight bench and every single booth at the shooting range were probably inhabited instead.

It was obvious that I didn't belong at St. Ignatius. Did the Program really think they could turn me, a brainiac, into an efficient soldier? I seriously had my doubts. I couldn't even shoot a gun.

On my fourth trip through the library with the cart, I realized that it was already 8:45 and that I only had a few more minutes of work detail left before I could head back to my room and start my homework. The time had gone by quickly, but Arabella was right, the Academy definitely didn't leave much room for down time. By the time I got back to my room, I'd have less than two hours for homework before it was lights out.

I rounded the corner into the *Wormwood* section and nearly screamed when I saw someone sitting at one of the tables. He was the first person I'd seen in the library all night, aside from Zelda of course.

The boy turned at the sound of my cart's squeaky wheels, and for some reason I wasn't at all surprised to see that it was Ozzy. He made it clear that he intended to talk to me, but about what, I still wasn't sure. All I was sure about was that Arabella had suggested I steer clear of him.

"How do you like your work detail?" he asked.

"I like it. It's nice and quiet. Nobody bothers me here," I answered, hoping he'd get my meaning.

"We need to talk," he said shortly.

"Actually, I'm on the clock and I need to re-shelve these books."

"Go ahead, I can talk while you work."

I glared at him in answer. It wasn't in my nature to be rude to people, but Arabella told me to stay away from Ozzy and given the fact that he was close friends with Quinnie, I had to agree. He was bad news.

"Okay, fine. I'll help you," he offered, grabbing a book.

"I don't need your help," I said, snatching the book back. I had a feeling his help came with expectations and I had no intention of indenturing myself to him for something I could easily do myself. I walked down the aisle and shoved the books into their places.

"You need to keep a low profile," Ozzy warned.

"I'm just trying to survive this place."

"What about Quinnie?"

I rounded on him, angrily. "What about Quinnie? I haven't done anything to her. She's the one harassing me."

"What about the pen exploding on her? What about the lights on the derby track?"

I laughed nervously. "I'm sorry your girlfriend had a couple mishaps, but you can't seriously be blaming that on me."

Ozzy scowled. "You can deny it all you want, Cleo, but I know more than you think I do. You need to get control of yourself or it could go very badly for you."

"Are you threatening me?" I asked angrily. "Do you honestly think I'm responsible for your girlfriend's clumsiness?"

"She's not my girlfriend."

I huffed. "Could've fooled me."

"Jealous?" he asked, a devilish grin playing at his lips. He raked his hand back through his dark curls, revealing intense, green eyes. And it wasn't just the color that was intense, it was the way he looked at me, as if he could read me like an open book.

"Jealous?" I repeated. "I don't even know you. Why would I care if you were dating a vicious hag queen?"

Ozzy smiled. "Don't worry, you still have a chance," he teased.

"I haven't chosen a date yet for the Autumn Formal."

"Then maybe you should stop wasting your time in here pestering me and get to work on that deficiency. Now, if you'll excuse me, my time's up and I have homework to do," I snapped as I put the last three books in their proper places.

"I'll walk you back to your room," he offered.

"Thanks, but no thanks. I know the way." Lie. I'd be lucky to find my way to my room before lights out.

"But, I need to talk to you."

"Not interested." Well, maybe a little interested.

"There are things I have to tell you."

I remembered what Arabella said about staying off his radar. I had to get rid of him. "Make an appointment, I'm a busy girl," I said as I steered the empty cart out of the aisle and headed for the checkout counter. I had to wait a few minutes in Zelda's office for her to return from the bathroom. Luckily, Ozzy didn't follow me inside.

After Zelda signed my timecard, I went back into the now empty library and picked up my backpack from underneath the counter. A piece of paper fluttered to the floor and I leaned over to pick it up.

The note said: "Meet me in the common room of your dorm at midnight. – O"

Not happening buddy, I said to myself as I crumpled up the note. I tossed it at the trash can and it missed by at least six inches, bouncing onto the floor. I cursed silently and bent to pick it up and drop it into the can.

Perfect aim.

Something I definitely didn't have — or want.

∞ 10 ∞

Dirty Secrets

There was a tapping noise coming from somewhere. I opened my eyes groggily and looked at the clock. It was one a.m. The tapping continued. I got out of bed and walked to the door, expecting Arabella to be the culprit of the late night disturbance. I peered through the peephole, but there was no one outside that I could see. Apprehensively, I opened the door, looked up and down the hallway, and confirmed it was empty.

The tapping continued and I followed the sound to the window over my desk. I pulled the cord on the blinds and nearly had a heart attack when I saw Ozzy on the other side of the window, hanging from the branch of a tree. He was holding a piece of paper up to the window that said, "I need to talk to you."

Jackass. I grabbed a piece of paper off the desk, scribbled a few words on it, and held it up to the window. My note said, "I need to sleep. Go away stalker."

Ozzy's reaction wasn't what I expected — he actually smiled. I rolled my eyes, let the blinds slam down, and then crawled back into bed. It was going to be hard to keep rejecting Ozzy's requests to talk. Not only was I curious about what it was he was so determined to tell me, but he was really easy on the eyes and a little part of me wanted to get to know him better, even if he was a little cocky sometimes. Actually, if I was being totally honest with myself, a BIG part of me wanted to get to know him better.

All I had to do, however, was remind myself that both Sterling and Arabella suggested that I avoid him. They must have good reasons. And on top of that, I didn't really want to give Quinnie another reason to hate me. If Quinnie had her sights set on Ozzy, she could have him.

The next day in Weapons class, Professor Farnsworth was back. I was relieved to discover that we weren't doing handguns again, and we'd be working with bows and arrows. I'd never used a bow and arrow and couldn't imagine how it was a skill useful to a soldier. Really, who was going to go traipsing around hunting an enemy with a bow and a quiver of arrows strapped to their back? This wasn't the Middle Ages or the back woods of Wyoming. But I wasn't going to complain. If shooting with a bow helped me avoid a fainting spell, I was all for it.

When Professor Farnsworth asked us to choose a partner, I looked hopefully at Helen, one of the girls from my roller derby team. Helen shrugged in apology and jerked her thumb at a girl next to her. I threw out a few other hopeful looks with even less success. Most people looked at me like I was a disease. Was it because of the fainting yesterday or the rumors of my argument with Quinnie? Either way, it was apparent that I was on the bottom rung of the popularity ladder.

I was calmly resigning myself to the idea that I'd be a team of one when someone stepped up next to me.

"Looks like we're partners today," he said in that infuriatingly confident voice.

"Fine. But just so you know, we're not here to talk," I informed him testily. "We're here to learn how to use the bow and arrow."

"Actually," he corrected me, "you're here to learn how to use the bow and arrow. I already know how to shoot, perfect aim and everything."

"Why are you even in this class?"

"Because I like to shoot stuff."

I shook my head and muttered something derogatory about boys and destroying things. Ozzy only smiled as we stepped up to our booth.

"Ladies first," he offered.

"No, no. I insist." I stepped to the side to allow him to go.

"Don't tell me you're afraid of arrows, too."

"With my aim, everyone here should be afraid of arrows when I'm shooting," I clarified.

Ozzy either didn't hear me or chose to ignore me. He wordlessly picked up the bow, knocked an arrow, and let it loose. It flew through the air in a blur of feathers and I immediately heard a thud. He knocked four more arrows in quick succession and there were four more thuds. He turned and handed the bow to me. "Your turn, Firecracker."

I took the bow clumsily, absolutely clueless as to what to do with it. I tried watching Ozzy so I'd have some idea of how to hold it and shoot, but he'd been so quick and fluid that I didn't even know where to begin. I held the bow out in front of me in my left hand, tried to knock an arrow, pulled back on the string with my right hand, and then let go. The arrow slid off the front of the bow and landed in the grass at my feet.

I turned to look at Ozzy — expecting a superior, arrogant grin — but he was looking away. I picked the arrow up off the ground and tried again. It didn't make it much further on its second trip. I tried three more times with no better luck. "Your turn," I said, attempting to hand Ozzy the bow.

"You have to hit the target at least five times."

"Says who?"

He pointed to a chalkboard behind them. "Must hit the target five times," was scrawled across the board in chalk.

"Well, clearly, I can't"

"Probably not without my help," Ozzy agreed.

I rolled my eyes. "Fine. Will you help me, please?"

"If you agree to talk to me." He wasn't smiling, but his eyes were.

"You can't bribe me!"

"And you can't pass this class without me."

"You're lucky I can't use this thing," I threatened, shaking the bow at him.

"You're lucky I'm a good teacher," he retorted, moving to stand beside me. "Now put the bow down."

"But we're supposed to be shooting arrows."

"And it will help if we know which eye is dominant."

"I'm right handed."

"I'm not worried about your hands. Not yet, anyways," he said with a grin.

I blushed in response even though I willed myself not to.

"Eye dominance doesn't really have anything to do with what hand you write with. Here," he said, standing next to me and demonstrating. "Put your hands in front of you and make a small triangle with your fingers. Position them so you can see the target through the small triangle." I did as he instructed. "Okay, now close your left eye and tell me what happens."

"I can't see the target anymore."

"Switch eyes. Close the right one."

"I can see the target again."

"Good. You're left eye dominant, like me. That'll make teaching you a little easier." He picked the bow up and put it into my right hand. Then he grabbed my hips and turned me sideways, standing behind me. Ozzy lifted my right hand, which was holding the bow, and then reached around to help me nock an arrow and pull the string back with my left hand. He was flat against my back and I could feel the rise and fall of his chest against my shoulder blades and his warm breath on my neck as he breathed slow and steady, helping me line up the shot.

"Make sure you keep your elbow up and pull the string back to your chin," he instructed. His deep whispers made me shiver. "Don't move," he reminded me quietly. He removed his hands from mine, but remained standing right behind me. "Let it fly whenever you're ready."

My fingers released their hold on the string and I briefly saw the feathers of the arrow as it streaked forward. Almost immediately I heard a thud. "I hit the target!" I exclaimed.

"Well, it was no bulls-eye, but it'll do. Now you have to do it four more times."

By the end of class, I'd shot more than 20 times. When Professor Farnsworth instructed the class to retrieve the arrows, I was delighted to discover that all but three of my yellow fletched arrows were impaled on the target. All five of Ozzy's green fletched arrows were crowded into the small, red, bulls-eye. Two of them were split down the middle from arrows being shot into the exact same spot.

"Farnsworth won't be happy about that," Ozzy mused as he pulled his arrows out.

"Then why does he let you in the class? He knows you have good aim, right?"

"Of course he does. That's exactly why he lets me in the class. Well, that and he frequently likes to take days off."

"Doesn't the Program have a problem with that?"

"Not really. For one thing, I'm a better teacher than he is. Secondly, I have a very important sponsor. I live by my own rules."

"So, you don't have to live by the rule of just enough? That only applies to me?"

Ozzy's eyes bore into mine; his face was completely serious for once. "It's too late for me, but you still have a chance. I'll talk to you later about it," he said quietly. "You owe me, remember?"

I was suddenly worried about exactly what I'd promised him in return for archery knowledge. "Just talking, right?" I confirmed.

"For starters. See you later, Cleo. And that's a promise," he said with a wink.

I set my tray of food on the table and then slumped into the chair heavily. "I don't think I'll ever be able to sit down properly again. My quads are destroyed."

"Peck?" Arabella asked knowingly.

"Yes! She made me do squats the entire class. She keeps telling me my legs look like twigs."

Arabella peeked under the table. "Twigs? That's unfair. I'd give you at least saplings."

I looked around the dining hall. "Where's Sterling? He's usually the first one here."

"Track practice."

"I thought he had practice right before dinner like we do."

"He does, but his first meet is coming up so he's putting in a little extra time during lunch. We probably won't see him much for the rest of the week."

I was disappointed. Meals were the few moments when I got to see my friends and talk to them.

"Anything else exciting happen this morning?" Arabella asked, shoveling bits of fruit into her mouth.

"Ozzy gave me a personal archery lesson in Weapons class."

Arabella frowned. "Personal, as in standing right behind you showing you where to put your hands like in those dorky romantic movies? That kind of personal?"

"Exactly that kind of personal."

"That boy is a stalker."

"You have no idea," I admitted, sneaking a quick glance toward Quinnie's table. Ozzy was staring straight at me as if he knew I was talking about him. I lowered my voice to barely above a whisper. "He showed up at the library last night." I relayed the events of the previous night, including the midnight window tapping. "Now he says that in return for helping me in Weapons class, I owe him. What do I do?"

"Avoid him."

"I'm trying."

"Try harder. If Quinnie finds out, she will be more pissed at you than she already is. She's already claimed him as her property. Besides, he's bad news," Arabella said, waving her fork at me.

"I know." I knew Ozzy was dangerous. And I had a feeling that wasn't necessarily just because of Quinnie. At the same time, however, he had secrets that he wanted to share with me, and I was a sucker for dirty little secrets.

"If you want, I can come do my homework in the library tonight after I get done with my work detail. That way, if he shows up again, I can scare him away."

I smiled at the thought of Arabella scaring away someone who was twice her size. "I think I'll be okay. By the way, I forgot to tell you how much I loved your hair today." Arabella's hairstyle for the day was numerous, braided ponytails — each one a different color and covered in something that made them sparkle. "It looks like a unicorn threw up all over your head. But in a good way."

"A unicorn?"

"Yeah, because they're made of rainbows and glitter and awesome."

Arabella laughed. "Ten points for effort. That's better than Sterling did today. He was too preoccupied with the Track meet to come up with anything good. It's definitely not my best work," she said, twirling one of the braids and inspecting the end of it, "but I couldn't make up my mind this morning on which color represented my mood so I went with all of them."

"How long does it take you to do your hair in the morning?" I reached out to one of the braids and rubbed it between my fingers. "I mean to get every single one so perfect looking, it must take you hours. Wouldn't you rather sleep? And you must spend a fortune on hair dye."

"It doesn't take as long as you think," Arabella confessed. "You might be surprised at how fast I get ready in the morning."

"You'll have to give me some tips sometime, I could really use a makeover."

"Don't worry." Arabella's mouth hooked up into a loaded grin. "I have some plans for your Autumn Formal look."

"Oh really?" I laughed. "I don't have a date yet, are you going stag with me?"

"Absolutely not," Arabella said indignantly as she popped a square of honey dew in her mouth.

"Why not?" I asked, pretending to be insulted.

"I don't know if you've noticed, but you're not entirely coordinated when it comes to physical activity. I totally plan to get my groove on and I can't let someone with two left feet hold me back. No offense, Sweetie."

"Maybe Sterling will go with me."

"No can do. He's already got a date."

"Seriously? Who?"

"Me, of course," Arabella stated, as if it were obvious.

"Oh, I didn't know you two were . . . you know . . . dating."

Arabella burst into laughter. "Dating? No. He's just the only guy here who would go with me," she admitted. She didn't look sad or upset about the fact, just accepting. "I don't know how much you've been paying attention, but Sterling and I are sort of unpopular. You've thrown your lot in with the wrong crowd, Babe."

"I like your crowd. And besides, I'm worse than unpopular."

"Don't worry. If you can smoke Quinnie in our first match like you did in the scrimmage, I'm sure you can rustle up at least a halfway decent date."

"We have a match before the Autumn Formal?" I squeaked. "You're joking, right?"

"Not even a little."

"How often do we have matches?"

"Four times a year. One for every season. Our fall match is in a little over three weeks."

I leaned over and put my head on the table. "Three weeks? I think I'm going to throw up."

"You'll be fine," Arabella said before tearing into a bagel with her teeth.

"With only a few weeks of practice? I'm going to die."

"Trust me, Honeycakes, you'll be great."

I wished I had that much confidence in myself.

A week went by and I was starting to learn my way around the Academy. I only got lost half the time and had managed to be on time to my classes most of the time. I was still late every once in a while. There were some things that would never change. The one class I made sure I was never late for was Professor Peck's class. That woman was sadistic enough without giving her another reason to dole out punishment. Peck seemed very concerned that I wasn't massively muscular like the rest of the Mandates and she was making it her personal mission to bulk me up.

Ozzy continued to be my partner in Weapons class and usually walked with me to Conditioning class, but he never brought up the subject of the secrets he needed to tell me. In a way, I was relieved. I'd promised Arabella I would stay away from Ozzy and aside from the two classes I had with him, I was keeping my promise. But at the same time, I constantly worried (and hoped) he was going to show up unannounced at the library or at my window again.

He didn't.

During my first weekend at the Academy, I spent all my free time getting in extra training on the derby track with Arabella. It was Wednesday and I'd been at St. Ignatius for eight days already. Most of Quinnie's bandages had been removed, I had finally learned to shoot a bow and arrow with consistency, and everyone was getting excited for the track and field meet that was scheduled for the weekend. When I showed up for work detail at the library that night, Zelda informed me that I had my first tutoring session at eight p.m.

"What subject?" I asked nervously, hoping it was something I knew well.

Zelda opened her appointment log and found the notation.

"Language. Spanish, I believe. You know Spanish, right?" Zelda asked, closing the book and going back to the work she was doing on her computer. I sighed with relief. Spanish was a breeze for me.

"No problem. Should I just re-shelve books in the meantime?"

"That would be perfect, Clementine. There aren't as many as yesterday, so it shouldn't take you long."

I was coming back for my last cart of books when a blur of color exploded out from behind a bookshelf. I yelped in terror, stumbling into one of the study tables in the middle of the aisle.

It was Arabella.

"There you are. I've been looking all over for you," she said.

"You scared the crap out of me." I leaned against the table while my heart rate returned to normal. "What are you doing here?"

"Lawless needed a book from the restricted section. Ms. Cain's back there now getting it and putting it into a locked box so I can't peek at it on the way back. As if I cared about anything *Wormwood* related."

I was surprised. "You're not even tempted to look?"

Arabella pretended to gag. "No. Would you be?"

I shrugged. "I'd probably be a little tempted to look at anything that was forbidden." Truthfully, I was a sucker for anything I wasn't supposed to know and right now I was itching to see the book that Ms. Cain was locking away for Professor Lawless. A book that needed to be under lock and key? I wanted to get a look at it so badly I was fantasizing about asking Arabella to bring it back here before taking it to Lawless so we could break open the box and get a good look at what was inside. I had every intention of eventually sneaking into the restricted room to look at all of the books, but I didn't tell Arabella that.

Arabella tilted her head. "True. But still. *Wormwood* is so boring."

"It's our history," I explained. "Aren't you even a little curious as to how we were made, who our parents are, and what our future holds for us?"

"We were made by scientists to be the best of the best," Arabella explained, holding up one finger. "As for my parents, I'm a commodity, not a child. They didn't care about me, so I don't care about them," she added holding up her second finger. "And right now, we're Mandates. Our only future is fighting," she finished holding up her third finger. "We're objects, Cleo, and that's all we are. No amount of anything we do can change our futures, so we might as well enjoy this while we can," she said, spreading her arms wide. "You want to know why the Autumn Formal is a big deal here? Because it's something to look forward to — something to help us forget we're just pawns in a war that's been going on for 30 years.

It's our chance to pretend we're normal, to pretend that we have a choice." The fire left Arabella's eyes and even her hair seemed a little lifeless. "I better go. Ms. Cain probably has the book ready and Lawless said I was off the clock once I delivered it to him, and I've got loads of homework. See you tomorrow."

I waved goodbye to Arabella, returned the cart to the front desk, and made my way to the tutoring room. I felt guilty that I was the reason my normally feisty friend was suddenly listless. Sophisticates didn't like to bring up their past and future — neither were a source of happiness. I should've known better. I'd make it up to Arabella later, somehow.

When I opened the door to the tutoring room, I saw the back of a guy who was sitting with his feet propped up on the table. A leather jacket was slung over a chair and from what I could tell, he was wearing jeans and a form fitting grey t-shirt. I couldn't wait until I'd earned enough from working at the library to buy some normal clothes. I'd ditched the sock tassels right after my last class, but I was still wearing the rest of the school uniform.

The guy turned when the door shut and I knew I shouldn't have been surprised to see that it was Ozzy, but I was.

"You're faking the need for a Spanish tutor to stalk me now?" I asked.

"I'm taking Spanish and I need your help."

"Honestly?"

"En realidad, no. Soy bilingüe en Español. Sólo quiero hablar con usted."

"That's what I thought," I responded, annoyed, as I reached for the door.

Ozzy got up quickly, hurried across the room, and put his

hand against the door, pushing it closed. "Don't do that. Trust me, this isn't going to hurt at all. You're not going to get in trouble or anything. As far as Ms. Cain's concerned, you're tutoring me. Besides, you owe me, remember?"

"What took you so long?" I asked, remembering his urgency to talk to me before. It'd been a week. Why now?

"What? Did you miss me?" He grinned mischievously. When I rolled my eyes in response, he laughed. "You told me to make an appointment, remember? Just following orders."

"You seemed desperate before, why wait a week?"

His smile reached his eyes and he shrugged, causing his muscles to ripple deliciously. "You've been behaving, so I thought it could wait. Besides, Ms. Cain wouldn't let me schedule a tutoring session with you the first week."

Ozzy was standing right in front of me and I could smell the fresh clean scent of his laundry detergent and shampoo. Must be nice to have time to shower after team practice, I mused. That's assuming Mr. Perfect Aim even has to participate in a sport like the rest of us plebes, I thought testily.

My curiosity — and involuntary attraction to him — won out over my sensibility. "Fine, let's talk. Then maybe you'll finally leave me alone," I said hopefully, but not too hopefully.

"Not likely." Ozzy's grin was rebellious and I had to fight the instinct to grin back.

I sat at the table. "Let's get this Q & A over with. I've got homework to do and I don't want you giving me a window wake up call again."

Ozzy sank into the chair across from me and leaned forward, his elbows on his knees. His constant invasion of my personal space always had me on edge. It was like he was invading more than just my space. I leaned back instinctively.

"What did you do to get sent here, Cleo?"

I looked away to mask my surprise at his straightforwardness and spouted my well-rehearsed lie. "I hacked into the Program's system to try to find out who my parents were."

"Bullshit. They took your Internet privileges away for that. Minor offense. Well, okay, not minor, but not worth getting sent to a Mandate Academy when you're clearly Vanguard material. Don't lie to me, I told you I don't like liars. What did you do?"

I pursed my lips, angry that he knew so much about me. Knowing my menstrual cycle and medical information was one thing, all the professors knew that kind of stuff. But Ozzy was a student; he shouldn't have access to my other records. "Did you look into some file of mine or something?"

"Of course I did."

"What? How dare you!" I vaulted to my feet, hands fisted at my sides. "You're a fellow cadet. That's none of your business," I said. Reading my file? That was like looking into someone's underwear drawer. "I'm done." I stalked toward the door, but Ozzy grabbed my arm and pulled me back.

"I'm trying to help you, Cleo. Why won't you let me?"

"I think you're only trying to help yourself."

"A little, maybe. But mostly I'm trying to help all of us."

"Who is 'us' exactly?"

"You, me, the other Vanguards. Haven't you noticed that you aren't the only one who doesn't belong here?"

"You mean like Arabella and Sterling?"

"And Quinnie, Sadie, Eva, Dexter, Marty, Theo, and Wesley."

I hadn't met Dexter and Marty yet, but I assumed they must

be the other two guys that regularly sat with Quinnie and her entourage in the dining hall.

"Maybe we're all just rule breakers, being punished for not doing what we were supposed to," I offered, even though I knew deep down that wasn't true.

"What did you do?" he asked again.

I looked away. If my best friend Cassie hadn't believed me, why would a stranger? There was no way I was going to tell him. "Isn't it in my file? If you have access to my file, you must know everything about me."

"Not yet, but I plan to." Ozzy stepped toward me, still holding my arm, hovering dangerously close to me, invading that personal circle of space that most people knew was off limits. But Ozzy didn't seem to care. He was so close. My willpower and anger were ebbing away and I was annoyed with myself for being attracted to him.

I pulled my arm free and stepped back. "Look, I'm not really sure what you want from me."

"Go to the Autumn Formal with me."

"What?" That was unexpected. "No way."

Ozzy looked surprised. I assumed he was used to his charm and good looks getting him whatever he wanted. "Why not?"

"You couldn't handle me, even if I came with instructions."

"A challenge, I like that."

"Too bad."

"Come on Cleo, go with me."

I said the first thing that came into my head. "I can't. I already have a date."

"No you don't. You've been here a week and the only friends you have are Arabella and Sterling and I know they're going together."

"I don't want to go with you."

"Sure you do."

"No, I don't," I lied. "And, I don't really want to give Quinnie another reason to hate me any more than she already does."

"Impossible." There was that smile again. "She absolutely loathes you. Her feelings for you couldn't get any worse. No harm done."

"I don't even know you."

"I'll change that."

"I don't trust you."

"I'll change that too."

"Doubtful," I scoffed. I had to get away from him before I was unable to counter his arguments. I was fairly certain that if I stayed much longer, Ozzy would get his way. I knew I had to keep my distance from him; he was too dangerous, and not just because he was good with weapons. "You read my personal file. How can I trust someone that invaded my privacy by reading my file?" I yanked open the door, ducked through it, and slammed it shut behind me. Ozzy didn't follow me.

I'd wanted to hear the dirty secrets Ozzy knew, but now that I knew they were mine, I was humiliated. I'd rather go to the dance alone than with someone who had been snooping in my file. At least that's what I kept telling myself as I hurried out of the library and back to my room.

11

SHOCKING TRUTHS

The rest of the week got easier as I got into the rhythm of classes and the relentless physical schedule. I wasn't getting much faster on the morning run and I was still Peck's squat target in Conditioning, but the other classes were bearable and I was surprised to find that I actually enjoyed roller derby practice. Younglove had us running various plays and maneuvers in preparation for our first match and I was often amazed to find I could still manage to walk with all the bruises and minor injuries I was collecting from collisions with all my hulking teammates. Quinnie finally returned to practice with her team, so I knew I needed to keep working hard. Quinnie would be.

I hadn't seen Ozzy since our pseudo tutoring session in the library Wednesday night. He hadn't come to any classes or meals. I had to admit that I missed his help in Weapons class. We were still working on archery, but we had moved from the traditional long-bow to work with crossbows. I struggled a bit, but I finally got the hang of it. However, on Friday, we started using compound bows. I was nearly helpless. The compound bows had so many bolts, wheels, strings, and other fancy parts that I was completely intimidated. Farnsworth insisted that the compound bow was easier to use than the long bow, but he quickly became frustrated with me and my clumsiness so he ended up ignoring me and allowing me to fumble around on my own. I tried to imagine Ozzy behind me, guiding my hands into the proper places and whispering directions into my ear, but the magic just wasn't there.

Where was he?

I had to remind myself that I didn't care.

Dinner on Friday night was a raucous affair. Everyone was excited for the fall sports season to get underway. Track and field was going to be the first competition of the year.

"Nervous?" I asked Sterling as he pushed his food around his plate.

"I just want to do well," he replied. "I don't need any more screw ups here."

"You'll do great," Arabella comforted him. "No one is faster than you."

"It's not all about speed, Arabella, you know that."

"Well, what you lack in brawn, you make up for with brains," she said, ruffling his hair. "And beauty," she added, squeezing his cheek, just like his aunt might. That is, if he actually knew who his aunt was.

"Thanks, Bella."

"You know I hate that nickname," she scolded, flicking him in the ear, just like his aunt might.

I smiled at my two friends. They were different from Cassie and the Homework Harpies, but they made St. Ignatius tolerable. One look at Arabella's cobalt colored mohawk and Sterling's sarcastic smile made me forget for a moment that I was at a military academy.

"How did you get that thing upright again after smashing it under your derby helmet?" I asked, indicating Arabella's massive hairdo.

"Talent, Sweetcheeks. Talent."

"More like black magic," Sterling suggested. Arabella glared at him, but we all knew it wasn't a legitimate glare.

Saturday morning, I decided that I rather enjoyed the morning run on the weekends. Without the cargo nets and other barriers, it took me less than an hour to complete it. I was still far behind the other cadets, but it was an enjoyable experience rather than a punishment. Halfway through, I urged Arabella — who was complaining about possibly dying from a lack of food — to run ahead. I intended to have a leisurely run alone, which would also mean an opportunity to shower in the communal bathroom alone. The one thing I did miss from the University was the private bathroom in each room. Here at St. Ignatius, I had to use the communal bathroom, sometimes standing in line to use the shower. Usually, with the time crunch of my schedule, I couldn't afford the luxury of waiting around to have the bathroom to myself, but today was different. Since it was a Saturday, the only thing I had to do was eat, do homework, and show up to the track and field meet.

The hallway was empty and quiet as I walked to the showers wrapped in a towel, lugging my bucket of toiletries and clutching a set of clothes that Arabella had loaned to me. The pants were a little short, but at least I wouldn't have to wear my uniform all weekend long. I was grateful to leave behind the brown, gold, and green plaid atrocity for a comfy pair of jeans and a t-shirt.

I set the clothes on the bench and stepped inside the shower to turn the water on.

"I've heard you're quite the little home-wrecker."

I spun around quickly, slipping on the wet floor of the shower, as my towel began to fall off. I met the malevolent glare of Quinnie, who was leaning against the wall, arms crossed.

"It's absurd to think you can even compete with me," Quinnie said, looking down her nose at me. "You may have gotten lucky at the scrimmage, but in the end, I'll crush you." She pushed off the wall and slowly walked toward me, hate rolling off her in waves of harsh, clipped words. "I know you had something to do with this," she said, pointing to her still-healing face. "I don't know what you did, but it didn't escape my notice that I was the only one injured."

Quinnie's beautiful face and bare arms were crisscrossed with red scratches and healing cuts. I grasped at the towel and pulled it tight around me, modesty overruling my common sense.

"Nudity is the least of your worries right now," Quinnie threatened, taking another step forward. "And I'm not sure what you think is going to happen between you and Ozzy, but you can give up on that dream now. Oh yes," she sneered in response to my surprise. "I heard all about your fainting spell and how you continually fawn all over him in Weapons class. It's pathetic, really. Do you actually think he'd be interested in you when he has me?"

I stepped back into the stream of water, my left foot making contact with the metal drain in the floor. My foot slipped on the wet drain and I grabbed the shower nozzle for support. Water rained down on me, soaking the towel and my face. I had nowhere to go.

Quinnie's smile turned sickeningly sweet. "The game's over now." She lifted her hand and I was sure I saw sparks flicker along the other girl's fingertips. I wanted to defend myself, to convince Quinnie that I wanted nothing to do with Ozzy, but I didn't get the chance.

"Don't look so shocked," Quinnie drawled, "I always win." She turned to leave the bathroom and flicked her finger over her shoulder. I saw a streak of blue light.

And then pain exploded through me.

I was being violently shaken as a series of massive and agonizing shudders went through my body. White, hot fire seared through my arms, legs, and torso as I convulsed uncontrollably. My hand and foot briefly felt like they were glued in place to the drain and nozzle but then I was released and thrown backwards against the shower wall. I hit the wall with such force that I broke several tiles before sliding down, crumbling into a pile of wet towel and twitching body parts. My fingers and toes were numb, but the pain lingered in my muscles, forcing them to tremble and spasm uncontrollably.

My nerve endings were being shredded into ragged bits and hot tears bubbled over my eye lashes. The water that ran off me and down the drain turned a pinkish hue, stained with the blood from the cuts on my back and head. I felt weak and twitchy and absolutely defeated. My fingers were burned and so was my foot. The pain was so incredible that I didn't want to do anything but lay there and give up.

The water had started to run cold and I was shivering when I finally heard someone enter the bathroom.

"She's in here," Arabella yelled, turning off the water, squatting down, and pushing the wet hair off my face. "What happened to you?"

I shook my head numbly. I wasn't sure if I could speak, but even if I could, I had no intention of telling her about Quinnie. As if being found by my friend, half-naked and barely conscious on the floor of the shower wasn't bad enough — Ozzy appeared behind Arabella.

"Move," he instructed, pushing her behind him. His usual cocky grin was uncharacteristically missing, replaced by concern. His lack of ego was the first clue I had that I was in worse shape than I had initially thought. He pulled me into his lap and held me against his chest as cold water dripped off my skin. I continued to shiver and tremble. "Go get a warm blanket," he ordered Arabella, who immediately ran off. Another sign that something was terribly wrong — Arabella was taking orders from Ozzy.

I couldn't stop shaking and Ozzy attempted to warm me up by rubbing my arms vigorously. "What happened?"

"I d-d-don't know," I stuttered, weakly lifting my hand to wipe water out of my eyes.

Ozzy gently grabbed my hand and turned it over. The skin of my palm was red and raw. He looked at the pattern of welts on my palm with curiosity, then turned to look at the shower, his gaze falling on the knob for the hot and cold water. He grabbed one of my feet and then the other, finding the polka dot pattern burn mark on my foot that had been caused by the metal drain. His curiosity mutated into righteous anger. "Quinnie!" he growled.

I shook my head, although I wasn't quite sure what I was denying. Quinnie had been responsible, there was no doubt about it. But I felt that accusing her would only make the situation worse. Or did Ozzy think that perhaps I did something even worse to Quinnie to have deserved this punishment? I wasn't sure about anything except for the fact that I was going to keep the truth about this incident a secret from everyone.

"Where did she go?" Ozzy asked.

"You sent her to get a warm blanket," I croaked as a shiver wracked through my body.

"Not Arabella. Quinnie. How long ago was she here?"

I shook my head. "I was alone."

"Cleo, don't lie. You know I hate that. Besides, you're a terrible liar. How long ago was Quinnie here?"

"I haven't seen her all day," I lied again.

Arabella rushed in with a blanket cutting off Ozzy's interrogation. "What happened to her?" Arabella inquired, helping Ozzy wrap me in the academy issued plaid blanket.

"She won't tell me," Ozzy explained, "But I think I have an idea."

"And?" Arabella nearly shouted.

Ozzy looked at me and I shook my head slightly. Arabella was too engrossed with Ozzy and what he apparently knew to notice. "Let's just get her to the infirmary first."

"Right," Arabella said, standing quickly and heading for the door to hold it open. Ozzy stood, cradling me as I continued to tremble and drip water everywhere.

"You have to go to Sterling's meet," I argued weakly. "He'll be upset if you miss it."

"He'll understand," Arabella answered.

"I'll be okay," I said, trying to keep my voice normal. "Put me down," I said to Ozzy, "I can walk."

He looked at me in disbelief, but set me down on my feet anyway, keeping a hand on my hip and one on my shoulder. "I still think you should go to the infirmary," Ozzy said. "Your back and head are bleeding. They need to be cleaned and bandaged." I was thankful he didn't mention the burn marks on my hand and foot.

"Sure," I agreed. When Arabella looked like she was going to offer to come with me anyway, I said, "Go watch Sterling and then you can come check on me afterward. I'll be fine. Really. Ozzy will make sure I get to the infirmary. Just tell Sterling I'm really sorry I'm missing it."

Arabella appeared torn, wanting to support both of us and knowing she had to make a choice. I also knew that Arabella wasn't keen on leaving me alone with Ozzy.

"It's just a few cuts, I'm sure Ms. Petticoat will have me patched up in no time. Maybe I'll even make it to the meet," I suggested helpfully, forcing my voice to sound strong.

Arabella was nearly bouncing on her feet trying to decide what to do. When she looked at me again, I did my best to look as if I had mostly recovered already, and it was decided. "You're going to keep an eye on her," Arabella said to Ozzy. It wasn't a question.

"Of course. I'll stay with her in the infirmary until you come, I promise."

Arabella sighed. "All right, I better hurry so I don't miss any of the meet." She glanced between us, her gaze finally settling on me. "You're sure you're okay?"

I nodded. "Hurry up and go," I urged.

"Okay," Arabella said, rushing to the door. She turned around and tossed me an air kiss. "See you later, Hot Stuff."

After Arabella left, I took a shaky step forward and almost fell.

Ozzy easily caught me. "You can't walk, can you?" he asked, somewhat amused.

"It would appear not. I'm not even sure I could crawl at this point," I whispered as another series of twitches and tremors rocked my body.

I attempted to sit down on the floor, but Ozzy gently scooped me up, careful not to rub the cuts on my back. "You're a good friend, you know that? Sending Arabella to the meet was the right thing to do."

"Are you just saying that because it gives you free reign to continue stalking me?" I asked, fighting the urge to smile.

Ozzy chuckled as he stepped out of the bathroom and began walking through the deserted halls. "She would've stayed with you since you were hurt, but it would've killed her to miss Sterling's meet."

"I know."

"Don't worry, I'll take care of you."

I didn't know how to answer that statement or even if I should. I wasn't exactly sure why he had such an intense interest in me, but I was fairly certain that it wasn't a healthy interest.

"Why did you guys come looking for me?"

"You didn't show up for breakfast so Arabella got worried and asked me to help her find you." He was breathing heavily with the effort of carrying me, but he didn't ask to stop and rest.

"She must have been desperate," I mused. "She can't stand you." Arabella made no secret about the fact that she wasn't a fan of Ozzy. She hated Ozzy perhaps only slightly less than she hated Quinnie.

"Well, Sterling had already left to get ready for the meet, so she couldn't ask him. Most everyone else had left for the meet as well.

I was her only option."

"So she was desperate. Sorry you got roped into this."

"I was already looking for you, too."

"Why?"

"My dear Clementine, I thought I made my interest in you pretty obvious," he chuckled. "I was worried when you never came down for breakfast. It's not like you to sacrifice a meal."

I didn't respond. It was true, I had a very loving relationship with food. However, I didn't want Ozzy being interested in me at all. He was cocky and patronizing and way too good with a gun. I didn't trust anyone that could handle a gun like that.

But I had to admit, the biggest reason I wanted nothing to do with Ozzy was the threat of Quinnie's wrath. No guy, especially one that was digging into my secrets, was worth getting my hand smashed for. He wasn't even worth being turned into a social pariah for. And he certainly wasn't worth getting electrocuted for. I hardly knew him, but so far his interest in me had caused me nothing but trouble.

Ozzy shifted my weight in his arms as he descended the stairs from the girl's dorm. I gasped as his arms rubbed against my cuts painfully.

"I'm sorry, I'm trying not to hurt you," he explained.

"I'm fine," I lied, sucking in my breath as each step jostled me around in his embrace.

He shifted my weight again, attempting to take some of the pressure away from my wounds and support me where I wasn't injured. I ended up leaning against his chest, my head nearly nestled into his neck. He smelled good — freshly showered and clean — like always. I reprimanded myself for knowing what he usually smelled like. That's the sort of thing couples knew about each other, but I closed my eyes and let the scent comfort me anyway.

I was suddenly tired. The violent shaking of my body and muscles after Quinnie's electrocution had exhausted me. All of the physical exertion of the last few weeks came crashing down on me and I surrendered to the fatigue and went totally limp in Ozzy's arms.

It wasn't long before Ozzy kicked open the door to the infirmary and laid me on one of the empty cots. "I'll go get Ms. Petticoat," he promised, making sure I was completely covered by the blanket before running off to find the nurse.

About an hour later, I was comfortably resting on one of the cots. Ms. Petticoat had cleaned and bandaged up my cuts and told me that I likely had a concussion from hitting my head against the wall. She gave me some pain relievers and an ice pack. Ms. Petticoat made Ozzy leave while she dressed me in some clean clothes. It was nothing but a white hospital gown, but it was still better than a blood soaked towel and dripping wet blanket. Ozzy was allowed to come back in to sit next to me once Ms. Petticoat finished.

"I don't understand," Ms. Petticoat started again. "How did you get those terrible burn marks on your hand and foot? It looks like you were electrocuted or something."

Ozzy looked up from the book he was reading.

"I don't know," I said. Again. "I don't remember. Maybe I was still holding my iPod or something when I stepped under the water? It's all a blank." I was horrible at lying and I was also aware that Ozzy was staring at me.

"Well, you need to be more careful, Clementine. Whatever caused it, you're very lucky it wasn't worse." Ms. Petticoat handed me the food that Ozzy had gone to get when he was forced from the room earlier. The kitchen had been closed for a while so I had no idea what strings he'd pulled to get me a hot breakfast. Whatever the case, I was grateful.

When Ms. Petticoat walked away, Ozzy asked, "An iPod? That's the worst explanation I've ever heard. I can't believe she bought it. And here I thought you were one of the best and brightest at the University."

"I never said I was one of the best and brightest," I said, taking a huge bite of omelet.

"You didn't have to, I read it in your file," Ozzy smiled. It was a handsome smile, but an annoying one.

I glared at him. "Don't think that just because you carried my bleeding body here and fetched some eggs and toast for me that I forgive you for looking at my personal info. I'm still pissed about that."

"As you should be. But I'm not going to apologize."

"You should."

Ozzy shrugged. "Maybe someday I will. But not today," he smiled. "Unless . . . "

"Unless what?" I asked uneasily. A price to pay for an apology? In that case, I could do without the apology.

"Go to the Autumn Formal with me."

I rolled my eyes. Again with the Autumn Formal nonsense. What was it with Ozzy and that stupid dance? "No."

"Is it because of Quinnie?"

"Well, I certainly have no intention of chasing after another girl's man."

"You're not chasing me, I'm chasing you," he said with a sly smirk.

"Whatever. Even without your girlfriend Quinnie being a factor, it's still a no."

"Why?"

Because, I thought, you smell and look so good that all I can think about sometimes is all the unmentionable things I want to do with you. I let my depraved thoughts burn out before I responded. "Because you spied on me and I don't trust you. And you play with guns. I hate guns."

"Give me a chance."

"Maybe someday I will," I echoed his words. "But not today."

I thought he would be angry, but he just smiled his cocky smile.

12

RESTRICTED SECTION

When Arabella arrived in the infirmary, she was breathless and her cheeks were flushed from the cool autumn air and bright sunshine. She settled into the chair next to my bed.

"How did he do?" I asked.

"Not too bad. His team lost, but he came in second in the overall race."

"So he's happy about that, right?" All I wanted to do was go to sleep, but I was dying to hear how Sterling had done.

"Sterling will never be happy with anything less than first place. He's the fastest person here at the Academy, he should easily win."

"Well, why didn't he? What happened?" I yawned.

"He ran the best race, but he got penalized. St. Ignatius track meets are sort of like decathlons on steroids. The teams have to run a five mile race. There are obstacles like hurdles, rope swings over mud pits, cargo nets . . . all sorts of stuff."

"So, like our morning runs. He's great at those. He always finishes first."

"Yes, but on the morning runs he doesn't have people from the other team throwing medicine balls at him or tackling him. Each team that competes in the meet has runners and gunners. The runners, like Sterling, compete in the race and obstacles. The gunners try to keep the runners from completing their tasks, and they're very good at what they do."

"How good?"

"Let's just say that Sterling is very lucky he's fast and dodges most of the attacks."

"Did he get hurt?"

"Nothing more than a few bumps and bruises. I think the worst pain is his pride. The target stations are always his downfall."

"You mean there's more than just running five miles, completing obstacles, and avoiding steroid-riddled muscle freaks?"

Arabella nodded. "There are ten stations throughout the race course. At each station, the runners have to stop and shoot at targets with various weapons. Javelin, shot put, long bow, cross bow, gun, throwing stars, knives — the works. The more accurate you are with your shot, the more time you get taken off your final race time. If you miss the target, you get time added."

"How good is Sterling's aim?"

"He had five minutes added to his finishing time." Arabella frowned.

I cringed. "He still got second, though."

"That's only because he's so fast. He would've gotten first if he hadn't missed any targets. You may be the only person in this school with worse aim than Sterling." Arabella shook her head.

"At least there's that comfort," I said as I shrugged. I really didn't care if I had the worst aim in the entire student body. To be quite honest, I didn't care if I never had to go to Weapons class again.

Arabella smirked. "Yeah, I'm sure he feels really manly that at least he's a better shot than the girl who faints whenever she touches a gun."

"Well, at least he's not worse than me. That would be tragic. For him, I mean."

The door to the infirmary opened and Sterling entered — laden with lunch, sporting a black eye, and managing a slight limp.

He held out one of the bags to me. "I heard you fell in the shower. I'm so sorry I wasn't there in person to find you half-naked and wet." He grinned.

"There is such a thing as secrets," I hissed to Arabella. "You could've at least told him I was dressed!"

"And what? Let him think you're mentally unstable and make a habit of showering with your clothes on? It's no big deal, this is Sterling we're talking about."

"Hey! I'm still a guy," he protested. "I do have a very vivid imagination," he continued, lifting his eyebrows and making a show of admiring me in my hospital gown. "So how long are you in for?" Sterling asked as he handed Arabella her lunch.

"Just overnight. Ms. Petticoat wants to keep an eye on my concussion. She said the burns should be better by then, too. Thank God for modern technology, I don't know if I could put up with this sensation for too long. It itches like crazy."

"Burns?" Arabella repeated in surprise. "What burns?"

I mentally kicked myself for slipping up. "I think I forgot to put down my iPod before I got in the shower. I electrocuted myself somehow," I explained, shaking my bandaged hand and foot.

"Your iPod? Electrocution?" Arabella repeated. "You're sticking with that absurd explanation?"

"That doesn't even make sense," Sterling accused me.

"I don't remember what happened, I'm just guessing. I hit my head pretty hard," I reminded them.

Arabella squinted her eyes and pursed her lips. "I hope you remember soon so we can help you with this problem. It's nice to let your friends help you out sometimes."

Sterling and Arabella obviously knew that I was keeping a secret, but if there was one thing I was sure of, it was that I wasn't going to get them mixed up in anything involving Quinnie.

"You can trust us," Sterling urged me. "Tell us what really happened."

"I do trust you, I just don't remember." I was getting tired of telling the same lie over and over again. It would be so easy to just tell everyone that Quinnie attacked me, but then it would only bring more of Quinnie's wrath. The hag witch was playing dangerous and dirty and I couldn't let Sterling and Arabella get caught in the line of fire. Quinnie always retaliated. She tried to break my hand for embarrassing her in the scrimmage and she electrocuted me for talking to Ozzy. What would she do to me and my friends if the truth got out? I wasn't willing to find out. The best course of action was to lay low, keep the truth a secret, and try to stay off of Quinnie's radar. I wasn't a coward, I just didn't want to risk the safety of my friends or cause any more trouble for myself.

"Whatever you say," Arabella quipped. "Too bad you'll miss our first match. I was looking forward to your rematch with Quinnie."

"I won't be missing the match. Ms. Petticoat said I could probably practice again as early as Tuesday or Wednesday. I have to wait a few days because I have a concussion. My burns might be totally healed on Monday, though. This medicine she put on me is amazing."

We spent the next half hour finishing lunch and recapping the track and field match. Although I winced at Arabella's graphic account of the opposing team's gunner attacks on Sterling and his teammates, I was sorry I missed seeing the meet. It sounded very exciting — like a modern day gladiator combat, without the fighting to the death part.

Soon, Arabella and Sterling had to leave to do homework and I was left alone in the empty infirmary. I took one look at the teetering pile of homework Arabella had lugged downstairs for me and decided that procrastinating and taking a nap were of the utmost importance.

Despite Ms. Petticoat's concern of a concussion, I gave in to the insistent need to sleep and barely had time to lay flat on my back before I was completely immersed in a disturbing dream. It was about Cassie, only it wasn't Cassie like I remembered her. Cassie was a sleek, black feline leaping from branch to branch as she climbed a tree next to a wall surrounding the University. When she was able to leap onto the edge of the wall, Cassie the cat looked behind her as if she suspected that she was being followed. Seeing she was alone, the cat then leapt to the ground, transformed back into Cassie the human, and took off running away from the wall and the University as fast as she could.

The wild images of the dream faded into dark, shifting shadows until the soft sound of paper brushing against paper brought me out of my shadowy thoughts and into consciousness. I was still too tired to open my eyes so I lay still under the covers, keeping my breathing smooth and slow as I listened to the rustle of the paper and the random scratching sound of a pen. Had Arabella come back to do her homework at my bedside to keep me company?

Soon I heard footsteps approach.

"She hasn't woken up yet?" It was Ms. Petticoat.

"Not yet, Ma'am." It was Ozzy's voice. What was Ozzy doing here?

"I thought for sure she'd wake up for dinner. And I need to give her another dose of painkillers. It probably wouldn't hurt to clean those burns and put another coat of medicine on."

I wasn't looking forward to having my burns scrubbed again. It hurt like hell the first time, not to mention the enormous needle Ms. Petticoat had plunged into my arm afterward. It must have contained some seriously strong antibiotics because the area around my tattoo still throbbed in pain. I continued to lay still and keep my breathing even and slow to feign sleep to put off Ms. Petticoat's ministrations as long as possible. Hopefully the pleasant nurse would feel too guilty about waking me up to cause me pain.

"You can go to dinner, Ma'am. I'll stay here with her, and if she wakes up I'll make sure she takes the medicine."

Ms. Petticoat seemed to welcome Ozzy's offer. "Well thank you, Osbourne. Her pills are right there on the side table. Just remind her to take them as soon as she wakes. I can always change the bandages on her burns when I get back. Would you like me to bring you anything?"

"I'm fine, Ma'am."

The footsteps receded, followed by the whoosh of the infirmary door as Ms. Petticoat headed to dinner.

"You can open your eyes now. She's gone."

"How did you know I was awake?" I asked, finally opening my eyes and cautiously sitting up. Ozzy was in the chair right next to the bed with an open book in his lap, a notebook resting on the edge of the mattress, and a pen in his hand.

"You're not only a terrible liar, you're downright pathetic at faking."

"Not true. I pretend to like you and look how convincing I am."

Ozzy, never one to be offended, smiled. "You're not faking. You like me, you just won't admit it to yourself."

"I forgot — the amazing Ozzy with perfect aim. Let me bow down and kiss your ass like everyone else around here does."

"I can think of better places for you to kiss me."

I refused to blush. "Don't you have anywhere better to be?"

"Probably," he retorted.

"Then why are you here?" I asked in exasperation. "Isn't it enough that I have a raging concussion headache? I don't really have the energy to banter with your ego, too."

"I'm here to make sure you're okay."

"Why do you even care?"

"Good question." He set his pen down and leaned forward, resting his forearms on the edge of my bed, invading my personal space.

"Well, why do you?" I repeated, accidentally focusing on Ozzy's full, very kissable lips. They were hovering ever so close to me and were lifted into a wicked grin. He seemed to be magnetically drawn to me as the space between us was slowly eroding. I reached up to tuck the insistently unruly lock of hair behind my ear as I leaned back into the pillows, trying to get my personal space back.

"I have a vested interest in your safety," Ozzy said, leaning in even closer and speaking in low tones, his breath tracing air kisses along my neck. He hadn't touched me, but my skin was screaming with pleasure as if he had. "I'm also very interested in your special skills." He was whispering now, his lips mere inches away from my neck.

I didn't know why I had the sudden urge to kiss him, but I knew all I had to do was turn my head and our lips would meet. I suspected the ridiculous urge probably had something to do with hitting my head — my judgment was all muddled. Don't go there, I reminded myself, Ozzy is dangerous.

"What special skills?" I whispered back, turning my head slightly, but not fully committing to a kiss. The chunk of hair came loose again and Ozzy reached up to tuck it behind my ear this time. I trembled as his fingers grazed my skin, but it was a pleasant tremble, not like the painful shudders from Quinnie's attack. Ozzy's hand continued to slide behind my ear and down my neck.

"I'm going to kiss you," he warned me.

"Don't . . . " I answered weakly as his fingers rested on the back of my neck and his thumb softly traced my cheek.

"Don't what?"

"Don't . . . stop." What was I saying? Was I telling him to stop or not to stop? I wasn't sure that my mind and heart were listening to one another.

Whatever the meaning of my mutterings, Ozzy took it as an invitation. He brushed his lips against mine and I closed my eyes, letting his mouth leave soft, smoldering, caresses on my lips. The light brushing of skin on skin mingling with hot breath was intoxicating and made me feel lightheaded. I tried to tell myself it was just the concussion and not a genuine reaction to the infuriating boy I couldn't seem to say no to. At least not successfully.

Ozzy's mouth took its time exploring me, trailing down my neck, across my jaw, and then back where it had started. When I reached up to thread my hand into his hair, I briefly felt him smile against my lips. This was nothing like any kiss I'd had before. This was perfect. His hands moved down over my shoulders, his arms wrapping around my back to pull me close. My breathing stuttered and became desperate as he continued to kiss me . . . gently . . . passionately . . . skillfully.

A little too skillfully.

How many other girls had he kissed just like this? Probably lots. Probably Quinnie.

And that killed the mood. I turned my head away and pushed on his chest to create some distance.

"What's wrong?" he murmured.

"I've had enough." Lie.

"Are you sure?" Ozzy asked, trying to catch my mouth with his again.

"Totally sure." Another lie. And another push to create more distance between us.

"Maybe I could convince you otherwise," Ozzy suggested, leaning forward, brushing his lips against mine, his breath leaving a trail of warm promises along my mouth.

I straightened my arm to keep him a safe distance away. Safe enough that I wouldn't be tempted. "Not necessary," I struggled to keep my willpower strong and the tremor out of my voice. "You weren't that great the first time around." The lie of my lifetime.

Ozzy backed away from me, the surprise on his face was quickly replaced by intrigued curiosity. I expected to see annoyance, not a smile. But there it was, a cocky smile. It seemed impossible to offend him.

"Well, I'll take that as a challenge," he announced.

"Don't. Take it at face value. I'm not interested." My heart was screaming. Don't listen to me, kiss me again. Now.

"Does this have anything to do with Quinnie?"

"It has nothing to do with Quinnie." Oh how the lies were piling up one on top of the other. "But now that you mention it, I certainly don't need any trouble from her. She's made it perfectly clear that you're her property."

"How so?"

She told me right before she electrocuted me. I couldn't admit that. The last thing I needed was a full on war with Quinnie. "You hang out with her at lunch, carry her trays . . . " I realized that my argument sounded more like jealousy.

"You eat with Sterling every meal and he brought you lunch today. Should I assume that you're an item as well?" Ozzy's egotistical grin was infuriating, especially when he was dominating the argument so easily.

"Of course not. It's just . . . everyone says you're together."

"And who's everyone? I hadn't noticed that you were such the social butterfly to hear that piece of gossip from everyone."

I glared at him.

"Ah. So Arabella said that we're a couple. Am I right?"

I didn't answer, but I looked away and began picking at the edge of the bed sheet, which was basically an agreement to his assumption.

"So if you're going to believe rumors about me, rather than what I tell you, then should I believe the rumors that you got sent here because you caused an explosion in your old dorm room at the University?"

My head snapped up to meet his gaze. I'd been caught off guard and was unable to hold back my surprise at his knowledge. I hadn't even told Arabella or Sterling about my exploding dorm room. "Who told you that?" I demanded.

"So, it's true?" He smiled.

"I didn't say that."

"You didn't have to. I read your updated file."

I crossed my arms. "I want you to leave. Now. I also want you to stay out of my file."

"Why don't you want to talk about this?"

"I already feel violated enough. It's creepy that you know all of my secrets."

"Would it make you feel better if you knew mine?"

Yes. I paused before speaking. "No."

Ozzy bent down and pulled a folder out of his backpack. It had a red sticker slapped diagonally across the front that said "Restricted Section." On the top right tab of the folder, the name "Osbourne Dracone" was typed neatly. Underneath of that it said "Deviant Dozen – Archerfish." He tossed the folder onto the blanket that was stretched across my lap.

"I'll leave this here overnight, in case you want to read it. I'll be back for it tomorrow morning. All I ask is that you don't let anyone else see it." Ozzy grabbed his backpack, stuffed his book and papers in it, and then slung it over his shoulder. "I hope you feel better soon," he called over his shoulder. When he got to the door, he stopped and turned. "Oh, and take the medicine on the side table. I told Ms. Petticoat I'd make sure you took it."

And then he was gone.

I stared at the folder like it was the apple from the Tree of Knowledge. In a way, it was. I knew once I opened it up and read it, there would be no way to put back the secrets I took out. Was it worth knowing? It would certainly even the score between me and Ozzy. That is, if he left everything in there. Who's to say he didn't take out things and leave only what he wanted me to know?

I put my hand on the cover; an internal war waged over whether I should take the small step to open the folder which would actually be a giant leap into someone else's privacy.

I was spared the difficult task of making a decision when the door opened up and Ms. Petticoat shuffled in, pushing a cart of food. The nurse was concentrating on getting the cart through the door without spilling anything so she didn't notice that I was awake, or that I was holding materials from the Restricted Section of the library. Before Ms. Petticoat looked up, I slipped the folder under my pillow and grabbed the pills off the table and popped them in my mouth.

"Ah, you're awake, Clementine. Excellent. I've brought you your dinner, and when you're done eating, I'll clean your burns. I think you'll be able to walk without a problem by morning."

Although I was starving, I forced myself to drag out my dinner so I could put off the painful promise of burn cleansing and redressing. Soon enough, however, Ms. Petticoat was back, eager to get her work done so that she could head off to bed. After an hour of having my raw skin diligently swabbed, purified, and rewrapped with medicine — I was mentally spent and happy to see Ms.

Petticoat walk out the door. I reached for the top book on my stack of homework and attempted to ignore the thick, restricted section folder hiding innocently under my pillow. I pulled it out a few times, but never quite mustered the courage to open it.

After pulling the folder out from under my pillow about a dozen times to stare at it, I realized my homework would never get done if it had to compete with the thrill of the unknown. I threw back the covers, swung my legs over the edge of the bed, and then hobbled to the nearest cot. I stuffed the folder under the mattress and then hopped back to my bed and scrambled under the covers before I could change my mind.

The next morning, I woke after a fitful night of bad dreams that churned with disturbing images of Cassie, cats, and restricted section folders exploding and catching fire. I opened my eyes to see that the sunlight streaming through the windows was strong and bright. It was at least ten in the morning. I smiled. It was nice not to have to do the morning run, even if it was because I was still recuperating from cuts and burns.

I soon realized that the infirmary was filled with the smell of freshly baked goods, cinnamon, and something chocolaty. I rolled over to find Ozzy in the same chair he had been in the night before.

"Arabella was here earlier after her morning run, but she left to do homework since you were sleeping."

"Don't you have homework?"

Ozzy held up the book that was in his lap. "Working on it." He picked up a tray on the table next to my bed and set it on my lap. "Hot chocolate and cinnamon cake. Hope that's okay."

I nodded. I wished he'd stop being so nice to me. It was hard to dislike him for spying on me when he was so irresistibly kissable, and freshly showered, and sweet, and ... I shook my head. He read my file — my secrets. And he's friends with Quinnie, most likely more than friends. I needed to stay away from this one.

"Did you read it?" Ozzy asked as I took a forkful of the crumbly cake and popped it into my mouth.

I shook my head. Ozzy reached over and lifted my chin so I was looking at him. He studied my eyes intently.

"You didn't," he agreed. He seemed disappointed and sighed. "Where is it?"

I pointed to the cot behind him and muttered, "Under the mattress."

Ozzy went to retrieve his folder and stood there staring at it despondently. "You didn't want to be tempted so you put it out of easy reach. Smart. I thought for sure you'd read it. At least, I hoped you would."

I shrugged. "It's not necessary to know everyone's deepest, darkest secrets. They're called secrets for a reason and everyone has a right to privacy."

"We're Sophisticates, Cleo. That means we have no rights and we certainly don't have any privacy. At least not from the Program."

"Aren't you mad?"

"Of course I am. I left this so you'd read it," he growled, shaking the folder.

"No. I mean, doesn't it make you mad that the Program knows every little detail about you?"

Ozzy shrugged. "It doesn't matter — it's too late for me. You still have a chance, which is exactly why I wanted you to read this."

I pursed my lips. I supposed being a favorite of the Program and having a sponsor probably made Ozzy's life fairly glorious. He didn't go around accidentally destroying things with fire or getting his Internet privileges taken away for trespassing. And he certainly didn't even have to worry about the whole cramp issue. He was the Golden Boy of St. Ignatius. What did he care if his life was an open book?

"I guess it's not a big deal to you because you have nothing to hide."

"That's not entirely true. The Program might know every little detail about me, but the rest of the world doesn't. I have secrets, I just want you to know what they are. I want you to read my file."

"I can't right now," I stammered, confused by his willingness to share his personal information with me.

"You have to. You have no idea what's in your future, Cleo. You, Arabella, Sterling, and all the rest of them. Even your little friend Cassie. Every last one of you are in more trouble than you can imagine. It's exhausting trying to keep you all off the radar," he said, raking his hand through his messy curls.

I perked up at the mention of Cassie's name. I hadn't told anyone about Cassie, not even Arabella and Sterling. I'd kept everything about the University and my past a secret. "What about Cassie?" I asked excitedly. "Is she okay?"

"She's fine. I'm sure you'll be seeing her soon enough, unfortunately."

My heart started to race. See Cassie again?

"Unfortunately? If Cassie came here it would make this place tolerable. She's like a sister to me," I said. "You mean there is actually a chance she could come here with me?"

Ozzy frowned slightly. "She's the last one to exhibit, but it's only a matter of time," he explained in a tone of resignation.

"What do you mean, exhibit?"

"Cassie is the last of the Dozen to exhibit her deviation. Cleo, haven't you ever wondered why you can do certain things?"

Dozen? Exhibit? Deviation? What was he talking about?

"I know why. I was genetically altered, just like every other Sophisticate."

"Yes, but you're more than a normal Sophisticate. You have to know that by now. Every single one of us in the Deviant Dozen is more than the normal Sophisticate. Quinnie causes electric shocks. I have perfect aim. And you, you can make things explode. The Program made you that way. They did this to us." Ozzy's face contorted with barely contained rage as he shook the folder again. "They didn't just change our genetic code, they added to it. We're aberrations of nature, Cleo. We're military experiments — experiments that they intend to make into human weapons."

I shook my head. I had no idea what he was talking about, but whatever it was, it wasn't true. I wasn't a weapon. I was a girl who could speak a lot of languages and hack computers. That's all. Definitely not a weapon. I fainted at the sight of guns, how could I possibly be a weapon of any kind?

But no matter how much I tried to convince myself that I was nothing more than the average Sophisticate, memories of an exploding dorm room, a busted pen, and shattered lights chipped away at my weak denials. I had no explanation for the things that happened — the things I knew I caused.

"I've tried to talk to everyone." Ozzy continued, pinching the bridge of his nose. "To discourage them from using their," he paused as if searching for the right word. " . . . powers. If they failed to deviate or didn't try to use them, I thought maybe the Program would spare them. Maybe the Program would think the experiment had failed and they ... you ... would be left alone. I tried to convince every one of them, but no one listened. Well, Sterling sort of listened, but then he freaked and tried to run away." Ozzy shook his head as if remembering something particularly awful. "I finally thought with you, I had a chance. I thought maybe I could save you." He looked up and his eyes were sad, as if he had failed me in some way.

Nothing he was saying was making any sense. He was rambling on like I knew what he was talking about. Powers and deviating? Maybe this was all part of some weird concussion hallucination.

"You're wrong," I said. "We may be extra smart or a little stronger than the normal person, but we're not weapons. You make it sound like we're superheroes or something."

"No. Being a superhero would require acts of bravery and saving the world. What you'll do — what I do — we're nothing more than ... "

"Than what?"

Ozzy sat down and leaned back in the chair, running his hand through his tousled hair again. He was muttering to himself and I couldn't quite make out what he was saying. His lack of usual cocky ego had me edgy and confused. More than anything else, that was what was making me nervous.

"I don't think what you're talking about is even possible," I ventured.

"It is. Trust me. You, of all people, should believe me. You nearly died at the hands of Quinnie just yesterday, didn't you?"

I didn't answer. I was too busy biting the inside of my lip and remembering what Quinnie had put me through.

"Don't worry," he said sternly. "You don't have to rat her out, your condition yesterday was proof enough. She's been severely punished by Overton. The Program doesn't mind when Mandates beat up on each other from time to time — they consider it good training. However, they're not ready to lose an investment. A few broken bones here, a sprain or bloody nose there, no harm done. But when a cadet almost kills another cadet — well, they just can't let that happen. Think of all the time and money they've invested in each of us. They can't let that go to waste, can they?" he said bitterly. "Especially not with one of the Dozen."

I ignored his comment about the Dozen. He was trying to lure me into asking about it. "What did they do to her?"

"Corporal punishment. It may not cure her hate for you, and it probably won't stop her from harassing you, but she'll definitely think twice before attacking you again." Ozzy stood and seemed to regain some of his swagger. "I've got to go," he said, looking at the folder in his hand. "Why don't you hold onto this for me until I get back? I trust you with my secrets." He tossed the folder onto my lap like he had the night before, only this time, some of the pages started to slide out of the confines of the mysterious yellow binder.

"Where are you going?"

"The answer is in there. Last page," he said nodding toward the bundle in my lap.

"You're trying to seduce me into reading something I don't want to."

Ozzy's cocky smile was finally back. "True. I definitely want you to read it. And even closer to the truth, I do intend to seduce you. But that will have to wait until I get back," he promised.

I tried to play it cool and act like his flirtations had absolutely no effect on me. In reality, it was exactly the opposite. My heart was racing and my pride was raging a battle to keep my embarrassed blush at bay.

"Why are you so interested in me?" I asked. "Is it because I won't give you what you want? Are you just interested in the chase of the elusive new girl?"

"I'm interested in you because I feel like I know you better than anyone else I've ever known."

"You've only known me for a few weeks. Actually, barely two weeks," I said counting on my fingers. "Fourteen days is hardly enough to warrant this level of obsession," I teased.

"The Program brought me here when I first exhibited at the age of ten. I've been watching you and the rest of the Deviant Dozen grow up from afar, knowing what you were expected to be able to do."

"Watching us?"

Ozzy shrugged. "Video surveillance . . . reports . . . I've even been sent to observe in person from time to time."

I cringed at the thought of being spied on, not only by Ozzy, but the entire Program. I always knew the Program watched and monitored us, I just didn't realize it was so invasive. I felt like a bug under a huge microscope — a butterfly pinned under a sheet of glass.

Ozzy continued as if spying was a completely normal and acceptable thing for him to do. "They've been training me to be the leader of this little experiment of theirs," he said as he approached me. "I know everything about you, Cleo. I know you'd do anything for your best friend Cassie. I know you desperately want to know who your parents are and have spent countless hours hacking into the Program's system. I know that by the books, you're fluent in four languages but in reality you know seven. I know your favorite color is red, but you never wear it. I know you used to make a wish every time you passed the terrapin on McKeldin Mall at the University. I know your favorite book is Jane Eyre and that your dog-eared copy was lost in the explosion. Cleo, you've only known me for the last two weeks, but I've been getting to know you for the last seven years." Ozzy moved closer and leaned on the edge of my bed. "And I've been wanting to kiss you for at least the last two years."

A thousand butterflies were battling in my chest as I listened to his confession. I still knew very little about Ozzy, but I knew that even after just two weeks, I was finding it impossible not to be attracted to him. And after a declaration like that, I wanted him to kiss me. Fiercely.

He moved toward me cautiously and when I didn't stop him or push him away, he gently put his hand behind my head and met my mouth with his. His soft, warm kiss — coupled with his intense admission — was exhilarating but way too short in my opinion. He pulled away and then kissed me one more time, soft and light like a lover's sigh.

"And it's even better than I imagined." He stood and deliberately backed away from the bed, keeping his gaze locked on me. When he reached the door, he grabbed the handle reluctantly. "I'll be gone for a week or two, but don't worry, I'll be seeing you in my dreams."

"You did not just say that, did you? That has got to be the worst pick up line ever."

Ozzy smiled. "See you later, Desert Flower." Then he turned and left the infirmary.

I felt a warm blush creep up over my cheeks. Corny or not, there was a certain thrill in believing that Ozzy would be dreaming about me. I reached up to touch my lips, which were still tingling. Why did I keep letting this dangerous boy kiss me?

I happened to look down at my lap and there in front of me was the mysterious folder with Ozzy's secrets peeking out of their hiding place. One piece of paper was hanging out farther than any other. It had a picture of a man in a turban and long beard. Above it in red were stamped the words, "Target: Rasool ur Ra'ahmah (Al-Qaeda)." Underneath the picture it said, "Mission: Execute target. Retain corpse for identification and authentication."

I shivered and delicately pulled the page out a little further so I could read more of it. It was dated and time stamped for earlier in the morning. Was this the reason that Ozzy was going to be gone for a week or two? Was he actually on a mission to assassinate someone? I hastily shoved the paper back in the folder, even more frightened than ever to read the rest of Ozzy's secrets.

Was he really an assassin?

He was only 17.

Apparently, age didn't matter when someone had perfect aim.

13

DERBY DAME NAMES

I was released from the infirmary Sunday evening and after a humiliating ride in a wheelchair from Ms. Petticoat's domain to the dorms, I was delighted to discover Monday morning that my burns were completely healed and I was able to walk. The good news was that I didn't need to show up to class in a wheelchair which was a relief since I knew that being wheelchair-bound would give Quinnie an overabundance of joy. The bad news was that I was healed enough to walk which meant I had to show up to the morning run along with the rest of the cadets.

"So, you're all healed? Burns gone?" Arabella asked, amazed.

"All healed. The one good thing about going to a military academy is that they have some serious, high-tech medicine here. I wonder how fast they can heal a broken bone?"

"Let's not test that theory, okay? I'm not lugging your homework to and from the infirmary again. There are limits to our friendship."

I was pretty sure Arabella was joking.

As we walked down the slippery grass toward the starting line, I noticed that my presence was garnering quite a few stares. Arabella promised me that what happened had been kept very hush-hush, but it seemed that it didn't escape the notice of the rest of the cadets that I missed the track meet. Nobody was allowed to miss the sporting events. I figured it was pretty much a given that everyone even knew I had been in the infirmary.

Quinnie sauntered up behind us and I noticed she was receiving her fair share of stares as well.

I looked over my shoulder apprehensively, and shifted out of the way, eager to keep her in sight. Quinnie was walking rather stiffly. In fact, she looked like she was in more pain than I was. She slowed her pace so that she and her sidekicks, Eva and Sadie, came up alongside us.

"Where were you this weekend, Cleo? I heard you missed the track and field meet on Saturday," Quinnie droned in her sickeningly sweet voice. "What happened?" she asked innocently, daring me to accuse her in front of all the other cadets.

Before I could come up with a clever, biting remark, Arabella jumped in. "Don't act like you saw much of the match either, Quinby," she sneered. I was sure if Quinnie could change one thing, it would be her first name. She visibly cringed whenever anyone used it.

Quinnie shot Arabella a look of pure hatred.

"Oh yes, darling," Arabella drawled in a fake, southern accent. "I know you were busy during the match taking your whippings, so you couldn't possibly have known from personal experience that Cleo missed it."

Quinnie instinctively reached for her back. "You don't know anything," she hissed, stomping off. Her two sidekicks followed, struggling to keep up in the wake of her seething shame.

"I know a whole lot of things," Arabella said airily. "For instance, I know she took at least ten whippings. Ten is standard. I also know that she won't be wearing a backless dress this year to the Autumn Formal." She clucked her tongue mockingly. "What a shame."

"What do you mean?"

"When you're accidentally injured here at the Academy, they patch you up in the infirmary, as you well know. However, when you're injured due to punishment, you get to heal on your own. Trust me, she's in much worse shape now than you are. Or, at least her back is." Arabella smiled wistfully. "She'll actually be forced to wear something rated PG this year."

"They actually whipped her, like medieval style?"

"What? Don't you think she deserved it?"

I was surprised at Arabella's easy acceptance of beatings as punishment. "What did they punish her for? I didn't accuse her of anything."

"You didn't have to, Ozzy did."

"But I thought he and Quinnie were friends. You know . . . a thing."

Arabella tilted her head toward me. "They are — which just goes to show you that what I said before is true: you can't trust Ozzy. He will rat out a friend as easily as an enemy."

"But I told Ms. Petticoat it was an accident. Why did they believe his word over mine?"

Arabella smirked. "Please. Ozzy can do no wrong; his word is golden around here. I tried to warn you about that. You may not admit that Quinnie was involved, but I know she was. Younglove determined it wasn't an accident and Quinnie's the only person that didn't have an alibi for when you were hurt. I'm just glad she was punished. This wasn't her first rodeo; it's just the first time she's taken it too far. Trust me, she earned what she got."

I didn't like Quinnie and I definitely thought she needed to be punished, but I wasn't sure I felt like Quinnie deserved to have the skin flayed off her back. It was barbaric.

Still lost in my thoughts, I barely heard when Dean Overton blew the whistle to start the morning run. Sterling, who was far ahead at the front of the line, turned to wave to us and mouthed, "I'll see you at breakfast."

I turned to Arabella. "I'm probably going to be a little slower than usual today. You can go ahead. I'll catch up with you at breakfast."

"No way," Arabella shook her head emphatically and her hair, which was fashioned into various shades of purple spikes, whipped around dangerously. She reminded me of an agitated porcupine. "I'm not leaving you alone again. At least not until you learn how to defend yourself."

"Defend myself? You're being a bit dramatic, aren't you?"

Arabella looped her hand around my arm and pulled me toward the obstacle course. "I'm sticking with you. I promised."

"Promised who?"

"Doesn't matter. Let's get going and see if we can get you through this thing in under an hour."

At breakfast, all the talk was about the upcoming roller derby match. Despite the faculty's effort to keep the shower incident a secret, the student body knew that something awful had happened and they knew it involved me and Quinnie. They just didn't know the details. It was a ripe, piece of juicy gossip right out of their reach and everyone was hungry for a bite, no matter how small. From what I overheard, people couldn't wait to see us face off at the match in two weeks.

Theo sat down between Sterling and Arabella and leaned across the table to whisper to me. "I heard you and Quinnie got into a cat fight. We know Quinnie got punished for something and you were in the infirmary. What did she do to you?"

"It's none of your damn business what happened, Donkeyboy, so get lost." Arabella threw a biscuit at him and it bounced off his forehead. "Well. Would you look at that! I guess Ozzy isn't the only one with perfect aim," she quipped cheerfully.

Theo kicked his chair back and left the table in a huff, flicking biscuit crumbs off his face. When he got back to his own table, I could see there was plenty of urgent whispering from his friends asking him what he found out. When he responded, at least a dozen heads turned to glare at me. I wondered how long the truth about what happened between me and Quinnie would remain a secret.

I hadn't even told Arabella and Sterling what actually happened, but I was pretty sure they had already put two and two together and figured it out themselves. They obviously knew Quinnie was involved and I had a feeling they also likely knew what Quinnie could do. I had burn marks and had still been twitching when Arabella and Ozzy found me. My friends weren't idiots. They knew. And if they didn't, they deserved to because they worried about me. I owed them the truth, even if there was a risk that they might not believe it. They also deserved to know that by being friends with me, they were at risk too. My conversation with Ozzy only confirmed all the things I'd been worrying about.

"You guys were right," I whispered, just enough that Sterling and Arabella could hear, but no one else. "Quinnie attacked me in the shower."

Sterling looked up from his breakfast, his fork poised halfway to his mouth. The eggs were falling off the edge and back onto the plate but he ignored them. "We figured that much out. Did she say why?"

"She told me she knew I caused the lights on the derby track to explode on her."

"Did you?" Sterling asked.

I shrugged. "Yes. Maybe. I don't know. Probably." I threw my hands up in surrender. "Anyway, she threatened me and told me to stay away from Ozzy. And then . . . she electrocuted me. I was standing on the drain with my hand on the shower nozzle and somehow she made the metal shock me. And since the water was running, it was a thousand times worse."

"Oh my God," Arabella breathed disbelievingly. "I always suspected she could do something like that, but I wasn't sure. I mean, static electricity is always a major bitch when Quinnie's around, but she's never done anything worse than that. She actually electrocuted you, like with her hands?"

I nodded. "I know, it doesn't make any sense. It's not logical, but that's what happened. Ozzy said —"

"Hold on. Ozzy said?" Arabella hissed. "When did you talk to Ozzy about this?"

"Did he give you that absurd spiel about deviating and exhibiting?" Sterling grumbled.

Arabella looked down at her plate and I had a feeling she was hiding something.

"Well, it kind of makes sense . . . " I started.

"I stand by what I said before. Stay away from that boy. He is nothing but bad news," Arabella said without looking up. She stabbed at her waffle a little more forcefully than was necessary. "Trust me, you don't want anything to do with him."

"Yeah, sure," I agreed. I knew Arabella was right. Ozzy didn't seem to be bringing me anything but pain and trouble. His interest in me was the main reason Quinnie went berserk in the first place. Now that I wasn't alone with him or at the mercy of his kisses, I could see the truth in Arabella's warnings.

"Look, we believe you," Sterling promised. "We just don't believe him. He's crazy and he'll only get you into more trouble than you can handle."

"All right," I agreed again as I looked over at Quinnie's table where Ozzy usually sat. He was unmistakably absent — the table consisting of just a battered looking Quinnie and her two very subdued allies, Eva and Sadie.

Ozzy's absence was like a missing piece of a puzzle. Something seemed very off. I was uncomfortably reminded of the yellow folder hidden under my mattress — a yellow folder that offered an unlikely and disturbing truth for his absence at breakfast this morning. After seeing the paper with Rasool ur Ra'ahmah's name and photo on it in the infirmary, I was too intimidated to read any more of the secrets contained inside. I hid the entire package, restricted section stamp and all, among my textbooks so Ms. Petticoat wouldn't find it. Then, I smuggled it back to my room and stashed it away under the mattress.

"We just want to help you; we know what it's like here. Everyone will try to use you, especially Ozzy. He is the antithesis of trustworthy." Sterling was earnest and I had no reason to believe he was being untruthful with me. At the same time, there was a small part of me that believed Ozzy. Something was definitely going on. Sterling and Arabella didn't blink an eye at my explanation that Quinnie electrocuted me. However, according to Ozzy, Arabella and Sterling had both heard of the Deviant Dozen, or at least knew about deviating and exhibiting (whatever they were), and didn't put any stock in it. Why? Were they in denial or did they know something I didn't?

The bell rang to announce the end of breakfast and the beginning of the first class in 15 minutes.

"I guess I better get to Foreign Language," I said, breaking the silence.

"What are you studying again?" Arabella asked.

"Arabic, with Professor Alcott." Rasool ur Ra'ahmah's face flashed through my mind again. I wondered if he was alive or dead. I wondered if he was the reason I was studying Arabic. Well, not him specifically, but terrorists in general. Was I really meant to be part of some secret assassination team with Ozzy? Were my friends? The thought made me sick to my stomach.

I got up and grabbed my backpack off the floor, now a lot less excited about learning a new language than I had been a few weeks ago. It wasn't fun when I equated it with the possible purpose of my learning it only to help kill someone.

"See you at lunch." When I hoisted my backpack onto my shoulder, I felt the burden of Rasool ur Ra'ahmah resting on my shoulders as well.

Without Ozzy to distract me in Weapons and Conditioning, the morning dragged on. Quinnie was on her best behavior during the afternoon classes, but I was lost in disturbing thoughts of Ozzy, guns, and human targets. By the time I finally made it to derby practice, I was mentally exhausted and was looking forward to an hour of mind-numbing physical exertion. The first lap around the track proved that my foot was well enough to skate, even if it was still a little tender from the newly healed burn.

I noticed that my team, although practicing the regular moves with precision, seemed unusually cold and aloof toward me. Was Quinnie spreading rumors about me? Did they think I brought bad mojo to the team? I was distracted by the thought that maybe they didn't want me as part of the group anymore.

Younglove turned on the obstacles, determined to get us in fighting condition for the match. I fell a lot, but I still thought I was doing pretty well for only two weeks of training. The good news was that when I did fall, I usually took down several people with me. I only hoped that during the match, I'd be taking down members of the other team and not my own teammates.

I was playing jammer when I took a pretty nasty spill after getting clothes-lined by one of the mid-level obstacles. I fell flat on my back and my helmet cracked against the floor, rattling my teeth. The cuts on my head had healed, but I still felt a little dizzy. Younglove must have recognized my vertigo because she called me over to the sideline.

"Take a break, Clementine," Younglove said. "I need to talk to you anyway."

I sat on the bench closest to Younglove's chair.

"How are you adjusting to St. Ignatius?" Younglove inquired, her words nearly drowned out by the hum of the skates as the girls circled the track.

"I'm getting used to it." This was really the first time that I'd talked to my mentor since the first day, but I had no intention of giving Younglove any details of my life. I was pretty sure the Program's disregard of personal boundaries meant that Younglove knew the answers to the questions she was posing — asking them was merely a formality.

"How about your work detail?"

"It's long, but I like it."

"What about your fellow cadets?" Younglove lifted a cigarette to her lips as smoke curled up around her head.

I swallowed. "I've made a few friends."

"And enemies?"

I shrugged. "I'd like to think they just don't know me that well yet."

"The Academy won't always be there to step in. Sooner or later you're going to have to learn to protect yourself, Clementine."

"Protect myself?" I did my best to keep the tremor out of my voice, as if I could deny the truth simply by pretending Younglove was talking about something entirely different. "I don't know if you've talked to Professor Farnsworth, but if I had a weapon, I'd be more of a danger to myself than anyone else."

"I'm not talking about using weapons. You're deadly enough on your own. But you already knew that."

I swallowed, not trusting myself to speak. This was a little too close to Ozzy's human weapon speech.

"Quinby won't be shy about using her skills on you," Younglove continued, "so you need to be prepared to fight back if need be."

She tapped her jade cigarette on the end of the metal tray on the table, knocking bits of ash over it. "Be creative."

I realized that Younglove was encouraging me to do the exact opposite of what Ozzy had suggested. And quite honestly, I wasn't sure I could trust either of them. I had a hard time trusting anyone that knew so many of my secrets without my permission.

"I'll do my best," I answered simply as I got up to go to the locker room. I would do my best to play roller derby to my utmost abilities and I'd excel in class. I might even put forth some extra effort in Weapons and Conditioning, but I had no intention of blowing anything up, either accidentally or on purpose. There was no way to ensure I wouldn't hurt someone or even kill them. I couldn't risk it. Definitely no more explosions, big or small.

"What did Younglove want?" Arabella asked as she slammed her locker door shut.

"She wanted me to stand up to Quinnie."

Arabella grunted. "For once, that woman is talking some sense. What did she suggest?"

I bit my lip. I still hadn't truly admitted to Arabella that I could cause things to explode. But to be fair, if Ozzy was correct about the Deviant Dozen having special skills, Arabella hadn't admitted her skill either.

"She just told me to be creative." That was true.

"Vague much? That's pretty crappy advice."

"Hey, you know what I was thinking?" I asked, hoping to change the subject. "I was doing some roller derby research online last night, you know, to get some ideas for moves . . . "

"That's a great idea."

"Well I did discover some new moves, but I noticed that the players always have clever names for themselves. Wouldn't it be cool if we did that? Come up with cheeky names and personas for the match? Do you think Younglove would let us?"

Arabella's grin nearly tore her face in half. "That," she said, poking me in the shoulder, "is the best idea I've heard all day. Younglove won't care what we do as long as we win. I vote yes, and we should come up with a team name too."

"I was thinking *Damsels of Distress*," I offered. "And I thought you could design some uniforms for us."

Jane, who overheard the conversation, slammed her locker door and to my surprise, joined in. "I like it. They'll be expecting us to show up in our regular uniforms. It will totally throw them off." She called the rest of the team over and had me repeat my idea. There was a resounding "yes" to the idea and my teammates couldn't wait to get started on inventing their new derby names.

I was excited. For once, I had something to focus on other than the Program.

The rest of the week was quiet and boring. I noticed that aside from Arabella's daily change in hair color, there wasn't much to discern one day from another. And with Ozzy gone, there was no hope for his unexpected and cocky appearances — or his stolen kisses. I didn't realize how much I enjoyed his company until he had been gone for a few days. I'd been so intent on pushing him away and rejecting him that it hadn't occurred to me that I might be genuinely interested in him.

When did he say he was going to be back? The end of the week? Two weeks?

I wondered if he'd be back in time for the roller derby match, and then I realized I wasn't sure whether I wanted him to watch or not. I reminded myself that he'd seen me faint in Weapons class and found me electrocuted and almost naked in the shower, so there weren't too many other ways I could really embarrass myself. And if my recent practices were any indication of how the match might go, I could even manage to impress him, that is, if Quinnie didn't metaphorically wipe the track with my clumsy carcass.

But being attracted to Ozzy was something I couldn't succumb to. My friends said he was dangerous and I was reluctant to think otherwise, especially after seeing the Rasool ur Ra'ahmah paper that had fallen out of the Restricted Section folder. Whatever I felt for him, it was completely physical and totally ridiculous.

Wasn't it?

During breakfast on Friday morning, reality crashed through the Academy, disintegrating the fragile layer of distraction the Program had so carefully constructed. I was steadily making quick work of my omelet when the blare of an alarm began to bounce off the stone walls like shrieks in a prison cell. Everyone looked around nervously, covering their ears as the emergency lights along the wall began to flash ominously. Arabella pushed back her chair, grabbing her silverware like weapons, her eyes darting around for threats. My first thought was that it looked like Arabella was ready to take on a monster pot roast or zombie tater tots. But the sirens continued to wail and I noticed with sickening dread that some of the cadets were scrambling for cover, hiding under tables or rushing to the outer edges of the room.

The sirens continued, and the wailing echoes shattered the

composure of the cadets. I could almost taste the fear and uncertainty coiling around the room and its occupants. The alarms clamored on for many long minutes, but no one moved.

"What's going on?" I yelled to Arabella over the screams of the alarms, as I pressed my hands against my ears.

"I don't know, but I doubt that it's anything good," she hollered back. Arabella's last few words suddenly stretched across the room as the blare of the alarms cut off unexpectedly. The cadets were motionless and I couldn't help but wonder if it was out of terror or readiness. Seeing as how Arabella was the only one who had bothered to attempt to arm herself, I had the uneasy feeling it was the former.

The great doors of the dining hall groaned open allowing the paunchy form of Dean Overton to squeeze through, Younglove fluttering in his wake like a leaf caught in a storm. He stopped in the middle of the room and held up a paper in front of his pudgy, sweat-glistened face. Without so much as an explanation, he rattled off a series of names — girls and guys alike. The cadets stepped forward, peeling themselves from the shadows of the walls or disentangling themselves ungracefully from table and chair legs. The knot of cadets surrounding Overton and Younglove was agitated and anxious. Unease gathered around them, thick and restless.

When he was finished, Overton glanced over his shoulder at Younglove. "Everyone accounted for?" At her nod, he folded the paper, stuck it in his coat pocket, and headed for the doors as Younglove herded the chosen cadets behind him.

Before exiting, Younglove turned back, scanning the room of frozen cadets. "Finish your meal," she instructed. "You don't want to be late for class." And then she was gone.

By lunch time, the rumor mill was in full gear. Terrorist attack. Las Vegas, Nevada. One of the extravagant hotels had been blown to bits not much bigger than the grains of sand in the surrounding desert. Thousands dead, a city in panic.

"I heard they were all set to graduate at the end of the year anyway," Sterling explained, referring to the cadets that had followed Overton out of the cafeteria, and who hadn't been seen since. St. Ignatius was caught in a whirlwind of theories and assumptions. It was the first time since I'd arrived that I had the impression that reality was finally breaking through to my fellow cadets. Life wasn't just about testosterone-fueled sports and meaningless work detail. St. Ignatius wasn't a forever destination, it was merely a mildly satisfying pit stop on the way to our violent futures.

The professors and administrators must have noticed the change in attitude among the cadets because on Saturday morning, they introduced a new distraction: gambling. They were allowing the students to place bets on the upcoming roller derby match. Gamblers could place bets on which team would win, who would score the most points, who would take the most falls, and most disturbingly — who wouldn't make it through the match in one piece. A large board had been erected in the cafeteria with a burly Mandate to take the bets. The missing cadets and sirens were soon forgotten and work detail money was swiftly changing hands. I didn't bother to look at the board. I didn't want to know how many people were hoping I didn't survive.

The weekend came and went and there was no sign of Ozzy. On Monday, he still wasn't in our Weapons and Conditioning classes. He wasn't at Quinnie's table in the dining hall. No surprise visits in the library, no tapping on my window after midnight, not even an email. I found myself constantly looking for him and it was always the same. No Ozzy.

Friday night, I returned to my room after dinner, too nervous to even think about starting homework. The match was less than 24 hours away and I was a ball of nervous energy. I sat down at my computer and, once again, attempted to email Cassie. Like before, I had no success. Cassie's email address was blocked and no amount of hacking had been able to remedy that problem. It killed me to think that I'd never see my friend again, or talk to her. I was a Mandate now and Cassie would specialize and become a Vanguard. We were destined for different futures.

Unless.

I swiveled around in my chair and stared at the bed.

Underneath the mattress was hope.

A hope that I might, in one variation of my future, get to see Cassie again.

If Ozzy was right.

If Cassie was part of what he called the Deviant Dozen.

I walked over to the bed and lifted the edge of the mattress. The yellow folder was still there, just where I'd left it. I pulled it out and sat on the bed, cross legged. I turned out the overhead light so that the Hounds would believe I'd gone to sleep. Then I turned on the small reading light on my desk and angled it toward the bed.

Oddly, the first page in the folder was labeled "Archerfish" and had a complete description of the fish and its unique abilities.

"The Archerfish uses a specially shaped lower jaw to shoot an arrow of water up to nine feet long to knock insects or small animals into the water. They are such skilled marksmen that they can routinely shoot and kill an insect six feet above the water while compensating for light refraction. If need be, an archerfish can shoot up to seven 'arrows' in quick succession."

Underneath the description of the archerfish was a detailed explanation of how the Program intended to genetically alter a Sophisticate to create a human archerfish — a human weapon with perfect aim.

The next few pages outlined the gruesome facts of how the Program initially experimented on a group of young children around ten years old, hoping to turn them into superior sharp-shooters. The experiment had massively unfortunate results.

"The genetic alteration of adolescents is a failure. The test subjects are deteriorating quickly. Their over-sensitivity to touch and their exceedingly powerful eyesight is inducing excruciating migraines and madness. We have attempted to blindfold them and cover exposed skin, but they are still unable to function. The decision has been made to exterminate the test subjects."

I was repulsed. Children. They tried to genetically alter children and failed. And then the Program put them down like dogs. I couldn't believe that the government allowed children to be tortured and tested on by the Program and then be killed as if they were nothing more than animals. Disgust pulsed through my body; I felt like retching. There were even horrifying pictures. My vision was blurry with angry tears, but I blinked them away and kept reading.

After the initial failed experiments, the Program decided to attempt the gene alteration on a fetus.

"Genetic modification of the inutero fetus has been successful. The subject, Osbourne Dracone, is flourishing and seems to be exhibiting flawless aim. In addition to the Archerfish Gene, he was also enhanced with a Coondog Gene. The hope is to combine both perfect aim and tracking skills to create a Sophisticate with ultimate hunting abilities."

And so, Ozzy was born. He wasn't really modified with anything from an archerfish or coondog; those were merely the names the scientists gave to the specific traits they were attempting to replicate. At the age when his predecessors were falling prey to debilitating headaches and madness, Ozzy was learning to shoot a bow and arrow, and was hitting the bulls-eye every time. No matter what weapon they put in his hand, Ozzy was able to master it immediately. He was moved from his training university in Colorado and brought to St. Ignatius Academy when he was only 10. Every weapon manufacturer wanted to sponsor him. If a company made something that could be thrown or shot or swung to kill something, they wanted a piece of Ozzy.

Although my childhood wasn't storybook material, at least I got to grow up with kids my own age. And when I was little, it wasn't all about the Program. My fellow Sophisticates and I got to play, and create, and imagine once in a while. But Ozzy grew up at St. Ignatius Academy among teenagers several years older than him

— completely submerged in military, battle, and strategic subject matter.

I felt a pang of sorrow for him. No matter how lonely I felt now, at least I'd always had Cassie and the Homework Harpies. Ozzy had had no one. As I flipped through more pages, my sadness for him increased, as did my anger at the Program. The things they did to him were nothing short of torture. No child should be put through the tests he suffered through.

I rubbed my eyes sleepily as I finished the scientific section about his genetic alteration, exhibition, and successful deviation. The Program considered exhibition when Ozzy started demonstrating perfect aim and superior tracking abilities. His successful deviation was when he learned to control those abilities — the point at which he evolved from a regular Sophisticate into something even more.

I was feeling less and less human with every passing page. If I really was one of these Deviant Dozen, how much of what I was was really me and how much was what the Program created? Maybe there was nothing about me that was truly real. It wasn't like I could even claim my choices and decisions as being real; those were made by the Program, too.

Dejectedly, I flipped to the next section: Career.

According to Ozzy's Career History, the Program started sending him on assassination missions when he turned 15. He went on them at least once a month. I found myself shaking my head in disbelief. He had over two dozen completed missions just in the last two years. Flipping through the pages, one fluttered to the floor. I bent to pick it up and realized that at the top was written, "Deviant Dozen." I swallowed back the lump in my throat and began to read it. It was a list of names, along with strange animal titles.

Ozzy was at the top of the list along with his Archerfish title. Underneath were eleven other names I recognized.

DEVIANT DOZEN:

Osbourne Dracone – Archerfish

Sterling Dracone – Hummingbird

Quinby Dracone – Electric Eel

Theodore Dracone – Bull Shark

Wesley Dracone – Bald Eagle

Sadie Dracone – Ring Tailed Cat

Evangeline Dracone – Tiger Moth

Arabella Dracone – Indonesian Mimic Octopus

Clementine Dracone – Malaysian Fire Ant

Cassandra Dracone – Horror Frog

Dexter Dracone – Spitting Cobra

Marty Dracone – Spitfire Caterpillar

I was appalled when I saw Malaysian Fire Ant next to my name. I concluded that the names were some sort of code for the types of skills that the Program had engineered into the genetic alteration. Malaysian Fire Ants were the suicide bombers of the animal kingdom.

Ozzy hadn't been lying. I really was designed to be a human weapon. I was shocked and devastated, but mostly I just felt dirty and wrong.

Tears swelled at the corners of my eyes, and then they angrily rushed down my cheeks, burning trails in my already flushed face. Fury boiled inside my chest. As if being genetically altered wasn't unnatural enough, I was a mutant with terrible powers. Did they really expect me to destroy things on command? What would I do if they told me I had to blow up a tank, or a plane, or a building that I knew had people inside?

I wouldn't. I couldn't.

I felt violated. I was nothing but a monster. My fingers shook as I tightly gripped Ozzy's folder, desperate for something to stabilize me. Suddenly, the folder burst into flames and I instinctively threw it in the trash can where it was engulfed in a tiny, angry, inferno. I watched as the pages, both read and unread, curled into a bright orange blaze. I was disgusted with myself. Did I not have any control at all? I poured a bottle of water over the smoldering papers to put the fire out.

My anger was far from being quelled, however. I was shaking and trembling. I could feel myself on the verge of doing what I'd done to my room at the University.

I clenched my hands, in a desperate bid for control. The tattoo on the inside of my forearm caught my attention, momentarily distracting me. I never thought much about it since every Sophisticate had the same mark. It was a symbol of being a Sophisticate. But what I never bothered to think about before, I now looked at with disgust. The tattoo wasn't proof of belonging to something. The mark was nothing more than a declaration that I was owned by the Program. I'd been branded. Like an animal.

Fury burned inside.

I rushed to the window and opened it. Below, the targets from Weapons class were lined up in a neat row. I took deep breaths but my control was tenuous, at best. Rage devoured all other thoughts, leaving only one desire — destruction.

No.

I didn't want to be a monster, but the beast inside was restless.

Stop. Please. Not again, I begged the animal inside me.

I stilled, clinging to the anger. Holding it tightly. Eyes pinched shut. Fists clenched.

The violation seeped deep into my soul. I was a storm of emotions.

Afraid. Angry. Tainted.

The fury was tearing me apart.

My hold was slipping.

Control it. Rule the fear.

I couldn't. I let go and the power screamed through me and straight into the nearest target which exploded into flames and canvas shrapnel, violently scattering across the lawn in fiery scraps. Relief flooded through me in cool waves as I continued to destroy the targets until each and every one of them was consumed in hungry little blazes of fire. I didn't stop until the anger was gone. I didn't stop until the monster within was sated.

Belatedly, I looked around to see if there were any witnesses to my fury. It was past curfew so all the cadets were supposedly in their rooms, sleeping. Luckily, there wasn't a Hound in sight either. My secret was safe, for now. But now I knew, truly knew, that none of it was an accident or coincidence. Not my dorm room, not the pen, not the rink lights. I'd done all of those things. The Program created me to destroy and I'd already begun to exhibit. Now, they were just waiting for me to deviate and perfect my skill. To truly become one of the Dozen. To become a weapon.

I watched the fire dance across the mangled targets, licking at the wood and painted canvas. Glancing over my shoulder at the new uniform that Arabella had designed, I cringed at the cruel truth of the name stitched on the back of the shirt.

Flame Fatale.

$\backsim\sim$ 14 $\sim\backsim$

DAMSELS OF DISTRESS

Breakfast the following morning should have been buzzing with talk of the roller derby match later that night. Instead, the destroyed archery targets had taken center stage and the theories were endless. Everyone had seen the ruined remains of ash and charred grass on their way out to the morning run and it seemed that many cadets were worried that it had something to do with the terrorist attack.

"Temper tantrum last night?" Arabella asked, plowing through a bowl of cereal. Assumptions and rumors were flying around us, the cadets a strange mix of worry and excitement.

"How did you know?" I sighed. There was no point in denying it.

"Lucky guess. Want to talk about it?"

I thought about all the things I'd read, all the things I now knew. And I wanted to talk about it to Arabella, but they weren't really my secrets to discuss. No matter how I felt about Ozzy, the information in the folder was still his. "I can't. I wish I could."

Arabella shrugged. "Well, when you're ready."

"Yeah," I agreed. I finished my breakfast quickly and headed off to class.

Younglove was quick to squash the terrorist rumors with an impromptu speech at lunch. She informed the skeptical cadets that the administration already knew who had vandalized the training arena and that the situation would be addressed. She ended the speech by reminding us that our final wagers for the match had to be made by dinner. And just like that, the vandalized targets were forgotten and there was a flurry of last minute betting.

On her way out, Younglove stopped behind my chair and stiffly leaned over, her mouth hovering inches from my ear. "I see you have decent aim," she said quietly, pride evident in her voice. "Please try to keep it under control tonight." And with that, Younglove disappeared, leaving me shaking so hard I barely managed to get the soup safely to my mouth.

The locker room was full of nervous energy that night. I allowed Arabella to crown my helmet with a punk rock tiara, which was adorned with a skull and spikes. It looked more like a weapon than an accessory and if push came to shove, I figured it could be used that way. Arabella had certainly hinted at that possibility more than once.

The rest of the uniform was just as outrageous as the helmet tiara. In lieu of the green tank top we usually wore for matches, Arabella had designed black corsets with purple ribbon lacing up the front and silver studs scattered throughout. The green shorts were replaced with white skirts that looked like they'd been in a battle of some sort, with a thick silver belt of skulls crisscrossed around the waist. There were also long, black and white striped knee socks that were enough to make anybody's eyesight go a little blurry. To top off the entire outfit, everyone had black leather bands around their wrists and biceps that were studded with even more spikes. Arabella suggested, or rather insisted, that these were to be used as weapons.

"Trust me, when you shove your shoulder or arm into them and grind those spikes into their skin, it won't feel good. Don't hold back," she encouraged.

When I voiced my concern ahead of time to Arabella about using metal on any part of the outfits, we both agreed that would be giving Quinnie an unfair advantage. Arabella had special ordered all the studs, chains, spikes, and skulls to be made of a special acrylic that only looked like metal. Metal or not, however, it would still be plenty painful when shoved into tender, unsuspecting skin.

I looked around at my teammates, impressed with the names they had come up with. Jane transformed into *Calamity Jane*, Helen was *Hellon Wheels*, and Misty was a feisty *Miss Chievous*. Jacqueline chose *Full Metal Jackie*, Katie was now *Katie Karnage*, and Maya was *Afro Dee She Smack* — complete with a massive afro wig. Anna selected the nickname *ANNihilator*, Susan was now known as *Susie Slaughter*, and Arabella, the genius behind the outrageous outfits, was fully in character as *Miss Demeanor*. And of course, I was *Flame Fatale*, a name that none of the other girls, except perhaps Arabella, truly understood. They'd never imagine in a million years it was based on some morsel of truth.

Younglove had enlisted Sterling to announce the match, despite the fact that he'd never done it before. She assured him that his most important job would be to point out the other team's faults and work the crowd into a frenzy for the *Damsels*. A free chance to insult Quinnie and talk smack? Sterling was more than happy to take on the job.

I bounced with excitement as I stood in the entryway to the locker room with the rest of the *Damsels* as Sterling introduced Professor Jediah's team into the skating arena. There were cheers and catcalls from all the male cadets in the crowd. Quinnie's team skated their obligatory introduction lap and then settled on the visitor's bench in the middle of the track. Immediately after, half the lights in the arena turned off and the cheers disintegrated into confused muttering. The colored spotlights and strobes that our team had installed earlier lit the arena up, making it look like an underground dance hall. I could hear Quinnie and her teammates shouting party foul, but we were the home team and there wasn't much in the rules that covered lighting, music, and announcing. I knew because we checked the rule book several times to be sure.

Quinnie's shouts of disapproval were soon drowned out when the music came on. Sterling had frowned when I handed him the ancient CD — *Bad Reputation* by Joan Jett — but I insisted it needed to be played during our entry. We also supplied him with a large stack of punk music, brimming with angry girls with sassy attitudes. He was instructed to make sure this music was playing in the background throughout the entire match.

Joan Jett's voice filled the room. *"I don't give a damn about my reputation . . . "*

"And now," Sterling's voice boomed. "Give it up for the *Damsels of Distress!*"

The guitar riffs bounced off the walls as Joan Jett wailed about her bad reputation and how a girl can do what she wants to do. We skated out onto the track as the arena erupted in cheers. The crowd loved the lights, the new and improved uniforms, and the music. The match hadn't even started yet and they were already chanting "Dam-sels! Dam-sels!"

Arabella whirled around the track, playing an air guitar and lip syncing to the lyrics. I was pretty sure that most of the crowd had probably never heard of the song, but they were singing along with it.

"I don't give a damn about my reputation . . . "

Arabella jumped up onto the railing to slap hands with the cadets in the front row.

"I've never been afraid of any deviation . . . "

Deviation? My breath caught briefly. I hadn't remembered that part of the song, and it was hitting a little too close to the truth. It made me think of Ozzy and I looked out into the crowd to see if he was there, but it was too dark to see anyone except the cadets in the first few rows.

The song ended and we skated to our bench in the middle of the rink. Quinnie's team was already gathered around their bench, dressed in their standard red and yellow uniforms. They were scowling, but the rest of the cadets in the stands were on their feet — cheering, stomping, and whistling for the *Damsels of Distress* as the crowd continued to grow wild with excitement. I could hear people yelling the names written on the back of our shirts, picking a favorite before the match even started.

We took our places on the bench as Younglove announced the five girls leading the first jam. *Katie Karnage* was going to be jammer while I sat out. I was fine with that. Quinnie was worked up enough already and I wasn't sure what sort of disaster would occur if the two of us were allowed to go at each other in the first jam.

Katie snapped the star adorned jammer panty on her helmet and then replaced her skull tiara over top. She put her fist out to me and punched it. "Kick some ass, girl," I told her.

"It's gonna be a bloodbath out there," Katie responded.

"You mean slaughter and carnage," Susie shouted happily, slapping Katie's helmet. *Susie Slaughter* was playing pivot in the first jam with *Katie Karnage*.

Both teams took their places on the track and when the whistle sounded the beginning of the first jam, the crowd went wild as Katie knocked the red and yellow jammer down immediately — just as she had done to me the first day of practice — and took off for the pack. Stunned by the unusual roar of the crowd, the red and yellow pack were easy pickings for Katie as she barreled her way through them, using her arms and the studs like meat tenderizers to shoulder her opponents out of the way.

"*Katie Karnage* is leaving a path of destruction in her wake," Sterling shouted into the microphone. "She easily skates through the pack and takes the position of lead jammer." Free of the pack, Katie sped around the track, slipping around the red jammer who was walled up behind Misty and Maya.

"Looks like the red team is having a hard time getting their jammer around *Miss Chievous* and *Afro Dee She Smack*. That afro is quite the blind spot." Sterling was right. Maya was using her enormous afro wig, which she had placed on the outside of her helmet, to keep the red jammer from seeing around her.

"*Susie Slaughter* just exterminated the pivot for the red team!" Sterling yelled happily. The crowd roared in approval as Susie blocked the other team's pivot, knocking her into and over the bar as Katie skated by. Instead of ending the jam, Katie continued around the track to pick up more points since Misty and Maya were so easily controlling the red team's jammer. By the end of the jam, the score was 10-0.

Younglove didn't put me in on the second jam, even though she substituted the rest of the girls. "You just had a concussion two weeks ago, let's not put you in until Katherine needs a break," Younglove explained. I was a little disappointed, but I couldn't deny that Katie was outscoring Quinnie's team with little effort.

I looked around the arena, hoping to see a sign of Ozzy's return. The sensory bombardment of all the colored spotlights and strobes, coupled with the atmospheric darkness, made it hard to see anyone in the crowd. I knew one thing for sure: my name was the only one not being chanted — I was the only one that hadn't been in a jam yet.

By the fifth jam, the *Damsels* were up 28-13. Quinnie had managed to score big on both of her outings and Katie was starting to wear down.

During the next to last jam, Quinnie skated over to the water jug in the middle of the two benches to get a drink of water. I was caught alone with her while the skaters changed spots on the bench. "Looks like your team doesn't trust you out on the track," Quinnie purred. "Not that I blame them, it's common knowledge you need supervision in the shower just so you don't require a trip to the infirmary again."

I ignored her. Younglove had told me to control myself tonight. Easier said than done with Quinnie around.

"I heard your girlfriend has to shower with you now to keep

an eye on you," Quinnie pressed. "Do you ladies wash each other's backs?"

"Leave off, Quinby," Arabella snarled as she skated up between us. "Speaking of backs, where are you ever going to find a dress for the Autumn Formal this year? I hear Puritan Party dresses is having a great sale, maybe you should check it out. They go all the way to the neck," Arabella said happily, miming the neckline of a dress right under her chin. "Wouldn't want anyone to see anything unsightly, if you know what I mean." Arabella spun around on her skates, giving Quinnie a good view of her back.

Quinnie angrily swung her arm forward, knocking the stack of paper cups off the table and all over the floor before skating back to her bench.

"She's a little sensitive, wouldn't you say?" Arabella asked innocently.

"Definitely sensitive. Maybe you should apologize," I feigned seriousness.

"What a fabulous idea," Arabella agreed, standing and taking the pivot panty from Susie and fitting it over her helmet. "I think I'll wait until after the match, though, because I'm not done offending her yet."

"I think offending is putting it lightly."

"Oh, I have no intention of doing anything lightly to her."

I laughed.

"Clementine, you're in," Younglove announced as Katie, breathing hard, collapsed on the bench. She tossed me the jammer panty and took a big swig of water.

"Last jam before halftime," Katie told me. "They're catching up, so try to put a few clicks on the board."

I nodded nervously and coasted out on the track.

"And we have a new jammer, ladies and gentlemen," Sterling announced as *Rebel Girl* by the punk rock band Bikini Kill blared through the speaker system. "*Flame Fatale* is taking the track and she'll be jamming against Quinby from the red team."

Quinnie glared at Sterling and I silently willed him to let go of the metal microphone before Quinnie decided to deal out a little payback to him for using her full name. Luckily, Quinnie didn't have a chance because the pack was lining up. The first whistle blew and Arabella and the pivot for the red team took off, leading the pack in a fast paced skate. Susie usually led her pack more slowly, allowing Katie to use her brawn to muscle through and score, but Arabella knew that my advantage was in speed and agility. She had to set the pace fast to allow me a chance to out-race Quinnie.

The whistle chirped twice and Quinnie and I took off toward the pack, neither of us wasting the time or energy to try to block one another. I had a feeling that Quinnie was protecting her back by avoiding as much contact as possible. Both of us entered the pack at the same time. The red team quickly converged on me, forming a diamond around me to keep me from grabbing the lead jammer position. Although the pack blitz slowed me down, it left Quinnie at the mercy of the *Damsels* who roughly jostled her around, nearly pushing her out of bounds.

I faked as if I was going to skate to the left and the diamond around me closed in on that side. I squatted low and skated in between the two large girls on my right side, squeezing free of the prison of bodies, struggling to pass the pivots before Quinnie could. Quinnie dodged Arabella and came up alongside her own pivot, who reached back and whipped her forward, propelling her into the lead jammer spot with me emerging from the pack right behind her.

We both raced around the track and entered the pack again, battling to get as many points as possible. Just as I was about to take the lead and pass my final blocker to escape the pack and go back for another lap, Quinnie kicked her foot out, tripping me. I fell to the track ungracefully, crashing into the wall. One of the large blockers from the red team didn't even attempt to avoid the collision and fell on top of me, forcing the air out of my chest and smashing my face into the floor.

The whistle blew, sending Quinnie into the penalty box, but by the time I had extracted myself from underneath the red blocker and had regained my footing, the jam was over. It was halftime. Quinnie and I had both scored four points, but it was obvious from my bloody nose that Quinnie actually won that jam.

Arabella handed me a paper towel for my bloody nose and lip. "Minor flesh wound, babe. It happens to everyone. Let's clean it up in the locker room. After halftime, we'll come out and give her the ass whooping she so deserves."

Halftime in the locker room was spirited and noisy. Sterling was playing some high energy techno music that I had picked out.

Arabella peeked out of the locker room door and into the arena. "They're dancing! I can't believe Sterling is deejaying a rave for Mandates!"

After I cleaned up my bloody face, I joined my teammates in twirling and dancing around the room while Arabella flashed the light switch on and off in a mock version of what was going on in the arena. With five minutes left in the intermission, the crowd started chanting.

"What are they saying?" Katie asked, moving to the door.

"It's kind of hard to make out since they have no rhythm whatsoever, but I'm pretty sure they're saying *Damsels of Distress*." Arabella laughed. "They totally love us. I bet Quinnie is pissed."

Arabella skated over to her locker and pulled out a box. She reached into it and then proceeded to hand each of us a stack of cards. I looked down at mine in disbelief.

"You made us player's cards?" I had no idea that when Arabella unveiled the uniforms on Wednesday and made each of us pose for a picture that she actually intended to do something with the photos. I vehemently wished I had done something more interesting than just stand there with my hands on my hips. Everyone else seemed pleased with their cards, however.

"Yeah, because I'm totally awesome like that. When we go back out there, toss a few cards into the crowd, really get them worked up."

Younglove entered the locker room, standing in the doorway. "Ready ladies?" She gestured to the arena and Katie was the first one to skate past her, clutching her player's cards in her fists like weapons.

The crowd went wild when we skated back into the arena. We sped around the track, tossing the cards into the stands which turned into a roiling mass of muscles and mild brawling. I couldn't believe it. Cadets were actually fighting over the cards. After tossing most of my cards into the crowd, I finally made my way to the middle of the track to take my seat on the bench.

Quinnie stood at the head of her team, arms crossed. "The score is 53-51 ladies. You're only ahead by two and it hardly warrants this kind of celebration. You're going to be humiliated 30 minutes from now when we take home the victory."

"Your mouth is writing checks your skates can't cash," Arabella sassed. "Even if we do lose, we still win. They love us," she said, indicating the crowd.

"All that matters is the score." Quinnie cocked her hip and her chin jutted out as her head did an annoying, cocky wobble that actually looked a little silly without the customary finger waggle that usually went along with that sort of thing.

"Really? Try telling them that." Arabella pointed to the crowd which was still fighting over the player cards that had been tossed into their midst. "They know us by name. You? You're just the red team."

"All right ladies, let's break it up," Professor Jediah said as she stepped between the girls and guided her team back to their bench.

The second half continued in a neck and neck fashion. Whenever I was jamming, so was Quinnie. Our jams were fast paced and it usually didn't matter who the lead jammer was since we seemed to score within one point of each other.

Going into the last jam, the score was 76-77. The *Damsels* were one point behind. We had dominated for most of the match, but since Katie had played most of the jams in the first half, she was losing points every time she went on the track during the second half. The last jam, however, belonged to Quinnie and me — the matchup the entire school had been waiting for all week. The rest of the cadets still didn't know the details of what went down between us, but they knew it was big and they hoped the drama would culminate on the track.

That's why everyone, including Quinnie, was surprised when I lined up as pivot instead of Arabella. There was a lot of noisy debating until Arabella took her place behind the pack beside Quinnie, wearing the star helmet panty.

The arena had gone almost quiet with confusion and I could easily hear Quinnie and Arabella arguing.

"What do you think you're doing, freak?" she yelled.

"I know you're not the sharpest knife in the drawer, Quinnie, but I thought even you would recognize a jammer panty," Arabella said pointing to her helmet.

"I hope you saved some of those cards for yourself, because they're going to be collector's editions after this match. *Miss Demeanor?* More like Missing in Action. You're going to need a fork for this jam because you're going to be eating my dust."

Arabella laughed. "Oh, Quinby. Please don't tax your brain with attempting to insult me. Stay with what you're good at — being a self-centered, egotistical bitchwad."

The whistle chirped once and I darted forward, eager to lead the pack as fast as I could.

The whistle blasted twice and I knew that the jammers were now in play. Quinnie was fast and so was I, but no one was as fast on the track as Arabella. And pound for pound, no one was as vicious either. She threaded her way through the pack, helped by the perfectly timed blocks performed by the rest of the team.

She passed me at the front of the pack to earn the lead jammer position. Then, to the surprise of everyone, except me and the rest of the *Damsels*, Arabella snatched the jammer panty off her helmet and reached back to grab my hand. She pulled me forward in a whip while handing me the jammer panty. I tossed the pivot helmet cover over my shoulder to Arabella and attacked the track in a burst of speed. Quinnie recovered her surprise just in time to be knocked out of bounds by *Hellon Wheels*.

I rounded the track coming up on the pack at top speed. The red team formed a wall across the track with the *Damsel's Full Metal Jackie* jockeying for position in their midst. As I came up behind her, *Full Metal Jackie* spread her legs wide and bent over with her hand down, creating a gateway for me to pass through. I squatted low, grabbed her hand, and Jackie yanked me through her legs, catapulting me through, and past, the wall of red blockers who yelled out in frustration.

The pivot for the red team turned around to see what was going on, just in time for me to slam into her shoulder and knock the much bigger girl into the side rail. The crowd erupted in whistles and cheers. As I passed the fallen giant, I whipped the panty off my helmet and handed it back to Arabella.

"It's your victory, you end the jam," I yelled over the noise.

In one smooth move, Arabella had the star panty on her helmet and her hands on her hips. The buzzer blared and the match was over. Just like that, we had won. Arabella grabbed my hand, pumping our fists into the air in victory. I couldn't believe Arabella's crazy idea had worked. We'd won. We'd really won.

The chanting of "Dam-sels" resumed as our team took a few victory laps. Sterling was yelling the score and recapping the last play, but no one could hear him over the noise, so he put another song on instead.

Arabella and I were coasting around the track, arms around each other, slapping hands with cadets that were leaning over the rink wall. Our celebration was cut short when we were pushed from behind. I whirled around to defend myself, anger chafing under my skin.

"You cheated!" Quinnie was furious, her hair nearly vibrating with electricity.

"You're mistaken," Arabella corrected. "We won."

"You can't just change jammers and pivots mid-jam!" Quinnie sputtered, spit flying unattractively from her mouth.

"Really? Cause I'm pretty sure we just did," Arabella said snidely.

"There's no rule against it," I added. I wasn't sure why I was trying to diffuse the situation. Somewhere deep in my belly I wanted nothing more than to give Quinnie a taste of her own medicine.

"You can't change mid-jam!" Quinnie repeated in frustration.

"We. Just. Did," Arabella said, enunciating each word like she was talking to a small child. "See the scoreboard? The match is over. Go slither back to your room and lick your wounds."

The air around Quinnie seemed to spark and flicker in response to Arabella's words. Quinnie stepped forward, hands thrust outward. There was a crackle of blue light snaking between her fingers. I immediately stepped in Quinnie's path, an undeniable urge to protect Arabella flaring through my chest. I didn't think about the pink, blood-tinged water in the shower or Ms. Petticoat's thin blade scraping over my burns. I didn't think about the agonizing moments slumped under the water when I was trembling uncontrollably from pain and fear. All I could think about was that I wouldn't let Quinnie attack Arabella. Ever.

Quinnie stepped forward.

I clenched my fists, expecting the pain of electric shocks to shoot through me. Instead, there was a fierce gathering of warmth that rolled through me from somewhere deep in my chest to the tips of my fingers and toes. Almost as if my body was exhaling, I felt the heat leave me, fast and harsh. Quinnie appeared to be hit with a blast of air as her helmet flew off, falling to the floor and rolling up against the rink wall. Her hair whipped around her head and her hands moved instinctively to her face for protection.

And then it was gone. The torrent of air had come and gone so quickly and silently, I wasn't even sure it had happened at all. However, when Quinnie pulled her fingers from her face, the skin underneath was raw and red, as if she had been either sunburned or windburned — or both. She looked wild-eyed at Arabella and me, her dry, cracked lips unable to find the right words. She clenched her fingers once more, snapping out a few residual sparks, and then she turned and sped away on her skates.

"What just happened?" Arabella's eyebrows were cocked in confusion as she watched Quinnie disappear.

"It seems that Quinnie is a bit distressed," I said warily.

The monster inside seemed to purr in satisfaction.

15

IN THE CLOSET

With Quinnie gone, Arabella quickly forgot about the alterca-
tion and joined in the celebration, much to my relief. I didn't want
to talk about what had just happened or what it meant. Or how
good it had felt.

The entire arena was celebrating, with some of the cadets
coming right out onto the track to dance and congratulate the
Damsels. Sterling came down out of his DJ box to give Arabella a
spin on the track-turned-dance-floor. For the first time in my life,
I saw Sophisticates being themselves — not brainiacs, not athletic
superstars, not militaristic drones, not what the Program told them
to be — just kids celebrating a sporting event and having a good
time. I wondered if this was what it was like to be a normal kid.
I considered what I would be willing to give up or suffer through
to have this kind of freedom and joy all the time.

But I knew those were dangerous thoughts. I knew that anything I was willing to give up didn't really belong to me in the first

place. I didn't even belong to myself.

Definitely dangerous thoughts.

I looked around the arena hoping and expecting to see Ozzy, but he was nowhere to be found. Everyone was required to come to sporting events. Did his absence mean that he wasn't back yet from his mission or had something happened to him?

As good as the victory felt, it was hard for me to completely enjoy the after party with my mind still on Ozzy. I'd been so sure he would be at the match. As the time for lights out approached, the professors were finally able to break up the celebration and send everyone off to their rooms. Theo, with his twin brother Wesley in tow, cornered me and Arabella at the bottom of the stairwell to the girls' dorms.

"Do you girls have any more of those player cards?" Theo asked.

"Why?" Arabella snapped. She didn't like Theo; it was obvious to everyone but Theo.

"Because I want to collect them."

"How many do you have?"

"All but yours and Cleo's."

"Well, if we give them to you now, that kind of defeats the purpose of collecting them doesn't it?"

"Why?"

"Because at that point you would have them and would no longer be collecting them."

"I don't follow."

"Theo, you're so thick-witted it's hard to believe you were genetically altered at all. I'm beginning to think that you had to share the brains with Wesley here."

Theo frowned. "Man, you're a hag queen bitch sometimes." He stepped back as if he expected Arabella to take a swing at him.

When Arabella threw her arms around his neck, he visibly flinched. "Really?" she crooned. "That is SO sweet. Just for that, you can have my card," she said, pulling it out of the skate she had slung over her shoulder and handing it to him.

Theo was beyond confused, but even he realized his good fortune at getting the card instead of an ass whooping. "Cleo?" he asked hopefully.

"Sorry, I gave them all away," I lied. I actually had one left in the waistband of my skirt, but I was saving it for someone, along with the hope that that someone would come back safely from his mission. I knew it was silly, but after reading the information in Ozzy's folder, I felt a connection with him. He wasn't just the Golden Boy with perfect aim and a cocky attitude, he was a boy who had probably suffered more than any of the other cadets at St. Ignatius. And I wanted to get to know him better, despite the warnings of my friends.

Arabella looped her arm through mine as we climbed the stairs. "I'm going to be walking on clouds all this week. Kicking Quinnie's derby ass and getting called hag queen bitch all in one night. I'm so happy."

I laughed. "Don't forget that incredible last jam you orchestrated, I'm sure no one will ever forget that."

"I don't intend to let them," Arabella promised, pushing open the door at the top of the stairwell. She sighed as we reached my door. "I'm going to be dreaming happy dreams tonight. But tomorrow, we start operation Autumn Formal. You need a date. I'm thinking either Dexter or Marty. Hey, did you leave your television on?"

I cocked my head, listening at my door. I hardly ever watched my television, but it definitely sounded like it was on. "That's weird. I don't even remember turning it on today."

"Could be a ghost," Arabella offered. "St. Ignatius is full of them. Most of them are harmless though."

"All right," I said slowly. I wasn't going to argue. First of all, I wasn't sure if Arabella was being serious. And even if she was, I didn't believe in ghosts. And . . . even if I did, I was fairly certain they couldn't turn on televisions.

I gave Arabella one last hug goodnight and then slipped the key into my doorknob. Once inside, it became clear why unexplained noise was coming from my room. There, sprawled out on my bed, was Ozzy. And he was watching my television.

I shut the door and stepped closer to the bed. "What are you watching?" I whispered, afraid that Arabella would overhear.

"Chimpanzees."

I glanced at the television. "Are they . . . are they ice skating?"

"Sure are. Which is why the show is called *Chimpanzees on Ice.*"

"But, they're wearing tutus," I said, shocked. Is this what I was missing from not watching television? If so, I didn't feel like I was missing much. The chimps were terrible ice skaters.

"Of course they are. It would be absolutely ridiculous if they skated in the nude," Ozzy explained.

"I can't believe you're actually watching this. Reality TV has really gone down hill."

"I had nothing better to do."

"Oh," I said simply. I wondered why I felt hurt that he'd rather watch chimps ice skating than see the roller derby match. I told myself that I didn't want anything to do with him anyway. I didn't, right? Well, Sterling and Arabella didn't want me to have anything to do with him and that was almost the same thing. My concern over his well being was just a typical human response for another person, that's all. I was just overly sensitive because of all the things I read in his file. "When did you get back?"

"A few hours ago."

"I didn't see you."

"That's because you were playing roller derby," he reminded me.

"It was a pretty good match."

"Actually, it was an incredible match."

"Who told you that?" I asked, sitting down on the edge of the bed, staring at the television where two monkeys were involved in a spinning move that was very hairy and involved a lot of strange noises and random butt scratching.

"No one told me, I was there. You were amazing," Ozzy added, sitting up as he pointed the remote at the television and turned it off.

I didn't say anything. I bent over to set my bag on the floor and the player card I'd saved for Ozzy fell out of my waistband. I tried to stuff it back into its hiding place before he could see it. Even though I'd saved it for him, I now felt silly handing it over.

"What's that?"

"Um . . . my player card. Arabella made them. You want it?" I tried to pretend as if I didn't care whether he took it or not.

"Sure, I'll add it to my collection," he said, reaching for it.

"How many do you have so far?" I asked out of curiosity, keeping the card just out of his reach.

"That one will make two."

"That's not much of a collection," I laughed.

"It is to me. I had to battle it out with a 300-pound Mandate who specializes in boxing just to get the first one."

I laughed again. "Who was it?"

"I think his name was Brutus or something like that. Hard to say for sure. All those Mandates look the same to me and I think half of them are actually named Brutus."

"No, I mean who is on your other card?"

Ozzy pulled the card out of his jacket pocket. "You, of course."

I could feel warmth rush up my neck, engulfing my cheeks in a burning blush. I looked away. "How did you get in my room?"

"Tree. Window. It wasn't hard."

"You know you're not allowed in here."

"You know I don't care."

I flicked the card nervously with my fingernail. "And why *are* you here?"

Ozzy snatched the card out of my hand and I looked up in surprise as he placed it on top of the other one and slipped both into the pocket of his jacket. A wicked smile claimed his lips and he leaned in toward me, drifting into my personal space, as usual. "Because dreaming about you just wasn't enough anymore."

I stopped breathing as he reached up and tucked the unruly lock of hair behind my ear. I was suddenly aware that I was sitting on my bed with Ozzy and my inhibitions were ebbing away. I knew that if I didn't get some distance between us, I might not have control over my willpower. And losing control with Ozzy wasn't an option, no matter what my body was whispering to my mind.

I slipped out of Ozzy's range and went into my large, walk-in closet to gather my pajamas. I was still in my roller derby uniform and felt uncomfortably grimy from the sweat and dirt of the match.

"You should probably go," I said without looking back at him. "It's getting close to curfew and I need to shower." I finished gathering my bathroom necessities and when I turned around, Ozzy was standing in the doorway of my closet, his hands resting on the doorjamb, casually blocking my exit. I hadn't even heard him get up from the bed and his unexpected closeness made my breath hitch in my throat.

I suddenly felt very vulnerable. And then I realized that was probably how Rasool ur Ra'ahmah felt right before he died — if that's what happened to him. Or, maybe he didn't even know he was going to die. I wondered what kind of an assassin Ozzy was. Did he sneak up and take out his prey without them even knowing it was coming, or did he flaunt it?

No, he wouldn't flaunt it. He wasn't cruel, was he? He'd do it quickly and painlessly.

And then I decided I didn't want to think about it. I didn't want to think about him killing anyone, no matter what manner it was done in.

"You should probably go," I repeated, although this time it sounded like a question.

"I don't want to." He stepped forward and reached for my waist, cautiously pulling me to him. "I've been thinking about this for two weeks."

"Thinking about what?" The words eked out, quietly. Apprehensively.

Ozzy leaned down toward me, slowly, giving me the chance to pull away. When I didn't, his mouth found mine, answering my question with a kiss that was barely there. His hands rested on my waist tentatively, as if he expected me to push him away like I had in the infirmary. His light embrace was a message that he wouldn't force me to do something I didn't want to.

I could hear Arabella's and Sterling's warnings to stay away from Ozzy echoing in my thoughts, but my lips seemed to have a mind of their own. I leaned into him and my mouth met Ozzy's once, twice, three times. And when my lips parted in invitation, his arms tightened around me and his breath quickened as his kissing became more eager, as if he was dying of thirst and only I could quench it. His tongue slid across my top lip and then he sucked on my bottom one.

He gently walked me backwards until my back pressed up against the clothes hanging from the rack behind me. I dropped my pajamas and toiletries to the floor and my hands went to his chest, roaming inside his jacket, working their way under his shirt to touch the tight skin of his stomach. Even knowing how dangerous this boy was and what he was capable of, I couldn't stop myself from touching him. The light graze of my fingertips caused his kissing to become more insistent. I reached up and tried to pull his jacket down his arms. There was too much clothing between us; I wanted to feel the muscles of his arms, the warmth of his skin.

When he continued to kiss me and run his hands through my hair, ignoring my desire to get his jacket off, I swung him around and roughly pushed him up against the clothes rack, ripping the offending clothing off his shoulders and throwing it to the floor. My less than gentle treatment caused him to smile through the kiss, our teeth grazing briefly.

"Flame Fatale," he murmured against my lips. "You're an animal."

I was surprised at my own actions. I certainly had never acted like this before. I'd tried kissing one of the Homework Harpies once, just to see what all the fuss was about, and I hadn't been impressed.

But Ozzy ... Ozzy's kisses tasted like mystery, and danger, and promises of things I never knew I wanted. His breath was intoxicating, his hands were persuasive, and I wondered why I'd been trying to prevent this from happening in the first place. I was crazy to push him away and I was crazy with the thought that he might pull away and take his kisses with him.

I leaned into him, gripping the muscles of his arms as his knees bent and he slid down the wall, pulling me down with him. We ended up in a heap on the floor, ripping half the clothes off the hangers on the rack in the process. Ozzy was sitting against the back of the closet and I was straddling him, pinning his wrists to the wall while I kissed him desperately. He tasted like cinnamon and his lips were hot and soft as I savored the feel of his mouth. I knew Ozzy easily could've broken my hold, but he let me hold him there, let me kiss him the way I wanted to.

When I stopped to catch my breath, Ozzy caught me in his gaze. "Go to the Autumn Formal with me."

"What is it with you and the Autumn Formal?" I panted.

"What is it with your reluctance to go? I thought girls loved dances. Just go with me."

"Why?" I was still breathing hard.

"So we can do more of this afterwards, obviously." His lips quirked into a grin.

The Formal I didn't care about, but his lips ... I wanted them back on mine as quickly as possible.

"What makes you think I'd let you get that far on our first date?" I asked. Clearly, I would.

"I like a challenge."

"So you've said before," I murmured. "But I can't go."

"Why not?"

"I don't have a dress."

"Is that the only reason?"

"Yes," I whispered, leaning in to touch his lips with mine again. Well, no dress and my friends don't want me to have anything to do with you, I thought.

"In that case, I'll come by at 7 p.m."

"I'm not going nude."

"Although that's quite a tempting notion, you won't need to. I got you a dress," he said, nodding to something behind me.

I looked over my shoulder and saw that a bulky white bag was hanging on the back of the closet door. I stared at it in confusion. "You can't be serious. Who goes around buying girls dresses? That's very stalkerish of you."

"Don't make me beg," he said, gently pulling his wrists out of my grasp. His hands roamed up my sides and along my back as he hooked them over my shoulders, pulling me in for another kiss. It was slow, and deep, and melted my willpower. He didn't have to beg, all he had to do was kiss me and I was pretty sure I'd say yes to whatever he wanted.

"Okay," I agreed quietly, knowing I was going to regret it later when Arabella and Sterling found out, but not caring one bit about that problem at the moment.

Ozzy smiled and then somehow lifted us both into a standing position. "I better go, I'm not sure how much longer I can resist this," he said, tugging on the ribbon laced through the corset of my *Damsels* uniform.

I blushed again and before I knew it, Ozzy was out the window, down the tree, and heading off into the darkness.

What just happened? I wondered, touching my lips with my fingertips. They were still burning with the stolen kisses of a boy I wasn't even supposed to talk to.

16

DELIRIOUS AND IN DISTRESS

As soon as Ozzy was gone, I couldn't resist the temptation any longer. I unzipped the bag and luxurious red material spilled out of it. He knew my favorite color was red, and that I never wore it. Like my fear of guns, my love of the color red and my avoidance in wearing it was just one of those things I didn't have an explanation for.

I pushed back the edges of the bag so I could get a better look at what was inside. It was a long, fitted dress that flared out near the knees and was ruched at the top. A glittering strap of beads draped over the right shoulder, down under the bust, and across the middle of the dress. I tried the gown on and it was a perfect fit. I realized there was no use in being surprised. Ozzy had read my file and knew everything about me, even my dress and shoe size. And to prove the point, there was a pair of perfectly sized, strappy, beaded shoes in the bag too.

After I took my shower and came back in the room, I noticed

that there was an instant message notification blinking on my computer screen. I wrapped my robe tighter and sat at the desk chair. Lights out had come and gone thirty minutes ago, so I turned off all the lights in my room, hoping that the dim light from my laptop screen wouldn't draw any attention.

I clicked on the notification. It was a message from Ozzy.

Ozzy: Did you like the dress?
Me: It's beautiful, thank you.

There was an immediate response.

Ozzy: It was my pleasure.
Me: Why are you still awake?
Ozzy: I wanted to make sure you liked it.
Me: I do. Now go to bed.
Ozzy: Put it on and send me a picture.
Me: I don't have a camera.
Ozzy: I was hoping to have dreams about you wearing it.
Me: Well, you'll just have to dream about me without it.
Ozzy: Okay.

I realized my mistake too late. I could almost imagine the cocky grin that was probably plastered across his face.

Me: That's not what I meant and you know it.
Ozzy: Too late. Good night, Cleo. Sweet dreams. I know mine will be.

I sighed and closed the laptop. He was charming and irresistible, despite my efforts to be unaffected by him. Once I was in bed, I finally let my mind wander to the problem at hand — finding a way to tell Sterling and Arabella that I was going to the Autumn Formal with Ozzy. And if that wasn't bad enough, I knew the backlash from Quinnie was going to be doubly awful what with the *Damsels* winning the roller derby match and Ozzy choosing me as his date to the dance.

How did I get myself into this mess? Was it worth the trouble? I touched my lips, remembering Ozzy's kisses — warm and insistent. I decided I'd risk going toe to toe with Quinnie any day if I could have Ozzy back in my closet again.

I woke up the next morning to the sound of my phone ringing.

"Hello," I said groggily.

"Get up and get ready. We're going to Baltimore," Ozzy ordered.

"What?"

"Arabella and Sterling are coming too. Get ready, and I'll meet you downstairs in 15 minutes." Ozzy hung up.

Before I could even put the phone back on the cradle, it sounded like someone was bashing down my door with a battering ram. The words: "Get up lazy bones. Just because they gave us the day off from the morning run, it doesn't mean you get to sleep till noon," told me that the battering ram was actually Arabella.

I opened the door and Arabella burst in, dressed in purple from hair to toe. Literally. Her hair was bright violet and looked like it was exploding out of her head. And she was wearing a traditional Baltimore Ravens jersey which just looked wrong paired with Arabella's typical punk rock clothes — purple mesh tights, black skirt, black boots, and a belt that looked like barbed wire.

"So, I hear we're going to a football game," Arabella stated, "with Ozzy." She scrunched up her nose. "You know how I feel about him, but it's not every day you get to see the Ravens play the Squealers, so I guess I'm just going to have to suck it up."

"Play the who?" I asked, still rubbing sleep out of my eyes.

"The Squealers. You know, the Pittsburgh Steelers? Archenemies of the Ravens?"

"Oh, yeah. Squealers. I've never heard them called that before." Ravens versus Steelers. Now that was a game worth getting up early for. At least, that's what I'd heard. I wasn't much of a football fan. I was usually nose deep in a book while the Harpies were busy commandeering the television remote and attacking a bowl of popcorn. I'd look up every once in a while to see what all the commotion was about, but the extent of my knowledge of football could be summed up in five words — running, throwing, catching, tackling, violence. I knew there was a ball involved too, but I didn't put much interest in anything with a name like pigskin.

"So tell me, why did Ozzy invite us?" Arabella asked, sitting down on my unmade bed while watching me stumble around the room aimlessly. "I mean, I know he's stalking you, but why invite me and Sterling? He knows we hate him."

"He's probably trying to soften you up," I suggested, finally locating a brush and attempting to tame my knotted hair.

"For what?"

"For the Autumn Formal."

"Hell no. I'm going with Sterling. Everyone knows that."

"Not you, me. He wants to take me to the Formal and he knows you don't approve. Maybe this is his way of winning you over to the dark side."

Arabella bit her bottom lip, flipping her lip ring back and forth with her tongue. I took a double take on the lip ring. That was a new addition today.

"Well, it's working," Arabella finally admitted. "If he buys me popcorn and cotton candy today, I might even let him get to first base with you."

I blushed, determined not to tell Arabella that Ozzy got a single last night in the closet. In fact, he had rounded first and was well on his way to second before he came to his senses and hopped out the window.

"What are you, my pimp?" I joked uneasily.

"Sorry, babe, I lose all sense of right and wrong when Ravens tickets are involved. By the way, what are you wearing to the game?"

"The shirt and pants you loaned me two weeks ago?" I asked, finding them in a pile in the corner of my closet with all of the other dislodged garments I hadn't bothered to clean up last night. "I haven't bought any new clothes yet."

"Don't worry, I have just the thing." Arabella left the room and came back five minutes later with a jersey and a hat. I took the clothes from her and quickly dressed. The Ravens baseball cap was a perfect way to hide my bed-head, which the brush had not been able to subdue. I put it on and checked myself in the mirror. Not bad for going from bed to out the door in less than 15 minutes.

I was disappointed when we got in the Academy SUV to go to the game and discovered that Professors Farnsworth and Youn-glove were chaperoning. My disappointment was quickly replaced by excitement, however, when we finally escaped the school walls and back roads and made it onto the familiar chaos of I-95. It had only been a month since I'd come to the Academy, but it felt like a lifetime.

Arabella and Sterling were in the middle row and Sterling was attempting to talk Arabella out of one of her remaining player's cards. Younglove and Farnsworth were up front, discussing the best way to reach the parking lot to avoid most of the game day traffic. Ozzy and I were sitting quietly in the back seat staring out the windows, avoiding the elephant in the room, which was the kissing episode from the night before. The memory of it seemed to be a yawning chasm between us, a chasm that neither of us were willing to risk leaping over just yet.

I wondered if he regretted it. No one seemed to be paying any attention to us and the silence between us seemed awkward after the closeness from the night before. I was confused since Ozzy was usually confident and outgoing.

"Where did the tickets come from?" I asked.

"One of my sponsors. They always give me tickets when the Steelers are in town."

"Why are they coming?" I whispered, pointing to the professors.

"A chaperoned outing is as close to freedom as it gets."

"What about when you go on your . . . missions?" I mumbled, glancing uncomfortably at Sterling and Arabella to make sure they weren't eavesdropping. They weren't. Sterling was threatening to take someone else to the Formal if Arabella didn't give him one of her cards. Arabella, in turn, threatened to take Theo.

"He'd never go with you," Sterling argued. "He doesn't even like you."

"Not true. He owes me because I gave him a card last night to complete his collection."

"That doesn't mean he likes you."

"Well then, I'll just have to rough him up a bit until he agrees," Arabella said haughtily.

Sterling sighed noisily and then continued his argument about how it would defeat the purpose of having a date if Arabella had to get it through threats. I knew the entire conversation was for show. Sterling and Arabella wouldn't dare think about taking anyone besides each other. Arguing was like foreplay to them.

"So?" I whispered when I realized Ozzy hadn't answered the question. "What about on your missions?"

He turned to face me, his green eyes were hopeful, and a little apprehensive.

"So you read it." Such a simple statement, but I could hear all the things he didn't say, or ask: Do you believe me now? Do you think I'm a monster? Do you hate me?

"Yes, I read it."

"Well, I guess that explains the destroyed targets on the Weapons field."

I shrugged.

Ozzy looked out the window again. "I've always gone with a team, but the deed itself . . . I've always done that alone."

Ozzy seemed to withdraw, as if admitting what he had done somehow transformed him into someone different. As if any of it was his fault. As if he had a choice. I wanted to reach over and put my hand on his, to comfort him, but I didn't feel it was enough. There was no gesture worthy of taking away someone's pain of knowing they were a genetic experiment. There was no way to unburden him from the things he had been forced to do, the guilt of the lives he'd been ordered to take.

"But even when I'm alone," Ozzy said quietly, "I'm not really alone."

"What do you mean?"

Ozzy's eyes found mine again. "Do you really think they'd let a weapon like me have that kind of freedom?"

I didn't understand what Ozzy was trying to say.

"He knows," Ozzy stated, tilting his chin to acknowledge Sterling. "I tried to tell him, but he ran anyway. And they found him." And with that, he turned to the window again, lost in dark thoughts that I couldn't bear to intrude on, even though I was now more confused than before.

Soon, the SUV was weaving its way through the crowded streets of Baltimore, which were packed with vendors selling souvenirs and food. Farnsworth parked at a VIP lot close to the stadium, and as we exited the vehicle, Ozzy seemed to shed the despondent brooding that had taken over his mood. We were on our way to a game and his cocky grin was back.

"So, Cleo tells me that you want to take her to the Formal." Arabella crossed her arms and was acting like she was my mother rather than my friend.

"She's already accepted." Ozzy's grin appeared to have no effect on Arabella.

She huffed. "I haven't approved of this whole idea yet. On one hand, Quinnie will be miserable that you won't be taking her and that thought makes me giddy like you wouldn't believe. But on the other hand, I still don't trust you."

Farnsworth and Younglove were busy paying the parking attendant, and were ignoring the discussion.

"So, how do I prove I'm trustworthy?" Ozzy asked. He was still smiling so it was hard to tell if he really cared what Arabella thought or if he was just humoring her for my sake.

"Well, you're off to a good start with tickets to the game. But . . ." Arabella said firmly, poking her finger into his chest, "I expect this to be the best damn game ever. Which means popcorn, cotton candy, a large soda, and a win over the Squealers."

"The food I can get you, but I can't promise a win," Ozzy argued.

"Well, for your sake, I hope the Birds protect this house today."

Ozzy laughed. "I had no idea you were such a fan."

"Any sports team that names itself after something in an Edgar Allan Poe poem is pretty damn awesome in my opinion. And you better hope they kick ass today or this date you have for the Formal," she said, waggling her finger between Ozzy and me, "will be Nevermore. That's a promise, Perfect Aim."

Ozzy grinned in response to Arabella's threats, either confident in the skills of the Ravens, or in his own ability to eventually win her over.

The parking attendant was finally paid, and Ozzy led us through the streets of Baltimore, weaving in and out of the surge of fans heading toward the hulking stadium ahead. The streets undulated in a sea of black and purple and I felt myself swept into the energy of the crush of people. There was a random shout of "Here we go Steelers!" that was immediately drowned out with insults about the visiting team and chants of "Protect this House!"

I felt giddy and normal. Not Sophisticate-normal, but average normal. Like I was part of something bigger — something more truthful and honest than my daily life. These people were alive and living in the moment. Despite the fact that Wormwood had taken so much from their future, despite the fact that the Program had kept them down so the Sophisticates could rise to the top, these people were happy. These people, these fans, they believed in the team.

I couldn't say that I ever believed in what I was a part of, I never believed in the rightness of the Program. It wasn't something I chose, it was something I was forced into. It was a little disturbing that a sport I didn't even understand could make me feel right and accepted in a way that my real life never did. I loved the feeling of being a part of the crowd and in a brief moment of daydreaming, I imagined what it would be like to not have to go back to the Academy. With the sun warming my skin and the noise of the crowd echoing in my ears, I imagined what it would be like to be free. As if sensing my thoughts, Ozzy grabbed my hand, threaded his fingers through mine, and pulled me close to his side.

On the walk to the stadium, Ozzy dutifully bought Arabella her cotton candy and promised her a box of popcorn inside. She seemed satisfied for the time being, tearing off the pink spun sugar with her fingers and stuffing it into her purple and black lipsticked mouth as we made our way through the gate.

The seats were amazing, right behind the Ravens sideline, close enough that our small group could smell the sweet scent of torn-up turf and hear the crack of helmets colliding. Arabella spent most of the game standing, jumping, and yelling — at the refs, the players, and other fans. I tried to pay attention to the plays, but the only thing my mind seemed to care about was the proximity of Ozzy: how close his hand was to mine when we both reached in the box of popcorn at the same time, how close his mouth was to my ear when he leaned over to explain the play that had just occurred, how close his knee was to mine as he lounged back into the uncomfortable stadium seat. And with every spark of electricity from his touch, I realized he was never close enough.

During the third quarter, I noticed Younglove pull out her phone and scroll through a few screens, clicking on various items. Her eyebrows furrowed into a tight "V" and she leaned over and whispered something to Ozzy. His easy smile disappeared as Younglove got up out of her seat and beckoned him to follow.

Ozzy leaned over to speak in my ear so I could hear him over the roar of the crowd. "I've got to talk to Younglove about something, I'll be right back."

"Is everything okay?"

He paused, as if he wanted to tell me something, but a glance back at Younglove and a shake of her head stitched his mouth shut tightly. "Yeah, everything is fine. Pay attention so you can tell me what I missed." His grin was far from genuine, like he was hiding something important.

"Bring me back a Coke, would you?" Arabella shouted, without turning to look at him. Before Ozzy could answer, she was yelling, "Interference! Interference! Where's the flag, ref?" Arabella shook her box of popcorn in the air like an old man shaking his fist at neighborhood kids — raining kernels all over the unfortunate souls in front of her. She didn't bother to apologize since they were Steelers fans. Sterling leaned forward, elbows resting on his knees, as he studiously watched the game while simultaneously ignoring the commotion otherwise known as Arabella.

The third quarter ended and Ozzy didn't return.

I leaned across the two empty seats between me and Professor Farnsworth. "When are they coming back?"

He took a sip of his beer and swallowed back a belch before answering. "They'll be back when they're back."

I was irritated, but settled into my seat and tried to pay attention to the game. The only thing I seemed to really comprehend was that the Ravens were winning. And that was a good thing as far as Arabella was concerned.

The fourth quarter dragged on and the seat next to me remained empty. Arabella took a break from her constant ranting and raving to notice the still empty seats. "Perfect Aim isn't back with my Coke yet? I'm dying from lack of caffeine here."

I shrugged.

"Do I have to do everything myself?" Arabella started to inch her way in front of me to make her way into the aisle.

Farnsworth snapped to attention, flinging his arm out to block Arabella's exit. "Where do you think you're going, Dracone?"

"Soda. Parched. Need sustenance."

"Sit down." When Arabella didn't immediately follow his order he added, "Unless you'd like to see Dean Overton when we get back to the Academy."

Arabella rolled her eyes and went back to standing in front of her seat and harassing anyone within earshot, and even those out of earshot.

The fourth quarter ended, the Ravens won, and Younglove and Ozzy still hadn't returned. The entire section cleared out and Sterling, Arabella, and I watched Farnsworth slowly and methodically drain the rest of another beer — visibly unconcerned by the fact that we were short two people to our party. Empty beer bottles rolled around under Farnsworth's seat and he carelessly tossed the new one on top of the haphazard pile. Finally, he pulled out his phone, checked his messages, and stood.

"Let's get going," he growled.

"Aren't we going to wait for Ozzy and Professor Younglove?" I asked.

"Nope."

"Why not?"

"They're gone already."

"Gone? Where?"

Farnsworth's bleary, drunken gaze finally found me and settled on my face as if looking at me helped him find his balance. "None of your business, cadet."

I was confused, annoyed, and anxious. Confused as to why Ozzy would say he was coming back and then break his word. Annoyed at being abandoned by him — even though it wasn't officially a date, I still felt jilted. And anxious about the look on Ozzy's face before he left. Most of all, I worried about what Younglove wouldn't let him say and what kind of secret would take him away.

Arabella and Sterling seemed unconcerned.

"I hope some of the vendors are still around, I'm going through caffeine withdrawal," Arabella hissed. "I'm moments away from having a full blown hissy fit."

"How's that going to be any different from how you've been acting for the last three hours?" Sterling asked.

"You're definitely not getting my card now," Arabella promised.

"I'll give you the rest of my Coke." Sterling swished the remains of his drink that was nothing more than flat backwash.

Arabella screwed up her nose, ready to throw back a biting insult. I interrupted her, "Aren't you worried about Ozzy?" Was I the only person to find the situation problematic?

Arabella looked at me like I just asked whether she'd like to kiss the Steelers' quarterback. "No. He disappears like that all the time. You'll get used to it."

I was positive I didn't want to get used to it.

Farnsworth led us through the concrete maze of the stadium, stopping briefly to let Arabella get a soda. At first, I thought the pit stop was merely an act to terminate Arabella's incessant whining, but I noticed that Farnsworth ordered himself another beer. He led us out of the stadium, and then collapsed onto a bench outside. We watched, disgusted, as he spent the next few minutes emptying his new beer.

"Um. Shouldn't we be heading to the parking lot?" Arabella was now fully caffeinated and ready to head home.

"No point," Farnsworth slurred. "Younglove and Perfect Aim took the SUV. They're sending someone to pick us up."

"When?" Arabella asked.

"7:30." Farnsworth belched and closed his eyes.

Arabella flipped up her hand and looked at the chunky watch strapped to the inside of her wrist. "It's only five o'clock! We're supposed to just sit around for the next two and a half hours?"

Farnsworth didn't respond, he didn't even move. His eyes were closed and I wasn't sure if he was dead or merely passed out. I inched forward, unsure whether I should bother to check for a pulse. I was even less sure that I wanted to touch him at all. And then I noticed that the useless lump, otherwise known as our Weapons teacher, was still breathing. At least he wasn't dead — just dead drunk and passed out.

Arabella flopped onto the curb. "If Ozzy thinks ditching us is winning him any kind of points in this whole Autumn Formal thing, he's sorely mistaken. This just might cancel out a Ravens victory," she complained, glaring at me as if it was my fault we were stranded in Baltimore with a passed out chaperone.

"I'm sure there's a good explanation," I said. But I was just as annoyed as Arabella, possibly more so.

"Doubtful. I mean, it wouldn't be so bad if we at least had something to do, but just . . . " Arabella trailed off, a dangerous gleam commandeering her blue eyes. "Poe's grave."

"Excuse me?" Sterling was as lost as me.

"Edgar Allen Poe's grave is at the Westminster Hall and Burial Ground. It's probably less than a mile away."

"So?" Sterling and I asked in unison.

"Farnsworthless is passed out," Arabella said hooking her thumb over her shoulder in the direction of the Weapons teacher. "We have over two hours to kill before our ride home gets here. When is the next time we'll be in Baltimore again with this kind of opportunity? If we catch a cab, we can be there and back in an hour. Mr. Can't-Handle-His-Liquor won't even know we're gone."

"Bad idea." Sterling shook his head.

"You mean awesome idea." Arabella was already up and brushing off the back of her skirt.

"Something could happen to him while we're gone," I argued, not really concerned for Farnsworth, but for the punishment we might face if we left him alone. Seeing some dead poet's grave wasn't worth whippings.

"I'll pay for the cab." Arabella offered.

I crossed my arms.

"I'll give you my card, you know you want it." she cooed to Sterling.

Sterling seemed to be softening up. "What do you think, Cleo?"

"No way. Bad idea," I repeated.

Arabella put her arm around me and pulled me close to whisper in my ear. "I'll let Perfect Aim take you to the Formal."

"Arabella . . . "

"Come on, it'll be fun. I promise."

A few minutes later, Arabella flagged down a cab and ushered us into the backseat.

"Where to?" asked the scruffy driver behind the wheel.

"Westminster Hall on the corner of Fayette and Green Street."

I was surprised that Arabella knew exactly where the gravesite was located.

The driver looked up into the rearview mirror so he could see his occupants. "Poe's grave? You're not up to no good are you?"

Arabella leveled a stern glare at him. "We're not paying you to ask us questions, just take us to Westminster Hall."

The driver glanced out the window. "He coming?"

Arabella followed his gaze which was fixed on a passed out, prostrate Farnsworth. "He's not with us," she answered simply, pulling the car door shut behind her.

Five minutes later, the car came to a stop in front of what looked like a church. In fact, the architecture looked a lot like that of St. Ignatius Academy, only on a much smaller scale. The front of the building had several tall, pointed arch windows set into it. In the middle was a towering structure that was nearly twice the height of the bulkier part of the building. Four spires sat atop the corners of the tower like fingertips reaching toward the sky.

Arabella leaned over. "Westminster Hall used to be a church, but the burial ground was here first. They built the church on pillars over some of the graves so now they have catacombs here," she whispered, waggling her eyebrows as if this was an exceptionally pleasant detail.

"Is that where we're going?" I asked warily. I was fine with entertaining Arabella's whim to see some poet's grave, but I wasn't at all sure I was up for going into any catacombs. The idea of being in a dark, dirty, underground graveyard frightened me more than I wanted to admit.

"Not unless you want to. Poe's grave has prime real estate." Arabella fished some cash out of her pocket and handed it over to the cab driver.

"This is only half," he growled, fanning out the bills.

"That's because I need you to wait here for us. Keep the meter running if you want. We'll only be about ten minutes."

"You can't just pay me half the fare. I'm calling the cops," he said, reaching for a cell phone.

"I wouldn't do that," Arabella warned, lifting her arm and twisting it to show him the tattoo on the inside of her forearm.

The driver looked at the mark, glared nastily at her, turned off his phone, and then turned to look out the side window. "Sophisticates," he hissed under his breath, like it was a word that didn't taste right. "I should've known."

Arabella ignored him, shuffled out of the car, and led us to the open gate and into the cemetery, which was located on the right side of the building. Immediately inside the gate was an imposing, white marble memorial. A circular medallion of a man's face was set into the marble of the monument and on the base it said "Edgar Allan Poe." Pennies were strewn all over the base of the monument. Just as I was about to ask why there were pennies all over the grave,

Arabella handed me and Sterling each a small coin before laying her own on the grave.

I held up the tiny piece of copper, inspecting it. "Why pennies?"

"Poe used to be buried in the back part of the cemetery but was moved here to be buried with his wife. He had an unmarked grave for years and in 1875 a local school teacher started this thing called Pennies for Poe to raise enough money to build him a proper monument. People still leave pennies as a sign of respect."

"So, do I make a wish or what?" Sterling asked, looking at his penny like it was a bit of dirt.

"No, you just leave it out of respect. Oh, just give it to me," Arabella snapped, snatching the penny out of his hand and placing it carefully on the base. I copied Arabella and laid down my penny as well.

We stood quietly, looking at the monument.

"All right then. Had enough?" Sterling asked. "Time to get back to the stadium before Farnsworth comes to."

"Are you kidding?" Arabella grabbed our hands, dragging us through the cemetery and around the back of the building. The light was starting to fade as the sky began to morph from pinks and oranges into deep purples. "Don't you want to see his original burial spot?"

"I didn't really want to see his current burial spot. I just wanted your player's card," Sterling admitted as she dragged him along.

We wove in and out of the ancient grave sites, making our way down a worn path, under trees, and to the back corner of the graveyard which was cloaked in too many shadows for my comfort. Soon, we were standing in front of a traditional looking headstone with a carving of a raven underneath words that said "Quoth the

Raven Nevermore."

Arabella stood there for what seemed like an eternity, staring at the tombstone that wasn't even the current resting spot of the poet anymore.

"He was an orphan, just like us," Arabella murmured.

"How did he die?" I asked.

Arabella tore her gaze from the raven. "It's kind of a mystery. He was found on the streets of Baltimore, delirious and in distress. He kept calling out the name Reynolds and the last words he spoke were, 'Lord, help my poor soul.' All of the medical documents have been lost. Some theorists think it was murder, some suicide, some cooping."

"What on earth is cooping?" Sterling asked, kicking at a pile of leaves at the base of the headstone.

Arabella turned to face Sterling. "Hard to explain, you'll have to look it up. But for the sake of simplicity, let's just say he was forced to do something he didn't want to do." Arabella turned back to the tombstone. "Just like us."

"That's all very fascinating, but I'm afraid story time is over," spoke a deep, strange voice.

I whipped around just in time to see half a dozen large men emerge from the shadows. Before I could even think about struggling, one of the men had caught me in a tight grip and another was putting something across my nose and mouth. I kicked out blindly, bucking in the strong grip of the man holding me. As a sickly, sweet, cloying scent filled my mouth and nostrils, Poe's words echoed in my thoughts. *Lord, help my poor soul.*

And then everything went black.

17

HALF-EATEN CRUST

My head was pounding before I even managed to lift my heavy eyelids. My throat was sore and there was a metallic taste thick on my tongue. I felt like I'd been licking a mound of Poe's copper pennies. As I opened my eyes, I realized that I couldn't see anything and a cold prickle of fear crept up my spine. My arms were secured behind my back with plastic ties that were cutting into my skin and I was lying sideways on something cold and gritty. It smelled like dirt.

Where am I?

I tried to work through the haze of memory. The last thing I remembered was looking at Poe's headstone in the graveyard . . .

Oh no. Not the catacombs. Please not the catacombs. Claustrophobia crashed over me in waves of suffocating panic as I kicked out frantically, terrified that I'd been entombed. I blindly thrashed and rolled, attempting to get away from the rotting remains and scattered bones that my fear had conjured all around me.

But my feet didn't make contact with walls. I wasn't buried alive. As I forced my breathing to slow, I noticed that I could make out a thin crack of light from somewhere in the distance. I wasn't actually blind after all — I was just in a dark, unlit place.

A distinct rustling nearby told me I wasn't alone. I went perfectly still, afraid to even breathe.

A grunt. "Oh, my head."

"Arabella?" I ventured.

"Yeah, it's me. God. Where are we? How long was I out?"

"I don't know, I was unconscious too." I managed to keep my voice level despite the panic that was still clutching tightly around my chest. "Sterling?" I asked.

"Yup. I'm here," he answered thickly. "Please talk quietly, my head is killing me."

"I hope that cab driver doesn't still have the meter running," Arabella muttered.

"Arabella," Sterling snarked, "I think that's the least of our problems right now."

"I know. Younglove is going to be pissed," she admitted.

"Another thing we don't have to worry about right now. Let's try concentrating on the problem at hand. Where are we? Who took us? And why?" Sterling asked.

Arabella didn't answer. Instead there was a flurry of rustling sounds and shoes scraping on dirt. I could hear Arabella grunting and moving around nearby.

"What are you doing over there?" I asked.

"I don't know about you, but I don't intend to lay here like a dead fish on a cold dirty floor. I'm trying to get my arms free." She grunted again. "Aha!" There were more rustling and scraping sounds and Arabella's voice was suddenly coming from much higher. She must have been standing. "This would be so much easier if there was a light. There has to be one somewhere."

Shuffling sounds came from somewhere near my head and I pulled my face out of the way as a whoosh of air informed me that I just missed being kicked in the head by Arabella.

"Ow!" Sterling yelled, after a thud and agitated swearing from Arabella. "You fell on me," he complained.

"If you hadn't noticed, it's dark in here and I can't see." More fumbling and cursing followed as Arabella tripped over Sterling again. "Oh. Here we go."

Light blossomed in the darkness as Arabella pulled on a string hanging from the ceiling which, as it turned out, was really low. A single, naked bulb hung from a chain, sending light swinging into the corners as it rocked back and forth.

We were in a small room with a dirt floor. The ceiling was a maze of ancient wooden beams laced with cobwebs. Dirt encrusted cinder block walls enclosed the small area, and a set of rickety stairs led upward to a closed door. There were no windows. The thin crack at the bottom of the door was where I'd seen the bit of light. There was also a small metal panel at the bottom of the door. In the corner of the room was a breaker box, a hot water heater, and a heating system. There was nothing else in the room with us. Arabella was short enough that she could stand without needing to bend over, but I knew Sterling wouldn't be so lucky.

Arabella's clothes were dusty, and her wrists were still fastened together with a plastic zip tie, even though she had managed to get her hands in front of her. Sterling was lying sideways on the ground about five feet away from me and still had his arms pinned behind his back. I started to wriggle and bend my body to get my legs through my arms like Arabella had. It wasn't as easy as I thought it would be; my feet kept getting caught in the fabric of my borrowed Ravens jersey.

Arabella briefly looked around the room and then grabbed the end of the zip tie in her mouth, wiggling it a bit, pulling it tighter, and moving it around her wrist. She lifted her hands as high over her head as she could, and brought her arms down in a quick movement. The zip ties popped right off.

"How did you do that?" I asked.

"Magic," Arabella said as she wiggled her fingers and then rubbed her wrists. "Actually, I learned it in my Tactical Threat Assessment class over the summer. We had a whole week dedicated to learning how to escape from various forms of imprisonment and capture."

I continued to stare at Arabella with my mouth hanging open. "Tactical what?"

Sterling seemed less impressed. "Great. That means you can bust us out of here, right?"

Arabella ignored him as she walked around the small room, inspecting everything.

I finally got my arms in front of me and stood up. "Show me how you did that."

Arabella was only too happy. "First you have to tighten up the cuff," she said yanking on the piece of plastic until the edges of it cut into my wrist even more.

"Ow," I hissed. "Are you sure it has to be that tight?"

"Did you not just witness my Houdini skills a moment ago? Trust me. Okay, now make sure the clasp is centered over that space between your wrists. That's right," she said, making sure I was following directions. "Now put your arms over your head. When you bring them down toward your stomach, pull your arms out in a chicken wing motion, like you're trying to pull your shoulder blades together. And don't forget to tighten your abs."

I did as I was instructed, but all I managed to do was punch myself in the stomach and nearly shear my hands off at the wrists. My cry of pain brought a look of disapproval from Arabella.

"We're not petting kittens here, we're breaking out of captivity. Do it with everything you've got. Every piece of rage, every moment of anger, every ounce of strength you have left. Think Quinnie and broken hands," Arabella encouraged.

I tried again, pulling as hard as my arms would allow and amazingly, the plastic tie popped off with only minor discomfort.

Sterling, however, was having no luck getting his long legs through the loop of his arms. His hands were still securely fastened behind his back. Frustrated, his breath puffed out loudly, lifting the long golden hair that had fallen over his forehead and into his eyes. "This is no use. Arabella, got any bright ideas how to get this thing off?"

"Break it over your ass."

"What?"

"Bend over, put your arms as high as you can, then swing them down over your backside and pull as hard as you can to the sides." She came over and positioned the tie where she wanted it on his wrists, tightening it up as she had done for me.

Sterling tried a few times and with the help of a few insults back and forth between him and Arabella, he eventually managed to break the tie on the fifth try. His wrists were red and raw but at least he was free.

Arabella checked her jeans pockets and frowned. "Either of you still have a cell phone?"

I shook my head. "I didn't bring one with me to the Academy."

Sterling checked his pockets and came up empty handed. "Damn, I just bought that phone," he complained.

"Why do you even have one?" I asked. "Who are you calling?" It's not like he had parents to call. And from what I'd experienced so far, communication with those outside of the Academy was mostly blocked anyway. I hadn't managed to get hold of Cassie via email or with the useless phone in my room.

Sterling glanced quickly at Arabella, and I thought I detected an embarrassed blush. "Hey, I've got friends besides the two of you. I call people," he argued.

I let him off the hook and didn't bring up what was obvious. He and Arabella were more than just friends, whether or not either of them would ever admit it. "What now?" I asked.

"We escape," Arabella suggested. "Through the door." She pointed to the only exit in the room.

Unsure of what lay on the other side of the door, we searched around the basement floor for some sort of weapon, a piece of wood or forgotten tool, but found nothing but dirt and useless trash. Finally, we decided to try our luck escaping, despite our lack of weapons. We crept up the stairs and my stomach was in knots wondering who or what was on the other side of the door.

Why were we being kept in a basement? Ransom? Torture? Murder?

I held my breath as Arabella gripped the old, rusted handle and tried turning the knob slowly. The door didn't budge. She then began spinning the knob forcefully, jerking it back and forth. When that produced no more success than before, Arabella began screaming and kicking the thick wood, determined to break it down with her bare hands.

No one answered. No one even told her to be quiet.

That was almost worse. Had we been left here to die? To disappear from the Program forever?

After ten minutes of us separately and collectively trying to smash down the door or pry open the small metal panel at the bottom of the door, we retreated down the stairs and huddled together on the cold, dirt floor.

"Who do you think brought us here?" I asked.

Unable to get comfortable, Sterling moved to the bottom step of the staircase and casually laid his arms over his knees. "Call me crazy, but I'm guessing the creepy men in the graveyard who were armed with chloroform."

"I know that," I said, rolling my eyes. "I mean, who are they though? Why do they want us? Do you think they're going to kill us?"

"Why would they do that?" Arabella asked. "Why go to the effort of bringing us here just to kill us?"

"Less witnesses," Sterling offered.

"No." Arabella shook her head, looking around the filthy cellar. "They want something from us."

"How do you know that?"

"Because we're Sophisticates," she said, lifting her arm and showing him the tattoo that we all had. "Somebody always wants something from us."

Suddenly a door upstairs opened and we could hear heavy footsteps crossing the floor above. We looked at each other and

Arabella motioned with a finger across her lips for us to be quiet. The sound of chairs scraping across the floor was followed by clatter that sounded like there were several people in the room above. Voices. Male voices. The owners of the voices were talking loudly, but we couldn't make out what was being said.

Arabella got up from her spot on the floor and crept like a spider, quietly and quickly, up the stairs. At the top, she sat on the step and pressed her head against the door. I followed and sat down on the top step next to her. There was no room for Sterling who stood several steps below us, glowering.

"Did you make the call?"

"Yeah."

"So what, then? We just hang out here?"

"Yup. We wait. It won't be like last time. These won't put up a fight, they'll be easy to break."

The men laughed and my eyes met Arabella's. I was wondering if I was the only one thinking of all the possible ways we could be broken. I swallowed back my fear and tried to reassure myself that we weren't completely helpless. We were Sophisticates. We were Deviants, although I wasn't sure exactly what that meant for Sterling and Arabella.

"Anyone want to order a pizza?" one of the men asked.

There was a resounding "yes" and the voices retreated to another room where we couldn't hear what was being discussed.

"Who do you think they are?" I whispered.

Arabella shrugged. "I'm more concerned with whether or not they'll give us any of that pizza. All I've eaten today is cotton candy and popcorn."

"Maybe you should ask them to order a couple extra for us. I like mushroom and green pepper," Sterling suggested.

"Good idea." Arabella began pounding on the door and before I could grab her arm to stop her, she was yelling, "Hey! Creepy dudes with the chloroform! Can we get some grub in here?"

The noise from the other room stopped momentarily, but there was no answer.

"I want some pizza, too!" she added. Arabella continued to yell out with requests, becoming more frustrated with every passing minute when they didn't answer her questions. She started out asking for food and pretty soon she was demanding to be let out. Eventually she slumped down, exhausted and dejected.

"Is that something you learned in Tactical Threat Assessment class?" Sterling wondered aloud.

Arabella's eyes narrowed. "It's important to know as much as you can about your captors."

"And you obtain this information by demanding pizza?" Sterling smiled, despite the situation.

Arabella looked away from him. "Shut up."

A while later, I awoke to the sound of metal sliding on metal and the crinkling of paper. I was curled up with Sterling and Arabella in an uncomfortable heap. We were trying to stay warm as the basement grew colder with what I assumed must be night-time temperatures. It was hard to tell what time of day it was since there were no windows.

We'd sat for hours hoping to get information from our captors and eventually decided to try to sleep. We needed to have strength for whatever was planned to be done to break us. The scraping metal sound was echoing through the silence of the room and

Arabella accidentally elbowed me as she pushed up from the ground and vaulted for the stairs. She reached the top of the stairs just as the metal panel slid shut again. She began pounding on the door.

"Who are you? What do you want? When are you going to let us out?"

When she received no answer, she picked up the white bag, which had been set on the top step through the metal panel, and carried it downstairs. She lowered herself to the floor and put the crinkled bag in the middle between us. Inside were dozens of pizza crusts — pizza crusts that had bite marks in them and had obviously been left over from our captors. And they were cold.

"That's disgusting," I said. "And they're probably poisoned or something."

"I suddenly don't have much of an appetite," Sterling added, tossing the piece he'd grabbed into the corner.

Arabella said nothing. She didn't have to. She was so furious she was shaking. After a few minutes of silence, she said, "Cleo, you know that exploding thing that you may, or may not, but probably can do?"

I picked at the seam of my jeans to avoid answering. I had a feeling I knew where this was going. I'd already considered it and discarded the idea hours ago.

Arabella wasn't deterred by my silence. "All you have to do is get rid of the door. Burn it, blow it up, whatever it is you do. What do you say?"

"No."

"Why not?"

"Because I can't control it. Maybe I could blast down the door, but there is also the very likely possibility that the best I could do is blow up the furnace or the electrical panel and then we'd be trapped down here with a fire we can't control and a door we can't open and we'd burn to death."

"But we have to try, we can't just give up," Arabella argued.

"I'm sorry, but I'm not going to risk your lives."

"Our lives are already at risk!" she screamed. It was the first time I'd seen any hint of fear in Arabella. "We have no idea what they plan to do to us."

I didn't say anything. I had plenty of ideas of what the men planned to do. I'd been obsessing over all the possible terrors for hours now.

"I wish I could blow things up," Arabella muttered.

"No, you don't, trust me. Anyway, what about you? Why don't you use your special talent?" I asked, staring Arabella down, daring her to deny the accusation.

Arabella looked steadily at me, biting the inside of her lip. Finally she answered. "Because my talent won't help us in this situation."

I was grateful that the pieces of Ozzy's story were finally coming to light, even if I didn't particularly like the story. "What is it?"

Arabella crossed her arms and stood, glaring at me. Suddenly, her wild purple hair wilted, smoothing into a blond waterfall that silkily snaked down her back. My breath caught in my throat. Arabella turned slowly as if she was modeling a dress and when she faced me again, her hair had curled up into a short brown bob, her skin had darkened so that she looked African American, and her eyes turned from her own vibrant blue to a warm brown.

"I can change my appearance," Arabella explained as her hair instantly grew out again into the purple mane she had for the game.

"Great for costume parties, but not really useful in hostage situations."

"That's amazing! Do Sterling!"

"What?" Arabella exclaimed, horrified.

"Make yourself look like Sterling," I clarified.

Arabella sighed in relief. "Oh, that's easy." She slowly exhaled and was immediately transformed into an exact replica of Sterling, only without all the wrinkled clothing.

"I can't believe it," I whispered as I reached over and touched Arabella-turned-Sterling's hair. "Do me!" I begged.

Arabella smiled and Sterling's golden, moppish hair mutated into my long, brown locks. His pale skin darkened into golden tones and the lips curved into a girly, rosebud mouth.

I felt like I was staring at my reflection and it was disorienting. "Incredible," I whispered, leaning in to get a closer look at my body double. "You look just like me, except for . . . "

"Oh, yeah." Arabella pursed her lips as she stared intently at me. Her eyes, which had changed into a dark brown color, lightened into the caramel colored brown I was used to seeing in the mirror. "I get the eyes wrong sometimes; they're hard."

"I'll trade you talents," I offered. "I'd love to be able to go from bed to beautiful in ten seconds flat. I know you said getting ready in the morning was quick, but this is so cool."

Arabella grunted. "Cool, yes. Useful, no. In fact, not even slightly helpful. This," she said, pointing to her Cleo-look-alike-face, "won't help us at all. It's a pretty crappy talent as far as skills go. I totally got the genetic alteration shaft."

"Well, there's that other thing you can do," Sterling mentioned offhandedly.

Arabella shot him a dirty look as her Cleo disguise faded away and she was once again decked out in purple hair and excessive black makeup.

"What other thing?" I demanded.

"It's nothing."

"I wouldn't say that," Sterling argued.

"You shouldn't have said anything," Arabella accused him.

"Are you keeping secrets from me?" I asked, hurt. I'd confessed about my knack for causing things to explode.

"It's not that," Arabella sighed. "It's just embarrassing."

"Do you summon squirrels?"

Sterling nearly choked he was laughing so hard. "That wouldn't be embarrassing, that would be downright awesome."

"What are you talking about?" Arabella looked like she had just eaten something rotten.

"You said your other talent was embarrassing. There was a superhero in Marvel comics called Squirrel Girl and her super power was that she could summon squirrels. I figured that would be pretty embarrassing." I smiled, happy to have riled Arabella's carefully cultivated composure.

"Summoning squirrels? Actually, that would be wicked cool. I could think of all sorts of things to do with an army of squirrels," Sterling mused dreamily.

"You two are impossible," Arabella complained. "It's like you're totally oblivious to the fact that we're prisoners."

"We're not oblivious, we just haven't thought of a good plan yet. So, tell me what the other thing is that you can do." I pressed.

Arabella sighed. "This other talent, it's pretty useless too. That's why I don't like to talk about it. I'm what you might call . . . flexible." With a resigned look, she reached out to the side and her arm stretched, flattened, and elongated until it had reached the corner of the room. She picked up the chewed piece of crust that Sterling had thrown, and then her arm shrunk and reformed until it was back to its normal shape. She was holding the crust, looking at it with disgust.

"Wow. That's impressive," I praised. When Arabella scoffed, I added, "Always able to reach things on the top shelf even though you're only five foot nothing."

Arabella was not amused. "I knew I shouldn't have shown you."

"Come on, don't be so melodramatic. It's a good skill," I encouraged. "I just have one question."

Arabella raised her eyebrows as if to say, "Yes?"

"If you can change the shape and size of your body, why didn't you just shrink your arm so you could slip your hands out of the plastic handcuffs?"

"What fun would that have been?" Arabella shot back, as if it was the stupidest question she'd ever heard. When I responded by shaking my head, Arabella continued. "Anyway, to prove my point, I have no useful skills with which to get us out of here. And Sterling's supersonic speed won't help us much either unless we get the door open. So, we're back to square one, how do we get rid of that door?" she asked, hopefully and suggestively.

I pretended I didn't know what Arabella actually wanted.

We brainstormed for hours, and then Arabella started banging on the door again, demanding a bathroom break. When no one answered, she was finally forced into the humiliation of squatting in the corner behind the furnace. We heard a television come on upstairs and I was wondering if we would get any sort of meal, or at least water. Nothing had been sent down since the pizza crusts and by the sounds of the television, Monday Night Football was coming on. We'd already been in the basement for 24 hours. I was hungry and was starting to feel lethargic. Too much longer like this and we wouldn't have a fighting chance to protect ourselves when the men came to break us.

"I've got an idea. I can't believe I didn't think of this before. I got a 100% in Tactical Threat Assessment and I'm just NOW thinking of the solution. I blame it on lack of caffeine." Arabella was pulling on a strand of purple hair.

Sterling was lying on his back, his arm behind his head, attempting to sleep. "Are you back to the exploding door idea? I think we've ditched that one a dozen times already."

"Cleo ditched it, I still think it's the best chance we have. But since she refuses, I say we start the hostage negotiation process."

"The what?"

"Hostage. Negotiation. Process. Since the initial assessment has proven that we don't know who took us or why we've been taken, and since they refuse to engage us in actual negotiations, I suggest we take away their basic needs."

"That's a great idea," Sterling piped in. "Or at least it would be if we weren't . . . oh I don't know . . . hostages trapped in a basement!" It was the first time he'd raised his voice, but it was apparent that Arabella was stressing him out.

"How long will they last without water, electricity, and heat?" she mused. "I say we take it away. At the very least, they'll probably talk to us. When I was in the corner going to the bathroom, I noticed that the electrical panel is back there, along with the main valve for the water. I think it's time for lights out," she said proudly.

"If they're without power, that means we won't have light down here either," Sterling reminded her.

"Not true. I can turn off everything but the basement. However, I'm going to turn the lights off down here too because it would be too much of an advantage for them if they could see down here. So, all the lights will go off. Eventually, I think they'll have to open that door." Arabella looked excitedly between Sterling and me.

"What do you think, Cleo?" Sterling asked.

I didn't like the idea of making our captors angry, but it also was clear that the men had no intention of opening the door any time soon, either to let us out or check on us. I shrugged, "I like it better than the exploding door idea."

Arabella grinned wickedly. "Let's start the negotiations then."

We briefly strategized our plan of attack. We knew that all six of our captors weren't upstairs since we'd heard several of them leave earlier. From the muffled conversation we could hear through the door, it sounded as if there were two men in the house watching television. Two was much more manageable than six. I started to feel a little hopeful that we might actually have a chance of getting free.

Sterling and I were crouching on the stairs, a few steps from the top, one on either side of the metal slot in the door. We knew the men would probably be too smart to open the door without at least peeking through the slot first. It would probably be our only chance. Arabella was at the bottom of the stairs, her arm stretched across the room to the electrical panel, ready to throw the switch. Once Sterling and I were settled in, Sterling nodded to Arabella. My stomach was in turmoil. I didn't know whether it was nerves, excitement, or hunger, but I felt like I was going to throw up. I heard a distinctive click as Arabella flicked the switch and the lights went off.

No electricity, no light. It was our only hope.

The cries of outrage were instantaneous. Apparently, the men were not happy to lose the Monday Night Football game. They were stumbling around and I could hear them arguing about where the flashlights were kept as they tripped over furniture. One of them wanted to come down and tie us up again so he could get the game back on. The other one wanted to wait for the others to come back.

"They're just kids, no threat at all. I don't know what we're waiting for anyway, we should just get it over with."

"We do what we're told. We wait."

"This is bullshit. I'm not missing the game."

"Man, don't do that."

Footsteps settled outside the door and the metal slot slid open. A flashlight ventured through the opening and there was an outline of a man's head behind it. Faster than I thought possible, Sterling's hand shot through the opening, pulling the man's arm through all the way. As Sterling wrestled the arm to the side, there was a snap that sounded suspiciously like a piece of wood cracking. From the sound of the screams coming from the man who was pulled halfway through the metal slot, I assumed it was his bone snapping in half. Despite the pain he probably was in, the man was violently screaming and struggling, trying to pull his arm back through the opening.

Unsure of how to help Sterling who was holding on to the man's arm, I reached through the hole and punched the man in the face. The blow slightly dazed him and he stopped moving. The hand

Sterling had trapped finally relaxed, causing the flashlight to roll down the steps and onto the floor where it was promptly picked up by Arabella at the bottom of the stairs.

The second man on the other side of the door attempted to pull his friend out of Sterling's grip, but it was no use. He only managed to further wrench his friend's broken arm which resulted in more strangled cries of pain. The second man finally gave up and the man in Sterling's grip stayed still, still whimpering. I could hear the second man walking throughout the house, flipping over furniture and making a racket. I couldn't decide if he was just angry and trying to decide what to do or if he was looking for something. The thought that he might have a weapon, a deadly one at that, made my heart race. Sterling held on tightly to the mangled arm.

The footsteps returned. "Let him go."

"Not until you let us out of here," Sterling shot back.

"You brats are gonna pay for this." The lock rattled and then the door was pushed open forcefully, crushing Sterling against the wall and bending the first man's arm back at an even more awkward angle. Sterling didn't let go and the trapped man didn't stop screaming. I couldn't see much about the second man except that he was armed with a taser and he was aiming it at me.

I started to back down the stairway just as something whizzed past my face. It was Arabella's arm and she was still standing at the bottom of the stairs. She grabbed the armed captor by the shirt and yanked him down the short flight of steps. He tumbled awkwardly down head first, but was still breathing and moaning in pain, when he landed in a heap at Arabella's feet. She picked up the taser, aimed it at him, and without hesitation, she pulled the trigger. Two pins fired out of the barrel and embedded themselves into the man's back. He jerked and tensed sporadically as the taser gun made strange clicking sounds.

"That's for threatening my friends," Arabella said, tossing the taser to the side after the man stopped jerking. "And for giving us half eaten crusts," she added as she used her foot to roll him over onto his back. "Let's go before anyone else shows up," she said.

Sterling let go of the first guy's arm, which was a mangled mess, and opened the door the rest of the way before dragging the man down the steps and laying him next to the guy that Arabella had zapped. The second guy, who looked like he had at least one broken bone, lay there on the floor, cradling his arm, making no effort to stop Sterling as he stepped over him. Arabella squatted down next to the unconscious man that she had tased and reached into his pockets.

"What are you doing?" Sterling snapped.

A little frown tugged at Arabella's mouth and she reached into the other pocket. Triumphantly, she held up a silver phone and stuck it in her back pocket. She then led us up the stairs, using the flashlight to pick her way through the darkness.

When we reached the top of the stairs, Arabella flicked the light both ways down the hallway to make sure we were alone. Sterling shut the basement door and slid the bolt in place. He also closed the metal panel and locked it.

Arabella located the front door and from the little I could see from the beam of her light, it appeared we were in a small townhouse. A decrepit one. The distance from the basement door to the front door was probably no more than 15 feet, but it felt like the Grand Canyon to me. Anything could be hiding in the darkness around us. From our earlier assessment, we'd been fairly certain there wasn't anyone else in the house, but we weren't positive. We crept across the room as quickly and quietly as we could. Sterling reached for the doorknob.

Just as he was about to turn the knob, a key was inserted into the lock from the outside and we watched in horror as the door began to open. Arabella turned, grabbing us by the sleeves and pulling us down the hallway toward the back of the house as two men entered through the front door.

"Why are all the lights out? I thought you guys were watching the game."

With a few unsuccessful flicks of the light switch coupled with Arabella's insistent cries of, "Hurry up!" it didn't take long for the man in the doorway to realize that the retreating figures in the darkness were the same ones that were supposed to be in the basement.

"Hey!" he shouted, running after us, his companion close on his heels.

Arabella pointed to the back door and Sterling lurched forward, yanked it open, and raced down the stairs, pulling Arabella with him. I swung the door shut behind me as I came out of the house last, hoping it would slow the men down. Just as my feet touched the grass, I heard the men reach the door, ramming into it in their haste. Sterling and Arabella were fumbling with a locked gate in a six-foot wooden fence that enclosed the small back yard.

We were going to be caught again. After all we'd been through, after all we'd managed to do in the last ten minutes, we were going to be caught and thrown into the basement again. I had a feeling that this time, there would be a punishment for what we'd done to the first two men.

That familiar burn of anger bubbled up through me and I could feel the heat building and spreading through my body. I heard the door finally open and when I glanced over my shoulder, I saw a taser pointed in our direction.

I wasn't sure which target made me angrier, that of my friends or myself, but the fury was there, threatening to overflow and burn everything in sight. I focused, released the energy, and the door and most of the wall surrounding it exploded. The explosion caused the men to be thrown back inside the house.

Sterling and Arabella stopped and turned to watch, in awe or fear I wasn't sure, as flames lashed across the floor and stairs. Brick and mortar fell off in jagged pieces and glass clattered to the ground from the windows that had been blown out.

I ignored the revulsion rising through my chest, ran back toward the steps to grab a trash can, and pulled it over to the fence. Using the can as a step stool, we hauled ourselves over the fence and into the alley.

And then we ran.

18

NIGHTMARES AND BEDFELLOWS

Once over the fence, we found ourselves in a sinister looking alleyway that was littered with liquor bottles, trash, and furry lumps that looked suspiciously like rat carcasses. We ran down the alley to the next cross street. We were on North Port Street which was little more than a large alley itself. It was dark out and the lack of street lights meant that we were at the mercy of Arabella's filched flashlight to find our way through the streets.

"I know where we are," Arabella said looking at the street sign. "We're still in Baltimore and I know where to go." She started running down North Port Street, crossing over Orleans Street, with me and Sterling following. We'd only run a few blocks and I was out of breath already. I was surprised at the lack of traffic we encountered as we darted across streets.

"Where is everybody?" I asked breathlessly.

"This area isn't what it used to be," Arabella answered between choppy breaths. "Let's just say we aren't in the best part of town.

It's no wonder no one heard us screaming in the basement, or if they did, they knew better than to care."

After three blocks, we reached a wide, open grassy area. "Patterson Park," Arabella informed us. She kept running as if the devil were on her heels. She ran diagonally across the grass to the right side of the park where a tall building resembling a pagoda stretched into the night. Arabella darted up the set of flared steps at the base of the pagoda. Before I could ask what was going on, she punched her elbow through one of the small panes of glass in the door, reached in through the jagged edges, and turned the handle.

"In here, quick," Arabella hissed. Sterling and I followed without question and Arabella shut the door behind us before pushing us to the floor. We crouched below the edges of the windows, hoping to stay undetected.

"What are we doing here?" I wanted to keep running. I felt like we were trapping ourselves by hiding out in a small building in a wide open expanse of park property.

Arabella reached into the back pocket of her jeans and pulled out the phone she'd taken from the man with the broken arm. "Hiding and calling reinforcements." She began punching in a phone number. "That's weird."

"What?" I asked, peeking over the edge of the window ledge to see if we'd been followed.

"St. Ignatius's phone number is already in here."

"How do you know?"

"When I keyed in the number, the identification bar said 'SI.' There would be no identification unless they had saved the number into the phone. Why would the Academy's number be in the phone of one of our captors?"

256

"Maybe they placed a ransom call," I guessed.

"Not from this phone. It would've been too easy for the Program to track."

"Maybe they just like to have their enemies on speed dial," Sterling joked.

"Maybe," Arabella agreed shakily. Her finger hovered over the phone. "You know, we don't have to call them." She turned to look at Sterling. "We could run."

He shook his head as he fidgeted with a hole in the knee of his jeans. "I won't do that again."

Arabella's lips pressed into a thin line and she nodded her head once before pressing the call button and putting the phone to her ear. I looked around our hiding spot, which was actually quite an intriguing and beautiful building. It was made mostly of glass windows and when I looked up, the spiral staircase in the middle of the pagoda reminded me of a conch shell as it twisted up into the ceiling, which was at least 50 feet above us. I wondered what a strange little building like this was doing in the middle of a park in Baltimore. I wondered who the men were that had taken us and what they'd wanted. And I wondered why the Academy's phone number was stored in the phone of one of our captors.

Absentmindedly, I tucked the stray clump of hair behind my ear. None of the answers I came up with made me feel any better.

An hour later, the phone rang and it soon made its way to Arabella's ear. "Hello." She got up on her knees and peered out of the window. "Yes, I see you. We're coming."

A short dash toward Patterson Park Avenue and Sterling, Arabella, and I were shuffling into the back seat of a black Academy

SUV. I didn't recognize the driver, but I wasn't surprised to see Twyla Younglove in the passenger seat. Somehow, I knew my mentor would be the one to fetch us home.

Younglove looked over her shoulder into the back seat. "Any injuries?"

"No ma'am," we answered, almost in unison.

"Very well, then. Rest on the way back. We'll talk about this tomorrow." She looked pointedly at the driver and I got the impression that whatever needed to be said, Younglove didn't intend to discuss it in front of the driver. "The phone," she said, stretching her hand back over her shoulder. Arabella put the stolen phone in Younglove's hand, careful not to touch her dry, brittle skin.

And that was it.

It was a quiet ride home. Younglove didn't press for details or discipline us for leaving Farnsworth drunk and passed out on a bench in the middle of the city. She didn't yell at us for taking off in a cab or for getting in trouble. The silence was more unsettling than an interrogation or punishment would have been. It gave me time to think about the fact that I'd been kidnapped and held prisoner by six men and I still didn't know why. I hadn't been physically injured or abused, but now that I was removed from the situation, I realized that either of those things could have happened at any time and I was very lucky to have come out of the ordeal only mildly hungry and slightly filthy. I could have been beaten, raped, or killed. I was lucky.

The fear of what could have been finally seemed to settle over me and I shivered uncontrollably. Sterling mistook the shivering as a reaction to being cold instead of what it really was — immense fear and relief. He reached up to the ceiling of the SUV to turn up the heat in the back seat and then instinctively put his arms around me and Arabella, drawing us in to his shoulders. I hid my face in his dirty, yet comfortably wrinkled, shirt to hide the tears that had forced their way out.

I hated feeling weak and scared. I hated crying. I hated feeling such a lack of control over my life. I pretended I was sleeping, hoping that Sterling didn't realize his shirt sleeve was now wet.

It was almost midnight by the time we got back to the Academy.

"Feel free to take showers and clean up before going to bed; you all look a mess. I'll have sandwiches brought to your rooms. Tomorrow morning instead of the morning run, I'd like you to come to my office for a debriefing." And with that, Younglove was out of the SUV, up the stairs, and through the front doors. She didn't seem angry or relieved or disappointed. She didn't even act like anything out of the ordinary had happened.

"Debriefing?" Sterling repeated. "She's acting like we were on a mission instead of victims of a kidnapping. Debriefing?"

"I'm tired," Arabella sighed. "Let's worry about it tomorrow."

A shower had never felt so good. I stood under the water until it started to run cold and my fingers were wrinkled beyond recognition. I shimmied into my pajamas, for once not even caring that they were Academy issued plaid. I trudged down the quiet hall to my room and slipped inside.

I nearly screamed when I saw a figure sprawled out on my bed. It was Ozzy. Again. Even though I managed to stifle a bloodcurdling shriek, the surprise of seeing someone in my bed caused me to drop my bucket of toiletries. The soap and shampoo rolled across the floor and under the bed, but I didn't attempt to retrieve them. I just stared at Ozzy, a storm of conflicting emotions raging inside me. For a brief moment, I'd thought it was one of the men come to take me back again.

Ozzy hopped up and crossed the room to stand in front of me. "Sorry, I didn't mean to scare you. I came to see you as soon as I got back. I was worried when you weren't here. But I saw the sandwich," he said pointing to the plate that Younglove had promised would be sent to my room, "and figured you must be coming back soon, so I thought I'd just wait." He reached up and tucked a wet strand of my hair behind my ear, his hand slowly tracing down my neck and to my shoulder. "I missed you." He leaned in, hoping to find my lips.

I avoided the kiss by stepping away from the door and out of his reach. "You left us. You said you'd be right back," I said testily, stooping down to retrieve my scattered toiletries.

Ozzy's playfulness eroded with the accusation. "I'm sorry. I figured Younglove explained."

"No, she didn't. I didn't see her again until tonight." I bit my lower lip, trying not to say anything I'd regret. Even though I knew that I'd made the decision to go along with Arabella's idea, deep down in my heart, there was a part of me that blamed Ozzy for what happened. If he'd never left, we wouldn't have had to wait for a car, and Arabella wouldn't have convinced us to go to Poe's grave.

Ozzy shook his head slightly, running his hand through his hair. "No wonder you're upset; I thought she would've told you what happened. I thought I was going to be right back, that Younglove just needed to discuss something with me. Turns out it was an emergency, I had to leave right away."

"To do what, exactly?" My tone was sharp and I was spitting

the words out.

Ozzy tilted his head and blinked, confused by my anger. "A job. I had to find . . ." He paused. "I had to track someone down."

I crossed my arms and looked down at the floor. I knew it was ridiculous, I knew Ozzy didn't have any say in the matter, but I felt as if he'd chosen the job over me. Not that we were dating or anything. Not really. It's not like we were a couple, but he had invited me to go to the game with him. And that was a date, wasn't it? And then he just left me there. And then everything had gone horribly wrong.

"And it couldn't wait?" I asked, biting the inside of my lip to keep back the self pitying tears.

"I was . . ." Ozzy seemed like he was going to say something and then decided against it. "I'm sorry, Cleo. I didn't want to leave. I would much rather have stayed and watched the game with you. I've told you this is what it's like for me. I don't get to choose when and where I go, as much as it seems that way to everyone around here. I'm more under the control of the Program than anyone else. Please, don't be angry." He reached up and lifted my chin so that I was looking at him. "Forgive me?"

I could feel my anger evaporating. Why did he have this effect on me? As much as I wanted to stay angry and blame him, I couldn't. "I don't know." I tightened the grip of my folded arms, determined to hold on to some of the bitterness, even if it was irrational.

"Please?" he begged, running his thumb along my jawline, allowing his fingers to trace lightly along my neck. I was putty in his hands.

I looked up into his eyes, resigned to give him another chance, but a chance he'd have to earn back. "You have a lot of work to do to make it up to me," I explained. "And not just me, Sterling and

Arabella, too. You're in so much trouble." I jammed my finger into his chest.

A smile jerked at the corners of his mouth when he realized that he was about to be let off the hook. Even if he had to grovel to get back into the good graces of me and my friends, he was still off the hook. He grabbed my hand, which was still angrily prodding him in the chest, and lifted it to his mouth to kiss it. "I look forward to it."

"Great. Now, if you don't mind, it's been a long day and I'm tired." I yanked my hand out of his, walked over to the bed, and crawled under the covers. "Do you mind hitting the lights on your way out?"

Ozzy grinned as he walked toward the bed and sat on the edge of it. "Come now, is that any way to say hello? I'm beginning to think you didn't miss me at all."

"You're still in trouble and I'm exhausted." I rolled over, putting my back to him. Part of me wanted to tell him about what happened, to have him hold me and tell me I was safe now and that everything was going to be all right. But at the same time, I wasn't sure I wanted to relive everything again so soon. I was afraid if I told him, I'd start crying and he'd think I was weak. And being weak was the last thing I wanted to be. All I wanted to do right now was fall into the oblivion of deep sleep and deal with it later.

Ozzy leaned back against the headboard and gently stroked my wet hair. "That's fine. I'll just sit here and watch you sleep for a while."

"Because that's not creepy or stalkerish at all."

He laughed. "I just want to be near you, what's wrong with that?"

I was quiet and he continued to gently stroke my hair, softly tracing patterns on my shoulder with his fingers. I felt myself relax, the fear of the last few days finally starting to fade as I allowed Ozzy's touch to comfort me. I tried to push my thoughts into the recesses of my mind, but they were as heavy and immovable as a mountain, demanding my attention. Men coming out of the shadows of a graveyard . . . waking up in a dark basement . . . a taser pointed at me . . . running down unfamiliar and dark city streets. I marveled at how confident and bold Arabella and Sterling had been. And all I could think about was how scared and unsure I'd been the whole time.

I went over the events again in my mind, trying to figure out what I could have done differently. The more I thought about it, however, the more I realized that being scared wasn't the same as being weak. When push came to shove, when my friends were threatened, I did what I needed to do to keep them safe. Even though it was something I'd promised myself I wouldn't do again, I did it to help those I cared about. Yes, I was scared, but that wasn't the same as being weak. Bravery is all about doing something you have to do even when you're afraid.

I kept telling myself I'd been brave. That was the only way my mind could tackle the haunting memories that seemed to be on a continual mental loop. Memories of an arm being yanked through a small metal door and broken by Sterling. Memories of a man being dragged down a set of steps and tased by Arabella. Memories of an explosion ripping open brick, mortar, and glass as the bodies of two men were thrown back into the gaping hole of the house. I'd done that. And honestly, it scared me.

I didn't tell Ozzy to go away and I allowed myself to take comfort in his presence. He was here and I realized I wanted his arms around me, that I needed him to say the words that would tell me everything was going to be all right. I needed him to tell me I wasn't a monster, that I was brave, even if I was scared of myself.

"You weren't there when I needed you," I admitted quietly.

"I'm here now." He gently twirled a piece of my hair around his finger. I let out a shuddering breath as he pushed the hair away from my skin and kissed the small crevice where my neck and shoulder met.

There was no way I was going to be able to go to sleep without talking to him about what had happened. He needed to know what I'd been through and I needed his strength.

"But, you weren't there when the men took us. You invited us into Baltimore, you left us, and you weren't there when they took us and locked us up," I accused.

Ozzy went perfectly still. "What?"

"Sterling, Arabella, and I were abducted, locked in a basement, and left for dead. And you weren't there."

He grabbed my shoulders and flipped me over so he could look into my face. The look in his eyes was the exact opposite of what I was hoping for from him. "Who took you?"

"I don't know. Six men."

"What did they do to you?" he asked, his eyes roaming over me, searching for wounds that weren't there.

"They tied us up and left us in a basement."

"How did you get away?" he asked hesitantly. His head tilted to the side as he glared at me. "You didn't use your powers did you?"

I bit my bottom lip as it started to tremble. Tears of shame filled my eyes, blurring my vision and I nodded slightly.

"You used your powers to get away? All of you?" He sounded

disappointed. Angry even. He had warned me not to use my powers. Of course he was disappointed.

I lowered my eyes, afraid to speak, afraid to admit what I'd done. This wasn't the reaction I was hoping for. Maybe bravery was the wrong word for my actions.

Ozzy nodded tightly and then stood. "Cleo, I . . . " He raked his hands through his hair as he cast his eyes around the room, refusing to look at me. "I'm sorry, I've gotta go." And without another word, he was gone.

I was left feeling alone and ashamed. I'd used my powers against those men. And not because the Program told me to, I made the decision all on my own. I made a monstrous decision. Telling Ozzy what I'd done was stupid. I didn't feel better, I felt worse. Much worse.

Half an hour later, I was still waging an internal battle on whether I wanted to actually go to sleep. My body was arguing that it needed to get some rest, but now that Ozzy was gone and I was alone, I was afraid to go to sleep with only my thoughts for company. A soft knock came at the door and I desperately hoped it was Ozzy. When I cracked the door open, I was shocked to see Arabella dressed in Academy plaid, her hair limp and black. No crazy hair, no wild makeup, just Arabella looking as emotionally stripped and raw as I felt.

"I don't want to sleep alone," Arabella admitted, fiddling with the hem of her t-shirt. "Do you mind if I crash with you?"

I opened the door and Arabella surprised me with a big, sniffling hug. I squeezed her back, relieved to not have to spend the night alone. I realized that most of Arabella's attitude was for show — she was just as distressed about the kidnapping incident as I was. For some reason, this made me feel a lot better, a lot stronger.

Once we were settled into my bed, back to back, Arabella's attitude seemed to come back to life. "Your feet are freezing cold."

"Cold feet, warm heart," I recited.

"Well, keep them on your side of the bed, Frosty. Haven't you ever heard of socks?"

"Who wears socks to bed?"

"Sterling does . . . " Arabella trailed off.

I felt the strange sensation of a smile spread across my face. After all we'd been through, I could still smile. Weird. "He does, does he? And how would you know?"

"He told me."

"Mm-hm."

"You don't know what you think you know," Arabella promised.

We both lay quiet for a few minutes — either avoiding sleep or the topic we were both afraid to talk about, I wasn't sure. Maybe it was a little of both.

"Arabella?"

"Hm?"

"How do you know so much about Baltimore?"

"Cleo, I'm a Vanguard reject. I know a lot about a lot of things."

"Yeah, but you're like an expert on all things Baltimore. Why?"

Arabella sighed and was quiet for so long I was afraid she'd fallen asleep. "My parents were from Baltimore."

"Your parents? How do you know that? We're not supposed to know anything about our parents."

"I asked and Lawless told me."

"I thought you said you didn't care about your donors."

Arabella rolled over so that she was lying on her back and staring at the ceiling, hands folded over her chest. "I guess I lied."

Morning came so quickly, I didn't feel like I'd slept at all. I envied the ease with which Arabella got ready. Her hair was already colored and styled before I even finished brushing out all of the tangles in my own hair. Of course, for Arabella, she merely had to create the thought and the result was instantaneous. My morning ritual was usually an all out civil war with my hair, which most often ended in a truce in the form of a ponytail.

We met Sterling down in the lobby after everyone else had already gone outside for the run. We weren't eager to answer the questions that would most certainly be asked about our absence, so it was just easier to avoid our fellow cadets altogether. We weren't even sure what we were allowed to say. Although relieved to miss out on the morning run for the third day in a row, a sense of unease settled over us as we trudged our way through the deserted corridors.

When we reached the door to Younglove's office, Arabella turned to Sterling, her hand poised to knock. "Still think it was a good idea not to run?"

He shrugged. "In their eyes, that's exactly what we did anyway. Leaving Farnsworth on a bench and taking a cab won't exactly win us any brownie points," Sterling answered truthfully. He left unsaid what we all knew, that even though it was Arabella's idea, we were all at fault. "I wonder what happened to Farnsworth?"

"Who cares?" Arabella retorted. "I don't regret what we did, I'm only sorry we got caught."

Arabella knocked on the door and Younglove's muffled voice

invited us into her office. "Please sit," she said without looking up, indicating the three chairs set out in front of her desk. The chairs were hard, wooden, and nothing but uncomfortable right angles — exactly the opposite of relaxing. Not that any of us would have been able to relax anyway.

Younglove finished writing something on the paper in front of her, allowing us to sit in awkward silence, letting our imaginations run wild with possibilities. She finally set down her pen, propped her elbows on the desk, and laced her fingers together. I could have sworn that the sound of Younglove's skin brushing against itself sounded like autumn leaves blowing over each other in the wind. I desperately wanted to get the woman some decent moisturizer.

"So, tell me what happened on Sunday after Osbourne and I left the game."

We'd already decided that Arabella would do the explaining. Not only was it her idea to go see Poe's grave, but she had a flair for the dramatic and if anyone could get us out of the mess we were in, it was Arabella. If she could keep her temper in check.

"After you left, Professor Farnsworth became increasingly intoxicated," Arabella began.

Younglove put her hand up to stop Arabella. "I'm well aware that Octavius Farnsworth is a worthless drunk. We found him on the bench outside of the stadium, passed out. It matters little to me whether he got there of his own accord or whether you dragged him out. I'm more concerned with what happened after that. Where you went, who you met, and why you were missing for nearly two days."

Sufficiently humbled, Arabella gave Younglove the facts of our visit to Poe's grave, our unexpected captivity, and our lucky escape.

When Arabella finished, Younglove smiled. "Excellent. It appears that you have passed this training exercise rather easily." She reached for a folder on the edge of her desk and opened it, preparing to write. "I'll have to wait to talk to the Hounds to confirm the events and details, but I'd say it was a successful exercise, especially for the first time."

"What do you mean, training exercise?" I asked.

A smug smile spread across Younglove's thin lips. "Well, what did you think it was?"

"We were kidnapped," I pointed out.

"For what purpose? There was no request for ransom. You were not physically harmed. You were merely restrained."

"We were taken by force," I persisted.

Younglove looked thoughtful. "I suppose technically you were abducted — taken by force and without your permission. Although that matters little. I have to admit that I was concerned that the original plan called for the Hounds to detain you outside the stadium where there might be witnesses. Thankfully, you removed yourselves to a less public space, which made it much easier. It all worked out for the best."

"The men in the graveyard with the chloroform were Hounds?" Sterling asked, dumbfounded.

"Of course. Who did you think they were?"

"But the Hounds are part of the Program, they're on our side," Sterling explained. "We could have killed them. I broke one of their arms." Guilt darkened his usually bright blue eyes.

"And he has already been mended," Younglove countered with an unconcerned wave of her hand. "Although," she added, looking at me, "the two men who were caught in Clementine's explosion are still recovering."

Still recovering? What had I done to them? I wanted to scream. I'd gravely hurt not one person, but two. It didn't matter that at the time I thought they were enemies, in the end they were Sophisticates. They were Mandates. It could've been any of my friends or classmates. It could've been the Homework Harpies.

"A fake abduction? Why would you do that to us? Why would you do that to them?" I barely got the words out. My emotions were a tangle of regret, sadness, and fear of my own capabilities. And I had thought I was being brave. What a joke.

"Let's be adults about this," Younglove said firmly. "I'm well aware that Osbourne has notified each of you of your capabilities as he was asked to do. All three of you know that you are not just genetically altered like every other Sophisticate, you have been genetically modified. Special abilities have been added to your genetic makeup. You're part of the Deviant Dozen, a group of Sophisticates who have been gifted with unusual abilities." There was something very menacing about the way she said gifted. "You were brought here to the Academy when you started to exhibit those skills and we've been waiting patiently for you to deviate them. Or should I say, master them. Some of you have been quite slow in this process, so we felt it necessary to put you in a situation to encourage you to harness and use these abilities. We figured a staged capture and imprisonment might encourage you to initiate your skills and put you on the path for deviation."

So that's what our captors had been waiting for. They'd been waiting for us to make a move, or break down and give up. That's why the Hounds didn't talk to us or feed us, they didn't need to. All they needed was to encourage us to initiate some sort of bid for freedom.

I wanted to reach across the desk and smack that stupid, knowing smirk off Younglove's face. Encourage? That wasn't an acceptable word for what had been done to us.

"Who is we?" I managed.

"Dean Overton, myself, and the leader of the Deviant Dozen, among others."

"The leader of the Deviant Dozen? As in Ozzy? You mean he knew about this?" I struggled to keep myself from screaming the words. Ozzy hadn't said anything last night about the kidnapping being a training exercise. Actually, to be honest, he started to say something a few times and changed his mind.

"Osbourne is familiar with our training exercises. He has been the subject of several and has overseen those of the other members of the Dozen."

Once I considered the facts, the more it made sense that Ozzy would've known about the training exercise. He knew everything about me. He'd seen my file. He had access to all sorts of Program secrets. He convinced me to come to Baltimore and then left me and my friends there to be part of Younglove's training exercise.

How had I not seen this? His affections toward me must have been part of the ruse to get us to Baltimore. As soon as I admitted to him that I'd used my power, he left. Arabella and Sterling were right; I never should've trusted him. If he cared about me as much as he kept insisting, he should've warned me. To bait me with platitudes of affection and then lure me into a traumatic situation forcing me to use skills I didn't want to use — it was unforgivable. It was worse than the fact that he looked at my file and knew all of my secrets. It was worse than ditching me on a pseudo-date. It was cruel.

"So, he knew? He knew what was going to happen to us before he left," I muttered. "Did he even have a job to do, or was that a lie too?"

"Of course he had a job to do. Osbourne was sent to track down a runaway University student. I believe you know her," Younglove looked at me. "Cassandra Dracone."

I felt like I was choking as my throat closed in a moment of panic. "Cassie ran away?" Ozzy's tracking mission was for Cassie, and he didn't tell me that either.

Younglove nodded. "She was tracked to Baltimore and since we were in the area, Osbourne and I were dispatched to find her and return her to the University. And once we arrived at the University to return her, he was directed to help the Hounds escort a few Mandates to their new Academy. Boys by the names of Justin, Bradley, and Samuel Dracone. I believe you know them as well?" Younglove's smile was slippery, ugly, and heavy on her mouth.

The Homework Harpies. Ozzy was with them, too. Cassie and the Harpies were the only family I'd ever really had and he didn't tell me he'd been with them. How could he not tell me? Because he's not actually your friend, I reminded myself. He doesn't really care about you, he's just another tool of the Program. I should have known better. Arabella and Sterling tried to warn me.

I was speechless. I couldn't think of a single thing to say, at least nothing that wouldn't get me into trouble. Sterling and Arabella seemed just as lost for words. Even though they didn't know who Cassie, Justin, Brad, and Sam were, they could see that I did, and that Ozzy's involvement with them was upsetting me.

"Now then," Younglove continued. "As I was saying, the training exercise was a tremendous success. I believe now that you are aware of the sort of situations you could be facing were you to be captured by the enemy; you may be more inclined to work a little harder on your deviations." She rifled through the papers in the folder in front of her. "To that end, in place of your first class after lunch, from now on you will be reporting to me for a Deviation Workshop." She handed each of us a paper which showed our revised schedules. "You're excused," she smiled humorlessly.

19

CROSS AND RED DRESS

I was numb, barely aware of where I was walking.

"Who are Cassie, Justin, Brad, and Sam?" Arabella asked softly.

"My friends." The backpack over my shoulder felt like it was pulling me into the stony floor of the hallway. I was ready to let it. I was so tired of all the lies, the loss, and the lack of choice. I was tired of the Program. I'd put my trust in Ozzy, against my better judgment, and he took that trust and shredded it into a tattered mess, scattering the remains of my life as if it were nothing. Justin, Brad, and Sam were gone, shuttled off to one of the other Mandate Academies, and Cassie was all alone now. Was that why she tried to run away? Did she know she was going to be left alone? "Cassie was my like a sister to me."

Arabella put her hand on my arm. "I'm sure she's okay. Cassie is back where she belongs."

"She belongs here."

"She's a Mandate?"

"No," I said, meeting Arabella's concerned gaze. "She's part of the Deviant Dozen. She's number twelve."

At breakfast, Sterling, Arabella, and I were treated like a communicable disease. No one, not even Theo, had the courage to come interrogate us. That lack of courage didn't extend to the surrounding conversations about us, though. I easily overheard at least a dozen assumptions being made about why the three of us and Farnsworth had been missing yesterday. Quinnie was loudly suggesting to anyone that would listen that Farnsworth had met an untimely demise because of me.

"I heard Ozzy has to take over the Weapons class for Farnsworth," Quinnie persisted, pleased to be the center of attention. "I mean, she can barely touch a gun without having convulsions. I bet she thought if she got rid of Farnsworth, she wouldn't have to go to class anymore," Quinnie speculated to her table of eager listeners.

"Don't listen to her," Arabella warned. "She's just glad everyone is talking about you and Farnsworth instead of the beating her team took on the track Saturday night."

"Gossip is always more fun than the truth," I agreed. "Do you think she knows what really happened?"

Arabella shrugged. "Even if she did, she's not going to tell anyone. Younglove would probably give her another set of whippings. I'm pretty sure the rest of the cadets aren't supposed to know we're different. Besides, if she told the truth, everyone would know you were kidnapped and held against your will before managing to escape. That would make you more likable and she doesn't want that."

"I'd think getting rid of Farnsworth would make Cleo more likable," Sterling pointed out. "Farnsworth is nothing but an assclown."

Arabella's face screwed up. "Sterling, check with me before you use words like that. You sound like an idiot."

"No, I don't. And he is," Sterling argued.

It continued on like that for the rest of breakfast, the three of us acting like we couldn't hear and didn't care what was being said about us, and the rest of the cadets repeating Quinnie's outrageous accusations to one another as if they were the truth.

Finally, to my relief, the bell rang and breakfast was over.

"What are you going to say to Ozzy?" Arabella asked as we lagged behind, letting the rest of the cadets filter out of the cafeteria first.

"I'm still trying to decide," I admitted.

"Well, don't let him sweet talk you. I'm totally going to rip him a new one when I see him," Arabella promised.

I knew one thing for sure — there wasn't going to be anything sweet about my conversation with Ozzy.

After Foreign Language, I was nearly having a panic attack about going to Weapons class. I couldn't confront Ozzy in front of the entire class and I also couldn't act like everything was okay. I decided my only option was to skip class. A few minutes before the bell rang, I was actually surprised to find myself opening the door to the library instead of marching out onto the Weapons field. Sure, I had a problem with getting to class on time, but I wasn't exactly a rule breaker; I'd never actually skipped class.

Ms. Cain wasn't in the library or her office, but I didn't think it would be a big deal if I re-shelved some books. I loaded up the cart and began the mindless task of putting the library back in order.

After about an hour, the bell rang ending the second class period. Ozzy was in my Conditioning class so there was no chance I was going to that class either. I continued re-shelving books, completely aware of the fact that I might not have much to do for work detail later on since I was getting it all done now. I was tucked away in a darkened corner of the library reorganizing some books about Foreign Politics when a nearby door opened. It was the door to the Restricted Section and Professor Lawless and Ms. Cain were coming out.

"Thanks for your help, Zelda, I really appreciate it."

"Not a problem, Geoffrey. It's not often I get to discuss *Wormwood* events with someone who is so educated on the subject."

"I know," Lawless said dejectedly. "Not many students, or professors for that matter, are that interested. This will be really useful to my research, though," he said holding up a book, "so thank you."

"Not a problem. Are you done with the books that Ms. Dracone brought to you last week?"

"I am, but I need to get back to my room to grade some papers during lunch. Can I have her bring them by this evening? I can put them in the lock box."

"I can come get them now and save you the effort. I don't have any pressing matters this class period."

And with that, Ms. Cain and Professor Lawless exited the library, neglecting to close the door to the Restricted Section, but locking the door that led into the main halls of the Academy. I stood in my shadowed corner, staring at the slightly open door with a mixture of fear and excitement. My fear of getting caught snooping was quickly overcome with a sense of anticipation. I'd already skipped two classes this morning, what was one more broken rule? If I was going to be punished, as I knew I likely would be, I might as well make it worth the effort.

I was drawn to the door. It was too enticing, too irresistible to ignore. I stepped out of my hidden nook, crossed the empty carpeted area, and squeezed through the open door of the Restricted Section before I could change my mind. It was a lot larger than I expected. The middle of the room was dominated by a large oak table, the walls were lined with packed bookshelves, and there were half a dozen stand-alone shelves, also full of books. Most of the table in the middle of the room was governed by two computers and the wall to the right was bordered with heavy, wooden, filing cabinets.

I stood there for a minute or two trying to decide where to start. The books, the computers, or the filing cabinets? Remembering the file Ozzy entrusted me with, I decided on the filing cabinets, hoping that this was where he had gotten his. If my file was in there, so was information on my parents and my history. I quickly found the Sophisticate section, located the Dracone cabinet, and rifled through the first drawer until I found the spot where my folder should be. Clementine — it should be between Clarence and Clinton.

It wasn't there. The blank space where my folder should've been almost made me feel like I didn't exist. I shut the drawer angrily.

Out of curiosity, I checked for Arabella and Sterling. It didn't take long for me to deduce that even though every other cadet at the Academy seemed to be represented in the various drawers, none of the Deviant Dozen were stored in this cabinet. Apparently, the Restricted Section of the library wasn't restricted enough for us.

Desperate to get something out of my risky trespassing endeavor, I sat down at one of the computers and wiggled the mouse until the computer screen flickered to life. I navigated to the database I'd found earlier in my hacking search back at the University. Even though I gained entrance into the database easily, I could find no mention of myself or anyone else in the Dozen. Not a history, not a class schedule, not even a birth record. It was like I'd been totally erased from the Sophisticate Program.

Frustrated, I slumped back into the leather chair, willing inspiration to come to me. Ms. Cain would be back soon. I glanced at the numerous shelves wondering if maybe I should grab a couple of books just to satisfy my aggravation. But even then, how would I choose? If I was going to take something, I wanted to make sure it was worth the risk. My eyes rested on a book whose binding read, "Technology and the History of News and Media." Definitely not that one.

I suddenly sat upright. That's it. The news! Why didn't I ever think of that before?

I opened an Internet search engine and used the keywords "Michael" and "Sarah" (which were the only tidbits I knew about my parents — their names) along with the words "Sophisticate Program" and "Baltimore." It occurred to me that since I'd always lived and studied near Baltimore that perhaps my parents were from there as well.

The search engine immediately came back with a list of news links from 16 years ago. I clicked on the first link, "Court Orders Michael and Sarah Cross to Relinquish Baby to Sophisticate Program." I eagerly read the article:

A Baltimore court has ordered the parents of a genetically modified infant to relinquish the infant into the care of the

Sophisticate Program. The parents, Michael and Sarah Cross, contend that they never agreed to be part of the Program's Reciprocity Covenant and that they were, in actuality, patients at Johns Hopkins University Hospital receiving IVF treatment.

"We didn't ask them to modify our child, we were there for fertility treatments," said the child's mother, Sarah Cross. "We are the parents and she is our child. They can't just take her away from us."

In accordance with Reciprocity Covenant exchanges, testing was done on the child to ensure genetic modification viability. The child tested positive and Judge Lorna Evans ruled against the parents, citing that the infant is indeed a Sophisticate and therefore property of the Program. The parents will receive the standard payment for a Sophisticate child, which includes a house and a yearly stipend. Mr. and Mrs. Cross requested visiting rights to the child, but they have been denied.

"We just can't allow that kind of thing to occur," said Jacob Overton about the visiting rights being denied. "The Sophisticate children can't have any attachments to people outside of the Program. They are not her parents, they are her donors. They haven't been her parents since the genetic modification occurred."

Jacob Overton, the Dean of St. Ignatius. I sagged into the seat. Could Michael and Sarah Cross be my parents? I had to admit that the names were common enough that there was a possibility that they weren't. There were probably hundreds or even thousands of Sophisticates born around that time. I wasn't even sure my parents were from Baltimore.

But I wanted them to be my parents; not just donors, but parents that had wanted me and had fought for me. If only the article mentioned the name of the baby, then I would know for sure if it was me. There was nothing to do but read more. There had to be more information. I sat upright and hungrily scrolled down the screen of search results, looking for something else to whet my appetite.

As I quickly scanned the article titles, I heard the distinct sound of a key in a lock and the front door to the library being pushed open. Ms. Cain was back. I was torn. I wanted to stay and read the articles, but I knew I had only about a minute or two before being discovered. I didn't know what articles were important and even if I did, I couldn't read them before Ms. Cain came back to the Restricted Section to return Lawless' borrowed books.

I glanced at the screen again, wanting to scream out in frustration. It wasn't worth it. Quickly, I closed the search window, crossed the room, slipped out of the door, and retreated into the dark corner I'd been in before. Moments later, Zelda Cain rounded the corner and then entered the Restricted Section room with an armful of books, closing the door behind her.

I scurried to the front of the library, grabbed my backpack, and silently made my way into the hallway. Once in the stony tunnel of shadows and silence outside of the library, I finally remembered to breathe.

The bell suddenly rang, making my heart leap into my throat. Lunch time. The cafeteria was fairly close to the library, so I hurried toward it in the hopes that I could grab something to go and take it to my room before I was forced into a conversation I wasn't ready to have. I knew Sterling and Arabella would be annoyed with me for skipping lunch and leaving them to face the accusations and assumptions of the rest of the cadets alone, but I wanted to avoid talking to Ozzy. I still hadn't decided what to say to him.

I clumsily balanced my tray of food as I attempted to unlock the door to my room. The guards at the front desk gave me a funny look when I walked by them, but didn't try to stop me from taking my lunch up the stairwell. Eating meals in one's room wasn't against the rules, but nobody ever did it.

I finally managed to get the door open without dropping my food and I set the tray on my bed before tossing my backpack on the floor. I closed my eyes and took a moment to lean my head to each side, stretching out the tightness in my neck, while the names Michael and Sarah Cross jostled around in my thoughts like loose puzzle pieces in a cardboard box.

"Why weren't you in class today?"

I jumped, nearly tripping over my backpack. Ozzy was sitting on the floor, his back against the closet door, his muscular arms draped over his knees. For once, I didn't find his smoldering good looks enticing in any way. When I looked at him now, I didn't see the kissable lips that tempted me; I saw the mouth that told lies and half truths.

"You can't just keep coming into my room uninvited."

"You didn't seem to mind last night." His voice was smiling, but he wasn't.

"Well, I mind today. If I wanted to talk to you, I'd be in the cafeteria right now."

"So. You are avoiding me. Why?"

I walked over to the window, which was already open, and gestured for him to leave.

"Not until you tell me why you skipped two classes this morning, and lunch, just to avoid me," Ozzy said, standing and hooking his thumbs into the pockets of his jeans.

I wasn't ready to have this conversation, but in all honesty, I probably never would be. I hated confrontation. I chewed on the inside of my lip, determined not to cry. Determined not to be weak. "You knew it was a training exercise. You took us to Baltimore and didn't even warn us."

Ozzy shook his head, holding his hands in front of his chest as if to ward off my accusations. "Cleo, I swear I invited you to go to the game with me, only the game. No ulterior motives."

"I'm sorry, but I don't believe you. I can't trust you."

"You can," Ozzy promised. "That's what I've been trying to tell you this whole time. I'm the only one you can trust."

"Really? Where did you go when you left the game?"

"You know where I went, I told you. I had to track a runaway Sophisticate."

"Who was it?"

The question surprised Ozzy, as if he never expected me to be interested in his job. Understanding transformed his features as he swallowed and licked his lower lip, catching it in his teeth. "You know who it was." It wasn't just a statement, it was a realization.

"Was it Cassie?"

"You know who it was," he repeated.

"Why did you take her back to the University?" I demanded.

"I was doing my job."

"Why did she run away? Where was she going?"

Ozzy stared into my eyes before finally answering. "Looking for you," he admitted grudgingly.

"Was she exhibiting?"

He shrugged. "I think so, but I'm not sure. I gave her the same warning I gave you — to keep it a secret."

"Why would you do that? If she was exhibiting you could have brought her here! Why would you do that to me? She's like my sister and she was looking for me! We could've been together again."

Ozzy's face twisted into a look of disappointment. "Are you serious? After what you've been through since you've been here, are you that selfish that you would want her here, going through the same things, just so you wouldn't be lonely?"

"She's the one that's lonely," I argued. "Younglove told me that you took the Homework Harpies away, too."

"They don't belong here either, Cleo. They're not St. Ignatius stock."

I stepped forward and pushed him angrily in the chest. "Who are you to decide who comes and goes, who deserves to be here and who doesn't? You think you're a God around here and that everyone has to listen to everything you say, but you're not. Cassie belongs with me," I shouted, slapping my hand on my own chest.

Ozzy shook his head and I reached out to push him again. He grabbed my hands to keep me from making contact, not that I was actually hurting him, but I assumed being pelted with ineffective and angry girly hands was probably annoying all the same. "You don't know what you're talking about, Cleo," he said, firmly.

"You're the one that doesn't know what you're talking about.

You don't know Cassie and you don't know me."

"I do know you," Ozzy said, releasing my arms and reaching for me.

Did he actually think he could hug me after what he'd done?

I avoided his embrace and walked to the closet, yanking open the door, and grabbing the bag he left for me Saturday night. I remembered the happiness I felt that night, the excitement in accepting his invitation to the dance — the kiss, the beautiful dress, the instant message. It all seemed petty and staged now. He didn't care about me; I was just a pawn in some power struggle he was playing. I didn't know what his motive was, but it was clear that it wasn't good for me.

I looked at the bag in my hands and then at Ozzy. "You read my files, you know my secrets, and you kissed me. But you don't know me," I said. I walked to the open window and tossed the bagged dress out of it and onto the ground. "If you did, you would have told me about Cassie instead of letting me hear it from Younglove. If you really knew me, you would've brought Cassie here. Having my sister back is more important than some stupid dress and games of intrigue."

I went to my door and wrenched it open. "You may be St. Ignatius' golden boy, but you chose the wrong person to cross this time." I started to go out the door and then turned to look over my shoulder. Ozzy hadn't moved and was staring at me in complete shock. "Oh, and in case I wasn't clear, you're going to have to find someone else to wear that dress and go to the Formal with you, I've got other plans."

20

DEVIANT WORKSHOP

The bell rang and for the first time since coming to the Academy, I was anxious to get to class. Although I still wasn't keen on using my ability — or power, as Ozzy called it — I was eager to learn how to control it. Sterling and Arabella caught up with me on the way to Younglove's Deviant Workshop. Arabella's annoyance at my absence at lunch was forgotten in the discovery that along with missing lunch, I skipped two classes, confronted Ozzy, and tossed the red dress out the window. The only thing I didn't tell my stunned friends was that I'd also been in the Restricted Section of the library. That wasn't something I wanted to discuss out in the open where just anyone could overhear.

"Wow. You were a busy little deviant today," Arabella smirked. "Skipping classes and arguing with golden boy. All I can say is, I'm proud. And I can't believe you threw the dress out the window!" Arabella was beaming. "You actually stood up to him; I didn't think you had it in you."

"Pretty bad ass," Sterling agreed, "but did you have to take it out on the dress?"

"I do feel kind of bad about the dress," I admitted. "I just wanted to make him as angry as I was about Cassie and the Harpies."

"And don't forget he invited us to the Ravens game, basically setting us up for a traumatic kidnapping fiasco," Arabella reminded me.

"I haven't forgotten about that," I promised.

"But, why do you think he's doing all of this? Why tell you not to use your skills? Why pretend to like you and ask you to the dance?" Sterling wondered.

"To gain my trust? To have some amount of control over me? I'm not really sure," I said.

"Maybe he sees you as competition," Arabella suggested.

I laughed. "I hardly think so. I'm the girl that faints at the sight of a gun, remember?"

"You're also the girl that doesn't need a gun, you can blow something up just by thinking about it. Making things explode blasts perfect aim right out of the water. If anyone can knock him off his throne, it's you. And he knows it," Sterling pointed out.

I hadn't thought about it that way. I was woefully challenged in Weapons and Conditioning and I was always the last person to cross the finish line on the morning runs. I knew my power was dangerous, but I never considered myself to be fearsome competition or a threat to anyone. "But I'm so weak."

Arabella tilted her head and looked at me from under her arched eyebrows. "You're many things, but weak isn't one of them."

When Arabella led us through the open door to Younglove's

office, my first thought at seeing the rest of the Deviant Dozen (minus Ozzy and Cassie) was, We are going to destroy this place in about ten seconds flat. I didn't know what the talents of everyone else in the room were, but given the chance, I knew I could demolish the office on my own with no problem. How did Younglove expect us to practice our deviations in here?

Quinnie was leaning against the back of one of the chairs in front of Younglove's desk. Her top lip curled in disgust when she saw us. "Are you three lost or something?"

"Oh, I'm sorry. We thought this was the Deviant Workshop," Arabella feigned an apology. She turned to Sterling and me as if to usher us back out into the hallway, "Come on guys, it looks like we stumbled on the remedial study group by accident." She turned and gazed around the room. "So proud of you all for resisting the urge to lick the windows and shove pencils up your noses."

Dexter mumbled something and started toward Arabella, but Quinnie held up her hand. "Keep it to yourself, Dex. She's not worth it." Quinnie eyed us up and down. "They really are scraping the bottom of the bucket, aren't they? I can't believe Younglove invited you three losers. Well, I guess every group needs —"

Slap.

The room suddenly went quiet. Before Quinnie could inform everyone what every group needed, there was a blur of color, a loud slap, and Quinnie's face was sporting a red welt in the impression of a hand. Arabella's hand. Which came from across the room.

"Sorry," Arabella apologized, "I thought you had something on your face, but I guess that's how hideous it normally looks." There were a few snickers, mostly from Sterling.

"You!" Quinnie's face turned a bright red and the handprint was suddenly lost in the sea of hot fury that was transforming her pretty features into red, splotchy, wrinkled rage. Just as she was about to leap at Arabella, Younglove entered the office and stepped between the girls. The bell rang indicating the beginning of the first afternoon class.

"Excellent. Glad to see you're all on time," Younglove said, glancing around the room. "Let's move into the training arena and get down to business." She walked past everyone to a door in the back of the room. "Oh, and do try to keep your hands and powers to yourselves. I'd hate to have to send any of you to Dean Overton's office," she said, looking at Quinnie and Arabella pointedly, "or to the infirmary. The Formal is right around the corner, you know, and punishment does leave its mark," she warned.

We filed out the door in the back of the office and into a large room that looked like a gymnasium, only with no windows. Florescent lights flickered to life when Younglove flipped the switch. The ceiling was high, lined with metal beams that arched up, giving the ceiling the appearance of a large skeletal rib cage of some dead, forgotten animal. Instead of being bordered with bleachers like a normal gymnasium, the walls were littered with stuffed dummies, targets, various weapons, and boxes shoved out of the way and piled high and haphazardly. Climbing ropes dangled from each of the corners of the room and along the length of the room on both sides, wooden rings hung from straps. At the far side of the gym where a basketball net should have been, there was a group of ten stuffed dummies lined up in a row.

Younglove led us to the middle of the glossy wooden floor and instructed each of us line up across from a dummy.

"I think it's about time we properly introduce ourselves to one another," Younglove announced, as she turned to face us.

Sadie jutted her hip out as it propped up her arm, snapping a piece of gum between her teeth. "We already know each other, Professor."

A glare from Younglove set Sadie's posture straight again. "I'm aware that you know each other, Ms. Dracone. My intention is that you get more familiar with what each of your fellow Deviant Dozen members can do. And, since you're so eager to share your thoughts, why don't you be the first to show us what your deviation is?"

Sadie looked unsure of herself. "What exactly do you want me to do?"

"Impress us."

I was glad to see that for all of her earlier attitude, Sadie was as nervous as the rest of us seemed to be. Everyone had become very subdued once they realized Younglove was going to make us perform one by one. Everyone, that is, except for Quinnie who seemed only too eager to show off. While most of the group was staring off into different directions, avoiding Younglove's gaze, Quinnie's shoulders were thrown back in confidence and she stared at Younglove, nearly begging to be called on.

Sadie reached up with both hands and pulled her multitude of long, black braids into a loose ponytail at the back of her head and then fastened it with a rubber band from around her wrist. She slowly looked around the room, apparently making plans for her attempt at impressing the group — or planning an escape route — it wasn't clear which. That's what I wanted to do. Escape.

"We've only got an hour for the workshop, Ms. Dracone," Younglove droned. "Let's get on with it."

"Yes, ma'am." Sadie then started running across the gym, silent as a cat. When she was still several strides from the rope in the corner, she leaped into the air and caught the rope about ten feet off the ground. Hand over fist, in a blur of plaid, she shimmied up the rope, disappearing into the rafters. As soon as her hand touched the ceiling, she pushed away and dove through the air, easily catching herself on one of the wooden rings that hung from the canvas straps. Her momentum carried her forward in a wild swing, which she used to propel herself along the row of rings like a child on the monkey bars.

"I'm not impressed," Sterling whispered as he leaned toward me and Arabella, "I can do that."

As if hearing Sterling, Sadie came to the last ring, swung her feet in the air, and then flipped twice before landing lightly on the ground. Her feet had barely touched the floor before she was scurrying up the dangerously stacked boxes. The stack looked like one wrong breath would send it tumbling to the ground, but Sadie scaled it without disturbing so much as one particle of dust.

Upon reaching the top of the teetering stack, she reached up and grasped one of the beams ribbing the inside of the curved ceiling. Using her hands and feet, she scaled the entire length of the ceiling, upside down like a spider. When she reached the other side of the room, she flipped her body and set her feet on another towering stack of junk and then proceeded to leap from one object to another, making her way toward the front of the room, never touching the ground.

Sadie finally reached the last structure of random junk and vaulted off it into the air. She flipped and twisted like a leaf caught in a tornado. The following thump was the result of her slamming into the body of the end dummy, taking it to the ground with deadly precision. She stood, releasing the dummy, which fell to the floor with a dull thud.

A few seconds passed and then a spattering of applause, led by Younglove, let Sadie know she was off the hook. "Meet Ring Tailed Cat," Younglove said, motioning to Sadie. "Skills — agility and acrobatics." The applause continued and Sadie smiled in satisfaction before returning to the group.

Dexter was called on next. His demonstration took a lot less time than Sadie's. He merely lined up in front of a dummy and from twenty feet away, he spit at it. I was grossed out and just as Sterling started to mime the universal thumbs down motion to give his opinion on Dexter's deviation, the dummy started to smoke and disintegrate. Dexter stood, unflinchingly, watching as holes wore into the dummy, pieces falling off and hissing away into nothing. When the demonstration was over, no one clapped. Everyone just stared.

"It's a little different with skin," Dexter informed us with a shrug, turning around. "There's a lot more bubbling, blood, and pus."

Still, no one clapped. And I didn't want to know how he knew how his spit reacted with skin.

"Meet Spitting Cobra," Younglove announced, slapping together her desiccated hands so that they sounded like two sheets of paper rustling together. "Skill," she continued, "poison via projectile, bite, and sting. "

"All right. Projectile is obvious and so is bite," Sterling mumbled, "but I don't even want to know how he stings."

Arabella and I giggled quietly. She leaned over to whisper in my ear. "I guess you can cross off Dexter as a possible date for the

Autumn Formal. Can you imagine that good night kiss? Having your heart melt is supposed to be just a metaphor."

I covered my mouth with my hand to stifle a laugh. This workshop was proving to be a lot more entertaining than I'd imagined.

Marty was next and upon facing off with his dummy, he took off his jacket and rolled up his shirt sleeves. He did a slow rotating move that looked like it might be tai chi. As he rotated, the hairs on his forearms grew longer and thicker. When he completed his circle, he flung his right arm out toward his dummy and dozens of the thick, prickly hairs disengaged from his arm and impaled themselves on the soft fabric of the target — all around the head and neck area. Some pierced clean through the neck.

Marty received more applause than Dexter, but it was still a cautious applause — nothing like Sadie received. Younglove introduced Marty as Spitfire Caterpillar, listing his skill as ejecting dangerous spikes and barbs. She informed us that Marty had only used small spikes for the demonstration but was capable of creating a spike large enough to decapitate someone. At her encouragement, Marty spun again and then took off the head of the dummy by flinging a razor sharp spike that was as long as his forearm.

Marty. Another guy I could effectively check off my dance card.

"I hope I get something more fearsome than Caterpillar," Sterling whispered. "I mean, Spitfire is pretty awesome, but Caterpillar?" He shook his head. I thought back to the Deviant Dozen list I'd seen in Ozzy's folder and had a feeling Sterling was going to be deeply disappointed when he learned his code name.

Arabella was called out next. She stepped forward and when she raised her arms to begin, Quinnie whispered to Eva, loud enough for everyone to hear. "I didn't realize ugly was a power. I just thought they forgot to genetically alter her looks."

Arabella lowered her arms. "Oh, I can choose to look as ugly as I want," she crooned, slowly turning to face Quinnie as her artfully messy, black hair lightened and fell into a dull, dirty imitation of Quinnie's usually luxurious locks. Arabella's face also took on Quinnie's appearance, but with the addition of huge, hairy moles dotting various spots on her face. The Quinnie look-alike that Arabella created also had a serious case of acne. "See? I can even look as ugly as you, if it pleases me." She smiled wickedly as there were gasps of surprise. "It doesn't." The look melted away and Arabella's purple and black makeup reappeared.

The look on Quinnie's face was pure hatred, but she didn't dare retaliate with Younglove as a witness.

Arabella turned back around to face her dummy. I expected her to lash out with her arm and hit the dummy from where she was standing, but Arabella seemed eager to prove a point — she wasn't just a one trick pony. The Dozen already saw her hit Quinnie from across the room, she meant to impress this time. Her leg shot out to the side, stretching across the room as she placed a roundhouse kick to a box at the top of one of the teetering stacks. It flew through the air, taking out one of the remaining dummies.

Then she flung her hands into the air and they elongated like a stretched rubber band until she was able to reach one of the rafters high up in the ceiling. Her body then rocketed toward the ceiling as her arms returned to their normal size and shape. She dangled by her hands for a few seconds as her legs stretched and circled around the beam, securing her. She then swung upside down and her hands shot out alternately, easily stretching down the 50 feet or so to knock two more dummies over with vicious punches to their heads. She grabbed another dummy by the arms and pulled it into the air. As it dangled 40 feet over the floor, Arabella proceeded to rip its arms off, allowing the armless corpse of canvas and stuffing to fall to the floor like a rock. She tossed the arms to the sides where they hit the walls and slid down into the piles of random junk.

Arabella finished her demonstration by swinging herself back down to the floor and landing next to Younglove. Her features instantly transformed into a mirror image of Younglove, her clothes the only indication of which one was the real Professor.

Stuffing was still floating in the air when Younglove started to speak. "Meet the Indonesian Mimic Octopus. Skills — preternatural strength, transformation of size and appearance, propulsion, and regeneration."

Arabella looked up in curiosity. "Regeneration? Really? As in I can grow a new arm if one falls off?"

Younglove studied her. "In theory. However, are you willing to try? I'm not sure Ms. Petticoat can fix something that drastic."

Quinnie raised her hand. "I'm willing to help out with the experiment."

Younglove pursed her lips. "I'm sure you are, Quinby. However, there will be no experimentation of such. As I said, Regeneration in theory."

It continued on like that for the next half hour — Younglove calling out names and nervous Deviants stepping forward to impress the rest of the Dozen. Sometimes, additional equipment was brought in or adjustments were made so that a deviation could be performed. At the end of the half hour, four more people had gone.

Eva was named Tiger Moth after she demonstrated her ability

to disrupt and change radio waves. Younglove informed the group that Eva was also skilled in affecting and creating sonar waves. Every one began to clap sporadically, unsure whether Younglove intended for Eva to demonstrate that as well. There was no water around, so it was unlikely. As the applause started to die down, Eva cleared her throat to get everyone's attention. "Ah, yes," Younglove agreed. "Tiger Moth has one more skill she would like to demonstrate."

Eva took a deep breath, opened her mouth, and began to speak. "You've got to go to Dean Overton's office," she said. Only it wasn't Eva's voice, it was Ozzy's. She imitated his pitch and tone perfectly. Theo's head snapped in Eva's direction in surprise, probably remembering the day those words were said to him by the actual Ozzy, when he was sent to the Dean's for pretending to shoot his brother with a loaded gun in Weapons class.

"Tiger Moth is also adept at manipulating sound waves and can disguise her own voice or mimic someone specific," Younglove explained. "Thank you, Evangeline." Eva nodded once and moved back with the group as Younglove dismissed her.

I decided I'd never feel comfortable talking to someone over the phone again. How could I trust what I heard when there was someone like Eva in the world?

Theo was next and smiled widely when Younglove revealed his moniker — Bull Shark. After the group created a makeshift maze with the boxes along the walls and turned out the lights, Theo demonstrated how he used electroreception to see in the dark to navigate the maze. However, since it was dark, I wasn't sure how we could be sure that he did as well as everyone thought. Anything could have happened in the darkness and no one could see. Just because we didn't hear Theo crashing about, it didn't mean that he was an expert navigator. It was clear we were just going to have to trust Younglove's confidence in him. Younglove pointed out that Theo's sense of direction and navigation was dead on, in the darkness as well as in the light.

Seeing as how Wesley was Theo's twin, it wasn't a surprise that his skill was also sight related. Not only was he able to read a handwritten letter from clear across the gym, but he was able to describe what was in most of the boxes along the wall, without opening them. He pointed to a box on the floor in front of the stack. "Five pairs of cleats, a football, two helmets, and a . . . " Wesley squinted and stared at the box intently, before blushing. "And a bra."

Younglove motioned Marty over to the box and he opened it, emptying the contents on the floor of the gym. Five pairs of cleats, a football, two helmets, and a bra that he held up between his forefinger and thumb like it was a dead mouse.

"Equipment from the girl's football team." Marty laughed, wiggling the massive white bra that looked like it belonged to a grizzly bear.

Eva wrapped her arms around her chest. "So, can you see through things?" she asked Wesley, timidly.

"Most things," Wesley said, clearing his throat.

"Clothing?" she asked. I noticed everyone was shifting position, covering parts they'd rather not be seen with Wesley's supposed x-ray vision.

Wesley blushed. "I guess if I choose to. It's not like I see naked people walking around all the time, I have to focus." He looked down at the floor, the only safe place to look after answering a question like that. He knew that answer wasn't winning him any points, even if it was the truth. I had to respect the fact that he answered honestly, knowing the answer wouldn't be well received.

"What can't you see through?" Arabella asked. I had a feeling that Arabella planned to fashion a wardrobe out of whatever substance was immune to Wesley's power.

Wesley looked to Younglove who responded. "That is information that is best left confidential. Wesley understands that looking through clothing is out of bounds, correct?" she asked, looking sternly at Wesley who nodded vigorously as if trying to convince the rest of the group of his good intentions. "Very well, then," Younglove continued. "Everyone, meet Bald Eagle," she announced, gesturing to Wesley who seemed pleased with his new identity.

Next up was Sterling. His turn didn't take long. A dozen speedy laps back and forth across the gym in less than a minute and he was done. It was no surprise to anyone; we'd all seen him in the morning runs and in the track and field meet. It was no secret that Sterling was abnormally fast.

His performance garnered a lackluster golf clap and then Younglove bestowed his name upon him. "Everyone, meet Hummingbird." The other guys started laughing and Sterling's face fell.

"Hummingbird?" he repeated, dejectedly. "I was thinking more like Cheetah or Wildebeest."

"How about the Mongolian Wild Ass?" Arabella suggested. "They run like 40 miles an hour. You were going at least that fast. And you're definitely an ass sometimes," she added happily.

Sterling glared at her. I shook my head and laughed, aware that this argument would be continued during dinner and would likely fuel more meaningless threats from both of them concerning the dance and going together or not. It was a daily occurrence that I recognized for what it was — their mating ritual. It was the strangest sort of flirting I'd ever seen in my life, especially since neither of them were willing to admit they were actually flirting or were truly attracted to one another.

Younglove looked at Sterling with a small grin. "I think you'd prefer to be a Hummingbird," she suggested as more laughter echoed throughout the room. Younglove gave a stern look at the group, quieting the noise before turning back to Sterling. "True, Cheetahs can run 70 miles an hour, but can only maintain that speed for about a hundred yards. A hummingbird's wings flap between 50 and 200 times per second. Hummingbirds are one of the most aggressive bird species and will attack larger birds like jays, crows, and hawks that infringe on their territory. During migration, there is a species of hummingbird that flies 500 miles nonstop. The hummingbird is the only type of bird that can fly backwards. And, most notably, the hummingbird can hover. I'd rather be a hummingbird." She crossed her arms, daring him to disagree. The room was unusually silent.

Sterling stared at Younglove, his mouth hanging open in disbelief. "Are you saying I can fly?"

"I'm saying that maybe you should research your namesake and investigate your deviation more thoroughly," she said evasively.

"But . . . " he started.

Younglove ignored him. "And, last but not least, Clementine."

"Wait," Quinnie interrupted. "What about me?"

"Very well, Quinby," Younglove sighed. "Everyone, meet Electric Eel. Skill — Electric Shock. No one is surprised. Now, let's move on to Clementine."

Quinnie looked genuinely offended. "But Professor, I didn't get to show my deviation," she pleaded.

"First of all, interrupt me again and you'll find yourself out of this workshop," Younglove scolded, a dangerous edge to her voice. "Secondly, you've been showing off your deviation since you arrived at St. Ignatius. Everyone in this room knows what it is so it would be a waste of time to display it. And lastly, even if they didn't know what it was, how would you demonstrate it? Do you think I would allow you to electrocute someone in this room? Do you think any of them would volunteer?"

Quinnie fidgeted with one of the pleats of her plaid skirt. "But, how am I supposed to practice my deviation then?"

"You've already mastered your deviation. What you need to work on is controlling your compulsion to use it. Understand?"

Quinnie nodded stiffly, one time, avoiding Younglove's gaze.

"Excellent. As I was saying, last but not least, Clementine."

I slowly walked forward, lining up across from one of the remaining dummies. Everyone leaned forward slightly, trying to get a better look at what I was going to do, and therefore, get a better understanding of the feud going on between me and Quinnie.

I looked at Younglove who nodded for me to continue. I looked back at the dummy. Nothing. I felt nothing and the dummy remained as fireless and intact as before. I concentrated hard, imagining the white canvas catching on fire, the flames eating away the faceless flesh on the head. Still nothing. I couldn't make anything happen and wasn't even sure how to begin. The raw power inside me was dormant and quiet and I had no idea how to call it to life. Someone coughed. I turned toward Younglove.

"I can't seem to do it," I admitted.

"Try harder," Younglove demanded. "Find that power deep

down inside of you."

I turned back to face the dummy, mentally begging it to burst into flames. I searched for the anger that caused me to throw the dress out of the window earlier, the fury I had toward Ozzy for his betrayal. I tried to coax it into a smoldering rage.

It didn't oblige.

After a few more minutes of strained silence, someone spoke. "You know, if you let me encourage her, we could kill two birds with one stone." Quinnie made it sound as if she was being incredibly helpful.

"No," Younglove said, the word dripping with more disappointment than I thought two letters should be capable of. What I didn't know was who the disappointment was aimed at — me or Quinnie. "She must learn to call on her powers on her own."

After a few more minutes of staring helplessly at the dummy, I heard a pinging sound that I recognized as a phone alert. Younglove pulled the phone out of her pocket, looked at it briefly, and then her voice cleaved through the silence. "I need to go take a call in my office, I won't be long. Clementine, I expect to see results when I get back."

The professor's heels clacked noisily on the gym floor as she made her way to her office. She'd barely closed the door behind her before the rest of the Dozen members were finding places to sit down and wait out Younglove's phone call.

I noticed that although the students knew each other beforehand, they hadn't really known each other as well as they thought. The displays of deviation were creating an even deeper division of cliques as the cadets found places to sit— Quinnie, Marty, Dexter, Sadie and Eva on one side; me, Sterling, and Arabella on the other;

and Wesley and Theo in the middle. Clearly, Wesley and Theo weren't wanted on Quinnie's side and they looked unsure about joining my side.

I sat down on the floor and Arabella sat down next to me, leaning over to whisper in my ear. "What's wrong?"

"I just can't do it," I said with a shake of my head. "I don't know how to turn it on, it usually happens by accident."

"Okay. Well what do those times have in common? Maybe there's some sort of trigger."

I shrugged, trying to remember. "Anger, injustice, maybe a little fear? Hard to say. I think mostly it's anger, though."

"Like the Incredible Hulk," Arabella mused. "Don't make her angry," she teased in an ogre-like voice.

"You're totally not helping." I laughed. "This is the opposite of anger."

A shadow fell across us. "You've got to be the most worthless piece of human being to ever come through the Program. You don't even deserve to be called a Sophisticate, let alone a member of the Dozen," Quinnie crowed, disgust hooking the left part of her lip and lifting it into a sneer. "You're the last one to finish the morning run, you faint at the sight of a weapon, and you can't even do the one thing you were designed to do."

Arabella started to get up to defend my reputation, but I held her back. "She can say whatever she wants about me; I don't care. She's just trying to goad us into a fight since Younglove wouldn't let her show off. Don't give her what she wants," I persuaded.

Arabella sat back down, gloomily. She was never one to back down from a fight and she didn't like the idea of letting Quinnie spout nonsense, but I was right. If we started going at it without

Younglove around, the gymnasium would quickly become a war zone. Or at the very least, a very vicious cat fight.

Quinnie smirked at Arabella. "Look at that. Just like a good little puppy listening to its master. Or should I say, good little bitch?" She turned to me. "Speaking of bitch, how will your girlfriend, Cassie, take it when she finds out she's been replaced? By a freak?"

Hearing my best friend's name coming out of Quinnie's mouth broke my resolve to ignore her. How did Quinnie even know Cassie's name? Arabella and Sterling hadn't even known about Cassie until this morning. "What do you know about Cassie?"

Quinnie flipped her thick curtain of hair over her shoulder. "Enough to know that she doesn't belong here and neither do you."

"You don't know anything then," I countered.

Quinnie licked her lips before allowing them to turn up into a self-satisfied smile. "I know that they returned her. She ran away, but Ozzy found her and he didn't bring her here; he took her back to that dump of a University."

I clenched and unclenched my fists, trying to release the slow burn that was creeping through my skin, scalding my fingertips and palms.

"Such a shame, too," Quinnie continued. "Deviant Eleven just doesn't have the same ring to it. But, don't worry. Maybe they'll send you both off to be with those mental rejects you used to hang out with. What did you call them? The Herpes? Cassie and the Herpes. Sounds like a band. A bad one."

I knew Quinnie was trying to get a reaction out of me, but as much as I tried to ignore the words and tell myself they didn't matter, my emotions didn't seem to get the message. My body was over-heating, a warm trickle climbing up my legs and over my stomach, turning into an uncomfortable heat. "Shut up. You don't get to say her name," I hissed, starting to stand. "You don't get to talk about any of them."

"What? Cassie? Or the Herpes?" Quinnie laughed. "You think it's all a big secret? That I don't know what I'm talking about?"

I looked around and noticed that everyone else was listening raptly. Arabella looked ready to step in and help, but was allowing me to deal with this on my own.

Quinnie noticed me inspecting the faces of our suddenly very interested audience. "Oh, don't worry, they don't know about Cassie," she promised. "But Ozzy tells me everything. Did you know when he found her she was crying? Like a baby. Crying and begging to know where you were."

"Shut up," I repeated. The burn was in my chest now, causing my heart to beat so hard I thought it was going to explode. I was so furiously hot I was sure my hair was going to catch on fire.

"He couldn't wait to get rid of her."

"Shut up!" I screamed.

I clawed at my hair, trying to put out the flames I was positive were there. Then I turned to the dummies and let go. I let go of my hair. I let go of the heat consuming my body. I let go of my anger. And I felt the release of a wall of invisible, powerful heat erupting from out of my chest.

When the unseen wrath reached the dummies, it engulfed them in flames before crashing through the back wall leaving a smoldering hole the size of a van. The explosion was massive, the noise deafening. I half expected to see a mushroom cloud billowing up into the ceiling. Outside of the hole, cadets were screaming in fear and running for cover. The stables were visible through the hole as were dozens of spooked horses whinnying in terror as cadets tried to regain control of them. It was pandemonium outside, a sharp contrast to the baffled and awed silence inside the gymnasium.

A slow clap began to echo through the room. I turned slowly to see Younglove leaning in the doorway of her office, a coarse smile stretching across the thin, dry skin of her face. "Very well done, ladies, very well done. Everyone, meet Malaysian Ant. Skills — explosions and spontaneous combustion."

I suddenly felt empty. There was no sadness, no anger, nothing. Just an overwhelming, lonely, void.

21

EAGLE EYE

Sterling and Arabella seemed unfazed by the large, smoking hole in the wall. They knew what I was capable of doing and didn't seem bothered by the violence I had unleashed. Younglove was nearly oozing with satisfaction, but the rest of the Dozen were apprehensive, cautiously peering at me as if I was a bomb that might go off again.

Quinnie was the exception. She ignored the jagged, gaping hole and stared instead at me as if mentally comparing our skills. I wondered in a duel, which one of us would be faster — me or Quinnie? A look at Quinnie's unconcerned smirk answered that question easily. Quinnie. I might be powerful, but when it came to speed, willingness, and know-how, the Bitch of Twitch definitely had the upper hand.

Although happy that I successfully used my deviation in the gymnasium, Younglove warned us not to use our skills outside of the workshop. She caught Quinnie and me in her glare. "I mean it.

Do not use your deviations. Not even a tiny bit. Especially you two. The other cadets and most of the faculty don't know what you are capable of. Some may suspect it, but let's not prove their suspicions. I shouldn't have to tell you that your skills are top secret, but seeing as how some of you fling them around haphazardly without concern for your safety or that of others, it seems necessary to say it out loud. It's not safe for you or the other cadets and staff. So I will repeat, do not use your deviations outside of this room unless you have my permission or express instruction to do so."

Sterling raised his hand. "So, I'm not supposed to run fast anymore? I don't see how that will make a difference. Everyone already knows how fast I run."

Younglove waved his concerns off. "You're running is an exception, and you," she said, looking at Arabella, "may still use your daily change in hair color. Those are activities that won't hurt anyone and are expected of you. I'm specifically talking about the skills that could put others in danger. Those must be controlled and kept secret."

The bell rang and the first workshop was over. Younglove made her way over to the gaping hole in the back wall to shoo away all the curious onlookers who had gotten over their initial terror and were starting to poke around through the rubble outside, trying to figure out what had happened. I took the opportunity to push past the rest of the members of the Dozen, retrieve my backpack from Younglove's office, and escape into the hallway. I was desperate to get lost in the crowd, to let the noise and vitality of the other cadets fill the yawning chasm of emptiness inside me.

I was ducking between two massive Mandates when I felt a tug on my arm. I glanced over my shoulder to see Sterling.

"You weren't going to wait for me? We have class together."

"Oh, right," I said sheepishly. Up until that point, I wasn't even sure that I'd been heading to class. I wasn't sure where I was going, but I knew that I wanted to lose myself in the clamor, to forget what I'd just done. To wipe away the memories of what I was capable of and ignore the truth that was echoing in my conscience. I could destroy things. Not just break them, but obliterate them with nothing more than a thought. And my power was triggered by anger. How could that be anything but corrupt and wicked?

"What's going on? You look like you're running from the devil," Sterling said, concerned.

"Can't run from myself," I mumbled.

"Okay." He was quiet for a moment as we threaded our way through the congested halls toward Lawless's classroom. "Are you going to explain that or do you expect me to try to puzzle that one out on my own? Because I gotta tell you, my brain is pretty much fried from trying to figure out all the crazy that Arabella is always spouting off."

I smiled in spite of myself. He was right. It wasn't fair to completely surround him with insanity. Arabella was normally moody enough for all three of us. "I'm sorry. I guess I'm just feeling sorry for myself. I mean, I'd much rather do what you or Arabella can do. I don't want to be the freak that makes things blow up. Arabella was right, I'm like the Hulk or King Kong or some monster. And you know what happens to the destructive monsters? People with pitchforks eventually hunt them down and kill them."

Sterling put his hands up in defense. "Whoa, whoa, whoa. Hold up there, Flame Fatale. You're not a monster. Did you hurt anyone back there? No. So you blew a hole through the wall and burned a couple target dummies. No big deal. If you were a monster, you would've turned Quinnie into a pile of ash because she was definitely asking for it. Actually, come to think of it, that would've made you a hero."

"Funny." I playfully punched him in the arm. "You don't get it. I don't want to be like this."

Sterling stopped and grabbed my shoulders, turning me to face him. "None of us want to be like this. Most of us would give anything to be normal, to be part of a family. But that's not going to happen, so we just have to make the best we can with the hand we were dealt. Just know that you're not alone. Okay? You've got me and Arabella. What more do you need? We're three parts of awesome. The best stuff always comes in threes."

I nodded as the corners of my eyes beaded up with stinging wetness and Sterling pulled me into a brief hug before putting me back at arms length. I kind of loved him in that moment. He was the brother I never had.

"Enough mushiness, let's get to class," he said, spinning me to walk down the hallway before smacking me on the ass like a pack mule.

When I walked into the cafeteria for dinner that night, I noticed Theo and Wesley sitting at the table that I usually shared with Sterling and Arabella. There were no other empty tables. I got in line for food and by the time I made my way back to the table, Sterling and Arabella were already standing there, trays in hand. Arabella seemed perturbed, which actually wasn't that unusual. I caught the end of the conversation as I walked up.

" . . . but this is our table, we always sit here," Arabella stated.

"It's big enough for all of us," Theo argued. "There are half a dozen more chairs," he said, motioning to the other empty seats around the table.

"But why do you have to sit here? There are dozens and dozens of other tables in this room. Why ours?" Arabella pouted.

"You don't own this table —" Theo started angrily.

Wesley interrupted him, "No one else will let us sit at their table anymore. Quinnie told everyone that I'm a pervert."

At the mention of "pervert," Arabella seemed to remember Wesley's special skill. She set down her tray and crossed her arms in front of her chest protectively.

"She did what? Younglove explicitly told us our powers were a secret, I can't believe she told everyone," Arabella hissed.

"I'm not looking through your clothes," Wesley said through gritted teeth as he glared at Arabella's crossed arms. "I'm not a scum bag, you know. And no, she didn't tell everyone about my deviation. She let them believe I've been peeking in through windows. She was telling a variation of the truth."

"But why?" Sterling asked.

Wesley threw a dirty look over his shoulder in the direction of Quinnie's table. "Because her sidekicks are uncomfortable with me around, so they want to make it uncomfortable for me to be around them. Or anyone else," he added.

I suddenly felt embarrassed at my earlier self pity, so I set down my tray next to Wesley. I was exhausted from derby practice and I collapsed into the seat next to him, too tired to stand any more and too tired to even care if Wesley was or wasn't using his powers to look through my clothes. It was the least of my worries.

"Come on, Arabella, it's no big deal," I said as I gnawed on a crust of bread.

Arabella sighed dramatically and then took a seat. "Sorry, Wes. I don't mean to be such a bitch, I just like my routine."

Wesley nodded and dug into his food, keeping his eyes to the table, probably the spot he thought was the safest to let them roam. We ate in silence and everyone seemed uncomfortable with the new seating arrangement that we'd been forced into. Conversation was nonexistent, as was eye contact.

After a few minutes, I noticed that someone was standing at the end of our table. I looked up and nearly choked on my dinner when I saw the newcomer. It was Ozzy and he was standing behind the empty chair next to me. He caught me in his gaze, but said nothing. Did he want to be invited to sit down? Was he going to yell at me? He continued to stare and I wasn't sure why, but I shook my head "no" at him. No, I didn't want him to sit next to me. And definitely no, I didn't want to continue our conversation from earlier.

His mouth tightened in annoyance and he looked around the cafeteria for some place else to sit. Quinnie, seeing his searching gaze, called him over to her table. Ozzy gave me another hard look that was tempered with a faint expression somewhere between hurt and betrayal. Maybe he was mad about the dress or the fact that I skipped a couple of classes this morning. Either way, I didn't care. For once, I wasn't jealous to see him heading for Quinnie's table. That's where he belonged. He looked back at me one last time as he sat down, his eyes pleading. Pleading for what, I had no idea.

I looked away.

"So," I said, breaking the awkward silence. "You boys have dates for the Formal yet?"

"Not anymore," Wesley answered without looking up. "Quinnie

has pretty much made us a social disease. I had a date, but she cancelled on me."

"Really? Who?"

Wesley finally looked up. "Eva. She ditched me right after the Workshop."

"Dude, that's messed up," Sterling said. "What about you?" he asked, motioning to Theo. "Did your date bail too?"

"Nah. I didn't have a date. Don't want one." He leaned back and stretched his arms back over his head. "Don't want to confine myself to just one babe. There's enough Theo to go around."

Arabella rolled her eyes. "Yeah. Good luck with that. I suggest first order of business you stop using the word babe or your mouth is going to get up close and personal with my fist."

Theo only laughed. "Wait and see. I'll be fighting the ladies off." He lowered his arms to put his hands behind his head to lounge back in what he must have thought was an alluring pose. "Don't worry, I'll save you a dance. You gave me your player's card. I owe you," he said with a wink as Arabella stared at him, her mouth open in horror.

She finally managed to close her gaping mouth. "In that case, do me a favor. Don't ask me to dance."

Theo grinned, leaned forward to snatch a grape off her plate, and then popped it in his mouth. It was hard to tell if he was disillusioned and thought he really was a ladies man or if he just didn't care what people thought about him. Either way, going stag probably wasn't going to be a matter of choice for Theo. It was a given. There probably wasn't a girl in the entire Academy deranged enough to accompany Theo to the Formal.

I chased my peas around my plate with my fork for a few

seconds, gathering the courage to speak. I finally caught three of the round, green, renegades and looked up at Wesley. "We could go together," I suggested.

He paused and chanced a look up from the tabletop. "You'd go with me?"

I shrugged. "Sure, why not? We're friends, right?"

"You're not scared of the whole vision thing?"

"What's it matter if I'm standing across the room or standing next to you? Seeing through stuff is seeing through stuff." I grinned.

"But I wouldn't," Wesley argued.

I put my hand on his arm. "Don't worry. It's no big deal. I don't have a dress anyway."

Wesley blushed. "You're teasing me."

I laughed. "Yes and no. I really don't have a dress. You might have to take me in Academy plaid."

Wesley finally smiled. "Fine by me." He began his own hunting of renegade peas with renewed vigor and then paused to meet my gaze. "And, thanks."

"For what?"

"For not judging me."

After that, dinner became much more relaxed and with a new target to torment, Arabella gave Sterling the night off as she relentlessly razzed Theo.

I was feeling both guilty and anxious when I entered the library for work detail later that evening. I felt guilty because I actually liked Ms. Cain and I felt bad that I snuck into the Restricted Section earlier in the day, dishonoring the trust that the librarian had in me. But, I was also anxious and eager to find a way to get back into that secret room and learn more, despite the respect I had for Ms. Cain.

I tossed my backpack into its usual spot under the front desk and was momentarily surprised when I checked the return bin of books that needed to be re-shelved and found it nearly empty. It was a few moments before I remembered that I'd re-stacked all the books earlier in the morning when I was hiding out in the library and skipping classes.

Ms. Cain glanced up from the paperwork she was filling out and looked over the top of her glasses. "Looks like you have a quick night tonight, there aren't that many to re-stack. You're free to go after you get those on the shelves."

I peered at the armload of books laying forlornly at the bottom of the bin and thought longingly of the room of secrets on the other side of the library. It'd be great to get back to my dorm room and get an early start on homework, but at the same time, leaving the library meant missing out on the possibility of finding a way back into the Restricted Section. "You sure you don't need me to help you with anything else?"

Ms. Cain smiled. "Take it easy tonight. My treat."

It only took me ten minutes to re-shelve the books and then I was on my way through the quiet halls to my room. Almost everyone was at work detail or in their rooms doing homework. When I passed the window overlooking the grassy area with the small track and weight benches, I could see several massive, shadowy shapes still at work outside, but the halls were empty.

Once inside my room, I flipped on my light and my breath caught in surprise. I wasn't sure why I was surprised, unexpected things in my room had become the norm. Clearly I needed to get some better locks for my window.

There on my bed was the dress. Or at least, I assumed it was the dress. It looked like the same white bag that Ozzy left in my closet Saturday night. The same bag I threw out the window a few hours ago. There was a note on top of the bag that I picked up gingerly, almost too afraid to read what it said.

Cleo,

I wish you'd let me talk to you and explain things. It's not what you think. I hope you change your mind about going to the Formal with me, but even if you don't, I want you to have the dress. You deserve to wear red.

-Ozzy

I unzipped the bag and sure enough, the beautiful red fabric spilled out of it. I was conflicted. The dress was so exquisite and fit so perfectly I couldn't imagine how I ever had the audacity to throw such a thing of beauty out the window. But, at the same time, I didn't want to wear it. If I accepted the dress and wore it, it felt like I was forgiving Ozzy for what he'd done and I definitely wasn't ready to forgive or trust him yet.

I sat on the edge of the bed rubbing the soft fabric between my fingers, trying to muster up the courage to let it go. Finally, despite my better judgment, I decided to keep it. It was bought for me, I needed a dress, and the last thing I wanted was to see Quinnie wearing it, which is where it might end up if I demanded Ozzy take it back. I hung the bag back in my closet before settling in at my desk to do homework. The message light was blinking ominously and even though I tried to ignore it, I found it impossible. I clicked on the link and sure enough, there was a message from Ozzy.

Ozzy: Can we talk?

I deleted it. He'd lied to me. He'd betrayed me. And even worse than that, he'd told Quinnie about Cassie and the Homework Harpies. He'd taken my most special memories and secrets and tarnished them by giving them to Quinnie, my enemy. I didn't know if I'd ever be able to forgive him for that.

I threw myself into my homework, eager to give my mind something benign to focus on. For three glorious hours I was a Vanguard again, attacking problems with my brain — not with brawn, skills, or bloodlust that I didn't have. For three hours, I wasn't the girl who could bring fiery hell with a spark of anger; I was Cleo, the girl that was good at homework. It felt good to be normal again. At least the normal I was used to. Just as I was closing my books and stacking everything in a neat little pile to get ready to turn in for the night, my message light began to blink again.

"Dammit, Ozzy! I'm not going to — " My words faded away as I realized the message wasn't from Ozzy, it was from Younglove. I opened it hesitantly.

Ms. Dracone,
Don't skip any more classes. You're getting a warning this time, but next time will require a visit to Dean Overton's office. See you tomorrow afternoon for Workshop.
–Professor Younglove

I breathed a sigh of relief and then groaned. I avoided punishment this time, but there would be no avoiding Ozzy tomorrow, which could be a punishment in and of itself. If the rumors I'd heard at breakfast earlier today were true, he was now the Weapons professor.

I was determined to survive Weapons class — which turned out to be all about knife throwing — without needing Ozzy's help. I paid close attention to his lesson and when it came time to put the lesson to practice, I stepped right up to a booth, not waiting to be told to do so. It was pretty easy. Grab a knife by the blade, throw, repeat. I wasn't hitting the target every time and I was only getting the blade to stick in the target once out of a dozen times, but the throwing was therapeutic.

"Don't throw it like a baseball, keep your arm in a straight line."

I knew it was only a matter of time before he came over. No matter how well I did, he would have something to say. I didn't look at Ozzy, I didn't even stop my rhythm of throwing.

"Do I look like someone who has ever played baseball?" I muttered. "I paid attention, I'm doing just fine." I threw a knife a little harder than necessary, intent on keeping my arm straight through the throw, and with a thud, it stuck into the target just as I said "fine." I merely picked up another knife to throw, wiping the sweat off my forehead with the back of my left hand.

"Yes, you are," Ozzy admitted. When I refused to turn around and talk to him, I heard him finally walk away to find another victim to harass.

With ten minutes left in the class, Ozzy sent us out into the target field to fetch all the knives that had been thrown so that we would have time to wipe down the ones that had found their way into the dirt. I had more to clean off than anyone. Ozzy silently came over with a rag to help me wipe off my knives. He didn't say anything, but I had a feeling that's because there were too many eager ears hovering nearby.

The bell rang and I still had quite a hefty stack of dirty knives. My fellow classmates started to file out of the room, ignoring me as they walked past. All except for one person. Wesley.

"Hey, you need a hand, Cleo?"

I looked up in surprise. "Oh. No thanks, Wes, I think I'll be okay. I'm almost done."

"Sure." He shifted nervously, chancing a glance toward Ozzy before steeling his nerves to speak. "Thanks again, Cleo."

"For what?"

Wesley shifted his weight again, another quick look at Ozzy who was ignoring him. "For inviting me to the Formal. It's really decent of you to go with me since I'm an outcast now and all." Wesley trailed off, but I sensed Ozzy's posture stiffen as he stopped wiping the blade he was holding.

"You don't have to thank me," I assured him. "What Quinnie did to you was wrong. I'm happy to go with you." That wasn't entirely true, but I was happy that Wesley was happy.

Wesley flashed me an appreciative grin and then headed for the door. "See you at lunch," he called with a wave.

Ozzy resumed cleaning the blade he was holding with renewed vigor. He tossed it angrily into the box of clean knives. "You asked Wesley to go to the Formal with you?"

I shrugged. "His date bailed on him."

"So did mine."

I pointed the knife I was cleaning at Ozzy. "You do not want to have this conversation, trust me."

"Of course I do, you won't even let me explain."

"What is there to explain? You were involved with setting me up for the training exercise and with splitting up my group of friends at the University. You could have told me the night I came back, but you didn't. I had to hear it from Younglove. You couldn't tell me, but you told Quinnie. Quinnie, of all people!"

"Quinnie? What are you talking about?"

"I don't know what kind of game you're playing, Ozzy, but I'm not playing it with you. Not anymore." I tossed the last blade into the box. "I have to go, I can't be late for class."

I carried the box of clean knives back to the appropriate weapons cabinet, with Ozzy trailing behind me. I shoved the box in an empty spot on the shelf and when I turned around, Ozzy was blocking my way, running a hand through his hair.

"Can we just talk about this so I can explain? Maybe I could meet you at the library for a tutoring session, or I could come by your room after work detail."

His green eyes searched my face, pleading. He seemed so tortured I almost felt sorry enough for him to agree, but then Cassie's face flashed through my mind along with the memories of the last few days. Quinnie's taunting voice was ringing through my ears, reminding me of his betrayal. There was no explanation that could make it right. I couldn't risk getting caught up in his lies and dishonesty again. It was hard enough surviving in a place where you didn't know who to trust. I was learning that in the world of St. Ignatius, you had to protect your emotions and heart. Trust was something that had to be earned and continually nurtured.

I didn't trust Ozzy.

I brushed him aside so I could get by. Instead of standing his ground and pleading his case further, he let me go.

The entire Academy was getting excited about the Formal, even the professors. While most everyone else was caught up in who was going with whom and were discussing all the other little details of the Formal, I was throwing myself into my studies. The only way I could keep thoughts of Ozzy and Cassie out of my head was to keep my mind busy and full of other information.

Deviation workshop became a lot less interesting since the initial class. In the last three workshops, Younglove insisted everyone do research on their namesake to better understand their capabilities and how to control them. As a result, we spent quite a bit of time in the large gym, at tables, reading books that Ms. Cain provided.

"I want you to stop thinking of yourselves as cadets," Younglove lectured as she stopped behind Eva's chair. "You're not Evangeline. You're Tiger Moth. You have to start thinking of your abilities not just as interesting skills, but as who you are. In this way, you will find that you have greater control and access to your powers."

Quinnie and her gang were hanging on every word coming out of Younglove's mouth, tantalized by the secret identity superhero propaganda that she was using to bribe them into mastering their deviations.

I wasn't swayed. Accepting a code name was the first step in completely relinquishing my identity. I had so little control over my life, and my name was the one thing I still owned. I wasn't, and never would be, Malaysian Ant. If anything, I was willing to be Clementine, but definitely not some freak-of-nature-killing-machine named after a suicidal bug. And yet, I continued to study and read, if only to understand myself a little better and fear my abilities a little less.

Rule the fear.

By the time the weekend rolled around, I was beginning to regret asking Wesley to the dance — not that I didn't like him, but my affection for him was born out of friendliness with a small dose of pity, not actual attraction. I felt bad for the way Quinnie, Eva, and Sadie were making his life a living hell. Wesley's reaction to his social banishment from the rest of the student body was to cling to me since I seemed to be the only person, aside from Theo, that was genuinely nice to him. He started walking me to many of my classes, insisting on sitting right next to me at every meal, and was often waiting for me after derby practice to walk me to dinner. I was starting to feel claustrophobic, but was too afraid to ask him to give me some space. I just couldn't bear to destroy any more of his injured confidence.

Ozzy, on the other hand, hadn't been around for days. I wondered if he was on another mission. And then I was annoyed with myself that I was often preoccupied with worry for him and what he was probably doing. I didn't want to admit that I missed Ozzy, but I did. As much as I told myself I didn't care about him, it was a lie. I didn't trust him, but I still cared. I knew that when I put on the red dress for the Formal next week, I'd be hoping for an approving look from him, coveting a slow dance in his embrace, wanting the taste of a forbidden kiss, and wishing that things were different. It seemed my heart and head were destined to be at odds when it came to Ozzy.

It was Sunday, six days before the Formal, and autumn was in full effect. The trees on the Academy grounds exploded into a chorus of vibrant oranges, reds, and yellows. The gentle fall breeze kept the grounds in a continuous flurry of blazing colors. The wind picked leaves off the ground or snatched them from branches and sent them sailing through the air, causing them to knock against the windows in soft whispers and cover the ground in a patchwork of burnt warmth. I was in my room doing homework as Arabella lay sprawled across my bed, reading an octopus book.

"Did you know that an octopus has three hearts?"

"No," I admitted.

"You don't think they put extra hearts in me, do you?"

"Doubtful. What would you do with two extra hearts? Besides, you don't seem overly compassionate to me," I joked.

"Good point. If anything, they probably removed some of my heart," Arabella played along. "I have been described as heartless by many."

"You mean by Sterling."

"Yes. Many times."

Arabella continued to read and I went back to my Arabic studies. Arabella suddenly gasped. "No way!"

"What?"

"Most octopuses don't survive mating!"

"Sex kills them?"

"Listen to this," she said, pointing to a part in the book that I couldn't read from where I was sitting. "After mating, the male octopus dies after a few months. Then, once the female lays her 200,000 eggs, she spends the next month caring for them. She doesn't bother to get food, she just watches those damn eggs, protecting them from predators. If she gets hungry, she eats an arm or two."

"Very funny."

"I'm not joking. That's what it says. She will ingest one of her tentacles for sustenance. Then, after the eggs hatch, she leaves her little birth cave, but she's so damn weak from watching her eggs grow, she pretty much gets eaten by the first thing that finds her. What a crappy life. I'm never having sex." Arabella slammed the book shut in disgust.

"Arabella, you're not an actual octopus, I think your future sex life is safe."

"I don't think I'm going to risk it."

"Not even for Sterling?"

"Ew. We're just friends. I'm only going to the Formal with him because he's the best dancer here at the Academy."

"Sure," I said. "And I'm going with Wesley because of his fine conversation skills."

Arabella shook her head. "I think that boy really likes you."

I twirled my ponytail in agitation. "I think he likes the idea of me. He likes the idea of someone accepting him for who he is. Everyone else in the Academy thinks he's a pervert."

"He's nice."

"True. He's nice, but he's not . . . he's not . . . " I fluttered my hands in the air, searching for the answer.

"He's not Ozzy," Arabella finished for me.

I lifted my head. "I didn't say that."

Arabella cracked her gum between her teeth. "You didn't have to. I'm your friend, I know what you're thinking."

"Well, if you're my friend, don't bring him up again."

"Cross my heart," Arabella promised with another snap of her gum.

"Which one?" I laughed.

"Someone got a sense of humor all of a sudden," Arabella mused.

"Are you going to do any actual homework or just read cephalopod books all day long?" I asked, stretching my leg across to the bed and nudging the edge of Arabella's book.

"Look who's grumpy and has a big vocabulary. I finished my homework already. How about you? Are you making any progress on controlling your deviation?"

"No. And would you stop calling it a deviation? It's more like a curse, a curse I'm never going to master."

"Want my advice?"

"Of course. As long as it's about the curse and not about my wardrobe again." I'd finally gotten paid for work detail and made my first purchase of non-Academy clothes. They came in at the end of the week and Arabella immediately declared them severely lacking in cool. That basically meant there wasn't enough black and purple.

Arabella rolled her eyes. "You have to figure out what triggers it."

"I know what triggers it. Anger. Righteous anger. But, it doesn't always work."

Arabella sat up on the edge of the bed. "What do you mean?"

"Well, there have been times since I've gotten here when I've been angry, really angry, but nothing happens. And then there are other times, like with Quinnie and the pen, where something little will set me off."

Arabella tilted her head thoughtfully. "Give me an example of a time you were angry but nothing happened."

I bit the inside of my lip. "The day I confronted Ozzy about the kidnapping and Cassie. You know, when I threw the dress out the window? I was thinking about that the other day and it occurred to me that nothing happened. I was so angry at him and nothing caught fire, nothing blew up. Why not? Maybe my deviation is broken."

"Maybe you weren't righteously angry," Arabella offered.

"What do you mean?"

"Maybe you were wrong and you knew it. Your anger wasn't righteous. You can still be angry and be wrong."

"I wasn't wrong."

"If you say so, I'm just trying to help you puzzle this out. Just a question though: have you read anything about the Malaysian Ant?"

"A little."

"And are you aware that they explode to protect their colony when it's threatened?"

"I read that much."

"Well, has it occurred to you that deep down, even though you don't like what he did, you know Ozzy did the right thing for Cassie?"

"She belongs here."

"Hey, I'm just trying to help. I'm not saying you can't be angry about it, but maybe your anger isn't righteous, that's all."

"So, you think Ozzy was right?"

Arabella put her hands up in defense. "You know I'm not a fan of that boy. I'm just saying you need to delve a little deeper if you're going to control your deviation. Think about it. They named you Malaysian Ant. They wouldn't have given you the power to make things explode without some kind of fail safe, right?"

I dropped my head in my hands. If Arabella was right, then I might have made a huge mistake, the least of which was throwing a perfectly good dress out the window.

22

MAKE UP OR MAKE OUT

On Monday, Ozzy informed the class that we would begin training with weapons that were traditionally thought of as ninja weapons. He picked up something that looked like a long, thin, piece of wood and showed it to the class.

"Wouldn't a gun work better?" Theo asked.

"Possibly, but what would you do if you lost your gun or ran out of bullets? You might have to improvise. The more you know about attacking and protecting yourself in various forms of combat, the better your chances of coming out alive. That's why we train you in so many different types of weapons. Today we're going to learn to use the bokken," he said as he held up the piece of wood again.

I could see that it looked somewhat like a crudely shaped sword blade.

"Generally, bokken are used as training tools when learning swordplay, but they can be weapons in their own right. Say, for instance, that you find yourself in an alleyway fighting for your life, what do you do? You look around for something you can use to defend yourself. If you find a broken board or pipe, you've got yourself a bokken. Now let's learn to use it."

As Ozzy was passing the bokkens out, he told everyone to partner up. Just as I was getting used to the idea that I'd be partnered up with Ozzy, like I usually was, Wesley bounded up to my side like a faithful, and annoyingly energetic, puppy. Ozzy showed no emotion as he gave us our weapons. Ozzy then partnered up with Theo to demonstrate to the class the moves he wanted us to work on — various parries to perform a forward thrusting cut and defenses against cuts to the side. He showed each move several times and then told us to practice and perfect those moves.

Soon the room was filled with the harsh cracks of wood on wood, grunts, sweating, and cries of anger when the bokken made contact with flesh and bone. The patch of training area I shared with Wesley was surprisingly quiet and tame. Wesley's attacks were half-hearted and useless. I frowned thinking that it probably would have been more dangerous if we were playing pat-a-cake.

"Wes," I hissed. "You have to actually try to hit me. I'm never going to learn if you act like I'm made of glass."

He made another passive stab toward me and I hit his bokken so hard it cartwheeled out of his hand.

"Sorry, I dropped it," he said.

Wesley jogged over to pick up his bokken, which had knocked up against one of the booths by the target range. He stopped dead in his tracks when he saw Ozzy bending over to pick up his lost weapon.

"Why don't you train a bit with Theo? I'll take over here with

Cleo," Ozzy ordered, slapping his own wooden blade in the palm of his hand like a jailor ready to deal out corporal punishment.

Wesley looked at me, hoping or expecting me to put up a fight and request he stay as my partner, but I didn't. I don't know why I didn't.

"Sure," Wesley agreed, a small frown forming on his face as he turned and walked over to where Theo was brandishing his sword, killing invisible enemies with cartoonish movements and overly exaggerated battle cries.

Ozzy stood in front of me, silently pointing the bokken at me. I adopted the stance he had demonstrated and before I had time to fully prepare, he jabbed at me. I barely dodged his blow and didn't even come close to parrying his sword with my own. He immediately came at me with a side cut and smacked me on the upper arm when I failed to bring up my blade to block his blow in time. I growled in frustration, but didn't complain. I merely brought my bokken up into the ready position again. Ozzy swung again, making a cut to my right arm which I managed to block, even if a bit clumsily. I missed the side cut he swung on the other side and the bokken smacked into my arm in the exact same spot as the time before, sending a sharp pain up into my shoulder. I squeezed my lips together, determined not to utter a single sound. And that's how it went for the rest of the class. I blocked about half of the blows and my body absorbed the rest. The more blows Ozzy landed, the angrier I got. And yet, nothing blew up. Nothing so much as even smoldered. I was mad, but apparently my blood wasn't boiling in righteous anger. There were no explosions.

When the bell rang, Ozzy didn't stop with the swordplay exercise and neither did I. I refused to concede even though it was obvious I was losing. The rest of the cadets watched for a few minutes until it became clear that they would be late for class if they hung around much longer. They tossed their training swords in a pile and left. Wesley was the last to leave, but when it was evident that I wasn't going to spare him so much as a glance, he left with everyone else. I wasn't trying to be rude, I was trying to avoid being whacked with the bokken again. And I refused to give Ozzy the satisfaction of giving up and admitting defeat.

Finally, Ozzy lowered his bokken and bowed his head with a slight nod, indicating he was done with me. He gathered up the wooden swords the class left in a pile and carried them to the weapons cabinet.

"Do you feel better?" I asked indignantly, tossing my bokken to him.

"Oh, are you speaking to me now?" He caught the piece of wood without dropping the pile he was holding.

"You're the only other person around, so it would appear so. You didn't answer my question. Do you feel better now that you've had your revenge? I throw your gift out the window and you beat me with a stick. An eye for an eye, I guess."

Ozzy rounded on me, "I'm doing you a favor, Cleo. As soon as you learn to control your little pyrotechnics, the Program will send you out on missions. They won't care if you're properly trained to protect yourself or not; they'll want to see their creation in action. I'm the only hope you've got."

"Oh, I'm sorry. So beating me to a pulp with a stick is good for me? I guess I should be thanking you then. Thank you," I said with a mock bow.

Chagrined, he looked at my arms, which were covered with

shirt sleeves that hid the bruises I was sure were forming. "Are you hurt?" he asked instead of arguing further.

"Well you certainly weren't tickling me. I vaguely remember you hitting me with a stick. Many times."

"Do you need to go to the infirmary?"

I looked at him steadily. "I'm not bleeding or broken, I'll be fine." I wanted to cross my arms, but I wasn't sure I wanted to risk lifting or touching them.

Ozzy nodded approvingly. "Sit here," he said as he indicated a table to the side of the weapons cabinet. I did as I was told and Ozzy went to the medicine cabinet. He returned, holding a jar and a towel.

"Take your shirt off," he said, tossing the towel to me.

"No."

He turned around. "I can't put the salve on if your arms are covered. Take off your shirt and wrap the towel around yourself. I won't look."

The bell rang as I slipped the shirt over my head and wrapped the towel around my chest. Being late to Professor Peck's class wasn't going to be pleasant, but I had a gut feeling that this was where I needed to be. "All right. I'm decent."

Ozzy made an unintelligible comment in reply and then turned around. He frowned as he surveyed all of the red marks up and down my arms. "You really need to work on your swordplay. Did you actually block any?" The old cockiness started to raid his mouth and tug his lips into a smile — the smile that held so much power over me.

"Stop being an ass. You know I did."

He dipped his fingers into the jar and scooped out a gob of

white, pasty cream that he rubbed onto my arms. It was cold at first and then I immediately began to feel the pain dissipate in healing warmth. The red spots faded as his hands gently worked the cream into my tender skin. He carefully worked the healing paste into every inch of my arms.

"Any on your stomach?" he asked. I nodded. "Lay down then," he ordered.

I did as I was told and lifted up the towel just enough that he could see the marks on my stomach. He rubbed the cream into my skin gently and methodically. When Ozzy was done, I felt his hand linger longer than necessary near my hip. Finally, he let go.

"I think I got them all. Ms. Petticoat's miracle cream," he said as he held up the jar.

I ran my hand over my blemish free abs, once again thankful to be in a military academy. Ozzy offered me his hand and helped me sit upright. I hopped off the table and accidentally stumbled into his arms. I looked up at him and our eyes met briefly. I could see the hunger in his eyes as his gaze shifted to my mouth. I only recognized it because the same hunger was burning in me. I pulled away, grabbing my shirt off the table.

"I have to go, I'm already late for Professor Peck's class."

Ozzy seemed to come out of the trance he was in. "I'll write you a note," he offered, turning back to the table, scrounging around for a piece of paper and pen. I took the opportunity to slip my shirt back on, letting the towel fall to the ground.

"You could just walk me to class and be my personal note," I suggested. Ozzy hadn't been in Peck's class since he took over Farnsworth's duties. He was given the status of Professor and had been removed from all of his other classes so he would be available to teach all of the Weapons classes.

Ozzy scratched the back of his neck. "Yeah, I suppose I could do that."

"Or, you could just tell her that I was injured in your class and get me off the hook."

"I can't do that," Ozzy mused as we entered the main building and made our way to Peck's classroom. "You need all the muscle building you can get. You're walking around on a set of twigs, remember?"

"So says Peck," I answered, looking down at my legs. "Arabella said they're at least saplings."

"Either way, you need Peck's class."

We walked in silence, the empty halls echoing the sounds of our footsteps. Confusion rattled around in my mind, keeping perfect time to the sound of our Academy issued boots slapping against the floor. Before I could decide whether or not I wanted to talk to Ozzy about Cassie and the Homework Harpies and everything else that had happened, we reached the Conditioning room. Ozzy's note-in-person was accepted by Peck and I was sent to the squat rack to turn my feeble twigs into mighty trunks.

I set down my tray and took my obligatory seat next to Wesley at lunch. It was Friday afternoon and the Autumn Formal was a little over 24 hours away. Wesley's chin was propped into one of his hands and he was pushing his lunch around his plate with his fork. I thought about asking him what was wrong, but honestly, I didn't really feel like having that conversation. I was saved the effort of small talk with my melancholy, food demolishing, date-to-be when Theo, Arabella, and Sterling arrived.

Theo crashed into the seat on the other side of Wesley, not even sparing a greeting before tearing into his lunch like a rabid dog. Sterling and Arabella were already deeply absorbed in a meaningless argument, as usual, which left Wesley and me sitting in awkward silence, with only the sound of Theo inhaling his food to keep us company. Theo paused to belch and noticed his brother sulking and smashing his lunch to a pulp.

"What's wrong with you?" Theo managed to get out past a mouthful of food.

"Nothing."

"Are you still pissed about Weapons class?"

Wesley glanced warily at me. "No," he said a little too emphatically.

Arabella stopped arguing with Sterling to join the conversation. "What happened in Weapons class?"

"Nothing," Wesley grumbled again.

"Yeah, if nothing means Ozzy," Theo joked.

"Shut up," Wesley advised.

"What's wrong with Ozzy?" Sterling asked. "He's a great teacher. Much better than Farnsworth. Everyone's been saying so. Our classes have been awesome."

"As much as I hate to admit it," Arabella growled, "Sterling's totally right. I'm finally learning to use some of those stupid weapons properly."

"Oh yeah. Ozzy's a great teacher," Theo agreed. "It's just lover boy here is jealous." He hooked his thumb toward Wesley.

"Don't," Wesley warned.

Arabella looked between the two boys. "What are you talking about?"

Wesley gave Theo another warning look and shook his head, but Theo ignored it. "Dude. I'm tired of hearing you whine about this. Better get it out in the open," he said to his twin. Theo looked at Arabella. "Our boy Wes thinks he should be Cleo's sparring partner, but Ozzy has been hogging her all week. Actually, beating her to a bloody pulp all week is a better description."

"I'm getting better!" I said defensively. It was true, I hadn't needed any of the healing cream today.

Arabella's eyebrows dipped low between her eyes as she looked questioningly at Wesley. "Why would you want to partner up with Cleo? She's hopeless in Weapons class. No offense," Arabella said apologetically to me, "but it's true." I shrugged in acceptance. Arabella continued, "You'll learn more by sparring with people better than you, not someone you can beat up on."

"He's not worried about getting better with his bokken sword-play," Theo laughed. "He's just jealous of Ozzy. He doesn't want Mr. Perfect Aim flirting with his girlfriend and impressing her with his moves."

"I never said that!" Wesley said defensively.

"I'm not Wes's girlfriend," I said almost at the same time.

Theo grinned sympathetically toward his brother. "I guess that's news to Wes."

Wesley, who was usually quiet and mild mannered, yelled at Theo. "Shut up, dude! Why do you have to be such an ass?"

Before a fight between the two brothers could break out, Ozzy suddenly appeared at the table, without a tray of food. He no longer ate his meals in the cafeteria and I couldn't imagine what he was doing at our table at such an inopportune time. Or maybe it was perfect timing since the twins were seconds away from a civil war.

"Cleo," Ozzy said, touching my shoulder. "I forgot to tell you that you have to make up the Weapons class you missed last week."

"Okay," I said, confused. I thought I'd been excused for those classes I'd skipped. All Younglove said was that I wasn't allowed to miss any more. Peck hadn't said anything about making up the missed Conditioning class. And if that woman knew she could punish me for a missed class, she definitely would've taken advantage of the opportunity.

"I wanted to tell you now because you'll have to make it up tonight after your work detail."

"What?" I blurted out. "Tonight? Why?"

"An investigation is being done on Farnsworth and Dean Overton is requiring all Weapons class cadets to be held accountable for the necessary requirements up until this point in the term. Only cadets that have done all of their required work will be allowed to go to the Formal. You missed a class last week and have to make it up before tomorrow."

"Why didn't you tell me about this earlier?"

He shrugged. "Just meet me at the training field at 9:15 tonight. And don't be late, I have to get my beauty sleep."

"Fine, it's a date," I grumbled, rolling my eyes. I immediately regretted my wording. "Not a date," I said hurriedly. "Because you're a professor and I'm a cadet and that's just against the rules. And I don't want to go on a date with you anyway." I tried to salvage the awkward conversation, but it was too late. The damage was done. Everyone was staring at me with odd expressions and Ozzy's cocky smile was victorious. "Never mind, you know what I mean. I'll be there," I muttered.

"Wear something comfortable," Ozzy suggested. As he swaggered out of the cafeteria, Wesley snatched up his tray and stalked off toward the trash can. I wondered how I managed to so easily get myself into such a mess — an unintentional boyfriend that I had no desire to date (or hurt) and an undeniable attraction to a boy that could easily hurt me in more ways than I could count.

I finished re-shelving the books in the library in nearly half the time, and Ms. Cain let me go early. I hurried back to my room to change, eager to shed the Academy plaid. As I stood in my closet agonizing over what to wear out of my slowly growing yet still miniscule wardrobe, I reminded myself that it didn't matter how I looked as long as I was comfortable.

This is just Weapons class, not a date, I kept repeating to myself. Who cares what Ozzy thinks?

Deep down, even though I didn't want to admit it, I knew I cared. Finally, I picked out a pair of black yoga pants, a green tee shirt, and a grey hoodie, and then hurried out to the training field. It was dark and the chilly October air forced me to cross my arms over my chest to keep in the heat. I looked at my watch and discovered I was a few minutes early so I sat down on one of the benches along the edge of the field, bent my knees up to my chest, and pulled the hood up over my head. I wondered what weapon Ozzy would be reviewing with me, and hoped it wouldn't be the bokken. Even though I was getting better, I was still pretty banged up from earlier in the day. Maybe we'd do more knife throwing; I liked that. There was less chance for bruises.

"Good. You're early."

I glanced up to see the outline of Ozzy, illuminated from behind by the training field lights. I couldn't see the expression on his face, but I could hear it in his voice. This was the Ozzy I first met, the one who was persistent and let nothing bother him. Cocky Ozzy.

I'd missed him.

"Let's get going," he said, as he shoved his hands in the pockets of his sweatshirt and headed for the door to the building.

"You told me to meet you here. If we were going somewhere else, why didn't you just tell me to meet you there?"

"So many questions. Just follow."

I hopped off the bench and jogged to catch up to him as he slipped through the doorway. He proceeded to snake his way through the many hallways and I soon realized why he hadn't told me to meet him at this mysterious location — I'd never been there before.

He led me through an arch that descended down a narrow set of stairs that spiraled into darkness. At the bottom we came to another long hallway with closed doors set in either side at intervals. We stopped at the end of the hallway and Ozzy pulled out a key to unlock the door. I was starting to get nervous, envisioning all sorts of horrifying possibilities, such as dungeons and torture chambers, so I was pleasantly relieved when he opened the door, flicked on the light, and I saw it was just an empty room. It looked somewhat like my old martial arts dojo at the University. The wall to the left was a floor to ceiling mirror. The floor itself was covered in rubberized mats — a red border around the edges and a larger tan square area in the middle. The other three walls were covered in padded mats.

"Take off your shoes," Ozzy ordered, putting his arm out in front of me to keep me from walking too far into the room.

I kicked off my sneakers and pushed them against the wall with my foot. "I don't see any weapons."

Ozzy shut the door. "They're at the end of your arms and legs."
His smile was wicked.

So it *was* a training room. "What's it to be then?" I asked icily.
"Tae Kwon Do, Karate, Kung Fu, Aikido, Judo —"

Ozzy interrupted me. "What's it matter? You know them all
anyway."

I strolled toward the middle of the room, hands on my hips.
"Was there anything that wasn't in my file?" I asked testily.

"Lots of things," Ozzy offered. "But don't worry, I plan to find
those out too."

Annoyed, I spun around, indicating the room. "Is there a point
to this? Surely there are better ways to help me with my Weapons
proficiency."

"You want another round with the gun?"

I frowned. "You know I don't."

"My main goal is to make sure that every cadet in my class
leaves prepared for the types of things they're going to face once
they leave the Academy. You're not going to be with an army of
Mandates, shooting at the enemy. You, and the rest of the Deviants,
are going to be on special ops missions. Do you know why Young-
glove had you kidnapped?" When I didn't answer, Ozzy continued.
"Because there is always the chance you're going to get caught
doing the missions they'll send you on. She needed to know that
you won't lose your shit if you get captured, that you'll be able to
defend yourself. And you might have to do it with nothing more
than your body and brains. Understand?"

Instead of nodding or saying yes, I just stared at him. I didn't
ever want to imagine being captured and held captive like I'd been

two weeks ago. Even though it wasn't a real kidnapping, it felt like it at the time. The terror was real. The nightmares I'd had since escaping were real too.

"Then let's get on with it," Ozzy said, acting as if I'd agreed with him instead of giving him the silent treatment.

I was ready for his first attack, easily blocking his punches and jabs. We circled each other for a few minutes, Ozzy throwing different combinations at me. He wasn't punching fast or hard enough to hurt me, he was testing me. He'd been rougher with me earlier in the day with the bokken training.

It didn't take long for me to get bored — waiting for Ozzy to make a move and then defending his attack when he finally made it. The next time he stepped back, I stepped forward, pivoting on my left foot and snapping my leg around in a round house kick. It made contact with the side of Ozzy's face and he dropped like a rag doll.

I yelped. I never expected to get past his defenses, I was just trying to mix it up a bit. I hurried to him, dropping to my knees beside his prone body. His eyes were closed and he was laying on his back, arms and legs splayed out haphazardly. Luckily, he was still breathing, so apparently I hadn't done any real damage. I touched the red mark on his face carefully.

"Oh my God. Are you okay? Ozzy. Ozzy!" I called, trying to rouse him, shaking his shoulder.

Suddenly, his eyes popped open, his left arm flew up at lightning speed, and he grabbed the back of my head, pulling me to him until his lips pressed firmly against mine. Then he let me go and rolled to the side and up to his feet with a mischievous grin. He was bouncing on the balls of his feet like a boxer.

"Ozzy - 1, Cleo - 0."

"What are you talking about? I just kicked you in the head, that's worth at least five. And I fail to see how you managed to score one."

"I let you kick me in the head, faked incapacitation, and then I delivered the death blow."

"Death blow?"

"You got close enough that I could've snapped your neck in two, stabbed you, or incapacitated you in a hundred different ways."

"Don't be ridiculous."

"For the next hour, every time I get close enough to kiss you, that represents a death blow."

"You can't just kiss me!" I shouted indignantly. "You're my professor. It's inappropriate."

"Then don't let me get close enough," Ozzy challenged, charging me.

I expected him to throw a punch or kick. Too late I realized he was tackling me. We went to the floor, rolling with the momentum of Ozzy's take down. I ended up flat on my back with Ozzy straddling my torso, my arms trapped by his legs, his hands holding my shoulders to the ground. He leaned down and kissed me lightly on the end of my nose.

"Ozzy - 2, Cleo - 0. That was too easy," he taunted. I struggled, but my strength was no match for his weight. Finally Ozzy disentangled himself and returned to the middle of the room. "Again," he ordered.

I got to my feet, glaring at him. "That wasn't skill, that was brute strength," I complained. "Emphasis on the brute."

"Hey, whatever works, darlin'. You think the bad guys are going to fight the way you want them to? You better learn to adapt," he suggested as he rushed me again.

I was ready this time and dodged him, throwing out an arm that almost made contact. There was a flurry of kicking, blocking, and punching as we danced around the room. I thought my hand-to-hand combat was good, but Ozzy definitely knew what he was doing. And he seemed to anticipate my every move, as if he'd memorized my fighting style. I wondered just how much he'd watched me fight and train over the years.

I dodged another punch and threw one that failed to make contact. Ozzy was no longer taking it easy on me and I was fighting for my life. Well, not actually my life, but for the protection of my dignity. With a series of side kicks, Ozzy forced me back toward the wall and as I threw a right hook at him to avoid being trapped in the corner of the room, he caught my fist in his hand and twisted my arm around behind my back, pushing me up against the matted wall, face first. He leaned in and dragged his lips down the side of my neck. His breath left a trail of hot desire that I tried to ignore.

"Ozzy - 3, Cleo - 0," he said, releasing me and jogging back to the middle of the room.

The next bout took longer. I was learning I had to stay out of his reach, keep him on the defensive, and not allow him to grab any part of my body. He almost had me again when I tried to throw another round house kick at him. He ducked under and came up in front of me, grabbing me around the waist. Just as he was about to plant another winning kiss on me, I brought my forearm up and rammed it into the side of his face. He stumbled backwards and I spun out of his reach.

"Cleo - 1," I said.

Ozzy merely laughed, dragging his hand across his mouth, wiping away the small drops of blood that were evidence of his newly split lip. "I'm still ahead," he taunted.

"Not for long," I promised. I went on the offensive, digging out every move and combination I'd ever learned in my training. We dodged, punched, and kicked — each of us blocking the other as if our bodies could read each other, as if our minds were in sync. Both of us were sweating and breathing hard from the exertion.

I tried to ignore the sheen of perspiration on Ozzy's muscles as they rippled and tensed with each move. Losing focus would cost me another death blow for sure. Instead, I concentrated on keeping him out of range until I was ready to strike. I feinted to the left as if I was going to punch with my right hand. Instead, I jabbed with my left hand. I hoped to catch him unaware and was already starting to follow through with a cross punch with my right hand when I realized too late that he'd caught my left wrist. The punch with my right hand missed its mark and soon, it too was trapped in Ozzy's iron grip. He smiled as I struggled to get free.

"What are you going to do, Ms. Dracone? It looks like kiss number four is on its way. Just give in now and pucker up already," he suggested with a tilt of his head.

"Never!" I shouted, trying to yank my hands back. I hurled my left knee up, intent on sinking it into his stomach, but he was expecting it. He leaned to the side to avoid the blow and in the same motion, used his left leg to sweep my right leg. We went down in a heap, Ozzy somehow managing to shield me from most of his weight as he fell on top of me. He was still holding my wrists, my arms stretched over my head.

"You must want me to kiss you. You're making this way too

easy," he teased, his lips inches away from my face.

I thrashed around, trying to get free, but Ozzy had my arms pinned to the floor and the weight of his body was draped over my chest. I couldn't kick him, but I bent my legs and tried to push my back off the floor and launch him off. It didn't do any good. He slowly leaned in and when his lips finally touched mine, my fighting instincts melted away. I could faintly taste the tangy, saltiness of the blood of his busted lip. He pulled back a fraction and our eyes met.

"Ozzy - 4, Cleo -1. I'm winning," he murmured, his breath intermingling with mine.

He let go of my hands and tensed, leaning on his elbows to keep his weight off me, clearly expecting another elbow to the face. Instead, I reached up and threaded my fingers in his hair, pulling his head back down, bringing his lips back to the heat of my own. I didn't want to fight with him anymore. Not for training, and certainly not for real. I couldn't even remember why I was so mad at him in the first place. Was Arabella right? Maybe my anger hadn't been righteous at all.

Our mouths seemed to dance together, just as in sync as our fighting had been. Ozzy rolled over, pulling me on top of him, so his hands could explore my curves as expertly as his tongue was exploring my mouth. I felt a flash of heat and tingling, a burning desire that was uncurling through my entire body. I leaned into him, kissing him more deeply and Ozzy moaned appreciatively, his hands making another round of exploration.

A small beeping sound echoed through the room. Suddenly, Ozzy sat up, peeling me away from his body. "Looks like our time is up." And just like that, the heat disappeared.

I shook my head in confusion. "What?"

He held his wrist up in front of my face so I could see his watch, which was making the beeping sound. "10:15. Class is over, you've fulfilled your obligations. You may go to the Formal tomorrow," he announced.

"Oh. Right," I said absentmindedly. After our tongue wrestling match, I expected Ozzy to ask me to ditch Wesley and take him to the dance instead.

I wanted him to ask me to.

He didn't.

Ozzy pushed himself off the floor and went to the wall to put his shoes on. "I'll walk you back to the dorm. I know it's hard finding your way back from the training rooms down here the first time. Besides, I'm going that way anyway."

"Okay," I said weakly.

After we both had our shoes on, Ozzy led me back through the maze of hallways, not speaking. I wished I knew what was going on in his mind. How could he just turn off desire like that? It was desire, wasn't it? It seemed like he wanted me. Or was the whole training exercise and kissing just a way to torment me for ditching him and inviting Wesley to the Formal? Maybe it was all just a game to him.

"All right, here you go," Ozzy said once we reached the main desk at the bottom of the stairway leading to the dorms. "See you tomorrow." He turned to go to the boys' dorms.

"Are you going to the Formal?" I asked.

"I'll be there."

I wanted to ask him who he was going with and desperately hoped it wasn't Quinnie. "Are you going as a cadet or as a chaperone?" That was a safe enough question.

He turned around, his green eyes looked sad and the smile on his face was a forced one. "Why? Do you need chaperoning?"

My face flushed. "No. Of course not. Wesley and I are just friends."

"Good," Ozzy said. "Then save a dance for me." And with that, he disappeared into the stairwell.

I'd save them all for you, I thought. I turned to go up the stairwell to my dorm room and reached up to touch my lips. They were sore from kissing Ozzy, but a delicious kind of sore that told me for the first time since the kidnapping-that-wasn't-a-kidnapping, I was going to have good dreams.

⤳ 23 ⤳

In Distress

It was Saturday evening and, to my relief, the football game was over. The guys won. Barely. After seeing the game, I was glad I'd been put on the derby team and not the football squad. I thought roller derby was rough, but it was nothing compared to the violence dished out on the football field. The girls hit just as hard as the guys and played even dirtier.

Currently, I was seated at my desk chair while enduring Arabella's brush, comb, and curling devices. I wasn't sure why she even owned such things when she could easily change her looks with just a thought. Arabella had already done her own hair — a black updo with a thin silver headband and blue, fuschia, and purple streaked pieces of hair straying down the side of her face. I wondered what Arabella's dress looked like since her hair was intended to match it.

After what seemed like hours, Arabella proclaimed me done. I went to the mirror and couldn't help smiling when I saw the miracle Arabella had performed on my usually disobedient hair. She took my unruly mess of curls and turned them into a work of art. The hair on the sides was pulled back into a loose, elegant bun with the rest of my hair falling into big, luxurious, auburn curls that cascaded down my back. Shorter strands curled and caressed the sides of my face. I tilted my head to see that Arabella had placed big, glittering beads throughout my hair to match the shiny beads on the dress.

"Wow," I said. "I can't believe you did this. Did you use your deviation to get it this perfect looking?"

Arabella smiled proudly. "I wish. Your hair is about as cooperative as a pissed off, twitchy-tailed cat. But I tamed it. Because I kick ass. He'll totally love it."

"Who?" I asked, fussing with the hair that tickled my cheeks.

"Uh, Wesley? Your date? Who did you think I was talking about?"

Arabella hadn't asked about the make-up Weapons class last night, but I was pretty sure she knew something was up. Her room faced the training field just like mine. She was sure to have noticed that Ozzy and I weren't out there last night.

"I thought maybe you were talking about Sterling," I fumbled immediately.

"Right. We'll be lucky if Sterling wears something that matches and has been properly ironed. Don't hold your breath that he'll notice what your hair looks like. Most guys won't get past the beaded bust of your dress anyway."

"Then, why go to all this fuss?" I asked.

"For your pride," Arabella said indignantly, scanning the tips of her fingers. She scrunched up her nose and the color of her nails changed from fuschia to a deep purple. "That's better," she murmured. "If you go in there looking like you rolled right out of bed, like you normally do, Quinnie will have a field day."

"She's going to no matter what. It won't matter how good or bad I look."

Arabella shrugged. "Well, let's hope Wesley notices then. Someone besides me should appreciate how hot that 'do is." She looked at the clock. "All right, time to get these dresses on. We're right on time to be fashionably late." Arabella snatched the two white bags that were hanging in my closet and handed me the smaller one.

I unwrapped the red dress and laid it across the bed. Ozzy was right. It was my favorite color, I just never dared to put it on. And I couldn't remember why. Well, it was time for things to change. I gingerly lifted the dress off the bed and stepped carefully into it. Before I could even ask, Arabella was zipping it up.

"Thanks," I said, turning around.

Arabella's dress was oddly breathtaking. It was dark purple satin, fitting her chest, waist, and hips like a second skin. Somewhere around her knees it puffed out, bunched and scrunched up in haphazard ruches that made the fabric billow out like a lumpy cloud. The bottom of the dress was dark purple and faded upward into fuschia, finally turning into a bright blue around the bodice. It was colorful, odd, and totally Arabella. And it matched her hair perfectly.

"Ready to turn some heads?" Arabella smiled.

"Absolutely." I didn't admit it, but there was certainly one head I hoped to turn and it wasn't the one whose arm I'd be on tonight.

Even though the Formal started at seven and we didn't come down until quarter after, the common area where the dorm staircases met was filled. It seemed everyone was planning on being fashionably late. I followed Arabella, pushing through the mounds of taffeta, high heels, and silk ties.

"There they are." Arabella pointed across the room to where our dates waited. It would've been hard to miss them. Well, it would've been hard to miss Sterling. He was wearing a black jacket and pants, but his shirt was a deep purple, perfectly matching Arabella's dress. The shirt was missing the obligatory tie and he neglected to button the top two buttons. He was also wearing matching purple Converse Chuck Taylor sneakers and it looked like his clothes were mostly wrinkle free. Wesley, on the other hand, was catalogue-perfect formal. He was wearing a black tux with a grey vest and matching tie that almost looked silver from across the room.

We made our way over to the corner where Sterling and Wesley were waiting. Theo was with them and dressed in a white tux. His grey vest and tie were the same color as Wesley's, and the two of them standing side by side reminded me of photo negatives of one another. Theo was the only guy dressed in a white suit and stuck out like a sore thumb, which was probably his intention.

"Wow, you look incredible," Wesley said, making an effort to keep his eyes on my face. I wondered how hard it was for him to not use his deviation.

"Thanks, you look great too," I answered honestly.

"Sorry, I don't match you," Wesley apologized, indicating his grey vest. "I ordered this to match Eva's dress." His eyes flickered momentarily to the other side of the room where Eva was dressed in a silvery sheath of a dress that didn't leave much to the imagination. She was hanging on the arm of a Mandate that I recognized from Weapons class.

"No big deal," I shrugged. "Matching is kind of corny anyway."

"I, for one, like corny," Sterling announced. "Don't hate on the purple. You know you love it."

"I actually do." I smiled as I nudged his foot with the toe of my high heel. "Especially the shoes."

Sterling looked down at his new kicks. "Yeah, I'm really hoping that Ozzy takes us to another Ravens game so I can get my money's worth out of these things."

"He took you to a Ravens game?" Wesley asked, astounded.

"Hey, I feel like dancing, let's get going," Arabella interrupted, keeping Sterling from revealing any information from the Ravens day fiasco. "I don't want to stand around in this hallway all night talking about shoes." She grabbed Sterling's hand and dragged him toward the hallway.

Wesley offered his arm to me and I slipped my hand over his elbow. He was dressed the right way, acting the right way, but everything felt wrong. Or was it just that he felt wrong? As we zigzagged through the mob of fancily dressed Sophisticates, I felt the strange sensation of someone watching me. More than just a fleeting sensation.

I glanced around and off to the right I saw him. Ozzy was leaning against the wall, arms crossed, right leg bent with his foot propped against the wall behind him. He was dressed all in black: black pants, black jacket, black shirt, black tie — except for the piece of silk peeking out of the breast pocket of his jacket. It was the same red as my dress.

Ozzy was watching me the same way he had the day I met him in the hallway before my very first class. For a moment, the sound and bustle of the crowd seemed to fade and we were the only two people in the room, tethered by a gaze that was stronger than words. Captured by Ozzy's presence, I wasn't looking where I was going and was bumped into a large Mandate which left me teetering precariously on my high heels. Wesley's grip steadied me and kept me from toppling into a pile of red silk and curses.

"Thanks," I managed, gripping Wesley's arm tightly and clamping my lips together to keep in the profanity that was trying to escape. I chanced a quick look over my shoulder, but Ozzy was gone.

The area where the Formal was being held was beautifully decorated. A huge tent was erected over the immense patio that stretched across the back of the building. White lights and amber-colored gauze were draped elegantly inside the tent, accented with burnt oranges, reds, and golds. A DJ was set up at the far end with a huge screen behind him that flashed with moving colors and images. Multiple tables covered with gold and white cloths were strewn on the grassy area alongside the patio. The air was just cool enough to keep dancing and mingling from becoming a hot, sweaty affair. Off in the dark distance, I could see the outlines of the woods where we did our morning runs. The woods looked decidedly less friendly in the dark than they did in the day.

Arabella and Sterling immediately headed for the dance floor and I had to admit that they weren't kidding when they bragged about their skills. A lot of people just stood and watched, and those that were brave enough to take a turn with the music gave them plenty of space.

"Want to dance?" Wesley asked.

It was a fast song so I accepted. I wasn't ready to be pressed up against Wesley, swaying in time to a slow song. He looked nervous as he took my hand and pulled me out onto the dance floor, so I smiled at him. I found that I spent most of my time laughing at Arabella and Sterling or searching the crowd for Ozzy. Wesley didn't seem to notice, he was just happy to not be lurking along the edges of the party, alone, like his brother.

After a few songs, a dreamy, slow ballad started easing its way out of the speakers. Couples slowed their gyrating pace and the space between them disappeared as arms pulled bodies close.

"You want me to get you something to drink?" Wesley asked, sensing my apprehension.

"Oh, you don't have to do that, I can get it myself," I said.

"No, let me," Wesley offered again. "What'll it be?" he asked, already on his way to the refreshment bar.

"Just water, thanks." I clasped my hands and leaned against one of the tent support poles as he happily jogged off.

"So, you're here with the pervert?"

I turned to see Katie, drink in hand, staring after Wesley.

"He's not a pervert. That's a pack of Quinnie lies and you should know better," I scolded her.

"I do," Katie smiled, taking a sip of her soda. "I just wanted to ruffle your feathers a bit." She cocked her head. "He's good looking, but a little on the small side."

I laughed. "More like you're a little on the colossal side." Katie looked sideways at me. "But sexy colossal," I added.

"You know it. So, how's it feel to have a steady boyfriend?"

"He's not my boyfriend," I said, defensively.

"Does he know that?" Katie asked, her eyebrows arching.

I looked over toward the line where Wesley was standing. He

turned and waved at me, smiling.

"Of course he does," I said past the hitch in my throat.

Katie's date came up from behind, grabbed her arm, and pulled her toward the mass of swaying couples. With a backwards wave to me, Katie disappeared into the ocean of colorful ruffles and lace that rippled with groping hands and teasing lips.

I wondered how I was going to avoid taking the plunge with Wesley. I didn't want to hurt his feelings, but I didn't feel that way about him either. What exactly would he expect of me? Could a slow dance with him be innocent? I hoped so.

"You owe me a dance."

I winced, hoping Wesley couldn't guess what I was thinking. When I looked up, however, it wasn't Wesley beside me. It was Ozzy. His brown, tousled curls were tamed into a slick wave which gave me a clear view of his deep green eyes.

The corners of my mouth lifted up without my permission. "How do you figure that?"

"It's the least you can do, seeing as how you ditched me." His eyes travelled up and down my figure quickly. It wasn't creepy, but I still felt the burn of his gaze as if he'd touched me with his hands. "You look knockout in that dress," he said as his eyes returned to my face. "I'm jealous," he admitted in a near whisper, leaning in so only I could hear.

"I'll let you borrow it when I'm done with it," I offered slyly.

Ozzy only grinned. "Come on, let me take you for a spin," he said, nodding his head toward the dance floor.

"The song's almost over and I have a date," I argued lamely. Right on cue, the song ended and another ballad started up.

"Your date's gonna be in line at least one more song. No sense standing around like a wallflower."

He took my hand and I let him lead me away from the edge of the dance floor and through the pulsating crush of cadets. Stopping on the far side of the crowd and in the shadows, far from the sight of Wesley, Ozzy pulled me close. I allowed my body to fit against him, curve for curve. My hands instinctively moved up his arms and draped over his shoulders, my fingers grazing the soft hair that curled down over the edge of his collar. His hands were innocently circling my waist and his jaw rested against the side of my head. My face was almost buried in the curve of his neck. The music coursed through me as I swayed with Ozzy, my body in tune with every movement of his.

I didn't notice when the song ended and a new one started. I didn't notice that I'd laid my head on Ozzy's chest and closed my eyes. I didn't notice that his arms had tightened around me. All I managed to notice was the sound of his heart beating and how perfect it felt to be in his arms. I lightly ran my fingers along the delicate curls at the end of his hair.

"May I cut in?"

I pulled away from Ozzy in surprise, my fingers still tingling from the touch of his hair. Wesley was standing next to us, a water bottle in his hand. Although his question was polite, it was obvious by the way he was looking at Ozzy that he was feeling anything but civil. And even though I'd never given Wesley the impression that he and I were anything more than friends, I felt guilty for the look of hurt on his face.

"Absolutely," Ozzy responded. He took my hand and brought it to his mouth. "Thank you," he said as his lips grazed the back of my hand. "Sorry, I borrowed Cleo for a dance or two," he said to Wesley who was looking even more irritated than when he first arrived. "She looked lonely."

"Well, I'm back. Feel free to track down your own date now." Wesley handed me the water and put his hand possessively on my lower back. I wanted to shake his hand off, to remind him that he didn't own me, but I didn't.

Ozzy's mouth pressed into a tight grimace, but he managed to turn it into a smile. "I think I will," he said, glaring at Wesley. "Cleo," he nodded his head toward me in a goodbye before melting into the crowd of dancers.

"Do you want to finish the song or start the water?" Wesley asked, hopefully.

"Whatever you want," I answered, wishing for the latter but not wanting to hurt Wesley's feelings.

He pulled his bottom lip through his teeth, clearly aware of the space between us and the lack of space that had been between me and Ozzy just moments ago. "Sterling has a table and Arabella is harvesting snacks from the buffet, why don't we go join them?" he offered.

"Sounds good," I breathed with relief. I felt guilty. Wesley was the opposite of repulsive and I shouldn't have been opposed to dancing with him, but all I could think about was Ozzy and how I felt incomplete now that he was gone. All I wanted was Ozzy's arms around me again, but instead I had Wesley's hand on my back, staking his claim. Wesley was a great guy, but compared to Ozzy, he was white noise.

As we skirted the edge of the crowd and found the table with our friends and the bounty of snacks, I realized I had no one to blame but myself. I was the one that reneged on my date with Ozzy.

I was the one that had invited Wesley to the Formal.

Sterling and Arabella, for once, weren't arguing. They were too busy complimenting each other on their dancing skills and planning which requests they wanted to make to the DJ for the remainder of the night. I sat down next to Arabella and was indelicately stuffing a pastry into my mouth when I noticed there was a commotion in the middle of the tent. Quinnie was storming across the dance floor, her hair nearly sparking with energy. People were leaping out of her way as if experiencing an electric shock, which from the way she was raging, was probably exactly what was happening. Quinnie was headed for the DJ and Marty was attempting to intercept her and calm her down. He was too wise to actually touch her though.

"What's going on?" Sterling stood, craning his neck to see what was sending Quinnie careening into a full blown hissy fit. "Oh." He laughed. "That's awesome."

I stood up with Arabella, but since Quinnie was drawing a crowd, we couldn't see. We had to stand on our chairs to see over the mob. Behind the DJ, the screen which previously had been just a blur of atmospheric shapes and colors was now playing a silent video. And not just any video. It was a collage of video clips of Quinnie on the derby track. Someone had taken a video of the last derby match and created an embarrassing montage of Quinnie in the most undignified positions as she took hit after hit after hit.

"I'm totally going to kiss whoever is responsible for this," Arabella cooed.

"You promise?"

I looked down from my perch to see Theo with a wide, self-satisfied grin plastered on his face.

"You did this?" I asked him, gesturing at the mayhem. Quinnie was screaming at the top of her lungs and the DJ was furiously attempting to get the video to stop playing as he helplessly punched at the buttons on his audio and visual system.

Theo laughed. "He's never going to get it to turn off by doing that." He dangled a small, black object between his fingers before flipping it around and pushing a button. To the surprise of the DJ, a new song started blaring out of the speakers. It was a country song and the first words I could make out were "Mean Girls." New video clips flashed across the screen. All of them of Quinnie, none of them flattering.

"Mean girls, scratchin' and spittin.' Mean girls, can't be forgiven. Mean girls, make mean women. Mean girls," the speakers bellowed as everyone watched Quinnie on the screen, acting out the words as if she had meant to. I had no idea how Theo managed to get all the footage of Quinnie, but it was doing what he meant it to do — sending her into an emotional breakdown. Younglove arrived on the scene and was calmly talking to the DJ. Meanwhile, Quinnie was still screaming, looking for a target for her humiliation.

"If they ain't out a-prowlin,' creepin' down the hall, you'll find 'em by the lockers, baby, sharpenin' their claws." The speakers rattled with the southern drawl of a female singer. Quinnie glared helplessly at the screen as a clip of her, Eva, and Sadie flashed across it. They were laughing, and cartoonish devil horns and claws had been childishly drawn onto them making them look like ridiculous, real life versions of the song.

Quinnie rushed the DJ's table, grabbed his keyboard and threw it at the offending video. The heavy piece of equipment sliced through the screen leaving a huge, ragged hole, but the images still played across the tattered fabric and the music was still going strong.

"Mean girls, make stuff up. Mean girls, just bad luck. Mean girls, stink."

Quinnie, now more enraged than ever, finally located me and my friends towering over the back of the crowd as we stood on our chairs. "You!" she screeched, pointing in our direction. "I know you did this!"

"Who is she talking to?" I asked.

"Probably whichever one of us she can get her hands on first," Arabella answered, getting down from her chair and pulling me with her. "Bring it on, witch," she added in a whisper, clenching her hands, already in derby mode. It didn't matter that she was in a sleek, purple gown. Arabella was always ready for a fight.

"I'm out of here," Theo said, taking off the opposite way.

"Coward," Sterling called after him. "But, you're an awesome coward!" he added.

Quinnie was pushing through the crowd, glaring at me, intent on only one thing. Revenge.

And then there was a wall of bodies between me and Quinnie. The *Damsels* were blocking Quinnie's path. Katie, Susie, Anna, Jane were all there, ready to protect me and Arabella.

"Get out of my way," Quinnie hissed at Katie.

"Ask me nicely and I'll think about it."

Quinnie reached out and pushed Katie backwards. Normally, Katie's bulk and size would have protected her, but at Quinnie's touch there was a loud pop and Katie collapsed, moaning. Small tendrils of smoke rose from two scorched handprints that marred the silk bodice of her dress. Everyone stared in shock, too stunned to even move. Before Quinnie could charge me and Arabella, she was grabbed from behind. One of Ozzy's arms was around her torso, pinning her arms to her sides. The other one was holding a dark object that he pressed to her neck.

"Party's over," Ozzy growled at Quinnie as he dragged her away from the crowd toward the back door of the building. Quinnie didn't bother to put up a fight, or if she was, whatever Ozzy had pressed to her neck seemed to be taking the fight out of her.

Younglove bent down to check on Katie who was still moaning, but not unconscious. She motioned to Katie's date and another Mandate that was standing nearby.

"Please take Katherine to the infirmary. Tell Ms. Petticoat I'll be there as soon as I deal with Quinby." She stood, spun on her heel, and then quickly disappeared into the building, following Ozzy.

As Katie was lifted and quickly carted away from the party, the regular playlist started up again and people moved back to the dance floor, excitedly talking about what had just happened.

I twisted my hands nervously. "I hope Katie's okay."

"She had no idea what she was up against." Arabella shook her head in disbelief.

"I can't believe Theo rigged that up," Sterling muttered. "No offense, but most of the time he seems like an idiot."

"There are cameras all over the Academy. It would've been easy for him to tap into them and get what he needed. When it comes to electronics, he's pretty much a genius," Wesley explained, staring after Katie regretfully. "I don't think he ever imagined Quinnie would resort to public violence like that, though."

"Why didn't you warn us?" Sterling asked.

Wesley held his hands up. "Hey, I had no idea he was planning that."

"I wonder where he ran off to?" Arabella craned her neck, looking for the unmistakable white suit that Theo was wearing.

"He probably went to cover his tracks, although that's pointless. Younglove knows what he can do; she'll know it was him." Wesley drummed his fingers nervously on the table, obviously worried for his brother.

We spent the next fifteen minutes working through the snacks Arabella had gathered earlier, worrying over Katie's condition, and wondering what kind of punishment Quinnie would be subjected to this time. I was trying to convince everyone to come with me to the infirmary to check on Katie when Theo finally showed up to our table.

"Katie's going to be fine," he said, taking a seat.

"You saw her?" Arabella asked.

Theo nodded. "After I saw what Quinnie did to her, I felt terrible. I checked out the video in the infirmary and she's talking and moving now. She's going to be fine."

I paused mid-bite, a square of cheese inches from my mouth. "There are video cameras in the infirmary?"

Theo tilted his head. "There are video cameras nearly every-where here except our dorm rooms and the bathrooms. Why?" A devilish smile crept over his lips.

"No reason," I lied, not looking at Theo just in case he could see the truth in my eyes.

Had anyone been watching when Ozzy kissed me that first time in the infirmary? And what about the training room? Were there cameras there, too? I was going to have to put my lips on serious lockdown from now on. All I needed was a public video montage of me tongue wrestling with Ozzy. I reminded myself to keep Theo on my good side from now on.

I was still nursing my water and stressing over the idea of cameras in the infirmary when my partner-in-kissing-crime came to stand next to me.

"Cleo, I need to talk to you." Ozzy's handsome face was etched with concern, eminent bad news evident in every feature.

"Is Katie okay?"

"She'll be fine. I really need to talk to you in private, though."

Wesley pushed himself between me and Ozzy. "I thought I made it clear that Cleo was *my* date."

Ozzy's eyes flashed dangerously as his fists opened and closed ominously.

I stood up, angrily pushing Wesley aside. "Wes, you don't own me. I'm perfectly capable of making my own decisions. Besides, Ozzy didn't ask me to dance, he asked to talk to me. And even if he did ask me to dance, I'm allowed to say yes." I turned to face Ozzy. "What's going on?"

He sighed. "It's Cassie. She's missing again."

∼ 24 ∼

TRACKING THE DAMSEL

Ozzy gave me the bad news. Cassie hadn't been seen since Friday afternoon. She went back to her room after classes were over and skipped dinner. No one really thought much of it — that had become her routine since I'd left. However, when Cassie didn't show up for a study session Saturday afternoon, the Hounds did a search of her room and found her missing. A subsequent search of the campus and interviews with the other students proved just as fruitless. It was as if she had fallen off the face of the earth, which in the world of Sophisticates, was impossible to do. Supposedly.

"Well, what are they going to do about it?" I asked as I emotionally crumbled into mild hysterics.

Cassie was missing.

My hands were shaking and my heart was hammering in my chest. I crossed my arms to keep myself from losing control and combusting right on the spot. Tears were squeezing their way out of the corners of my eyes and making their way to my cheeks, in full, humiliating view where everyone could see.

"They're sending me to find her," Ozzy responded, putting a hand on my shoulder.

I sniffed. "Oh. That's good, right? You'll find her won't you?"

"We'll find her," he answered. "You're coming with me this time."

"I'm going, too," Arabella interrupted.

"Me too," said Sterling. "This party's gotten kind of lame ever since Quinnie went psycho and trashed the DJ's stand."

"Good," agreed Ozzy, looking at Arabella and Sterling gratefully. "Younglove wants this to be a Deviant search and rescue mission."

"This isn't a training exercise, is it?" I asked. Despite the way I phrased the question, I was desperately hoping it was, that Cassie was safe and sound at the University. I was starting to realize that Ozzy was right. Cassie was better off at the University, preparing to be a Vanguard. I'd been selfish to want my best friend with me. I'd never really considered the danger that being a Mandate at St. Ignatius would present to Cassie. At least I'd been trained in martial arts as my leisure activity. She'd done ballet. They'd tear her to pieces here. Why hadn't I realized that?

Because I'd been selfish.

Ozzy shook his head. "Not a training exercise. She's missing and even the Hounds can't find her. I'm not going to lie, Cleo, this is bad. Sophisticates don't go missing. We can't."

"What do you mean?" I sniffed.

Ozzy held up his arm and pulled back his shirt sleeve, pointing to the tattoo on his forearm. The same tattoo that I, and every other Sophisticate, had. "This isn't just a brand, it's a tracking device. This is how they know where we are at all times," he said, stealing a knowing glance at Sterling. "But Cassie, she's no longer on the grid."

"What does that mean?"

"It means we have no idea where she is."

"How could that happen? Could she just cut it out or something?" I shuddered at the thought.

"No. It's embedded too intricately for that. She'd have to cut her arm off, and even then, we'd still be able to track her arm," he explained, ignoring my horrified look. "I don't know why the device isn't working, but it means we have to find her the old-fashioned way. We sniff her out. I have the tracking skills, but you know her best. You'll see clues that I might otherwise miss, that's why you're coming with me."

I sniffed again and wiped away the tears that were straggling down my cheeks, resolving to find my strength — for Cassie. "Let's go."

"We're going," said Theo, indicating himself and Wesley.

"Younglove knows what you did tonight," Ozzy said to Theo.

"I figured." Theo suddenly found his thumbnail exceedingly interesting. "You know, I only did it because of how Quinnie's been treating Wes."

"Younglove thinks you should come," Ozzy continued. "You're not in any trouble. You know how she likes to see people standing up for themselves. And you," Ozzy looked at Wesley. "I guess you might as well tag along, too. We can't exactly leave you to the wolves." He nodded toward the rest of Quinnie's entourage.

Thirty minutes later, the six of us were out of our formal wear, belted into an Academy SUV, and exiting through the front gates and down the long lane that cut through the dark woods. This time, there were no professors along for the ride, just one Hound acting as what I guessed was the equivalent of a chaperone. Not that it mattered.

With our tattoos, I realized we were walking homing devices anyway.

Why wasn't Cassie's working anymore?

Ozzy was driving and I was sitting shotgun, Sterling and Arabella were in the middle row, and Theo and Wesley were sharing the back row with the requisite adult supervision. His name was Stanley. At least that's what I thought he said. I hadn't really been paying attention. Wesley didn't seem happy with the seating arrangement, but since he was along only under the good grace of Ozzy's generosity, there wasn't much he could do about it.

I was silent for most of the ride, anxious about Cassie. I turned to study Ozzy's profile by the light of the passing cars on the interstate.

"Why do you think her tattoo isn't working anymore?" I asked.

Ozzy turned to look at me briefly, his green eyes soft with sympathy. "I don't know, Cleo. This has never happened before. When she went missing before — " He paused guiltily. "When the Hounds finally realized she left campus, they were still able to locate where she was by tracking her tattoo. They called and told us exactly where to find her and Younglove and I went to pick her up. Now, she's just gone. No trace."

I swallowed down a sob. "So, how does the tattoo work? How do they know hers didn't just malfunction? I mean it wouldn't stop working if she wasn't . . . living anymore. Would it?"

"Don't think like that," Ozzy reprimanded me sternly. I noticed he didn't actually answer the question.

After a few moments he spoke again. "I honestly don't know how the tattoo works, but I don't think death is a trigger for it to stop working. I don't think Younglove would send us on a search and rescue mission if that were the case," he said, trying to comfort me. He reached over and grabbed my hand. "Don't worry, we'll find her."

I clung to his words as if they were a life raft. Search and rescue. That's what it was. We would find Cassie.

We had to.

At the University, Ozzy parked the SUV in the parking lot closest to my old dorm. Following Hound Stanley and the rest of the Deviants, I scaled the familiar steps and looked up at the building where most of the windows were already dark. It was already Lights Out. In the lobby, we were met by two Hounds, one with blond hair, one with ginger-colored hair — both large.

Ozzy looked around. "Where's Dean Younglove? I was under the impression she was meeting us here."

The University Hounds looked at each other nervously. "We haven't been able to contact her," Ginger said. "We don't know where she is."

"Fine. We don't need her," Ozzy said. "Take us to Cassandra's room, please."

Ginger Hound nodded and then led us to the elevator. When the doors opened on the eighth floor, we walked down the quiet hall, stopping in front of Cassie's door. The blond-haired Hound fit the key into the lock before letting the door swing wide open. I held a few steps back from the group, hovering in front of the door of the room next to Cassie's.

The wood on the door was old and familiar and I could still smell a faint burnt odor leaking from the cracks along the floor. My old room. I wondered if it was already occupied, given to a new Sophisticate. I felt sick, realizing how easily I could be replaced. The Program could make a new Sophisticate like they were minting money. Sure, I held some intrinsic value merely because of the time and effort put into raising me, but ultimately, I was a possession, a tool to be used by the Program.

And Cassie — was the Program worried about her safety or about the fact that she was the last puzzle piece to the Deviant Dozen? What was most important to them? The loss of a Sophisticate, a missing Deviant, or a human being in trouble? I was pretty sure I knew the answer and it didn't make me feel any better.

Everyone began filing into Cassie's room and Ozzy turned to encourage me to follow as well. The University Hounds were standing outside the door talking to Stanley. It was obvious they all knew each other well.

"How could she just disappear?" Stanley was asking, hands shoved deep in the pockets of his jeans.

Blondie shrugged his shoulders, unconcerned.

Ginger Hound laughed. "After the whippings she got last time, I thought that little bitch was thoroughly tamed. Apparently not."

Before I could stop myself, my hand lashed out and connected with Ginger's meaty face. He stared down at me with a look of surprise that quickly turned into rage. His wrath was nothing compared to mine, though. I could actually feel the air around me getting warmer. Vaguely, I wondered if I could make people explode as easily as pens and lights.

"You stupid — " Ginger started, cocking his hand back, fully intent on bringing it to meet my face. I was ready to let him. All I needed was an excuse.

Before he could follow through, he found himself slammed up against the wall outside Cassie's room, Ozzy's forearm pressed against his neck. It was ridiculous to see Ozzy, a normal-sized guy, manhandling a Mandate who was not only a decade older, but probably 50 pounds heavier and a foot taller. Despite his size, however, Ginger made no move to fight back. I had a feeling it had more to do with not being able to fight back than not wanting to.

"I wouldn't do that if I were you," Ozzy hissed menacingly through clenched teeth. "You know who I am, don't you?"

Ginger's eyes met Ozzy's, the rage instantly disappearing in recognition. "Perfect Aim," he swallowed.

Ozzy's head nodded fractionally. "Don't touch any of my friends, especially her," he emphasized, indicating me. "I wouldn't want to have to put you out of commission. Too much paperwork," Ozzy threatened coldly.

Ginger nodded once, his mouth set into a grim line and I felt a coldness brush over my skin, quenching the fiery rage that had filled me only moments ago. A big, muscular Mandate brought to heel just by the sight of Ozzy. It was a little frightening and I was reminded just how much I didn't know about him and what he did for the Program — what he could do.

Ozzy released the Hound, took my hand, and pulled me through the door. He leaned over to whisper in my ear. "You're the one he should really be afraid of," Ozzy laughed quietly.

I didn't laugh. I was already afraid of myself.

The room was just as I remembered it. Makeup and styling products littered the dresser in colorful disarray, pictures of Cassie and me were still scattered across the desk, and clothes were discarded haphazardly across every available surface.

I walked over to the desk and picked up a framed picture of us from when we were about eight years old. Our arms were slung easily around each other's shoulders — our gap-toothed grins childish and naive. My heart clenched with recollection, desperately yearning for the innocence of those long lost days. I set the picture back on the desktop, the memory of that day rushing back in harsh clarity.

****

I thought that going to the ice rink with my best friend to celebrate my eighth birthday was going to be the best day of my life. The Program never did anything special for birthdays, but this year, they decided to have a group birthday party for all the Dracones. It wasn't my actual birthday, but it was as close as I'd ever get to a celebration like the normal kids got.

Cassie and I had been talking about it nonstop all week and were so excited we could hardly concentrate on our schoolwork. I'd seen the elegant girls in the sparkly costumes in the skating competitions on television. I imagined that it would be the same for me — I would be like an angel on the ice, spinning, twirling, and leaping through the air. After all, I was one of the best of the best. Things were supposed to be easy.

But they weren't. Not this time.

Ten minutes in, my knees were bruised, my rear was wet, and my pride and confidence were injured to the point that I was counting down the minutes until the party was over. I sat down on the bench outside the rink and did my best not to cry as the rest of my fellow Sophisticates easily glided around the ice.

As I sat there moping, a body crashed into me in a flurry of cold air and breathless giggles before settling on the seat next to me.

"What's wrong?" Cassie asked.

"I can't do it. I keep falling," I admitted, ashamed.

"So? I keep falling too. Just get back up."

"But it hurts."

"Well, if you keep trying, you'll get better, you won't fall as much, and it won't hurt."

"But I'm afraid."

Cassie sighed in her little girl way. "Okay."

I thought she would get up and go back out on the ice but she didn't.

"Aren't you going to skate?" I asked.

"No," Cassie said. "It's no fun without you." Then she smiled and flung her arm over my shoulder. "We can just watch. As long as we're together, it's still the perfect birthday."

"Smile, girls," said one of the nannies as she pointed a camera at us.

I put my arm around Cassie and grinned, realizing that the pain of missing out on some fun with my friend was worse than any pain I felt from falling. Once I had a new goal — having fun with Cassie — I found that ice skating was a lot easier and the falling was hardly noticeable anymore.

It ended up being the perfect birthday.

Because of Cassie.

****

I swallowed back my tearful memories. I glanced around the room, my eyes straying over the walls, which were plastered with familiar ballet posters of toe shoes and ballerinas in frilly tutus. Cassie loved everything ballet. I wandered over to the dresser and lifted the lid of the old, tattered box on top. Music faintly tinkled as the tiny, plastic, ballerina spun in front of the small oval mirror. I let the lid slam shut.

"What do you think?" Ozzy asked as my fingers toyed with the small metal clasp on the front of the old, pink music box.

"It doesn't make any sense. She didn't take anything with her, at least not the things she valued. I can't be sure about the clothes without going through everything in her closet, but if she ran away, she didn't really take much."

"Maybe she wasn't running away."

"Do you think she was kidnapped?" I asked worriedly.

"Not from campus," Ozzy assured me. "Security is too tight for that to happen. I think she wasn't so much running away from, as running toward something."

"What do you mean?"

"I think she was trying to find you," Ozzy explained.

I chewed my bottom lip, watching Arabella, Sterling, Wesley, and Theo walk around the room, picking up random things and looking at them hopelessly. They didn't know how to find Cassie any more than I did.

Unless . . .

I scurried past Ozzy and sat down at the desk in front of the computer.

"Did the Hounds check the computer?"

Ozzy nodded. "They didn't find anything. They checked her files and the history on her search engine. Not a clue."

I rolled my eyes. "Well, if she didn't want to be found, Cassie was probably smart enough to clear out her search engine history." I pulled the keyboard closer and started digging through Cassie's computer files and internet history as only a hacker could. Information could be deleted and trashed, but it always left a trail and I knew how to uncover it. Just like a digital archeologist, I would dust away bits of useless information until I found the precious information I wanted buried deep in the computer's memory.

Ozzy turned toward the others to give them each something to do as well. "Arabella, go through everything in the closet. See if anything looks odd or out of place. Theo, have Stanley take you and Sterling to the video surveillance room. They're still sifting through hours of footage from all over campus looking for a sign of where she's gone. See if you can help."

Wesley sat down on the bed while Arabella rummaged through the closet and I tapped away at the keyboard. "What can I do?" he asked Ozzy petulantly.

Ozzy stared at him thoughtfully before answering. "Can you take a look around the room? See if the Hounds missed anything Cassie might have hidden away?"

"Okay."

"I mean look. Look as only you can," Ozzy explained. "Just keep your looking away from the ladies, okay?"

Wesley flushed a beet red. "Oh, right," he answered, embarrassed, finally understanding Ozzy's request.

I lost track of time as I scoured the computer in silence, restoring trashed files, and digging through the once deleted history. Ten minutes later, or maybe it was thirty, I found what I was looking for.

"I think I have something," Wesley called.

"Me too," I said triumphantly. I stood up from the desk chair and walked to where Wesley was standing at the dresser. He was holding the music box.

"There's something in here, tucked under the liner. Do you want to do the honors?" he asked, pushing the box toward me. "I don't feel right dismantling something so personal."

I took the box from Wesley as Ozzy and Arabella joined us. I carefully peeled back the stiff satin, careful not to knock the tiny ballerina from her delicate perch. Under the lining was a small piece of folded paper that seemed to be a hastily written note that looked like it had been unfolded and refolded numerous times. It was rather hard to read.

St. Ignatius Academy, Forest Hill. North of Baltimore
Tattoo. Electric shock. Maybe a taser?
Last of the Deviant Dozen?
Horror Frog. WTF?
1:30 pm Friday

Where did Cassie get this information? And, what did it mean? Some of it made sense. It seemed that somehow Cassie had discovered that I was at St. Ignatius Academy and where it was located. Everyone else knew that Cassie was the last member of the Dozen to deviate, but how did she find this out? Ozzy? He hadn't mentioned that he told her anything about the Dozen, only that he had suggested she not use her powers. As for Horror Frog, I knew that was Cassie's Deviant Dozen moniker, but how did Cassie get that information and did she know what it meant?

In any case, none of that was what I was really worried about. What I couldn't wrap my mind around was the line about a tattoo, electric shock, and a taser. That made no sense. I handed the note over to Ozzy and shrugged.

Ozzy frowned as he read it quickly. "Not very helpful in telling us how she got away undetected, but at least we know where she was going and when."

"And I think I know how she planned to get there," I offered. "I found a search that she did on cab companies. She only clicked on one. Chances are, that's the one she called and that's how she got away."

"Right then. Let's go see if Theo and Sterling were able to find anything in the video surveillance footage." He grabbed the music box, slid it into a plastic bag with the note, and tucked it under his arm.

Luckily, the video monitoring room was located in the security office on the North end of campus just beyond the dormitories. It wasn't a far walk. The large grassy area between the dormitories that we were crossing through was better known as La Plata Beach. I had many fond memories of lounging on the grassy beach with Cassie, soaking up the sun, and studying with the Harpies. Even though the darkness was swallowing the area in quiet shadows, my memories were bright enough to help me see. I could even make out the vague outline of the volleyball net and the sand underneath that was shining brightly in the moonlight. I soaked it in, knowing that this was probably the last time I'd ever be at the University. If we found Cassie and she had exhibited, we would take her back to St. Ignatius for sure. There wouldn't be a reason to come back here.

The automatic doors of the security building slid open with a slight whoosh and our group stepped inside the brightly lit interior of the foyer. In front of us was a shiny black desk with a Hound lounging behind it, his arms behind his head. The Hound behind the desk nodded when he saw Ozzy and pressed a button that allowed us to go through the secure doors to the right side. After a short walk down a fluorescent lit hallway, Ozzy opened a door to his left and ushered us inside.

The room was enormous and filled with video monitors. There must have been nearly a hundred television screens, all of which were intermittently changing views every 30 seconds. There were a dozen Hounds in this room and they each seemed to be in charge of a group of monitors which they stared at listlessly. Theo was seated behind a large computer screen on a desk and Sterling was standing behind him, leaning on the tabletop and pointing to something on the screen.

"Find anything?" Ozzy asked.

Sterling turned with a triumphant smile. "We think so. Cleo, come here and take a look at this."

Theo rewound the footage and I stood next to Sterling, looking over his shoulder at what he was pointing at. It was footage of the southwest side of campus. The Cornerstone Grille, a bar that locals liked to frequent, was just barely visible beyond the campus gates. I'd never been there, but I'd seen it before. It was the middle of the day and the glassy blocks of the exterior of the bar were glinting in the sunlight, but it looked quiet. No one was going in or coming out.

"I don't see anything," I complained, squinting at the screen.

"Just wait," Sterling shushed me, holding up his hand.

At that moment, a taxi cab eased into the picture from the right side of the screen and stopped in front of the building. The words Crabby Cabby and a logo of a crab designed to resemble a taxi cab adorned the driver's side door. A figure emerged from the bottom of the screen where the gates of the University were no doubt located. Her slight build was familiar and her long, black, straight hair trailed out behind her as she ran across the street and opened the door to the cab. The girl tossed in a rucksack and then slid into the backseat, pulling the door shut behind her.

"Cassie," I breathed.

"I knew it was her," Theo said as he leaned back and crossed his arms proudly.

"How did you find it so quickly?" Ozzy asked, amazed.

"If I was going to try to run away from this place, I'd pick the gate farthest away from security headquarters," Theo explained. "Once we found out which camera it was, it was just a matter of scanning that footage for the timeframe she had gone missing."

"Good job, I'm seriously impressed," Ozzy complimented Theo.

Theo's eyebrow quirked up. "As you should be. This was a piece of cake compared to the Quinnie collage I compiled earlier tonight."

"You do realize, though, that she'll have her revenge," Ozzy warned.

"Oh, I seriously doubt that," Theo quipped, unworried.

"How so?"

Theo merely grinned. "I can't give away all my secrets."

"Dude, are you going to blackmail her?" Sterling asked hopefully. "Because if so, I want to see the dirt you've got on her."

"Look," I interrupted. "Let's all agree that we're not fans of Quinnie and move on. Can we please just go find Cassie?"

"Right," Sterling agreed. "I guess we need to find out where this Crabby Cabby place is located."

"Not a problem," I answered. "I found the information on Cassie's computer. Let's go."

Crabby Cabby wasn't too far from campus, but it was still far enough that we needed the Academy SUV. Ozzy drove us through the University campus to the main entrance, circling around the traffic circle adorned with a large, flowery "M."

Even though the Sophisticate Program took over the University years ago, they had allowed all of the landmarks to remain. The big 'M' circle at the entrance, the various bronze Testudo statues, and the reflection pool on McKeldin Mall all stayed. The pi statue and sundial on the mall also survived the hostile takeover.

I was glad. I hated to think of all the history at the University being swept under the rug as easily as the histories of the Sophisticates themselves were erased. I frowned, thinking about the restricted room and the names of the people who may or may not have been my parents. Maybe the Program thought my history was erased, but I was determined now, more than ever, to reclaim it.

Ozzy continued down Campus Drive and crossed Route 1, leaving the campus and continuing on Paint Branch Parkway. We'd barely gone a mile when we saw the obnoxious angry crab sign for the taxi company. It was a run down place — a drab, one story building with open cargo door bays that were filled with cabs on lifts and grease-covered men mingling about. It was nearly 2 A.M., but the place was busy. At this hour, I assumed there was probably a huge demand for cabs because of the local bar clientele.

Ozzy parked the SUV in front of what appeared to be the office and then turned around in his seat. "Cleo and I will go in. The rest of you just hang out here with Stanley."

There was grumbling, but no one was brave enough to contradict Ozzy, not even Arabella. I noticed that there was a chorus of yawns spreading through the interior of the vehicle, which probably had a lot to do with the lack of argument.

The main office of the company was just as grungy as the rest of the building. Inside, the only piece of furniture was a filthy front counter behind which sat a very dingy man. He appeared to be snoozing, his feet propped up on the grease-smeared top. That didn't last long, thanks to Ozzy. He repeatedly pounded the bell until the sleeping man managed to rouse himself.

"Can I help you?" the man grumbled.

"I need to know who was driving cab number 43 and where it took the passenger it picked up at the Cornerstone Grille at 1:32 Friday afternoon."

"Who are you?" the man growled sleepily.

"The beginning of a very bad day for you if you don't tell me what I want to know. Now."

I would've rolled my eyes at Ozzy's overly dramatic answer if I didn't know that it was backed by truth. If only the man knew what he was up against. The dingy man pulled his feet off the counter and put his hands behind his head as he leaned back in the chair, assessing Ozzy.

"I don't think I'll be giving you that information, son. See, we got something here called client confidentiality." He took his time saying confidentiality and I was actually surprised he knew that word. He looked like a two syllable word kind of guy.

Ozzy glared at the man. "And I've got something here that makes that null and void," he said, lifting up his sleeve and showing the man his Sophisticate tattoo.

"That's a nice tattoo, boy, but I'm still not telling you anything."

"Perhaps you can be persuaded," Ozzy hissed through gritted teeth.

The man leaned forward, resting his elbows on the countertop and steepling his hands in front of his face, tapping his thumbs together. His mouth turned hungrily up in a greedy grin that appeared to be missing more than one tooth and had far too much glinting gold for my taste.

"I guess that depends on how much you got, boy. Persuasion and client confidentiality don't come cheap."

"Is this enough?" Ozzy asked icily, his hand settling on the chipped laminate with a dull clank of metal. His hand was wrapped possessively around the grip of a gun, his finger nestled against the trigger. The barrel of the gun was pointed straight at the chest of the man who was now struggling unsuccessfully to free himself from his chair. His wide eyes stared down the barrel as his mouth opened and closed noiselessly like a fish out of water.

"Ozzy!" I hissed. "What are you doing?" It was the first time I'd seen Ozzy on a mission. In some ways he was the same — fearless, confident, and in control. But in many ways he was different — cold and calculating. This heartless side of Ozzy was the side I always feared existed. This was the Ozzy I couldn't bring myself to trust. This was Ozzy the assassin.

"Persuading the man," he said flatly.

"You can't just pull a gun on someone!" I admonished him.

Ozzy ignored me. "Tell us," he demanded, squinting at the man's nearly illegible name tag, "Chuck. Who was driving cab 43 and where did they take their fare Friday afternoon?"

The man nervously eyed the gun. "Let me just check the records," he grumbled. "They're right here on the computer."

Ozzy nodded and the man pulled the chair closer to the desktop, tapped a few keys and moved the mouse around, his hands shaking with undisguised fear. His eyes were constantly drawn to the barrel of the gun, which was still pointed squarely at his chest.

"Here it is," he muttered with relief. He frowned slightly, tapping the computer screen with his finger.

"Well?" Ozzy snapped impatiently.

"The driver was Jay Martin. But — "

"But what?" Ozzy growled, his gun hand twitching ominously, stirring the man out of his confusion.

"Jay took the fare to Overlea Friday afternoon, but never returned."

"Where in Overlea?" Ozzy was beginning to get exasperated at having to nudge the information out of the man.

"A place on Route 1 called The Rink." When Ozzy continued to glare at him, the man explained. "It's an old roller rink. It's been abandoned for years."

"That's where the fare asked to go?" Ozzy asked impatiently. "I have a hard time believing that."

"I can't be sure about that," the man explained. "All I can tell you is that's where Jay went and that's where the car still is."

"And you know this how?"

"GPS," the man replied, turning the computer screen around and pointing to the glowing red light. It was settled along the line labeled Route 1, between I-695 and Glade Avenue on the map of Overlea.

"What's this Jay Martin like?" Ozzy asked.

The man shrugged. "He's a cab driver. Not much different from the rest of the guys out there," he said with a nod of his head toward the side of the building where the cargo bays were located. "But, it doesn't make sense that he wouldn't have come back. He should've been back on Friday."

"And why did this go unnoticed?"

"Look, the guys rent the cars, okay? I don't babysit them. They call in, I give them a new fare. Jay isn't the most trustworthy cabbie out there, but he's money hungry. He would've called in for a new fare as soon as he was back in the area. We don't really check up on them. The fact that he didn't return his cab yesterday after his normal shift just means that he would be charged for the extra time.

It happens. Sometimes guys just want to make some extra cash and pick up fares we don't give them."

Ozzy reached in his pocket, causing the man to flinch involuntarily. Instead of another weapon, he slapped a business card down on the laminate countertop.

"This is my number. If that dot moves, you call me. If that dot disappears, you call me. If you see or hear from Jay, you call me. I'm going to track down that cab," he said, pointing to the dot with his gun. "If I get there and the car is gone and you haven't called me, I'll be back and I won't be happy. I will, however, be more than inclined to give you your payment." Ozzy waved the gun at the man. "Understand?"

The man nodded his head rapidly.

"Good," Ozzy said, re-holstering the gun somewhere inside his leather jacket. "Let's go, Cleo, we have an hour drive." He grabbed my elbow, steering me out of the office and into the chilly night.

Stanley took over driving to The Rink and Ozzy asked Wesley to ride shotgun. I couldn't be certain, but I was confident that Ozzy was keeping Wes as far away from me as possible. Ozzy's excuse was that when we got closer to our destination, he wanted Wesley to have a good view so that he could use his skills to look for hidden danger. Wesley's accepting grimace was a silent declaration that he didn't believe that explanation, and frankly neither did I. When Ozzy and I climbed into the car and settled into the back seat, Theo got up and scrambled to the middle of the SUV.

"Scoot over," he insisted, pushing Sterling closer to Arabella. "The back seat gives me motion sickness."

And with that, Ozzy and I were alone in the third row, shrouded in the darkness of the pre-dawn hours of a Sunday morning.

"Another morning run we can effectively skip out on," Sterling announced happily. "No way Younglove will make us run after being up all night."

"Let's worry about surviving the night first," Ozzy warned. "I have no idea why Cassie was taken to this abandoned roller rink, but I guarantee you whatever the reason, it isn't a good one. Everybody rest up, we have to be on our game."

"Yeah, yeah. Of course," Sterling agreed. I couldn't see him blushing, but I could hear it in his voice. Nothing like being scolded by Ozzy to make you feel like a child.

I tucked myself into the corner of the seat, resting my head against the glass, thinking about Cassie being alone at an abandoned building with a creepy cabbie.

Ozzy leaned over, his lips to my ear. "You tired?" he asked quietly, his breath stirring my hair.

I turned to look at him, my mouth within striking distance of his, and shook my head. "Not really, I'm just worried about Cassie."

The words tumbled out of my mouth in a choked whisper as tears welled in my eyes. I blinked rapidly to make them disappear, but that only seemed to encourage them to rush forth. Ozzy reached up and wiped them away with his thumb.

"We're going to get her back," he promised.

THE RINK

I was startled awake by the sound of a phone ringing.

"Hello?" Ozzy's voice was loud as it shattered the silence in the SUV. I couldn't hear what was being said on the other side of the conversation but I could hear the drone of a voice and felt Ozzy's posture stiffen in response.

"Yes, this is Osbourne. Did the car move?"

I could hear muffled conversation in response to Ozzy's question.

"You found Jay? Where?"

A hurried explanation.

"Really? How long has he been there?" He switched the phone to his other ear. "I understand. Did anyone see anything? Have you called the police?"

More muffled conversation.

"No. I'll send a cleanup crew from the University. They'll be there shortly. Don't move him. Don't touch him."

Ozzy pressed a button on his phone to end the call and then immediately typed in another number and put the phone to his ear. After a few rings, someone picked up.

"This is Osbourne Dracone, I was there earlier this evening reviewing video surveillance. We have a code 419 at Crabby Cabby on Paint Branch Parkway. This is in connection with Cassandra Dracone's disappearance. Please send a few Hounds out there."

I could hear a deep voice asking a short question although I couldn't make out the actual words.

"Yes, I'll do the paperwork," Ozzy snapped, exasperated. "Just get over there and clean it up before the crime scene is completely compromised." Annoyed, he ended the call with a push of a button and then he turned off the phone and slipped it in his pocket with a sigh.

"What's going on?" Sterling asked blearily, rubbing sleep out of his eyes as he peered over his seat.

"They found Jay Martin, the cabby that was supposed to be driving the taxi that picked up Cassie."

"Supposed to be? He didn't pick her up?"

"I don't think so. I think someone took the cab from him before he could."

"Why do you think that?" Sterling quizzed him.

Ozzy stole a look at me, his mouth in a tight grimace. "Jay Martin was found in the trunk of one of the unused cabs. Dead."

Stanley approached the area around The Rink from side roads so that if someone was watching, they wouldn't see and recognize the Academy SUV. Ozzy seemed to think that Cassie had been kidnapped by someone who knew who she was and what she could do. Chances were if they knew that much, they would probably be expecting the Program to eventually send out a search party. Stanley pulled into the parking lot of a seafood restaurant about a quarter of a mile down the street from The Rink and parked behind the unlit building.

Ozzy opened the hatch of the SUV and unlocked the metal box that was nudged up against the back seat. He started pulling out handguns and ammo and handing them out. When he got to me, I put my hands up in protest.

"I'll pass." I eyed the gun warily, feeling faint at the thought of it in my hands.

"You have to have some kind of protection," Ozzy insisted.

"I'll stay with you," I suggested. "Plus, I have the whole raging inferno thing going on." I waved my hands around my head in a half-hearted attempt to remind him of my deviation.

Ozzy sighed. "And that's still hit or miss. Here," he said, pulling something out from behind the box and handing it to me.

I eyed the piece of wood in my hands. "A bokken?"

Ozzy shrugged. "Just in case there's a glitch in your explosive temper."

"Fine," I agreed. I actually wasn't opposed to using the bokken; I just felt useless in comparison to everyone else who could not only handle guns, but use their deviations at will.

"Theo, Wesley," Ozzy barked at the brothers. "I'll need you two to lead, be our eyes. Take us through the shadows behind all the buildings from here to The Rink. Once we get closer, Wesley, tell us what's waiting for us inside." The brothers nodded and took their positions up front with Ozzy right behind. Stanley took up the rear with Sterling, which left Arabella and me sandwiched between all the gun-wielding testosterone.

"You okay?" Arabella whispered.

I tried to repress the fear that was building inside of me, the nightmares from our staged kidnapping still fresh in my mind. Arabella seemed to be completely nonplussed, but she seemed that way when we were held prisoner in the basement, too. Despite Arabella's bravado, I vividly remembered her showing up at my door, emotionally damaged, and requesting a sleepover so that she wouldn't have to be alone. Arabella looked like she was holding it together, but I knew she was probably just as scared as I was.

"I just want to get Cassie back safely," I murmured, my voice wavering.

Arabella tucked her non-gun-toting hand through the crook of my arm and pulled me close. "We will. Don't worry."

As we approached The Rink, we could see the Crabby Cabby taxi parked behind the building.

"Wes, can you see anything from here?" Ozzy whispered.

We were huddled in the dark shadows of the building next door with an unimpeded view of our destination. Theo wasn't able to see any video cameras, which both comforted and bothered me. Was the kidnapping random or planned? If it was planned, the attacker was certainly pretty confident if they didn't even have security cameras.

The Rink was a large building with the distinctive, classic arched roof that gave it that iconic roller rink look. The lettering on the front of the building was dilapidated and discolored, but still legible. Huge, chunky letters in a vintage 1970s font spelled out "The Rink" above the front doors which, like the windows, were covered with plywood.

"It's limited," Wes admitted and I realized he was referring to his ability to see through the walls. "I'm a little too far away to get much detail, but there's a lot of activity in the back of the building beyond the taxi cab. It looks like they're loading up boxes or something into a big moving van."

"How many?" Ozzy asked.

"People? Eight, maybe nine. It's hard to tell."

"Can you see Cassie?" I interrupted.

"I can't really make out anything specific from this far away, but I don't think so."

Ozzy frowned. "For now, let's avoid the back entrance. We'll just have to go in through the front door."

"Do you think that's a good idea?" Stanley asked. It was the first time he'd really spoken other than when he was talking to the University Hounds earlier. I'd almost forgotten he was with us.

Ozzy glared at him. "If I didn't, I would've suggested something else."

Like Chuck back at Crabby Cabby, Stanley withered under Ozzy's threatening demeanor. I didn't blame him. I felt myself recoiling from this harsh, unyielding side of Ozzy.

Before I could spend too much time dwelling on it, however, Arabella pulled me forward. We were all heading for the front door of the building and I let my random thoughts scatter silently out of my mind as I concentrated on the anxiety that was seeping into every nook and cranny of my body.

Quietly, we crossed the open area between the buildings and huddled in front of the main doors. Plywood was nailed across the glass portions of the doors, as if in preparation for a hurricane. There was chain looped through the handles of the doors with a plain combination lock keeping the chain secure.

"This is their security?" Ozzy huffed, lifting the lock up.

"Not very sophisticated," Stanley agreed.

Ozzy pulled something out of his jacket that was small, thin, and silver. He bent over the lock and less than a minute later, he was untangling the chain from the door handles. He quietly gathered the chain into his hand and then set it, and the lock, into the neglected landscaping to the side of the entrance. Ozzy slipped through the doorway first and then silently signaled for the rest of us to follow.

Inside, the vestibule was completely dark and smelled like old carpet, mold, and sweaty feet. Beyond, I could see the rink itself, a curved, waist-high wall circling the worn, wooden floor. The red, white, and blue stripes painted on the wall were chipped and faded, and the weak lighting from the bulbs in the ceiling ricocheted off the silver disco ball that still hung from the middle of the room.

"What the hell?" Sterling whispered, echoing my thoughts.

The Rink, which at one time had been filled with awkward teenagers on wobbly wheels, was now filled with military style bunk beds along one side, rubber gym mats on the other side, and targets on stands along the far wall.

"Come on," Ozzy encouraged. "Don't worry about that right now. Let's look for Cassie. You guys check out that side," he said, pointing to Sterling, Arabella, Stanley, and Theo and motioning for them to go to the left. "We'll go this way."

The first room Wesley, Ozzy, and I came to looked like it at one time had been the concessions area. The battered orange and brown tables were clearly original from the roller rink's heyday, but the gleaming silver kitchen appliances behind the counter looked new. Ozzy beckoned for me and Wesley to follow him behind the counter and back through a doorless opening. The empty doorway led to a storage room with shelves lining one side that were filled with canned goods and other non-perishable food. Along the other wall were two refrigerators, humming softly. At the far end of the room, there was a door that was slightly ajar. Ozzy crossed the small closet-sized room, opened the door quietly, and stood at the top of a set of stairs, peering down into the darkness.

"Shhh. I hear someone." He cocked his head. "And I can smell her," he whispered.

"Smell who?" I asked, warily.

"Cassie. She's here."

I looked at him doubtfully. "You can *smell* her?"

Ozzy frowned. "Yes. I was in her room only a few hours ago. I know her smell."

"Oh. That's right. Bloodhound," I remembered. "One of your deviations."

Ozzy nodded and I briefly wondered what Cassie smelled like. I was distracted by thoughts of a perfume made of ballet shoe leather, chocolate Cadbury eggs, and crab cakes — Cassie's favorite things. It sounded disgusting.

And then it hit me. If Cassie had a smell, then I did too. What did Ozzy smell when I was around? Oh God. I hoped it wasn't embarrassing.

"Yes, you have a smell too," Ozzy whispered as he descended the steps, answering my unasked question.

"Do you read minds too? Another deviation I don't know about?"

"No, I just know how your mind works." When I raised my eyebrows in disbelief, he added, "Years of stalking someone has its benefits."

I should've known. "Well, what do I smell like?" I finally asked, carefully following him down the stairs and gripping my bokken tightly.

"Trade secret," he answered quietly, and I could hear the smile in his voice. I heard Wesley huff in annoyance behind us.

At the bottom of the stairs, Ozzy held his arm out to prevent me from going any further. He turned to Wesley, pointed to his eyes with two fingers, and then motioned around the room with the same two fingers. Wesley nodded and squeezed around me so that he could get a better look.

The room itself was filled with boxes and discarded furniture. I could see roller skates and shoelaces tumbling out of the tops of most of the boxes. All of the stuff down here was probably just the abandoned carnage of a forgotten business.

Wesley was scanning the clutter when he suddenly stopped. He tapped Ozzy on the shoulder, pointed to the door at the end of the room, and held up two fingers. Two people. There were two people on the other side of that door. And not surprisingly, that's where the noises seemed to be coming from.

Ozzy ushered us across the cluttered area and held a finger to his lips as he signaled for me and Wesley to go on the opposite side of the door. Standing against the wall, I could now clearly hear a voice from inside the room. It sounded familiar, but I couldn't place it.

"Do it!" the familiar voice snarled.

"Can't," a low voice sobbed.

"Yes, you can!"

Silence. Then a slapping sound.

"Please don't make me do it again," the low voice moaned.

"Do it!" the familiar voice shouted. Her demand was followed by the sounds of sickening, dull thuds and more sobbing and pained cries.

"Stop. Please stop," the low voice begged.

"Protect yourself!" The thudding sound became more violent, echoed by cries for help.

Ozzy motioned to Wesley, asking what was going on inside. Wesley grabbed my bokken and mimed that he was beating me with it. As Ozzy prepared to kick down the door, the begging inside the room suddenly transformed into a heart-wrenching keening. It was a wail of pure pain. The screams tore at my heart and I lunged for the door, desperate to get inside. I didn't know what was going on, but I had to do whatever it took to make those screams stop. Ozzy got to the door first.

The door shattered as Ozzy drove his foot through it, his gun drawn. Inside, weak light seeped down from a bare bulb that hung from the ceiling. Against the far side of the room, a cot was shoved up against the dirty wall. The mattress had no sheets or blankets and had mysterious dark stains all over it. In front of the cot stood a girl with a bat who turned toward the sound of the shattered door like a caged animal. I recognized the brown hair and familiar profile — I'd seen them both many times before.

In the mirror.

And now I knew why the angry voice seemed so familiar. The girl, who had moments before been using the bat to beat the wailing figure on the cot, looked exactly like me. The hair, the hands, the face. Everything was exactly the same. Except for the eyes. The eyes were different. Empty. Furious, but empty.

The small Asian girl on the bed continued to thrash and scream as her body bucked and flailed, her hair a tangled mess, her skin bruised and blood-spattered. She wasn't being beaten anymore, but it was clear that she was still in considerable pain. I couldn't look away and I couldn't move. I couldn't tear my eyes away from my best friend.

It was Cassie on the bed. It was Cassie shrieking as if her skin was being peeled off.

We were shocked into inaction by the state of Cassie, but it didn't take long for my doppelganger to realize she was outnumbered. She swung her bat at Ozzy and he dodged it neatly, spinning to lunge at her from the side. She swung the bat at him and he dodged again.

Why was he messing around with this girl? All he had to do was shoot her in the arm or leg and she'd be out of commission. With his aim, he could've disarmed her easily. Instead, he kept looking between her and me as if he couldn't believe his eyes. It was like he couldn't make the decision to hurt her.

The girl swung at Ozzy again as he spun away from her. Annoyed, she threw the bat at him and it exploded into a fireball that hit him in the chest, knocking him onto his back, causing him to hit his head on the floor. And just like that, Ozzy was unconscious and no longer a threat.

I was still immobile, trying to decide whether to help Cassie, who was still screaming, or check whether Ozzy was okay. Wesley was just beginning to fumble with his gun. Bat Girl, despite her lack of body weight, easily pushed Wesley to the side where he tripped over Ozzy's prone body and went down in a heap, his gun clattering off into the corner of the room. At the door, my twin paused to look back, a wicked smile stretching across familiar lips. It was as if she were making a challenge to me — or was it a promise?

Footsteps on the floor above us broke the trance and I watched as the girl disappeared into the darkness of the cluttered basement.

With the threat gone, I finally found myself able to move. I rushed to the bed where Cassie's screams were finally fading. Her eyes were rolled back into her head and her body was arched unnaturally off the naked mattress. I was about to grab Cassie's hand to calm her down when I noticed long white slivers slicing through the skin of her hands, accompanied by what sounded like twigs snapping.

Cassie was convulsing as her hands were growing claws. Long, white, bony, claws.

She let out another scream and started slashing at her own arms as if to rip the new talons off. Blood splattered everywhere as she cut herself over and over again. Finally, she went rigid, her body stilled, and then she collapsed onto the mattress. Cassie was passed out — peaceful, but bloody. Eventually, the white blades slowly receded back into her skin, leaving nothing in their wake but puffy, vertical welts where the claws had once been.

Finally able to get near the bed, I grabbed Cassie's arm and tried to lift her unconscious body up. "Cassie!"

"This is Cassie?" Wesley asked, incredulous. He had somehow disentangled himself from Ozzy, who was still lying unresponsively on the floor.

"Yes, she won't wake up." I gently shook Cassie, who started breathing rapidly. "Is he okay?" I asked, nodding toward Ozzy.

"He's breathing, so I think so," Wesley said. "I'll just go get some help — "

He was interrupted as Stanley entered the small room, surveying the scene with the expertise of a veteran soldier.

"What the hell?" Stanley murmured.

"Long story," Wesley said. "Did you guys find anything?"

"Long story? What happened to Perfect Aim?"

"Exploding fireball trumps Perfect Aim, I guess." Wesley seemed a little too pleased with the outcome.

"Exploding?" Stanley whipped his head around to look at me. Apparently, Stanley was in on the Deviant Dozen's secret skills.

"It wasn't me!" I swore, holding my hands up in front of me. "Well, not exactly. It was someone who looked like me."

Stanley raised his eyebrows.

"Never mind," I said, shaking my head. There was no time for an explanation now. "We should get out of here. This is who we came for," I said, indicating Cassie.

"Right," Stanley agreed, taking notice of Cassie for the first time. "Theodore," he yelled through the doorway, "help me carry Perfect Aim. You," he said, pointing to Wesley, "get the girl. The rest of you lead the way. And be careful, I have a feeling they're not going to just let us waltz out of here."

"Yeah, Cleo's evil twin will probably be back with more sports equipment," Wesley mumbled. He grabbed his gun from where it had skittered earlier and tucked it in his waistband. He then scooped Cassie off the bed like she was merely a pillow and held her tightly to his chest, not even concerned about the blood that was smearing on his clothes and skin. Cassie was still limp and unresponsive.

Sterling and I took the lead up the stairs, bokken and gun drawn, although I knew they wouldn't do much good against exploding fireballs. Bat Girl was nowhere to be seen as we made our way through the old concessions area and into the mildewed, shadow-rich foyer.

"I'll get the door," Arabella called, pushing her way to the front of the line past Stanley, Theo, Wesley, and the limp bodies they were carrying.

"Going somewhere?" A voice called out from behind us.

I recognized the smell before I remembered the voice that belonged to it. Wet cats. And mixed with moldy carpet, it was enough to make me want to retch. I turned slowly to see Delia Younglove, my former Dean at the University, standing on the other side of the rink wall, arms crossed. Three figures stood behind the Dean and for a moment, I was confused as to why Quinnie, Sadie, and Eva would be here, of all places.

Shouldn't Quinnie be recovering from punishment for attacking Katie at the dance? Did they come as reinforcements?

Twyla Younglove had to be around here somewhere. She would explain. It didn't matter though. We found Cassie and now we could leave. I didn't care who came to help as long as Cassie would be all right.

Just then, my look-alike walked across the old rink floor and joined the group, standing next to Quinnie.

I finally understood. It wasn't Quinnie. I recognized the same hollowness in the eyes of all four teens. What were they and why did they look like Deviants? Were they twins? Evil twins? Siblings? Coincidence?

No. Not coincidence. There was no such thing as coincidence where the Program was concerned.

Dean Younglove turned toward the girl who looked exactly like me. "Everything ready, Persephone?" she asked. Persephone nodded and the Dean turned her attention to me and the rest of my confused companions. "You have something that belongs to me."

I moved protectively in front of Cassie, who was still in Wesley's arms. "What's going on here, Dean Younglove?"

The Dean smiled, or at least I assumed that the grimace was meant to be a smile. "Leave Cassandra and go, or I'll be forced to let Elysia have a little fun," she threatened, indicating the Quinnie look-alike that stood next to Persephone.

"What do you want with Cassie?" I asked. My voice sounded a lot braver than I felt.

"I need a complete set," Dean Younglove said bluntly, unfolding her arms to inspect her nails. She then licked the back of her hand and used the wet side of her hand to smooth down her hair.

Holy shit, I thought. Did she just lick herself? Like a cat? Out loud, I said, "You can't have her."

"Elysia," Dean Younglove purred dangerously, "Get me my property."

Elysia's self-satisfied grin turned Quinnie's beautiful, familiar features into a mask of depravity. She raised her arms as she walked forward, electricity crackling between her hands in arcs of blue and yellow light.

Remembering the damage Quinnie had done to me in the shower, I worried for my friends and knew that with two of them injured and unconscious, we had very little hope of getting out unscathed.

"Wait. Take me instead," I offered to the Dean, stepping forward.

She cackled. "I already have one of you, I don't need another," she said, indicating Persephone. "Especially one that can't control her deviation. Elysia, if you'd be so kind. Or rather, don't bother with any kindness, just get me Cassandra."

I could hear whispering behind me and desperately hoped that my friends weren't planning to do anything stupid. I turned around and whispered, "Get Cassie and Ozzy out of here, I'll create a diversion or something."

The monster inside was stirring.

"Too late," Sterling grimaced.

"What do you mean too late?" I quickly looked around at the ragtag group of my friends. It was dark and I could barely see everyone. Wesley, Theo, and Stanley were still holding Cassie and Ozzy. They were backing up toward the front door with their unconscious cargo, presumably to get them to safety.

"Hey, where's Arabella?" I asked worriedly.

Sterling inclined his head and his eyes settled on something behind me. I spun around to see that Elysia was advancing, working her hands around a crackling network of sparking light, pulling and pushing it like it was pizza dough. Before I could get properly frightened, however, my gaze was drawn to the area behind the Dean and her collection of empty-eyed teens.

In the middle of the rink, Arabella quietly crept across the worn floor, stopped underneath the disco ball, and reached up. Her arms elongated and stretched until her hands disappeared in the darkness above the ball. I returned my gaze to Elysia. I couldn't worry about what Arabella was doing and I also didn't want to give away her vulnerable position by continuing to stare at her. My immediate problem was dealing with the high-voltage girl in front of me.

Elysia lazily flicked her right hand at me, a teasing bolt of electricity snaking out and tagging me on the forearm like the snap of a whip. I grimaced and jerked my arm back as my skin burned, the bolt leaving a black mark where it bit me.

I lifted my bokken, fully aware that a piece of wood wasn't going to be of much use to ward off what Elysia had in mind. But I wasn't going down without a fight and I had no intention of letting Elysia anywhere near my friends. I hoped to get in at least one good swing. I had to do something to give them a chance to get away.

Elysia whipped her hand out again and another bolt snapped forward, catching me across the shoulder. I swiped at the rope of electricity with my bokken, causing it to ricochet back at Elysia like a broken rubber band. Elysia dropped her hands, and the rebounding sparks sizzled into nothingness around her.

Dean Younglove sighed in annoyance. "I grow impatient. Persephone?"

Persephone stepped forward, another bat dangling from her hand. I moved into a defensive position and Persephone tilted her head — a predator surveying its prey. The bat came up so swiftly, I barely had a chance to duck and avoid it before it was coming at me again. Holding the bokken with both hands, I swung it up and across my body, knocking the bat away. Persephone stumbled from the bokken's contact with her bat, growling in frustration. Abandoning any attempt at a fair fight, she resorted to the same tactics she had in the basement. Her bat burst into a flaming torch and she hurled it at me.

I didn't even have to think about what to do. Instinctively, rage rocketed though my body, exploding from my chest in a blast of heat that deflected the bat and sent it whirling in a cartwheel of flames toward Dean Younglove. She dodged out of the way, howling at Persephone and Elysia to attack me.

I took my defensive stance again, the bokken ready to swing at anything that moved.

Persephone lunged at me just as two more bolts of crackling electricity shot out of Elysia's hands. One wrapped around my right ankle, the other around my left wrist. The bolts burned, causing my skin to bubble and scorch where it was touched. I growled, biting back the screams that were fighting to be heard, just managing to jab at Persephone and land a blow to her shoulder with the bokken.

Elysia released me, grinning at the raw, raised marks now circling my ankle and wrist while Persephone rubbed her shoulder and stepped back. It seemed she was going to let Elysia take charge.

Elysia raised her electrified hands over her head, but before she could unleash her charged fury, there was the distinctive sound of wheels on wood echoing through the room. She broke eye contact with me and turned just in time to see Arabella come hurtling down the center of the rink, carrying the huge disco ball, using it to knock the unsuspecting empty-eyed teens down with the ease of a seasoned derby skater. I was confused at first until I noticed that Arabella was wearing a pair of roller skates, still coated with dust and cobwebs from storage in the basement.

Coming to her senses, Elysia pulled her arms back to attack Arabella, but she was too late. Arabella had already taken out the three unsuspecting Deviant look-alikes and a cat-scented Dean with the disco ball that she was wielding like a weapon. She grunted as she tossed the glittering ball at Elysia.

The nearly three-foot sphere arced through the air, tossing glittering rays of light around the room. There was a blur of color as Arabella seemed to magically disappear at the same time the ball made contact with the electrified space between Elysia's hands. I covered my eyes and dove to the ground behind the rink wall as the disco ball reflected the sparking light in a thousand directions before glowing orange and exploding outward in a shower of glass and screams.

The lights went out and the room was in pure darkness as shards of the mirrored disco ball rained down on the floor in a cacophony of shattered tinkling. On the other side of the rink wall, I heard the crunch of glass and cries of pain as the Dean and her teens tried to remove themselves from the carnage. Dean Younglove was calling out loudly for help.

I crawled along the floor looking for my friends, desperately hoping none of them had been injured. A rectangle of light blossomed where the front door was and I felt a hand grab my arm and pull me toward the opening. The fingers dug into the burn on my forearm and I hissed and instinctively pulled my arm back.

"It's me," whispered Sterling. "Let's get out of here while we still can."

Relieved, I let Sterling pull me through the front door. Once outside, we darted across the clearing to the building we first used as cover when we arrived at The Rink. This time, however, we were standing in front of the building, close to the road. Theo and Stanley were still supporting Ozzy, but it looked like he was starting to regain consciousness — he was groggily rubbing his forehead. Wesley was there too, with Cassie still pressed against his chest like a small child.

"Where's Arabella?" I became frantic, preparing to rush back into The Rink.

Sterling grabbed my arm. "She went back for the SUV, she's picking us up."

"Wouldn't you have been faster?"

"She had skates on."

"I've seen you run. She's fast on wheels, but you're faster," I argued.

Sterling shrugged. "I don't know how to drive."

"Oh." I glanced nervously at the doorway to The Rink, expecting the Dean and her teenage minions to come rushing out at any minute. There was the sound of an engine starting and wheels squealing, but I couldn't tell what direction it was coming from.

"What happened in there? Arabella just disappeared. Is that another deviation?"

"Ah, no. That was me and my so-called hummingbird speed. Had to get her out of there before that glitter ball shattered into a zillion pieces. I don't envy that woman and her toadies or the places they'll be picking glass out of," he mused. "Did you get hit? You were pretty close."

"No," I murmured, absentmindedly checking myself just to be sure. "I think I'm okay, except for all these burns."

Headlights illuminated us and we all took a step back as the black SUV crossed the center line and screeched to a stop along the curb in front of us, facing the wrong way on the four lane road. Luckily, the street seemed deserted. The driver's side door swung open as Arabella jumped out, her skates still on.

"No wonder your driving is so bad," Sterling said. "You couldn't bother to take off the skates?"

"Blah, blah, blah," Arabella sniped back, using her hand as a puppet mouth. "At least I know where the key goes."

"Shut up, you two," Stanley growled. "Get in before Little Miss Spark Plug shows up." He glanced nervously back at the front door of The Rink, which was still hanging wide open, yet vacant. He pulled a phone out of his pocket and typed in a number. It rang only once before someone picked up on the other side.

"We have Cassandra," Stanley said curtly.

Pause.

"Yes, there were a few injuries, but nothing severe, I hope."

Pause.

"There's something you should know. Delia Younglove was there."

Pause.

"No. Not to help. It appears that she kidnapped the girl."

Pause.

"No, she had help. She has other . . . " Stanley looked at me and Sterling briefly before glancing back at the empty doorway. "She has other Deviants."

Five minutes later, I found myself in the back seat with Ozzy and Arabella. Despite my begging, Wesley was unwilling to give up Cassie's limp body and he was sitting in the middle row protectively cradling my best friend on his lap. Sterling was next to him, already asleep. Stanley was driving and Theo was riding shotgun, keeping a lookout for anyone that might be following us. I didn't think it really mattered. Delia Younglove was part of the Program, she knew we'd be heading back to St. Ignatius.

The real question was, if she was part of the Program, why was she kidnapping Cassie and more importantly, why did she have other Deviants?

Ozzy leaned forward with his forehead resting on the back of the seat in front of him. "You said she has other Deviants besides the one that looks like Cleo? How many others?" He reached up and rubbed the back of his neck.

"At least three others," Arabella said. "She had a Quinnie, an Eva, and a Sadie. But from the way she talked, it sounded like she only needed Cassie to make her Deviant collection complete. I'm guessing that means Cassie would've been the last of a dozen."

"It just doesn't make sense," Ozzy mumbled. "We're supposed to be one-of-a-kind. Well, twelve-of-a-kind, I guess."

"Is that what's bothering you?" I asked. "That you're not one-of-a-kind?"

Ozzy lifted his head to look at me with bloodshot eyes. "No. That's not what bothers me. That's what worries me."

~ 26 ~

THE KING AND QUEEN SEAT

Younglove — the brittle-skin-non-cat-smelling one — was waiting for us outside the Academy when Stanley pulled the SUV around the circular drive. She was leaning against one of the stone lions, accompanied by Ms. Petticoat, a handful of Hounds, and a few nurse's aides. While Stanley and Ozzy gave a quick rundown of the events to Younglove, Ms. Petticoat had the still-unconscious form of Cassie shuffled away on a stretcher, which I tried to accompany.

"I'm sorry, Clementine, but you can't come along," Ms. Petticoat said softly, blocking my way.

"Why not?"

"Cassandra has suffered tremendously, both physically and mentally. She's going to need special care and it wouldn't be good for her to have distractions. Especially you."

"Why not me?"

"Well," Ms. Petticoat explained, embarrassed. "I'm not sure she's going to understand that it wasn't you who was forcing her to deviate."

"She knows I would never do anything like that!"

The nurse shrugged apologetically. "We won't know what she believes until she wakes up and talks to us. I think it would be best at this point if you weren't one of the first things she sees when she regains consciousness."

That didn't seem fair. As Cassie's best friend, I should be there by her side. I had a duty to be there, but Ms. Petticoat was adamant.

"Why is she still unconscious?" I asked, trailing after the nurse. "Is she going to be okay?"

"At this point, she's technically in a coma," Ms. Petticoat explained.

"Coma?" My legs buckled as the breath rushed out of me. A coma. That was one step away from death as far as I was concerned. Arabella was suddenly at my side, supporting my weight and wrapping a comforting arm around my waist.

"Is she going to die?" I could barely get the words out.

Ms. Petticoat stopped and turned, a kind smile on her face. "Don't worry, Clementine. I'm quite certain that she's not going to die, she's just been severely traumatized. I'll take good care of her. As soon as she's awake and well enough for visitors, I'll let you know."

I nodded numbly as I watched my best friend — my sister — lying as still as death on the stretcher while the Hounds took her away. A coma was better than the hell Cassie had been going through a few hours ago. At least that's the thought I comforted myself with.

After having one of the nurse's aides bandage up my burns and the other minor injuries the rest of the group had sustained, Younglove sent us all off to our rooms with the orders that we were to stay put for the next 24 hours.

"You'll need time to rest and decompress." Younglove looked sternly at each of us in turn. "I don't want you coming out of your rooms and I don't want you talking to anyone else until we've had time to debrief in my office Monday morning."

"So, we don't have to do the morning run?" Theo asked, hopefully.

"No."

"But, we're on house arrest," Arabella grumbled, crossing her arms.

Younglove blinked once, slowly. "It's nearly dawn and you have been awake all night long. What you've been through tonight was shocking. I think you all need some time alone to rest and think. Right now, our main concern is Cassandra's health, everything else can wait. And besides," she looked around the group, "the rest of the cadets are unaware of your deviations. I don't want them to know about the Others."

"We won't tell anyone," Wesley pressed.

"Rooms. Now," Younglove insisted. "And don't forget. There are cameras," she said with a waggle of her finger in the air. "I'll know if you're not in your rooms where you're supposed to be."

We obeyed, making our way into the foyer and to the dormitories. I noticed that Arabella had the roller skates slung over her shoulder.

"I can't believe you stole roller skates."

"Why not? They came in handy."

"Who goes on a search and rescue mission and steals abandoned junk?"

"I was curious. Besides, they're not junk, they're antiques."

"They're prehistoric."

"They're kick ass."

"They're dirty."

"Just my style," Arabella smirked. "Don't hate the skates."

Lying in my bed, I expected a knock from Arabella requesting a sleepover, but none came. Knowing Arabella, she was probably in her room polishing her new four-wheeled treasures. I considered turning on my laptop and sending her a message, but before I knew it, the sun was starting to rise and exhaustion overtook me.

When I finally started to wake from my fitful sleep, I had the feeling that I wasn't alone, which was strange because I remembered locking both the door and window before climbing in bed.

I opened my heavy lids. Soft evening light was seeping in through the window and soaking the entire room in a flood of gold and shifting shadows. I must have slept nearly 12 hours if it was already evening. One of the shadows separated from the dark corners of the room and approached my bed.

Shaking off the remnants of sleep that clung to my brain, my vision cleared and the figure came into frightening focus. It was Persephone, my twin. How had she gotten into the room? Younglove said there were cameras everywhere, this shouldn't be possible. There was no way Persephone should be able to get on Academy grounds, let alone in my room. But then again, it shouldn't have been possible for Cassie's tracking tattoo to go on the fritz either.

What did Persephone want? Kidnapping? Revenge?

My twin continued to approach the bed and belatedly, I realized that Elysia was at Persephone's side. Their eyes were as empty as before, but the smug looks smeared across their faces were full of lethal promise.

I sat up and scooted backward on the bed until my head bumped against the wall. Every fiber in my being was firing warnings, demanding that I scream or run or both. But I couldn't. I was frozen with the same fear that immobilized me when I saw Cassie's horrific, wailing transformation on the filthy mattress in the basement of the roller rink.

Persephone had a baseball and was tossing it between her hands menacingly. She tilted her head. "What do we have here? Another fool who can't control her deviation?"

Elysia's hands sparked at the fingertips as she cracked her knuckles. "I think she just needs a little encouragement."

Persephone's sneer widened. "Oh, I can be very encouraging." She tossed the ball up in the air and caught it, watching it with fascination. "My dear Clementine, what do you say you give us a little display," she cooed. She pointed to my television. "That would look divine in a million pieces."

I shook my head. There was no way I was going to cause any explosions and even if I could, I wouldn't choose the TV.

"I was hoping you'd say that," Persephone grinned. "It's much more fun my way. When you have to be persuaded."

She pulled her arm back and threw the baseball. It hit me in the shoulder, exploding in a mass of fiery leather that caught my shirt on fire. I immediately threw myself face first on the bed, rolling around to snuff out the flames. Once the fire was out, I pushed up into a crouch, staring at the other girls like a cornered animal. My shirt was burnt away at the point of impact and the skin was raw and blackened at the edges of the wound where the flaming ball hit me. The pain clawed at my skin but still, the screams wouldn't come.

"My turn," Elysia chirped excitedly. "Defend yourself, Clementine."

She playfully snapped out a line of electricity like a wet towel. I felt pain slash across my back as the bolt snaked around my shoulders. The bite of the lightning whip was accompanied by the sting of electricity and I felt my teeth clench as my body trembled uncontrollably. My mind was a maelstrom of shrieking and yet, no screams escaped my mouth.

It continued like that. Persephone battering me with objects that exploded on contact and Elysia whipping me with bolts of electricity. I couldn't find the righteous anger to defend myself and I couldn't find the strength to speak. Eventually, I collapsed face down on the bed. My skin felt like it was being ripped and burnt off my body. I prayed for unconsciousness so I could no longer feel the pain.

"Fight back!" Elysia screeched as a network of shocks exploded across my back again. It was scorching and sticky like the tentacles of a jellyfish. Over and over again Elysia flogged me. How could no one else hear what was going on?

I was all alone.

Finally, the screams came.

I woke up to the sound of my own voice yelling out in pain and fear. My legs and arms were tangled in the sheets and I was drenched in sweat. It was early evening, but Persephone and Elysia were nothing more than fading phantoms of a nightmare. A very realistic nightmare.

I was alone in my room and my body was unblemished, although I couldn't say the same for my mind. A quick look at the clock confirmed that it was 6 P.M. and that I'd slept almost the entire day.

I untangled myself from the sheets and noticed that there was a tray of food and drink on my desk. Younglove must have had meals delivered to discourage anyone from leaving their rooms before their 24-hour enforced rest period was over. So much for the safety of locked doors.

My stomach was growling, but I took the time to change out of my sticky, damp clothes first. Freshly clothed in a pair of sweatpants and a tank top, I sat down at the desk to eat my dinner and check to see if anyone was awake and chatting. I turned on my laptop, taking a quick bite of the cold sandwich as the machine hummed to life.

I wasn't surprised to see that Arabella and Sterling had invited me into a private chat room and were discussing the events of the previous night. It took me a good fifteen minutes to read their previous posts and catch up to the conversation. Not surprisingly, they were talking about the Other Deviants.

Sterling: But where do you think they came from?

Arabella: The same place we came from. A test tube.

Sterling: No, I mean, I thought we were supposed to be one-of-a-kind. Not only do they have similar powers as us, but they look like us, too.

Arabella: Actually, as far as we know, they look like Cleo, Quinnie, Eva, and Sadie. I didn't see any Arabella or Sterling duplicates.

Cleo: You're lucky. It was disturbing seeing myself and hearing my voice.

Arabella: Ah! She's alive! Where have you been?

Cleo: Sleeping. But not well. I'm thinking about crawling back in bed as soon as I'm done eating.

Arabella: No! We have to talk about this.

Cleo: We'll be talking about it plenty with Younglove tomorrow morning.

Sterling: Exactly. Don't you think it's smart to hash out some of this before then?

Cleo: Hash out what exactly?

Arabella: Oh, I don't know. Maybe the fact that there was a crazy ass Younglove look-alike with an army of counterfeit Deviants who wanted to destroy us with flaming sports equipment and electrical whips! Where exactly did they come from and what is their purpose? We know what our purpose is, but I bet you my favorite Ravens jersey it's not the same as theirs.

My head started to ache. I didn't want to think about my own purpose, let alone that of a cruel group of teens led by a cat-scented woman who condoned and encouraged the torture of Cassie. All I really cared about at this point was that Cassie was safe and would recover. That's all that mattered.

Cleo: Any word yet on Cassie?

Sterling: No. I haven't heard a thing. I think we're in solitary confinement.

Arabella: Why are you changing the subject?

Cleo: Because I don't want to talk about what happened at The Rink. I have to go, I have a headache.

Arabella: Hey. Wait a minute. I heard you screaming about fifteen minutes ago. Are you okay? What happened?

Cleo: Bad dream.

A few seconds pause.

Arabella: Me too. I'm still having them about the kidnapping-that-wasn't-a-kidnapping.

Cleo: I keep thinking about that, too.

Arabella: Want me to come over?

Cleo: No. It's not worth getting in trouble for. I'll be fine.

Sterling: You can come over here, Bella, and help me take my mind off things.

Arabella: Don't call me Bella! I'm so gonna punch you in the mouth for that.

Sterling: I have other ideas for what you can do with my mouth.

I smiled. I could only imagine the horror on Arabella's face at seeing what Sterling was writing — and in front of another person no less. I had to admit, it cheered me up.

Cleo: Wow. I totally feel like a third wheel. I'm out of here. See you guys in a few hours.

I signed off the chat room before I could see the fallout from Sterling's comments, but I didn't shut down the computer. I opened my search engine and browsed my way to the Maryland Department of Assessments and Taxation website. From there, I located the SDAT: Real Property Search and typed in the Overlea address for The Rink and waited. I wanted to find out who owned The Rink. Was it Dean Younglove? Was it someone from the Program? I thought if I could find out who owned it, I'd have some clue as to what Delia Younglove and her bad-tempered minions were up to.

I held my breath while the page loaded, expecting to see Delia Younglove's name under the listing for property owner. Instead, I saw the name Janus Malleville. I scrolled down the page to see how long he'd owned the property — nearly 20 years. That told me nothing.

Who was Janus Malleville, how did he know Delia Younglove, and why was his building being used to house the unauthorized offspring of Program experimentations? Clearly the bunk beds and training equipment proved that the place had been inhabited for a while.

I took out a pad of paper and wrote down all the information on the taxation page about the property, as well as anything I could remember about The Rink, including my theories about the other Deviants. Under the heading "Others" I described the way they looked, acted, and the few names that Younglove mentioned. I even tried typing "Janus Malleville" into my search engine to see if I could find out anything about the man who owned the building, but all I found was an article dated nearly 20 years ago that stated that The Rink ownership transferred over to Malleville when his father died. Not soon after, the business shut down due to lack of clientele. It appeared he was nothing more than an unsuccessful businessman. Perhaps he was just renting the space out to Younglove and had no idea how she was using it.

I jotted down all of my theories and was just finishing up my sketch of the layout of the building when I looked up at the clock to see it was nearly 2 A.M. With a sigh, I closed my notebook and turned out the light before climbing back into bed.

This time, my sleep was nightmare free.

My eyes flew open and for a moment, I was worried that I wasn't alone. I'd heard something. I lay quietly, not moving, searching my room for a clue as to what made the sound that jerked me out of slumber. I was almost too scared to breathe.

There was the sound again, a slight knocking.

My eyes followed the noise to the window and I sat up slightly so I could see if maybe a branch from the tree outside was hitting the glass. Instead, I saw Ozzy's face on the other side of the window, barely illuminated by my desk lamp. A lamp which I'd left on every night since the kidnapping-that-wasn't-a-kidnapping. Ozzy motioned for me to open the window. I tossed the blankets aside and scurried over to the window, sliding it open.

"Is it Cassie? Is she okay? Did she wake up?"

Ozzy's eyebrows dipped in confusion momentarily. "I don't know . . . Oh, I see." He pulled his bottom lip through his teeth. "I wouldn't come knocking at your window if it was about Cassie, I would've just called you."

My heart fell into my stomach. "Then, why are you here?"

"I'm breaking you out."

"What do you mean? What about the tracking tattoo? I can't just leave Cassie! Not after everything that's happened. What about Sterling and Arabella?"

Ozzy laughed. "Not a real breakout, a temporary one. This one is approved. Come on, I want to show you something," he said, holding out his hand.

"If it's approved, why didn't you just come up the steps and knock on my door?" I asked skeptically.

Ozzy tilted his head as a smile spread across his face. "Now, what fun would that be? Grab a jacket, let's go. We have to get there before the sun's up."

"You're not telling me where we're going?"

"As I said, what fun would that be?"

I grabbed my jacket off the back of the desk chair. "And you say this has been approved?"

Ozzy reached his hand through the window, beckoning me out onto the tree limb. "Yes. Now stop being a coward."

"I'm not a coward!"

"Prove it."

It was a challenge and it was more than just proving that I wasn't afraid of getting in trouble, he was asking me to trust him completely.

He hadn't exactly earned it.

I stood inside my room, the muted darkness playing havoc with all of my uncertainties. Ozzy was motionless, perched on the limb of the tree, his hand held out in invitation. But an invitation to what? I knew that whether or not my heart could make the decision to trust Ozzy, my curiosity already decided to take the leap. I shrugged into my jacket, climbed onto my desk, and allowed Ozzy to guide me out onto the limb and down the tree.

He led me through the darkened grounds, past the training area, and down a slight hill. The grass was slippery with leaves and the morning air was chilly and dark. The branches overhead still clung desperately to a few brittle leaves, but I knew it wouldn't be long before the trees were bare and the crisp autumn air would fade into the harsh clutches of winter.

Ozzy, still holding my hand, led me to the far side of the Academy grounds to a large, stone outbuilding I'd never been in before. He typed a few numbers into a keypad, pushed open the door, and flipped the switch just inside. As the lights flickered to life, I was surprised to discover that it was a garage. I wasn't sure what I was expecting, but it certainly wasn't a building full of black Academy SUVs and other vehicles.

"You woke me up to show me cars?" The exasperation was evident in my voice.

Ozzy merely grinned. "No, not cars." He pulled me by the hand and led me to the back of the building. He stopped next to a motorcycle. It was shiny black and chrome, with the Harley Davidson logo stamped proudly on the side of the inky black gas tank which was decorated with silver flames. Ozzy reached into a cubby hole next to the bike, pulled out two helmets, and handed me one. The smile tugging at his lips was sinfully daring.

"Put this on."

I didn't obey right away. "Whose bike is this?"

"Mine."

"One of the perks of sponsorship?"

Ozzy's look darkened and his cocky grin slipped a bit. "Something like that," he murmured.

I felt guilty, but for what, I didn't know. I did the only thing I could think of to get his smile set straight again and put the helmet on.

Ozzy's eyes blazed happily. He reached over and buckled the strap under my chin, allowing his hand to linger against my skin.

"This looks good on you," he smiled.

"Is that some kind of joke about covering up my head so I look better?" I challenged.

"Not at all, I just like seeing you wearing my things." Unexpectedly, Ozzy leaned in and brushed his lips against mine. It was brief and feather light, a temptation beckoning me to trust him.

He put his own helmet on, mounted the bike, and fished a key out of the pocket of his leather jacket. When the bike roared to life, I had to fight the urge to cover my ears and I briefly wondered if our departure would wake anyone else.

Ozzy backed the bike out of its parking space and I had to admit that seeing him confidently straddling the growling motorcycle was thrilling. Butterflies were fluttering uncontrollably in my stomach and I couldn't wait to sit behind Ozzy and wrap my arms around him.

He turned to look at me. "Trust me?"

I didn't hesitate. I swung my leg over the seat and settled in behind him, the inside of my thighs hugging the outside of his legs intimately. I clutched the edges of his jacket in my fists.

"You're gonna have to hold on tighter than that unless you want to get left behind," he suggested as the garage door began to slide up into the ceiling. He let the bike jerk forward in a small burst of speed causing my arms to clutch around him, erasing any space between our bodies.

"Good girl." He laughed. "Now we can ride."

I felt the muscles in Ozzy's arms tense as his hands gripped the handlebars and the motorcycle shot out into the dark morning.

The first time I'd travelled down theses thick-wooded, desolate, back country roads, I'd been anxious. This time, however, I was overcome with a sense of mystery and adventure and I knew it had everything to do with the fact that I was with Ozzy and only Ozzy. I also knew that the danger of hurtling down the dark, curvy roads on the back of a motorcycle gave me a different perspective. It was new and exciting and normal.

All too soon, Ozzy slowed the bike and turned down another side road, maneuvering past a metal swing gate and parking next to a ranger's station. As we got off the bike and removed our helmets, I could see the promise of the sunrise as it threatened to steal across the sky. The royal blue of the autumn night began to glow with the warmth of the coming sun.

"We have to hurry," Ozzy said, grasping my cold hand in his warm one. "I don't want you to miss this."

We quickly made our way past an old pavilion with deserted picnic benches, followed a hiking trail, and plunged into the quiet solitude of the sleeping woods. It was that magical time when the creatures of the night were sleeping and the creatures of the light had yet to stake their claim on the day. Aside from us, only the light autumn breeze seemed to be awake to welcome the sun.

As we made our way along the path which was covered in pine needles, I could see a patch of sky ahead. Silhouetted against it were lumpy shadows I couldn't quite identify. I had no idea what Ozzy intended to show me.

"Hurry," Ozzy encouraged, pulling me toward the massive profiles as we exited the woods and came to a clearing.

The large shadows turned out to be huge rock formations. Ozzy began to climb the tallest one, holding my hand, and pointing out to me where I should put my feet. At the top, I stood next to him and my breath caught. The rock formation we were on overlooked a valley that was about 200 feet below us.

"Sit here," Ozzy ordered, pointing to an indentation in the boulder that looked like a seat. There was another one next to it that he sat in.

Below our perch, an outcropping of rock jutted into the open air like a finger reaching out into the empty sky above the valley.

"This is the King and Queen seat," Ozzy explained, indicating the rock we were sitting on. "I'm the king," he said regally, "which would make you my queen." He nudged me and I laughed. "This used to be a ceremonial gathering place for the Susquehannock Indians. We're about 190 feet above Deer Creek Valley."

"It's beautiful," I breathed.

"Just wait," Ozzy promised, leaning back in the King's seat. "Trust me."

"I do trust you."

Ozzy's green eyes searched my face. "Do you forgive me yet?"

"For what?" I was apprehensive.

"Reading your file."

"Oh, that." I thought about it. I'd read his file, too. Well, most of it anyway. And in a way, I discovered that I felt like I knew him better because of it. Maybe I could understand why he would be so desperate to know about others like him. To be brought to St. Ignatius when he was only ten — he must have been lonely. Of course he'd want to find out as much as possible about those who were like him. At least, those who were as different as he was.

"Yeah, I think I do," I said and I realized I meant it.

Ozzy reached for my hand and I could almost feel the happiness rolling off him. Suddenly, a thought occurred to me.

"Ozzy, you've read my entire file, right?"

He nodded warily.

"What is my last name? Please tell me about my parents. I

know their names are Michael and Sarah, but that's all."

His eyebrows dipped over his dark lashes. "Cleo, I'm sorry. I haven't read that file."

"What do you mean?"

"They may want me to be the leader of the Deviants, but there is information about us that even I haven't seen. I don't know anything about your parents. I don't even know anything about my own."

"Oh." I looked down at my lap and my hopes faded away as quickly as the night was receding across the sky.

Ozzy reached over and lifted my chin so I was looking at him. "But if it's that important to you, we'll figure it out, okay?"

I nodded.

"Good, now let's climb down and get a front row seat before this show gets started." He helped me descend the throne-like rock structure and then led me toward the thin finger of rock that hovered out over the valley.

I stopped halfway, nervously eyeing the absurdly dangerous bridge of rock and how far down the floor of the valley was below it.

Ozzy tugged my hand and once again I found myself putting my trust in him. He helped me sit at the edge of the cliff, never letting go of my hand. With the rock digging into the backs of my knees and my legs dangling in the open space, my heart sped up. I could hear the refreshing sound of the river that wove in and out of the trees, tumbling over rocks and rushing off through the wooded hills below.

"Any minute now," Ozzy whispered.

I sat in silence as the sun broke over the horizon, spilling golden light down over the valley, setting the autumn leaves ablaze in riotous golden color. Far below us, the morning light rolled over the carpet of trees, seizing the day in a slow, glorious immersion of morning light. I watched as the sun climbed into the sky, chasing away the night.

Sitting at the edge of the cliff with nothing but open sky all around, I could almost imagine that freedom was within my grasp — that I could make my own choices and decide my own fate. It was a gift, however illusory, that I could treasure. A moment, a feeling of freedom, and a hope for something more than I knew I would ever have.

I tore my gaze away from the sunrise and stared at Ozzy. The smile on his face spoke volumes. For once it wasn't the usual cocky smirk or the confident grin. It was pure, unadulterated happiness.

"Why did you bring me here?" I asked.

"You've seen and been through so much ugliness lately. I wanted you to see something beautiful."

"Thank you." My voice was a whisper. I didn't want to break the spell.

Ozzy's eyes met mine. "This is one place I feel like I'm truly me. I feel like the fingers of the Program can't touch me here."

Sitting on the ledge, with nothing in front of us but a valley of sun-drenched trees, I understood. "I feel it, too."

He looked at me a moment longer before speaking again. "A roasting creamsicle," he said.

"What?" I laughed.

"At The Rink, you asked me what you smell like," Ozzy said with a smile. "That's the best way to describe it. You smell like vanilla, and oranges and a match that's just been struck." He noticed my look of uncertainty. "It's a good thing."

"You sure?"

"Very," he assured me.

Ozzy's eyes searched mine and he reached out to touch my face. I leaned my cheek into his hand and soon found myself against his chest. His arms snaked under mine, reaching up my back to my shoulders, pulling me to him until my lips met his. His kiss was urgent, as if I were the only thing he needed to survive.

My hands threaded into his hair and he groaned low in his throat. Desire burned warm inside me, deliciously exploding through me like the sun had burst through the sky only moments before.

"Cleo," Ozzy murmured, his voice low and throaty and pleading.

My mind began to race as fast as my heart — visions of a different life shifting around in my mind. Visions of a life where I was a normal girl with normal problems and choices. A life where I could make my own possibilities and future — maybe even a future with Ozzy.

High above the golden valley near our throne of boulders, it seemed like anything was possible.

Intoxicated by the feel of Ozzy's mouth on mine, my hands roamed down his chest, slipping inside his jacket, and exploring his body. I let my hands venture inside his shirt and trace the hard muscles of his chest and stomach. He moaned appreciatively and his hands tentatively left my shoulders, skimming around my sides, and finding the zipper to my jacket. I pressed myself against him, letting him know I wasn't going to stop him. At least not yet.

When his fingers found their way under the hem of my shirt, excitement tingled along my skin in anticipation. I reached down between our bodies to touch him, his jeans suddenly an unwelcome barrier. He seemed to come unraveled at my touch.

"Cleo," he groaned as he clutched me tight, need heavy in his words.

There was a sudden ringing and Ozzy's lips stilled. He pulled away, his eyes full of apology.

"What?" I asked, my breathing still heavy, my hand still mid-exploration.

He reached into his jacket. "It's my phone."

"Don't answer it."

"I wish it were that easy."

"It is."

Ozzy didn't say anything as he shifted to put the phone to his ear. "Yes?"

I self-consciously straightened my shirt as Ozzy quietly listened.

"Just now?" he asked, his gaze flicking to me. "Has she said anything?"

I bit my lip and re-zipped my jacket, shoving my hands into the pockets. Without the warmth of Ozzy's body, I shivered in the cool morning air.

"Of course," Ozzy said in a clipped tone. "We'll be there in ten minutes." He turned off the phone and hid it away in his jacket.

"Do we really have to leave?" I asked.

Ozzy reached forward and ran his thumb along my lower lip. "Don't look at me like that, it'll make it that much harder to drag you out of here."

"Let's stay a little longer," I suggested. "We have to finish what we started."

I didn't want to go back to the Academy. I was intoxicated with the feeling of freedom I felt in this place. I wanted to stay here and let my hands and lips discover every inch of Ozzy. And by the look on his face, he wanted the same thing. Ozzy's gaze darkened and I knew he was remembering the last place my hands were. He took a deep breath.

"If I were selfish, I would. Trust me, you'll want to go."

"I don't think so." I couldn't think of any reason I would possibly want to leave.

"I know there's at least one place you'd rather be right now."

"Hardly."

Ozzy licked his lower lip. "Cassie's awake. And she's ready to talk about the Others."

Epilogue

She pulled the pool ball out of her pocket as she watched them, tossing it back and forth between her hands. The black eight on the ball spun dizzily with each toss. For Deviants, they had been way too easy to follow, they hadn't even suspected she was there. In fact, they still didn't realize they weren't alone. She had been concerned about the unpredictable autumn breeze, but luck held out and her hiding place was upwind from the Tracker.

From her perch in a nearby tree, she watched the entire lip locking scene unfold. It was entertaining, but at the same time, she had a serious urge to push them off the cliff and just be done with it. Well, maybe not the guy, he looked as if he could be worth keeping — he did seem to have very talented lips. And his body, well, it was top-notch, too. She was feeling a little sorry she had roughed him up on their first encounter. But, there were always ways to make amends, especially under the right circumstances.

She smiled as she remembered the look the girl gave her when the door came crashing down — surprise and horror, as if she were looking in a mirror and seeing her worst nightmare come to life. The monster inside.

That girl. She could definitely do without the girl. There was only room in this world for one Fire Bringer and all it would take was one little push. Maybe even a strategically placed, exploding eight ball.

Effie eyed the ball in her hand. The urge was loud, yelling in her ear, begging her to fulfill the itch. But, she was reluctant to give in. She'd lose the ball in the process and she wasn't willing to give it up. Plus, D.Y. would be angry. She told the urge to be quiet. When it wouldn't shut up, she broke off a small piece of a nearby branch and started scratching deep lines into her forearm. The pain was a blessed distraction. It made her forget the voices, if only for a few minutes.

Suddenly, a phone started ringing. Effie looked up from the deep, bloody scratches on her arm to see the guy take the offending object out of his pocket and answer it. Soon he and the girl were stumbling to their feet and rushing back down the path and through the woods.

She pocketed the eight ball. Her opportunity was gone, for the moment. Besides, D.Y. gave her strict instructions to just watch and report back. Sometimes that was easier said than done; the voices were rarely cooperative. But, soon she'd have her chance — once the Dozen was complete.

Effie couldn't understand why D.Y. was so intent on having that other brat be part of the group. She couldn't even deviate at will. And it wasn't for lack of trying. Effie spent hours forcing that bitch to deviate, but that's the only way she could manage it, only when she was forced. Effie would be happy to just forget about the brat, but she knew that once D.Y.'s mind was made up, that was that. And so, now they had to get the brat back. D.Y. definitely wasn't happy about what happened at The Rink. She blamed Elysia mostly, but in all honesty, everyone suffered once that disco ball shattered. Effie looked down at her arms and winced as she remembered how all of the raw, jagged cuts had gotten there in the first place.

The girl and guy were now far enough ahead that Effie could safely get down out of her hiding spot and report back. She had some news to give to D.Y. Good news and bad news. The bad news — that worthless deviant, Cassie, was now awake and was no doubt spilling all of the information she knew about her captors. Luckily, that information wasn't much. The good news — the two Deviants that D.Y. was most worried about definitely had weaknesses. Each other. And Effie had every intention of exploiting that.

She was going to have fun.

She smiled as she cut her way through the woods, taking a shortcut so she could make sure they were headed back to the Academy.

For once, having the face she had was going to be a good thing. A very good thing.

ACKNOWLEDGEMENTS

I'm extremely lucky to have such an amazing supporting cast of people who have helped me make my dream of being an author a reality. Writing a book is a long and difficult journey that takes an enormous amount of time and dedication. I'm thankful to be surrounded by people who constantly lift me up and motivate me.

First and foremost I want to thank Johnny Manzari, the love of my life and my ruggedly handsome muse. When I told him I wanted to write a book, his response was: Do it. Start now. Don't wait. Simple as that. I started that night and he has been there every step of the way to encourage and enable me to make my wish come true, whether it be to give me a goodnight kiss and let me write into the wee hours of the morning without complaint, or to listen to me ramble on about my progress (or writer's block). He even built me a library so I would have an inspirational place to read and write. I couldn't have done this without you, Johnny. I love you more than you could ever possibly know.

I'm not sure if she'll ever see this since she is a very successful author in her own right, but thank you to Jeri Smith-Ready for joining NaNoWriMo in the fall of 2011 and tweeting/facebooking about it. You inspired me to challenge myself too. *Deviation* was conceived on the fly during that month of insanity and if it hadn't been for your inspiration, this book might not have ever been birthed. (By the way, check out Jeri's books . . . she's awesome.)

I want to thank my beta readers, and sisters: Laurie Marin, Shelly Burch, and Amber Englehart for taking the time to read the first draft of *Deviation* and give me invaluable feedback. You helped me turn my NaNoWriMo experiment into a real story, and you gals really are the most kick ass sisters anyone could hope for. And Laurie, I think you may be the only person who has read this book as many times as I have . . . that's love. I always know your feedback is going to be helpful and insightful.

Many thanks go out to my generous friends who took the time to get out their virtual red pens to edit my words and who also asked the difficult questions I forgot to ask myself (and my characters). Thanks to Todd Supple, Noel Lloyd, Rich Sanidad, and Shelly Burch for your eagle eyes and for making my story better.

And of course I have to thank those who asked to read my manuscript and gave me much needed fangirl/fanboy love. Patti Blakeney, Dan and Jen Sekowski, Sandy Vogelman, Jennifer Ramey Schmoll, and Danielle Clark Fisher — you're the best. Tiffini Crown, Kay Redding, and Jessica Holmgren . . . thanks for being part of the book request fan club too. And Johnnie Redding and Jonathan Szczepanski, thanks to you boys for being willing readers for me when I first started writing. Jon, I promise there are no vampires in this one, it's completely safe to read.

My deepest gratitude goes to all my family and friends who have always been there to give me virtual high fives or words of inspiration in person and on social media. It means so much that I have so many people that believe in me. Thanks to Pop, Hon, Kay, and Mimi for asking me for updates and being interested in my dream.

Lastly, I have to thank the two people who created the weird little monster that I am today. Mom and Dad, thank you for being the kind of parents that let me believe I could do anything (no matter how weird or crazy that thing was) and for always being there (no matter how far you had to travel to support me). I've always expected to succeed at the things I set out to do and I know this strange confidence I have has everything to do with your love and support. You let me know it was okay to be different. You allowed me to make my own mistakes and achieve my own victories and I'm forever thankful for the beautiful, unconditional love you've always given me. I hope this book makes you proud of me.

P.S. An extra thanks goes to Vania Stoyanova for the amazing photography for the new cover of *Deviation*, VLC Photo for the new cover design, and Krista Gibson for being the perfect Cleo.

ABOUT THE AUTHOR

The first thing Christine does when she's getting ready to read a book is to crack the spine in at least five places. She wholeheartedly believes there is no place as comfy as the pages of a well-worn book. She's addicted to buying books, reading books, and writing books. Books, books, books. She also has a weakness for adventure, inappropriate humor, and coke (the caffeine-laden bubbly kind). Christine is from Forest Hill, Maryland where she lives with her husband, three kids, and her library of ugly spine books.

CONNECT WITH CHRISTINE MANZARI:

Website: www.christinemanzari.com

Facebook: www.facebook.com/ChristineManzari

Twitter: www.twitter.com/Xenatine

Instagram: http://instagram.com/xenatine

Pinterest: www.pinterest.com/xenatine

Goodreads: www.goodreads.com/Christine_Manzari

BOOKS BY CHRISTINE MANZARI:

Deviation (The Sophisticates Book 1)

Conviction (The Sophisticates Book 2)